Next Stop
HOLLYWOOD

To Jim.
Aloha from
Hawaiian Jay Ryan

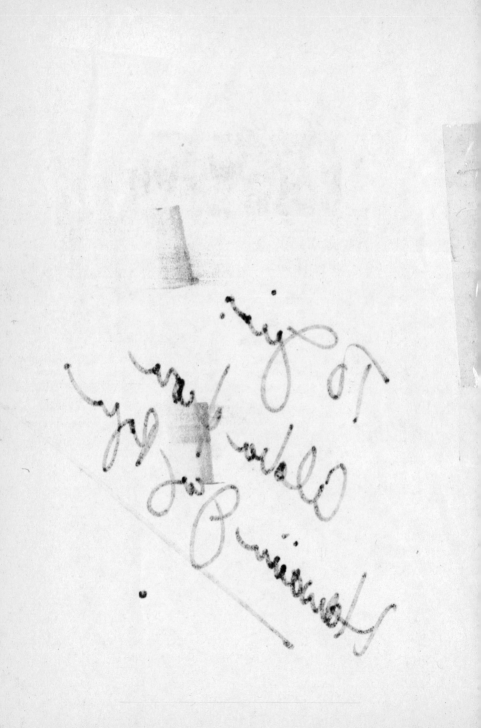

Next Stop HOLLYWOOD

Short Stories Bound for the Screen

EDITED BY
STEVE COHEN

 St. Martin's Griffin ❧ New York

NEXT STOP HOLLYWOOD. Copyright © 2007 by Steve Cohen.
"An Age of Marvels and Wonders" copyright © 2007 by Perry Glasser.
"Dirk Snigby's Guide to the Afterlife" copyright © 2007 by E. E. King.
"Mexico" copyright © 2007 by Perry Glasser.
"The Adam Collection" copyright © 2007 by Therese Mageau.
"Gone to Mum's" copyright © 2007 by Barry Simiana.
"The Injunction" copyright © 2007 by Don Wallace.
"My Stunt Wife" copyright © 2007 by Michael Guerra.
"A.K.A." copyright © 2007 by Gerald O. Ryan.
"The Door Beast Nine Vee Bee" copyright © 2007 by Ed Jesby.
"Some Pig" copyright © 2007 by Nancy Davidson.
"The Good Kid" copyright © 2007 by Brian Richmond.
"Blind Man in the Halls of Justice" copyright © 2007 by John Minichillo.
"The Piano" copyright © 2007 by Janet Neipris.
"Waltzing Matilda" copyright © 2007 by Russell Bittner.
"The Equation" copyright © 2007 by J. Paul Cooper.

www.stmartins.com

Design by Phil Mazzone

Library of Congress Cataloging-in-Publication Data

Next stop Hollywood : short stories bound for the screen / [edited by] Steve Cohen.—1st ed.
    p. cm.
  ISBN-13: 978-0-312-35789-4
  ISBN-10: 0-312-35789-3
  1. Short stories, American. I. Cohen, Steven Martin, 1953–

PS648.S5N48 2007
813.0108—dc22

2007061721

First Edition: June 2007

10 9 8 7 6 5 4 3 2 1

Contents

Contents

Introduction

It started with a bar bet. "Dinner says you don't know what these movies have in common," said Jon Davis, my longtime friend and collaborator. As a movie buff, I thought this was a pretty safe wager. I was soon to find out it was a sucker bet that I would lose this time; and then go on to use dozens of times over the next ten years—and win every time!

"*All About Eve, It Happened One Night, Rear Window,* and let's say, *High Noon,*" asked Jon.

The left side of my brain kicked in: they didn't have a common director. They all had different stars. And they all had different themes, styles, cinematographers. Hmmm.

"Here's a hint: add these to the others. *Guys and Dolls, The Absent-Minded Professor,* and *Terminator,*" smirked my about-to-be-former friend.

I was baffled. "Okay. I give up. You win. What do they have in common?"

"They all started as short stories."

Jon went on to explain that he had been browsing at an obscure bookstore, and picked up a copy of an interesting paperback called *No, But I Saw the Movie.* He handed it to me and I saw that it was a collection of short stories that became successful movies. The book included an appendix of some fifty other well-known, successful, and often critically acclaimed films that started as short stories.

What was also apparent, was that there were very few recent films that had originated as short stories. (Remember, this conversation was taking place in 1995, so *Brokeback Mountain* and *Minority Report* had not yet been made.) Why weren't there more recent films based on short stories?

Jon, true to form, had a pretty good theory: the magazines that had published commercial fiction were all gone. *Saturday Evening Post, Colliers, Mademoiselle*—all shuttered. Yes, there were literary journals that published short stories. But they were, well, "literary" and not likely to publish the types of stories that had more prosaic elements like plots or characters one cared about; or beginnings, middles, and endings.

Jon then took his observation to the next level: "I will bet that writers still write short stories. And some will have real potential to be good movies."

It was a bet that we were on the same side of. I had an idea where Jon was going with this, but for once I stayed silent and let him finish.

Jon's conclusion was as logical as it was provocative: Hollywood can't produce them if they can't find them. If the stories aren't published, it's almost the same as them not existing. True, an author can self-publish—in print or on the Web—but finding those publications is near impossible, and one could waste months sifting through the truly horrible looking for that one gem. In self-publishing, no one—other than the sometimes self-delusional author—vets the material and says "This is pretty good."

We both sensed that if short stories had once been a major source of successful Hollywood material, they could be once again.

But so what? Why had Jon raised this particular subject in the first place? Because among our many projects together were a few television shows. In my youth I had managed to get *Time* magazine into the television business as the creator and executive producer of the *Time* "Man of the Year" TV specials; and Jon had written or produced a few of the annuals. He knew that producing was something that had gotten under my skin. The unspoken implication was clear: If we could find good short stories that had movie potential—and control the film and TV rights—we were, de facto, producers.

Every once in a while Jon has a brilliant idea—among the dozens of truly horrible ideas we pitch to each other over dinner. We both knew this had the potential to be one of the great ones.

The ball had shifted to my court.

I began to talk to writers whom I knew. I asked them if they happened to have a short story sitting in a desk drawer, or on an old hard drive or floppy disk somewhere. To a person, they said they did. Journalists, novelists, O. Henry winners, Pulitzer nominees. To a person, they all looked at me as if I were clairvoyant. *How did you know?*

This was becoming a safe, if not a sucker bet. That's what writers do: they write. Most prefer a particular form or genre, but many experiment. Journalists try their hand at novels. Novelists write a spec screenplay. Aspiring authors attend writing programs where short stories are a preferred form of teaching. In short, the stories were out there.

From my own background in publishing—plus Jon's prescient analysis of the demise of the commercial fiction-friendly magazines—I also knew about the challenges of getting a single short story published. Whether one prefers Deep Throat's (ill-attributed) advice to "follow the money" or Jerry McGuire's client's instruction to "Show me the money," the reason these stories were sitting unread in their author's "dead projects" file was simple: There is no money chasing them.

With few outlets to sell short stories—and almost no money being paid if a story is accepted—agents had very little incentive to pitch their clients' work. Thus they stayed in the writers' drawers and on their hard drives.

Several weeks after our sucker-bet dinner, Jon and I got together again. I reported on my discussions with authors. He one-upped me: he handed over a short story written by a Pulitzer Prize winner. (It didn't make the final cut for this volume.) So, clearly, there were stories out there—at least from established writers and no doubt with budding authors—and agents were doing nothing with them. Terrific. Now what do we do? Really, was there anything we could do?

Let's face it: we weren't film industry insiders. And there were few industries where the barriers to entry were higher. We agreed that we should probably just relegate the still-unbaked-idea to the "Nice idea but . . ." pile, and move on to other things. It was an interesting dinner conversation topic and it would always be good for a sucker-bet.

But something kept gnawing at me, and I wouldn't let the idea drop. I had just finished lecturing at the Stanford Professional Publishing Program where my topic had been "Turning Books into Magazines." Not surprisingly, I pushed the short-story-as-movie-material idea through the magazine sieve. Whether it belonged there or not was secondary. At least Jon and I had a business model that we could start with.

Having started three magazines during the previous ten years, I knew a couple things for sure: magazine start-ups were unbelievably costly. And most fail. Nevertheless, we started noodling.

Since neither of us had the capital to start a magazine, or knew enough rich (foolish?) folks who might like to finance a new, guaranteed-to-lose-money magazine, we quickly side-stepped our way to a variation. We would approach established magazines and pitch the idea of short stories as an advertiser-supported special section. We had, as part of our team, a former book editor who had migrated to Holly-wood as a script reader for several producers. One magazine publisher was interested, but the financial model didn't really make sense for us. The idea lost steam.

A few years later, I read about a new magazine to be launched by the renowned film director Francis Ford Coppolla. It was called *Zoetrope*— now known as *Zoetrope: All-Story*—and its theme was short stories. Moreover, he would be acquiring the film rights to the stories he pub-lished. Someone with the same vision—plus the deep pockets to do something about it—had validated our idea. Oh well, on to the next venture.

Over the next several years I looked for *All-Story*, and occasionally found it. The magazine's distribution was spotty—even in a magazine-friendly, artsy place like New York—and I wondered how many prospective contributors or readers were really aware of *All-Story*. The Internet was starting to change that, but I noticed something else about my (at least in my mind) "competition." *All-Story* had become notice-ably, well, literary.

Literary is okay. But it wasn't what Jon and I had in mind.

There was one other thing we noticed. *All-Story* was fond of uti-lizing "guest editors." Some of these guest editors were artists; others were writers; a few were filmmakers. The results, in terms of story selection, were interesting. But also, not surprisingly, highly individ-ualistic.

And that is when I had the "Aha!" moment.

For me, the "Aha!" moment is that remarkable intersection of rig-orous, logical analysis and serendipitous insight. It is creativity born of hard work. In this case, I admit that I was influenced by *American Idol*. At first I wasn't willing to admit it publicly, and found a more "re-spectable" analogy: the Zagat guides.

One of my gnawing fears throughout the gestation of this entire project was who was going to choose the stories? Certainly I wasn't qual-ified to choose stories that ought to be movies. In our earlier attempt to put this together, Jon and I had settled on the former "D-Girl" (producer's development person/reader) Andrea. But we both knew that that was a weak link in our proposal. I had long been a fan of Oscar-winning writer William Goldman and his oft-quoted assessment of the movie business, "Nobody knows anything!"

Now I thought we had the perfect approach.

First, we would put together an editorial advisory board of movie-industry insiders. Nobody may know anything, but at least with their guidance we would know what we didn't know. If we could get any of them to actually read some story submissions, that would be great. But we didn't expect too much in that regard.

The second step was the crux of the Aha moment: we would ask lots of "regular people" to read lots of stories. It wouldn't be my taste, or Jon's, or that of any single guest editor or smart D-kid right out of college. Instead, we would rely on the "wisdom of crowds" to tell us what they thought would make good movies.

But we started by seeking the industry insider guidance and validation.

Never accused of being shy, we approached everyone we knew who had any connection to the film business. Typically we started with the movie quiz—at least having the judgment not to set it up as a sucker bet—and then asked if what we had in mind made sense. Were we onto something or just dreaming?

The insiders told us it was a bit of both.

Some thought it was a nifty idea; others said Hollywood just gave lip service to the notion of "new sources of talent." And still others just didn't get it. But we were able to put together a list of criteria by which we might judge short stories for their movie and film potential. And several of the insiders gave us permission to use their names.

By this time we had moved away from the magazine idea and settled on a book format. We approached John Sargent, the CEO of St. Martin's parent company Holtzbrinck. We started with the quiz, and moved on to the pitch. John, who is on the board of the NYU Publishing Program where I am an adjunct professor, "got it" immediately. (*Duh*, there's reason why he's CEO.) He shared it with his colleagues at St. Martin's, and we had a deal in record time.

Now the challenge was to find the stories.

We knew they were out there, but where?

One place was through the established literary agents. Here, we didn't actually have a disagreement, but more of a . . . oh hell, yes we

did. One of us wanted to get stories from as many well-known, established writers as possible. The other wanted to limit the project to un-
knowns. After lots of shouting we came to a Solomonic decision: we'd
solicit and accept both. The objective was to find the best short stories
that had film potential, and we simply didn't care whom they came
from.

We sent e-mails to every creative writing program we could find.
We sent press releases to college newspapers. We posted "submissions
wanted" posters on Web sites and in writing rooms. We attended story-
telling slams, and encouraged friends and acquaintances to get the word
out.

At first, the submissions were both sparse and, to be kind, awful. We
suddenly had a new perception of *American Idol*. One of us had always
been under the impression that the early rounds were filled with people
who were out having fun; karaoke with a bigger audience. Now we
knew differently: those people—and many of our early authors—truly
think they have talent. They don't.

But word started getting around and the submissions got better and
better. At the same time, we put out word that we were looking for vol-
unteer readers; people who liked movies, short stories, and thought
they had a sense of what might make a good film.

Here, our instinct about how to transform the Aha moment into a
viable process worked. We sent out each story to lots of readers, along
with an evaluation form. We weren't looking for detailed "coverage"—
synopses of the stories—but rather gut reactions. We asked each reader:
did a particular story work *for you* as a potential film? Were there
characters—either heroes or villains—that you cared about? Was there
a plot with a beginning, a middle, and an end? Would this be an easy or
a hard story to adapt to the screen? And lastly, would this story have
narrow or wide appeal?

Some of our readers read dozens of stories; others only evaluated a
few. On the flip side, every story was read by several evaluators; and the
real contenders were read by more than a dozen judges. In the end we
had more than six hundred submissions and some sixty evaluators.

Did it work? That is for you to decide. We might have said "That is
for Hollywood producers to decide." But we didn't, for a very specific
reason: The voice of the marketplace—indeed the wisdom of crowds—
is far more powerful than the taste of any one studio executive. True, the
studio executive can "green-light" a project. But they can't ignite a trend,
build word of mouth, or get people to watch films they don't want to.

We believe there is a fundamental transformation taking place in the entertainment business. It is a shift in power from a few "experts" to the consumer—and *Next Stop Hollywood* is part of it.

That is why we are asking you—the readers, the moviegoers, the trendsetters—to tell us what you like and what you don't. Tell us, via our Web site www.nextstophollywood.org, which stories should be made into movies and who should star in them. We are also conducting competitions for the best movie poster and trailer based on these stories. So please check it out.

Will Hollywood decision-makers listen? We hope so, and we actually believe they will. But only if you participate.

Will there be a second volume of stories? That too is up to you. Our editor and publisher are watching this volume with interest. So, if you think this is worth doing again, please let us—and them—know.

Our e-mail address is contact@NextStopHollywood.org

Again, thanks for your interest in this project. We hope you enjoy the stories—and their potential as movies—as much as we do.

—**Steve Cohen**
New York City
Winter 2007

Next Stop
HOLLYWOOD

An Age of Marvels and Wonders

by Perry Glasser

Raylene is a single mother, down on her luck and on the run from an abusive husband. Bob, a retired college professor living in small Midwestern town, is slowly going blind from diabetes. Their paths cross, and someone lies dead in Bob's driveway. This cross between Thelma and Louise *and* Mr. Holland's Opus *is poignant, surprising, and wonderfully uplifting.*

The man pinned between my car and my neighbor's house screamed at first, shouted, threatened, cursed, bargained, pleaded, then finally wept, but now that he is quiet, I risk a close look. My car door strikes the gray stucco wall. The space in which I can maneuver is only a few inches because the driveway is so narrow. Taking my time, I emerge by first extending my neck and head. Then, after I push my left arm and left leg out, I raise my arm to the sky, twist, turn, and my right arm and leg follow. The driveway is that tight.

In the dark, cold rain, it's difficult to see much of anything. Twenty-five yards up the street, just beyond the oak that dominates the block, a streetlight sputters, but we are in dark shadow. Wind rustles the wet leaves; shadows shift. This neighborhood is known for its tree-lined streets, shallow lawns, driveways, and pitched roofs with old-fashioned vinyl and cedar shingles. Close to campus on this side of the river, housing is modestly dense. Despite the rain, the air carries the sweet smell of fireplace smoke. People like living here.

The man is bent forward at the waist, sprawled across my car's trunk, his arms wide, his right cheek flat on the black metal, mouth open. He mumbles, but I'm damned if I can make out what. The wind fusses the trees. Their leaves sigh and shake. Thunder grumbles far off, but I see no lightning. By morning, horizontal rain and wind will strip the last leaves off the trees. But not yet. Now the weather is a heavy, whirling mist that blots out everything. Nothing is distinct. My driveway is suddenly a dangerous place.

The young man is tall and thin, near haggard, but that's a fashion statement, not the sign of hardship. We've met. We're old friends, he and I. Men of the world, he thinks, the kind that share understandings of work and women. I have a well-honed imagination, but I can't explain how the short woman ever became involved with this man. *Just a guy with a baseball cap and a mullet.* What could that mean? She's better than that. His cap brim is tight and low over his eyes. He tries to push himself erect, but his hands slip feebly on the wet metal. The crimson satin baseball jacket might be new. He's an Expos fan. Red, white, and blue, but Canadian, a team that no longer exists, for God's sake. There's devotion, for you. The sleeve is ragged and torn where it snagged on the wall. I draw close enough to see from across the car that he is breathing, so I gingerly slide back into the driver's seat, race the engine, and put the car into reverse.

That causes me to back into him, another mistake. It's not panic; I am just a confused old man. I go forward a bit and straighten my wheels, but as I back out the length of the driveway, I oversteer and my car's front left fender crumples sickeningly when it scrapes the wall. My headlight shatters. The amber turn lamp falls intact out of its socket, dangling from black-taped, snakelike electrical cords.

All told, I've run the young man down three times. Will the short woman forgive me? I go directly into the house and call 911.

After I give the dispatcher all she needs to know, on a stool at the table in my dark kitchen's breakfast nook, I dry my hair and neck with a dishcloth until the pulse of a red and blue strobe douches the night. As I open my front door, I lift my old woolen jacket from a wooden peg, shrug into it, step onto my enclosed porch, and push my screen door out as far as the spring will allow it to go. Wet wool. It's a smell all about manly action, about being in charge. I should have a Labrador retriever. Duck lures. Things like that. I lean into the night and welcome the cool rain to my flushed face. Two policemen holding long flashlights come up my walk. I take a deep breath and remind myself to sound frightened. Anything else could prove suspicious, and I am a cautious man.

Almost a year earlier, two days before she follows me home, the short woman stands ahead of me in the checkout aisle. She is short like you could put her in your pocket, but she is hardly a dwarf. Just short. She glares at me. She says, "No," biting off the word, bitter on her tongue.

The cashier is none too happy with me, either.

I offer the short woman money because I'm hoping that for five or ten dollars I can save myself thirty minutes and score points with God. I am not looking for some medieval indulgence here, no Get Out of Purgatory Free card, but just maybe, if the Good Lord wills it, a small miracle; say, some July day my sandals might be guided past the bubblegum. All I want is to pay for my Muenster cheese, the soft kind. It will go with the unpretentious Riesling chilling in my refrigerator at home. I like the tapered neck of the brown bottle. The label with the milkmaid and the cat and the woodcutter pleases my eye. On impulse, I've picked up some Rye Crisps, something to vary from my usual Ritz. These Rye Crisps are my low-threshold adventure of the week.

My entire purchase is my dinner: cheese, crackers, and a glass of sweet, yellow German wine. Maybe two glasses. My doctor would kill me about the cheese. She'd give me a long, scary lecture. Then I'd go home and regret I had not bought a creamier Camembert.

The short woman is not slow. She pushed a full cart to the register, and she took only a minute or two to empty it, her hands darting swift as nesting birds. She's entitled to the time; I am not impatient; I have no place to go and no one waits for me. The only problem is she doesn't have enough money to pay.

The cart also contains her kids. They ride with the groceries. That's not unusual. Lots of people do that. It's a longsight better than the ones who lash the kids to their wrists with clothesline. These two might be a boy and a girl; it's hard to be certain. One wears a pink nylon jacket and the other wears a blue nylon jacket. You don't need to be Charlie Chan to figure this family out. The boy is four, tops—closer to three. The girl, maybe six. The frayed stitching on the jackets' quilting is unraveling, and on the girl's chest a dirty tuft of the fill leaks. The kid picks at it like it was a pimple. Beneath their unzipped jackets they wear candy-colored, striped T-shirts and generic jeans with lots of room to grow, the cuffs rolled up. They are roiling around on each other, squirming, needy, whiny, and loud. Their identical black knit hats stretch almost over their eyes, and they both have thick-knit maroon mittens clipped to the sleeve ends. Outside in early March, it is still cold enough to mist breath; but inside? There's no need for woolen hats, so both kids are pink with heat and shine with sweat. They have crusty, chapped running noses and what might be the glistening remains of a couple of pur-loined lime lollipops rimming their lips. They strain to touch their mother. The boy says, "Uppie uppie," a shrill mantra that in the past must have got him lifted into his mother's arms. It doesn't work now. On and on he goes, like a dentist's drill through Novocain. The girl's sticky hands pull at her mother's breast, yielding beneath a stained yellow sweatshirt. The neckline stretches; we all see the pink strap of Mom's ratty bra and the delicate line of her clavicle under translucent skin.

Mom's fingers part her sky blue nylon wallet. She probes compart-ments. She separates Velcro. The thing is jammed with crumpled slips of paper and folded photos, but none of that crap is money. Money is what she needs. That's why I offer.

Beth Anne, our cashier, has efficiently pushed the little mother's groceries over the register scanner. Beth Anne languidly chews gum, her mouth slightly open, and though her hand has twice drifted to the post to switch on the problem light to bring Frank the manager, she has not flipped it yet. She touches her nameplate and rolls her eyes, at six-teen having seen from the vantage point that is Register 4 all life has to offer.

Beth Anne is jaded because she is destined for better things. Beth Anne's chronic impatience for her real life to start has already chiseled frown lines in her young face. Despite all she has discovered about her-self since she was eleven, the details of her bright, glowing future re-main vague to her. As long as her skin stays clear and she keeps away from the Debi Cakes and Ding-Dongs, she'll be fine. Perfect, in fact.

I don't try to be judgmental, but ever since Dr. Feldman told me that macular degeneration would sooner or later leave me blind, I see more. It is one thing to be in the world, it is another to see it. What I do not see, I fill in. It amuses me. The blank spots in my eyesight may spread, but my mind supplies a different kind of vision.

Look at Beth Anne, for example. The knowledge of her special des-tiny is why trailer-trash, loser mothers plunge her into despair; they are irritating reminders of the capriciousness of Fate. She is not going to think about that. No sir. Customers are spittle afloat in the clear pool of her existence.

Look at the short mother, for another. Payment is due: $177.58 worth of groceries. She is down to searching for coins. Most of us want to avert our eyes at such a time; we read checkout aisle literature— pondering the aliens that despite monitoring TV and radio broadcasts for generations, choose not to appear to world leaders in the company of diplomatic envoys, but instead taunt us by causing cellulite, arthritis, and the rare form of leukemia that puts boys in bubbles; we read about the talking dog in Guatemala that in perfect English has predicted the end of the world for Tuesday next; we're enchanted by winners of the genetic lottery for whom fame and fortune does nothing but plunge them into heartbreak and life dramas filled with pathos so much more acute than our own, suffering the curse of being gorgeous, talented, or God-forbid rich. We wonder what the fifteen secret new ways to have sex that are guaranteed to keep a man faithful could be. Where is this research conducted? How long has it been going on? Can they use a sixty-two-year-old subject? Are we certain the camp followers of Caesar's legions were ignorant of these techniques? How about the courtesans who flourished in the Kremlin at the time of Catherine the Great? Fourteenth-century geishas? Have they checked the carvings on Hindu temples in Burma? Fifteen new sex techniques. Think of it.

Oh, we are lucky to live in an age of marvels and wonders, an age of daily miracles that inexplicably cannot ascertain why fatty deposits swell behind the retina. Maybe the aliens know, but choose not to tell us. Perhaps they are the cause. Perhaps we should journey to Guatemala to ask the dog.

The little mother dumps her purse onto the checkout counter. An errant nickel rolls free like an illegal immigrant sprinting across the Rio Grande, but the little mother slaps it flat. She pushes a single finger through the pile of crumpled pink tissues, a rainbow-colored kerchief, one of those clever, clear plastic rain bonnets that once unfolded never seem to be able to be put right again, four postage stamps, an open roll of butterscotch Lifesavers, a knobby hairbrush, two lipsticks, what might be a tampon holder, maybe a dozen keys on a single key ring, two pointless pencils, one of those fat pens with four different color points, Sunday giveaway food coupons that are irrelevant to today's purchases, a bus schedule, one half of a crumbling Lorna Doone cookie, and three packets of McDonald's ketchup.

I do like to account for details.

The little boy has already torn open his box of animal crackers.

I repeat my offer. "Let me buy the little boy the cookies. It will be my pleasure. A gift." I ask Beth Anne, "How much more does she need?" and the cashier's eyes cloud. Why is this old fool asking her to perform subtraction? Beth Anne's inchoate glowing future does not include higher math. Eyeliner, yes. Body piercing and tattoos, of course. She already gives head better than Paris Hilton. Ask Frank the Manager. But subtraction?

"You say you don't want nothing?" the little mother says to me.

I say "It's a loan. Or pass it forward. Whatever works for you." I withdraw a ten from my wallet. It has several older and younger brothers snug and warm beside it. I live alone, my needs are simple, and the pension is adequate. The ten I offer her is crisp.

"A loan," she repeats, and snatches the money from my fingers without touching my hand. "A loan."

Beth Anne taps a few buttons. The register bursts open. Beth Anne hands me $5.42. I gesture it goes to the little mother, but Beth Anne hands it to me anyway. This means the little mother won't have two cents on her as she makes her way home, but by the time I drop my Muenster onto the rubber belt that feeds everything across Beth Anne's magical laser scanner, the young mother is gone. If she suffers a flat tire, she will have to barter Doritos for assistance. Once past Register 4 and the magisterial Beth Anne, I figure I am done.

But outside, I see her beside a red pickup truck just two spaces away from my black Ford Taurus. This is how strange life can be; despite an acre of parking spaces, Chance makes us neighbors.

The kids are strapped into their car seats. The truck motor runs and the groceries are secure beneath a restraining elastic net in the pickup's bay, but when she sees me open my car's door, she comes over. With her fists on her hips, she says, "You don't buy me so cheap."

"I'm not trying to buy you."

She snorts.

"Not that cheap," she repeats and returns to the truck. She has to haul herself up to get behind the wheel. It's an extended cab, just large enough to have a back seat where the kids are strapped in. The engine roars as she drives up the rpms, so when she jerks it into reverse, she pops the clutch and the tires grab the macadam. They spin and smoke before she steers to the parking lot exit. By then, despite the cold, the truck exhaust is colorless.

Buy her?

———

The Riesling turns out to be more challenging to the palate than I'd expected; it's respectable, though a long way from distinguished. As I slice the cheese to precise proportions of a Rye Crisp, I reread *The Magic Mountain*, Thomas Mann's doorstop of a novel. I am at the wonderful passage about Old Castorp's silver baptismal bowl, that symbol of propriety, the family's station in life, and the continuity that is about to be disrupted by history. The irony is exquisite; we know how events will engulf the family, while the family, of course, does not. The print is small, but if I hold the book close to my face, I have no trouble. I read while the university's classical music station plays the usual, pleasant, undemanding material. Tchaikovsky. Berlioz. Mozart's shorter pieces.

I used to teach a night class at our fine second-tier state institution. We are proud of its basketball and football teams, manic about wrestling, and civic leaders point to the university's proud tradition of serving the citizens of the state. The students are not always of the most astonishing quality, though they are willing enough.

The chair of the department is new. Young, hired away from a school on the East Coast, he was no doubt lured by better public schools and housing that is comparatively low in cost. I suppose he has children or is planning to. I hardly know him, but he called a few months ago to ask if I could once again offer my winter session night class. The department secretary supplied him with my name. She keeps the Rolodex.

"Do you have any available day sections?" I asked.

Well, no, he did not. Only regular faculty teach day classes. I had to turn him down. He thanked me, did not ask me why I was uninterested, and told me he'd call if the situation changed.

I miss teaching. My class in Finance for Non-Finance Majors began on the very first night with my writing on the chalkboard in letters a foot high:

ASSETS = LIABILITIES + EQUITY.

We then spent fifteen weeks exploring what that means. It's as practical as Swine Science and has many more applications.

Last year, the last time I taught, I had a nice group. At 9:30 at night, after class, one or two students often walked beside me to the parking lot over the winding footpaths that lace the campus like fine wrinkles above an old woman's smile.

They'd ask the most extraordinary questions, seeking advice on credit card debt, mortgages, equity loans, life insurance, and even sometimes retirement planning. Inevitably, their questions about personal finance led to my questions abut their lives, and that's when I'd learn about sickly parents, untrustworthy spouses, too many children, rotten bosses, bad spending habits, thwarted ambitions, sudden medical bills, and unobtainable dreams. I'd meet husbands with all the financial restraint of teenagers, young wives who read too many magazines that told them they should want to "do it all."

My counsel mattered. I'd ask, "Why not stay home with the kids for five years?" and you'd think they'd been granted a license to follow their heart's desire. As if they needed one. But here was hard evidence. The professor told them what they already knew; they were wearing themselves out and doing their kids no favor.

I'd hear it all in that quarter-mile walk. At 10:00 P.M., when the bell tower clock chimed, those leaden notes rolled over us, our signal to stop chatting and head home. But we'd always stand a heartbeat more, to prolong our sense of embracing peace, silent beneath the splendor of winter's starry sky, and I'd imagine the globe of leaden sound expanding outward over the entire prairie. Our footsteps broke the frozen patina of the snow. If we looked back, we saw the tracks of where we had been.

Last year on just such a night, I said to a twenty-seven-year-old woman, "Be more aggressive with your savings and don't let the money your mother left you stand idle." She was terrified of an inheritance. Too many zeroes. What if she squandered it? "You've paid off your credit cards?" I asked, and when she said that she had, I suggested she undertake risk via the stock market. "Youth is a great advantage," I said. "Time will heal any bad luck. Look, you owe it to your mother that her future grandchildren will afford college and grow up in a nice house. Isn't that what she wanted?" She nodded. These were the things she needed to hear.

She walked with me all the way to my car and helped me brush an inch of powdery snow from the windshield and rear window. As I climbed into the driver's seat, she said good night and thanks, and that's when I nearly killed her.

I backed out of my parking space and stopped six inches shy of running her down. I'd turned around in the driver's seat. I'd checked my mirrors. I backed out very slowly. Never saw a thing until she cried out.

My night vision, I learned, was deteriorating faster than my day vision. Macular degeneration is a funny thing. No one understands it. I've got idiopathic spontaneous drusen, which means that for no known reason in no predictable pattern and at no predictable rate, crap accumulates in tiny spots under my retina.

Try planning your life around "idiopathic" and "spontaneous."

I finished the semester, but I could no longer kid myself. I am a hazard. In the day, I compensate by moving my head as I drive, I suppose, to teach at night, I could simply hire a car service—teaching hours are regular enough—but the idea is humiliating. My doctor says I was still okay to drive, but not to kid myself, either. Bright sunshine only.

Besides, I do not need to teach. For twenty-four years I worked for Great Plains Doll & Figurine. I still have my office door plaque: MR. ROBERT EVANS, CFO. Every woman under fifty owned a Birthday Betty. But when Jake Feinstein died, his sons, those blockheads, exported its processes to Brazil and Taiwan and closed the headquarters. When the word spread that Birthday Betty had her hair curled and lipstick painted by nine-year-old Malaysian orphan girls who worked fourteen-hour days, the company tanked. Now, original Birthday Betty clothes and accessories are hot on eBay, but the code word is "original," which means American-made. My pension . . . forget it. Not half of what it should have been, because of the early buyout; but, as I said, adequate until I go blind.

Jeanne was the teacher: an anthropologist. Summers she would travel to the most obscure places on the planet while I balanced the books. Ovarian cancer burned through her like prairie fire in a season of drought. Once she was gone, I could think of several reasons to leave, but I could think of no place to go.

So I will die here. Nowhere else.

Midwestern college towns have their charms. True, snow is not one of them, but the movie theater is first-rate, and I never stand on line to obtain a ticket. Live theater at the university means a new production nearly every week except for summer; *Othello* last year was first-rate. Our bookstore serves coffee with cinnamon or nutmeg, and they load the fireplace with hardwoods. Cybele, the older woman who owns the place, calls me "Professor"; her husband once attended my class. I hold the magazines closer and closer to my face. The letters appear to shimmy and dance. When the dark spots grow too large, I will say farewell to books. If I have the courage, I will say farewell to everything else, as well.

I rinse my glass and replace the remainder of my cheese into my refrigerator. I own a set of plastic containers in all sizes for such leftovers.

I think: *Buy her? Buy her? What could she mean,* buy *her?*

Tuesday, after a chicken sandwich at lunch, I head for the market, but I don't see the little mother. I like fresh produce, and I am out of lettuce. Beth Anne reigns again at Register 4, but she sees right through me. Not my motives; but her eyes pass through me as though I were glass. Men my age are invisible. The more blind I become, the more invisible I seem to be, though I see more and more.

On Wednesday the little mother sees me in the parking lot before I see her. I wasn't looking for her. Not really. I often go to market. She comes right up to me.

"I don't have your money," she says.

"That's all right," I say. She really is short. Her head comes to my chest.

Her hands are deep into her back pockets and she stares at the ground near my feet. It makes her seem earnest. She wears faded jeans and brown boots. Her chin is a hard line, her jaw set, and when she turns her head, I see her fine profile. Without children pulling at her, she is pretty. Lladro, porcelain white skin, pink and radiant with inner light generated by the cold and her inner heat. I recall the glimpse I had of those bird-thin bones of her chest when her daughter grabbed at her.

"I might have it in a week. I have a thing happening, and if it works out I will have your money." We walk beside each other toward the market's front doors. "It was kind, what you did. It was kind. Are you a kind man? I need to know if you are a kind man."

"I'm fifty-seven," I lie.

She nods. Her hair is tied back. I don't know how women do that. Oh, I realize it is all rubber bands or elastic, but the knack of it is something more. Jeanne never did it. Her hair was full and loose and brown, and she gave it one hundred brush strokes every night before she went to bed, but that did not stop it from falling out from the chemo. The little mother's hair is red; not bright red, but red like burnished copper.

"My kids are with my sister," she says. The electric-eye door of the Stop-N-Go swings open for us, but we stand in the cold. It shuts and opens, shuts and opens, because we are right in the sweet spot that makes the electric eye crazy. "That's me over there," she says and points to the bulletin board in the Stop-N-Go's entranceway. "That's what I have going on."

We walk closer. She shows me a sheet of paper that reads HOUSE-KEEPING. REASONNABLE RATES. Along the sheet's bottom she has neatly penned her phone number on a dozen or so small slips scalloped from the main sheet, so they may be torn off one at a time. The little mother has done her work with a computer that, she tells me, is at the library. They charged her a quarter for the green card stock. The page is headed by a graphic of a mop and pail. I don't tell her she has misspelled a word, and I solemnly tear her phone number from the sheet and place it in my shirt pocket. "There," I say. "I am first. I hope it brings you luck."

"You *are* a kind man," she says. Some people, when they smile, smile just with their lips; some with their lips and maybe their eyes, but the little mother smiles with her whole face. It is something to see. Her teeth are crooked but fine. His eyes are bright green. She tells me I am kind as if she were a prospector who discovered gold. She says, "I have to leave now. She's not really my sister, just a good friend. I miss my blood, but they are far off and gone, so I make my own family."

"What's your name?" I ask.

Her lower lip curls inward and she chews it, as if she is thinking. "Call me Raylene," she says. "The name on my license is Raylene Goodheart." She looks at me as if expecting a challenge. When I say nothing, she adds, "I have to go. Lynette has the kids."

Her red truck is parked far off. It's huge, the Dodge diesel, she tells me. Raylene walks quickly, nearly running. Her copper red hair flounces as she runs. Her hair is why her skin seems so pale. I can still see her distinctly when she pauses, turns, and pulls her hands from her rear pockets to wave to me. She probably had freckles when she was a kid.

Goodheart, I think. I almost believe it.

I buy a tin of cashews, a new hairbrush, a small bottle of Old Spice aftershave, and after thinking about it, I buy Grecian Formula, the blue goo in a tube for graying hair. It's not a dye or anything, but it enhances a man's mature look. It smells of lavender. It's masculine. What can it hurt? I need hardly any food, but I select a few apples. Fruit is tasteless this time of the year.

I am most of the way home when I see the red truck in my rearview. I pull into my narrow driveway, and as I walk from my car across the untidy front lawn to the front door I pretend I do not see Raylene in her idling pickup.

Two days later, twelve of the fifteen slips with Raylene's phone number have been torn from the forest green sheet at the Stop-N-Go. I stand close to count them. The day after that, Raylene's announcement is hidden beneath a yellow piece of paper announcing the formation of a soccer league for girls ages eight to twelve. I must have passed this bulletin board a thousand times, but I have never thought how it speaks the hurly-burly of life in this community. I stand close enough to read. A used snowplow is for sale. Someone collects money for African orphans. These are real lives, not my fabrications to fill in blanks. I've never looked. A new church is forming. There are announcements: childcare, resumé preparation, support groups for abused women, for alcoholics, for children of alcoholics, offers of jobs and free kittens, tutors for the SATs, people who want to stay still sell cars and trailers to people who want to travel. There is no support for anyone going blind.

I rearrange some thumbtacks to give Raylene more visibility, but just a few days later her ad is gone.

A week after our talk in the parking lot, one morning before I have my oatmeal and toast, Raylene appears at my front door. I have not yet shaved. I'm wearing a T-shirt and tan slacks. She stands wordlessly on the three cement steps, looks up at me, then walks past as though she has been invited and there is just no question of what must happen next. As she passes the doorframe, she sidles to make room between us for her plastic carryall filled to overflowing with cleansers, rags, paper towels, glass cleaner, Endust, and lemon-scented furniture oil. She has pulled her hair back with the scrunchy thing again, and in her dirty, flat-soled canvas sneakers, she is even shorter than I thought before. Even tied back, her hair hangs lower than her collar.

She makes a second trip to the red truck, and as she passes me again she says, "Nice place. Coffee would be good." She is halfway up the stairs when she calls over her shoulder, "I hope you own a vacuum."

She starts in the upstairs bathroom. Her pants are scarlet. They call them Capri pants today, but I called them pedal-pushers, once. Jeanne owned a pair, thin, sky blue cotton. She wore them when she was a girl. I may go blind, but I will always be able to see that. The summer we met, she was on a red-and-white, three-speed girl's Schwinn with a big brown leather seat, fenders on the wheels, and pink-and-white streamers that fluttered from the handlebars. We were kids. She buckled a white wicker basket over the front wheel, and she loaded it with food and a gunmetal gray steel thermos so we could ride together to Harris's field where we picnicked beneath a willow, the only tree in that field. Toward evening, the mosquitoes came up awful; but that afternoon was the first time we kissed. Jeanne's lips were salty. Neither of us closed our eyes, we were so damned eager to see.

"My neighbor has the kids," Raylene calls down to me, shouting over the roar of water in the bathtub. She is filling a zinc pail. "I only have two hours," she shouts. "The thing I said. It's happening, but not fast enough. I cannot pay you money. Do you mind ammonia?"

"You don't have to do this," I shout up to her as I measure out the coffee and try to remember if the bathroom soap has my pubic hair on it.

The water stops running. Her head appears over the balustrade. "Yes, I do," she says, "I do have to do this." When she steps back her head vanishes, but then reappears. "I should know your name," she says. "You should tell me your name."

"Bob."

"Bob," she says. "Bob is good."

Later, after she asks if it is all right if she stands on one of my wooden chairs, I watch as she wipes grime from the refrigerator's top. Her shirt rides up, and I see that across her back she has that tattoo, a curlicue of some kind from kidney to kidney. It looks Gaelic.

I notice this tattoo on many young women. It is not as though I am inspecting. It is the fashion. They wear short shirts to bare their midriff, and they wear low-rise jeans, so when they turn or move I can't help but notice the tattoo. They are none too careful about appearances in front of an invisible man, though I am beginning to allow myself to believe that, for Raylene, I may no longer be invisible. The tattoo is ubiquitous. For all I know, my daughter in Australia has such a tattoo. I do not know what it means.

Two hours later, Raylene sits at my kitchen table. She drinks a second cup of coffee. "This is what I do," she says. "I am sorry I did not get to finish. I can vacuum another time."

"I must pay you." When she does not argue, I find a twenty. "Is that enough?" I ask, and Raylene says that this time it is, but if I want her to come back, she will need to charge me regular rates. That seems fine to me, and we shake hands. Her hand is tiny, but raw from housework.

As she stands, she touches my bookstand on the kitchen table. Some people who are alone have a TV. I have my bookstand. It is a chrome, tubular thing designed to hold a book open and erect, allowing me to keep my hands free while I read. I want to read as much as I can before I cannot read anymore.

"That's a big book," Raylene says. "Are you going to read all of that?"

"I've already read it. I am reading it again."

She stares at me as if to see if I am making a joke at her expense, but then she says, "Like Scripture?" and I say, "Yes. But it is not a holy book. Some books are worth a second and third look."

Her finger touches the page, drawing back her hand as though she has touched something sacred. She lifts the heavy book from the stand, and her lips move when she reads the title, *The Magic Mountain*, but then she sits again and, aloud, she flawlessly reads:

> *"Then, seventy-five years ago, I was the youngster whose head was held over this selfsame basin; that was in the dining-room too, and the minister spoke the very words that were spoken when you and your father were baptized, and the clear water flowed over my head precisely the same way—there wasn't much more hair than there is now—and fell into this golden bowl just as it did over yours."*

Her eyes shut; she seems to be considering something far away and long ago. "I cannot abide Baptists," she says. "Were you baptized?"

I nod. "When I was a baby. My children were not. It did not seem important."

"I did not see any pictures of children," she says, and though she does not ask, I tell her about Geoffrey in Manhattan and Irene in Sydney. I don't like to visit Geoffrey; I tried it once. There is nothing to do in New York City except hurry to the next overpriced restaurant. If Irene could have settled on the moon, I think that's where that girl would have gone. She could never travel far enough away. She spent a semester abroad, and that should have been the end of it; but she met a man, stayed, and finished her degree in environmental sciences. "Irene and her mother . . . something was wrong there," I say, and Raylene nods as if she recognizes an old story. I do not mention the seven-year-old grandson I have never seen.

Jeanne flew eighteen hours to Sydney to stay three months when the baby was born, but I stayed here. From Chicago to San Francisco to Hong Kong to Sydney. Think of it. The world in a day. My wife and daughter patched things up. Jeanne and I planned to return together. We had plans, but no amount of planning helps if there is not enough time.

"The photo on the bedroom bureau. That's your wife?"

"Was," I say. "Jeanne."

"Pretty woman. They used nice wedding dresses in those times. They call that kind of brown finish 'sepia,' right?"

"Yes."

"Like henna rinse, but on a photograph. The veil she wore—it's pretty. That's called a mantilla, isn't it?" I say that it is. Raylene purses her lips. "I thought I was born-again when I was fifteen. I gave my life over to Jesus Christ, Almighty. Everybody was doing it. I will not argue that good can come of it, but I was knocked up six weeks later." She laughs as she washes our coffee cups and places them in the proper cabinet. "So much for the power of prayer. I have made a deal with the Lord that if He stays out of my life, I will stay out of His, provided He watches over my children. I hope that does not shock you."

I tell her it does not.

"It would, some." Her green eyes flash to my bookstand and she says, "I read a lot to my kids. It's important."

I tell her I agree. "Tell me about the tattoo on your back," I say.

"It's my tattoo," she says after hesitating. Have I been too personal? "I don't know about other people. Mostly I see girls with Celtic braids. They'd be Irish, I guess. But mine is the symbol of Albania. I found it in the encyclopedia. It's a two-headed falcon with a crown. My grandma was from Albania." She stands up and turns her back to me, lifting her shirt just enough. "I just love it."

And then she quickly gathers up her carryall tray of cleaning stuff. Since I live alone, she thinks she should only have to be at the house twice each month, a fact that will make her schedule difficult, though she is willing. I ask her to come once each week, anyway. She shrugs. "There's always work to be done," she admits. "I don't do laundry, though," and I agree to her terms. No laundry. She will do windows every other month or so, "But not in winter." Fifty dollars, cash, each week.

She asks me to put up some supplies—more paper towels, rags, Murphy's Soap—and she will leave them in a plastic bucket in my garage.

I buy a better vacuum for the upstairs carpets. An upright would be awkward for the short woman, so I buy one on casters. It's a tradeoff between power and weight with these things. The vacuum is made of an alloy created by NASA. Is that a miracle, or what? It costs nearly four hundred dollars, but who cares?

Each week, Raylene cleans my kitchen and both bathrooms, and every other week she vacuums. The little unit follows the little woman like a greedy puppy. She is careful not to let it collide with the furniture. The first time she vacuums under my bed, as we sit over our coffee she asks, "Why do you have a baseball bat under your bed?"

"I forgot it was there. Is it still there?"

"I moved it to your closet. It was in my way. Do you need it under the bed?"

"The closet is fine." Houses breathe at night, but Jeanne was sure every creak and sigh was a burglar. She would not abide a firearm, but she insisted I keep the baseball bat. It is a genuine Louisville Slugger made of wood. Pondering blindness, I wish I'd bought the gun.

From time to time, Raylene takes care of other things. She wipes mirrors. She dusts. She washes crystal. She kneels to wipe dust from the decorative carvings on the bedroom furniture. She oils the mahogany pieces in the bedroom and the oak pieces in the living room. Raylene informs me that once it gets warmer she will have to spend a day doing nothing but my upstairs windows, but on another day she will do downstairs. "It's amazing you can see anything at all outside," she says with feigned pity. "They are awful dirty and awful dim. Don't you ever want to look outside?" One day, with my permission she climbs a chair and disassembles the glass prisms of the fixture over the dining room table. She washes each piece in a bucket of soapy water. When she is finished, she flips the light switch. "Isn't that fine?" she asks with satisfaction.

Raylene is grateful when I buy her a white enamel folding stepstool. It's lightweight, and when she stands on it, she can near touch the ceiling. When she admires what a good idea the stepstool is, I tell her she can have it. I have to persuade her to take it, but she agrees when I point out her other customers will be happy if she does not stand on their furniture.

She works three hours each Tuesday, and she always takes the time to share coffee and talk when she is through. She usually stays an hour more. "Do you chat with all your customers?" I ask.

"Do I look crazy to you, Bob?" she says and helps herself to milk. She finds sugar as well.

Her business grows. First, they stop watching her every move; then they trust her with a house key. She is able to clean more quickly when no one stares over her shoulder, and she never shows up to learn she has been locked out. "That's the important part," she says. "I hate wasting time."

I take the hint and have a key to my door made for her, but I am always home on Tuesday mornings.

Another Tuesday, as she comes in my door, when she hears my radio. Her head lifts like a startled deer's. "Mozart," she says "*Eine Kleine Nacht Musik*." She wrestles a dust mop through my door. The long handle is taller than she. She's wrong. It's one of the Brandenburg Concertos, but right or wrong, that's not the surprise, is it? I don't correct her. It's startling. The short woman who cannot spell *reasonable* confuses Bach with Mozart.

I ask about her children as she moves a dust rag over the bureau top and around Jeanne's framed photo. "Lee D. and Amy," she says.

"Lee D.?"

She pauses to explain. "The D is for Danger. His Daddy wanted his son to be able to say, 'My middle name is Danger.' Isn't that a hoot?" She smiles that bright full-face smile. "It was the only good thing about the indecent son of a bitch."

I imagine the hellish life Lee D. will have in junior high school when the word gets out. "Amy is a nice name," I say. "What does their father do?"

"I have no idea where Amy's father is. Lee D.'s daddy is in jail."

"I am sorry to hear that," I say.

"Don't be. I put him there." She pauses as if to decide how much I need to know. "Eligible for parole next fall. I don't know what I will do then." She shakes her head with resignation. "Why is there such a thing as parole? Three years should mean three years, right? But now there is talk of rehabilitation and good behavior. That man would not know 'good behavior' if it came up and bit him on the ass."

I wonder about the rest, but it is not forthcoming, and I lack the courage to ask. As she mounts the stairs to start her work, she says, "He was a guy with a baseball cap and a mullet," as if that explained something, "and he could name his son 'Danger.' And I was that stupid."

Her silence the rest of that morning is like an August day when humidity and sun accrue clouds that turn a blue sky the color of a bruise. Over our coffee, she is less talkative than usual. Instead, she asks me to tell her more about the big book. Mystery, comedy, or adventure?

I explain that *The Magic Mountain* is none of these things. "It's about ideas," I say.

"What ideas?"

"Complicated ideas."

She stares at me. Raylene knows when she is being patronized. So I take a deep breath. "It's about a young man with no special opinions who goes to a mountaintop sanatorium for tuberculosis. He meets a lot of people who have different ideas about how the world works. He tries to decide who might be right and who might be wrong."

"I liked the little bit I read about the baptism. You wonder, what is it like to have family like that? My kids will never know anyone from their fathers' sides. As for my mother . . ." She shakes her head. "The less said the better. My grandma raised me, and I am not so sure she was my grandmother. Gamma was a good soul, I'll give her that, but she rode me hard. Hard, I tell you." Raylene stares into her coffee as what I can only call a sardonic grin flits across her lips. "I probably should have listened to her, but when I was fifteen I was not smart enough to think an old lady knew anything." Her green eyes hold me over the lip of her coffee mug. She is trying to determine if I have told her enough about the book. She waits, like a feral cat. "I have a brother, somewhere. A half brother."

"My grandchild will never know me," I say. She nods and allows the silence to weigh on us both until I speak again. "He's in Australia. That's a long way to go."

"You should go anyway," she says.

"I couldn't."

The unasked question hangs in the air. I don't know an answer. Why can't I go? I have no idea. I should, while I can still see. I won't, I know.

"Is the book exciting?" she finally asks. "How about the magic?"

It takes me a minute to realize she refers to the title. *The Magic Mountain*. "Not in the way you think. The weather is strange, so the young man loses track of time. Everyone at the hospital is in bad health. They expect to die. They think that excitement and movement is not healthy. It's a place for rest. So they don't talk about anything unless they think it is important. They don't have time."

She stands to rinse her mug. "I would like to read a book like that; it sounds to me like they are dead already, though. If they can't do much else except talk, I mean."

"I can lend it to you."

That makes her laugh as she rinses her coffee mug clean and places it in my dishwasher. "Oh, no. 'I would like to' doesn't mean 'I think I can.' Right now, when I make it to the last page of *The Cat in the Hat* I celebrate. I bet I read that book to Amy and Lee D. a million times.

That Dr. Seuss, he has ideas, too. You have to look close, but they are there."

Later that day, I open the bureau drawer beneath Jeanne's wedding picture. From time to time, I like to touch Jeanne's things, and while I have long ago given away all her clothing, I kept her jewelry. Her jewelry lies in a tin box that once held Danish butter cookies. Jeanne had no use for a fancy jewelry box. I suppose I should send the stuff to Australia, but I can't bring myself to part with any of it. I run my fingers through the beads and bracelets when I notice a piece seems to be missing. I no longer trust my memory when it comes to Jeanne, but the cameo cocktail ring I gave her one Christmas is missing, a young woman in profile surrounded by a dozen seed pearls, little things, delicate as Jeanne's tiny hand.

I decide I want to be wrong, but still I check the jewelry box every Tuesday. As I said, I am prone to imagining things when I cannot see.

One morning Raylene does not appear. I am annoyed, but then concerned. I dump her undrunk coffee into the sink. She should call. I don't care about the housecleaning, but what if she had a car accident or something? Does she have my number? She must have my number. I pace through the house like an idiot. Should I go to the Stop-N-Go and wait to see if she shows up there? If she wants more money, she should ask. I know I am paying her less than I should. I call information. No Raylene Goodheart lives in this town, at least none with a telephone. Then I remember that Raylene's number is on a stub of green paper that I tore from her advertisement. Fifteen minutes later I locate it in the nightstand drawer under the telephone. I crammed it into my address book like a bookmark.

Her phone rings and rings and rings. I call her three times, every hour. At least the phone is not disconnected. I will buy her an answering machine. She is in business; she needs an answering machine. She could be losing clients.

I write her number in big, bold black Magic Marker, triple ordinary size, under "R" and under "G". *Raylene Goodheart*. I will be able to see it until I cannot see anything at all. Beneath Jeanne's precise script, my block letters seem peculiar. Here are George and Marilyn Robinson and Harriet Ritter and Jane Rogers and Harold Reichart. Betsy Gallaway and Iris Gordon and Jane and Max Gottlieb. Jeanne knew and liked so many people.

The next day, Wednesday, Raylene shows up at her usual hour. First,

I hear her struggling with the lock, and as she backs through the open door she calls, "Are you decent?" Lee D. squirms in her arms. I am standing nearby, relieved and happy to see her. She is not ill. She has not left. She pushes the wiggly boy into my hands. "Here," she says and hurries right back out to the truck for the girl, Amy.

Lee D. is cleaner than last I saw him. It has been months. Without a hat, he looks neater, his hair a shock of brownish silk that falls across his forehead. He goes rigid in my grip, but soon relaxes and sucks his thumb, his dark eyes examining me. His head smells shampoo-clean. He is unafraid to be in the embrace of strangers.

Raylene returns with the girl and passes Lee D. and me in the door-way. She is a fury of motion, shouting in my kitchen as she runs water into a pail. "I just cannot do it. I am so sorry I did not come yesterday. Lynette is an airhead. An absolute flake. I don't know why I call her 'sis-ter.' She stood me up. She did not call. She did not leave a note. For all I knew, she was dead. Now, would blood do that? I ask you, Bob, would a real sister do that? What am I supposed to do? I should have called you, Bob. I know. But I thought it would just be an hour or so and I'd be here any minute, but no one was available, and this morning it's just as bad. Just as bad. I was able to postpone Mrs. Anderson to Saturday morning. She is good that way. Stand still, Amy, help Mommy. Lee D.! You be nice to the nice man. Do you have any cookies? They can watch TV, if that is all right with you. I don't know if I'll be here to finish the job today and you won't have to pay me. Amy, I said *stand still*. Lee D., if you need the bathroom you speak right up, you hear? No accidents. No accidents today. Now we add ammonia. Yes, I know it smells funny, Amy. It's ammonia. It's supposed to smell funny. I told you the nice man has cable, but I don't know if *SpongeBob* is on right now. Just tear me a few squares from the paper towels, honey. That's right. I am really so sorry about this, Bob, I know you don't care for children. No, I do not mean it that way, Amy. Mr. Bob likes you. Don't cry, honey. Please don't cry. I don't know if Mommy could stand it if you cry." She dashes up the stairs with the pail in hand, Amy close behind her. Amy pauses to peer at me through the balustrade. Pressed against two wooden columns, her face is her mother's, etched softer, her skin just as lumi-nous, but hair pure black. "I am Amy and I was born in May," she says. "I am Amy in May." She scoots up the stairs to be with her mother, and calls back, "I start school next year, but I already know how to read." Maybe she wears heavy shoes; maybe she deliberately clomps her feet. Each step is a cannon shot. *Boom. Boom. Boom.*

"I like children," I shout after her. I am still in my entranceway, frozen to the spot between the living room and the porch.

Lee D. squirms in my arms, serious enough about being uncomfortable that he takes his thumb from his mouth and with two hands pushes against my chest. "Down down down," he says, but I am not considering anything like that. Jeanne's collection of Hummel figurines on the living room coffee table look too much like toys, and her Wedgewood and Royal Doulton Toby mugs stand on the shelves of the baker's rack at the kitchen door. And while I do not think Lee D. can reach the china, the rack itself has a short leg and is unstable. He could confuse it with a jungle gym or something. So we struggle a little bit until I ask him, "Do you want a cookie?"

He stops squirming. "Cooooookie," he says, rolling the word like the Sesame Street Muppet, and he giggles.

"Cookie," I say.

"Cookie," Lee D. repeats.

I cart him to the kitchen, holding him at the waist as if he were a large, animated loaf of rye bread. I open and shut cabinets, but I already know there's nothing close to a cookie in the pantry. The best I can do is a Ritz Cracker.

Lee D. stuffs a cracker into his pink mouth, I give him another, and shortly we are both covered in a sprinkle of golden crumbs.

"Good cookie?" I ask.

"More."

It has been a while since I had a satisfactory conversation that called for fewer than five vocabulary words. My fingertips brush his corn silk, brown hair from his eyes. I sit on one of the two high stools I have in the breakfast nook, my arm loosely circling his belly as he sits on my lap. I spread four crackers in a square array, then line them up on the counter surface. We try a few configurations. Three in one line, with another on top. Three above and one below. This game makes him laugh, and when I use a cracker to tickle his nose, he laughs more.

One by one, he downs the crackers.

Then he squirms uncomfortably, and suddenly, remarkably, clambers up to my shoulder, his head goes flat against my chest, and by the soft regularity of his breathing, I am sure he is instantly, happily, blissfully asleep. His clean scalp is right under my nose. It has been a long time since I've felt life and warmth cling to me. So we sit still, Lee D. and I, while upstairs Amy and her mother dust and vacuum and scrub and rinse and wipe and polish.

Age of marvels? This is the same filthy kid I saw weeks ago in a shopping cart at the Stop-N-Go. He has not grown all that much; so it must be my vision that changes. I go blind, but I see more clearly every day.

After a time, Raylene puts up the coffee and returns her materials to the garage. Amy has followed her from task to task, silent, dark eyes enormous. When Raylene pulls herself up on the stool opposite mine in the breakfast nook, she says "Amy wants to know why you have so many books and if she can read one. She wants me to read to her from the one about the magical mountain, if there is a kid version. I told her I did not think there would be, but I also promised I would ask, if she was good. She was. She was good. A big help to her mother."

"How did you help?" I ask. Lee D. breathes softly on my shoulder.

Amy's large eyes blink. Her hands are folded neatly on the table before her, little thumbs intertwined on top. She sits on Raylene's lap. She slowly nods. "I was good. I watched the Cartoon Network the whole time. You have cable TV."

"Yes. I do."

"Do you have the book about magic?"

Raylene takes two sugars with cream. She pours milk for Amy. I take coffee black, but sweet.

Amy's lips are red and round. She speaks slowly and carefully, as if conversation were something new and required special effort. Which, of course, for her, it does. Think of it.

"*The Magic Mountain*?" She nods with great seriousness. I say, "That's not a book for little girls."

My mommy will read it to me. She reads to me all the time."

Raylene's coffee is hard to explain. It's my coffee. Same stuff from the Stop-N-Go that I always buy. Folger's. The water is from my tap. Same water I always use. It's my Braun pot. Same filters. Nevertheless, when Raylene makes coffee it is better than my coffee, more rich and more fragrant.

"I have a better idea," I say, and gently, so as not to wake Lee D., I stand. He bobs on my shoulder, a pleasant weight.

We'd look like a parade, if anyone watched, as we march to the garage through the door at the rear of the kitchen and down the three green wooden steps. Since Lee D. fills my arms, I direct Raylene to turn on the light. The wooden scaffold against the rear wall holds a dozen plastic storage boxes.

"It's in one of those," I say. "Look for a label that says 'Irene.'"

Raylene wrestles two boxes from a rack. Amy stands behind me;

there's no real danger, but with kids, you want to be careful. What if something fell? Raylene finds a crate sealed by masking tape on which Jeanne wrote "Irene" in black marker. "Just pull the tape off," I say. It sounds like cloth being ripped, or a zipper. "Open it," I say when Raylene hesitates. "Most of the stuff is junk."

But Irene's abandoned junk is Amy's discovered treasure. There's Mr. Mouse, a blue stuffed animal that went everywhere, everywhere but Australia. The jewelry box plays a selection from *Swan Lake* and the little ballerina pirouettes in front of the mirror. I forget. All the stuff a kid can have. I say to Raylene, "If you see any clothes that might fit, take them. If it does not fit now, it may in a year or two." Or three. Or four. Why haven't I donated this crap and taken the tax deductions?

The crate's bottom is lined with books. I tell them to look for *Charlotte's Web*. They find *Little Women*, a hardcover edition with a torn dust jacket and full-page color picture plates, a dozen "original" Birthday Betty outfits, and a coloring book that has never been touched. But the real discoveries are the copies of *Madeline* and *Eloise*, appropriate to her age. Amy seizes them along with Mr. Mouse and an untouched coloring book. I have no crayons. I promise Amy a box of Crayolas, and when her mother says nothing, I say, "The deluxe box. The biggest they have. Fifty colors. A hundred, if they have it. More."

When first I saw the short woman at the Stop-N-Go, Raylene could deny anything offered to her, but the tiny mother is unable to refuse anything for her children. I see her, new, and I begin to understand.

"This is a happy box of memories," Raylene says, looking up to me. She kneels on the concrete garage floor beside her daughter.

Amy hugs Mr. Mouse. She holds books against her chest. Raylene tells her how to refold the top panels of the plastic storage container. "There'll be more to find another day," she says. They push the box back against the wall on the floor. The space above the shelf where the box had been looks terribly empty.

Lee D. stirs and I hand him to his mother. The parade reforms; we march back to the house. In the living room, Raylene softly reads to Amy.

> *In an old house in Paris,*
> *That was covered with vines*
> *Lived twelve little girls,*
> *In two straight lines.*

"What's a pendix?" Amy asks later as Raylene turns the pages. Lee D. lies on his back beside me on the sofa, his dark eyes wide and open, soothed by the lilting music of his mother's voice. He twirls his hair as he drifts in and out of sleep, his sneakers against my thigh.

"It's a part inside you," Raylene explains.

"Is Madeline sick?"

"A little bit. She needs an operation."

Amy nestles in what I guess is her customary place in her mother's lap, her arms folded about Mr. Mouse. Raylene's voice explores syllables as if each word were a new taste on her tongue.

Lee D. fully awakens just as Amy sinks into sleep. This is the shape of Raylene's life, I realize. When one sleeps, the other awakes.

That's too hard, I think. Too hard for the short woman.

"There are five years between our children," I say.

"That's nice timing," Raylene says as she gathers up what she must. I carry a pail with a mop in it to the big red truck. First she buckles sleeping Amy into her seat, then Lee D., who resists only a little. He's not a fussy kid; just a boy. She climbs behind the wheel, starts the engine.

"I'll be here my usual time next week, if that is all right. This is usually library day."

"You didn't have to be here."

"Yes, I did," she says. "You keep saying stuff like that, Bob, but I don't do nothing I don't have to do. Or choose. You must have noticed that by now."

I have, I tell her. "I like this second trip down this aisle," I say.

"What?"

So with one foot on the running board, talking through her truck window, I explain my theory of how the Stop-N-Go is the paradigm of life. "We all start with the same empty cart," I say. "You might have bad luck and draw a cart with a sticky wheel, but once it is your cart, it is your cart for as long as you want. You can walk any path you want through the store. No one cares what route you take. You can explore any aisles in any order. You can omit whole aisles; you can stroll up and down the same aisle two or three times. Haven't you ever gone down an aisle a second or third time and spied things you did not notice before? We fill our carts as we see fit, and we live with what we take."

Burdened by babies and weary from work, Raylene listens to my metaphysics. She allows me to finish, but as I utter each sentence more pretentious than the last, I can see her incredulity tempered only by politeness. Jeanne had a facial expression like that. I'd ramble on, and the more I prattled on, the more her face deflated me.

I leave out the part about how some of us persist in pushing sticky wheels despite the fact that we are free to turn in our carts at any time, when Raylene says, "Bob, are we going to be friends?"

I tell her I think we already are.

She nods, pleased. "Bob, you are maybe the smartest man I will ever know, but Bob, the Stop-N-Go ain't nothing but a grocery store."

I hear her laughing as she pulls away, and the sound makes me smile.

I don't soon see the children again, but Raylene arrives as ever on the next Tuesday and begins her chores by saying, "Amy says 'Hey.'" She can already read *Madeline* herself. She likes the watercolors of Paris. "Tell her the crayons are here," I say. (When did they change the names of all the colors?)

On another Tuesday, Raylene discovers a carrot cake muffin in my pantry. After her chores, and after asking my permission, she slices it in half as if it were a rare delicacy. Muffins become a regular part of our time together. We take the occasional flyer on banana nut or poppy seed, but carrot cake remains our first true love. Our muffin ceremony consists of Raylene swearing she will only have half, and then breaking down to eat the second half despite herself. It not so incidentally means she lingers thirty minutes more with me, so every Monday I make certain to buy four muffins at the Stop-N-Go.

Raylene becomes harried and frustrated by how word of mouth has made her clientele more than she can handle. She reschedules me to Tuesday afternoons instead of mornings, because she needs the morning for a house on Elm in Pinehurst. She keeps Wednesday afternoons redlined. That is inviolable library time for Lee D. and Amy. Worse, some of her first clients become insulted when they recommend her to their friends or neighbors and Raylene has to say no. She could not work for a Mrs. Williamson, but just two days later Mrs. Freeman's husband, Arthur, accepted the transfer to the Milwaukee office. With her schedule opening up, Raylene called Mrs. Williamson back, "But by then, she'd hired someone else."

"What did you tell her?"

"That if it didn't work out, to be sure to call me. But she won't, Bob. That woman did not hire nobody else. Her pride was hurt when I turned her down. People get weird when they come to housework.

Weird, Bob, weird." Raylene receives special requests, too. Anniversaries. Birthday parties. There was a first communion party thrown by an Italian woman who did not want to be a regular, but just wanted one day of help. "But I was not about to wear that uniform she wanted to rent. Where do folks get such airs?"

More and more of her clientele is from west of Grand Street and east of the river, north of the bend, which means big Queen Anne homes with lots of woodwork and lots of old money. She is becoming frazzled and tired, but the pay is too good. "I need to learn how to say no," Raylene says.

"I disagree," I say. "You need to hire help."

She puts down her mug with a bang and stares at me. "Well now I know you are a crazy old man," she says. I can tell by how she says it that the idea is one she came to herself, but has no idea how to go forward. She is probably frightened of the prospect.

So I give her the short version of the three-week university lecture about entrepreneurship. Her business has attained critical mass: her clientele is self-sustaining and self-renewing on the demand side, but Raylene is up against the limits of her capacity to match demand with supply. "You are fresh out of labor," I say, "unless you are willing to quit going to the library or want to work on weekends."

She shakes her head.

I explain that the crucial issue for expansion of a service business is training. Hardee's is a pit and Starbucks thrives because Starbucks learned the trick of teaching people to make a double decaf latte or a skim milk double-shot espresso while burger places will let any acneridden high school flunky flip beef. Every business has its finesse. Donut makers go to Donut College. So I say, "Can you train other women to do what you do?"

"There's nothing to teach," Raylene laughs. "You start on the left, go around the room, and apply elbow grease. In a big room, don't try to clean more than you can reach with two steps; you have to sort of divide the room up in your head."

"If it were that easy, then everyone would be cleaning houses. Why do you think all the women who are making demands on your time aren't first going to lots of other cleaning services?"

She listens as I tell her how she might plan, and as I do her green eyes first widen and then narrow as I answer each of her doubts. There's Geoff's room upstairs we can turn into an office. All we'll need is a phone, a desk, and a filing cabinet. New employees must first go out with Raylene to watch and learn, not to mention build confidence in the client. Eventually, the new employee can be sent out alone. "But only after I say okay," Raylene interrupts me.

"The chief asset of a service business is your reputation. You have to guard it," I say, and the little woman nods.

"And that's why no one but me holds the keys to the houses," she says. "After a while, I just open the lock and let them in. That's right, isn't it, Bob? Think of it. We might be doing three or four houses at the same time."

I think of Jeanne's cameo ring, but instead I ask, "What's your schedule now?"

"One house in the morning and one house in the afternoon, if neither is too big. What kills me is when they are far apart. There is no time for lunch, hauling myself from one place to the next. I suppose with enough business, I can make better schedules," she says, and five minutes after saying that Raylene is asking me if it might be better to send three girls to a single address all at once. "Maybe as a team they can handle four or five houses in a day. One of them would have to be in charge. Like a team captain."

Logistics and deployment? Piece of cake. Raylene is quicker than any student in my university course has ever been. Don't explain excess value-add or hierarchical organizational structures to Raylene—she is way ahead of you. She calls Lynette to say she will be late.

Our customary thirty-minute coffee stretches to three hours. Raylene brews an unprecedented second pot and picks the walnuts from the top of a second muffin without any pretense of slicing it. She can only hire women with cars, she can see that. She likes the notion that we ask them to buy their own brushes, rags, cleaners and such, but she is willing to lend any new employee whatever money she needs to get started. "That way, they already like us for helping them out," she says, rolls her eyes, and adds, "and they pay us back, guaranteed. It's so sweet. We just deduct it from their first pay. It's not like a loan." I wonder how soon she can get the job as chair of the university management department. Maybe dean of the business college.

Her good soul wants to supply free daycare for employees, but I say that so kind an idea has to wait, because of what it will cost in insurance. She says, "Insurance?" and I explain how she cannot go forward without it. "Someone, sometime, someplace is going to break a bowl or something, and you can expect people will expect you to pay for it." She chews her lip at this. "Look, it's better to pay a few dollars to an insur-

ance company than it is to go bankrupt because someone dumps bleach
on a Karastan. You carry insurance on the truck, don't you?"

"Well, that's the law."

"Now you know why it is the law."

Maybe it is the extra caffeine, but the little woman becomes animated. I've seen this a few times with students, not many; but it always
makes the small hairs on the back of my neck stand on end. Raylene's
vaguest dreams are coalescing into a graspable vision.

We talk about limited liability partnerships and incorporation; we
talk about Social Security taxes, and when she looks a little doubtful and
a little fearful about the enormity of what we are discussing I say, "Why
don't you just let me take care of it?"

"You've got to explain, though, Bob. I won't go ahead with anything
that I do not understand. I could not allow that."

I agree. And so, without much conversation, we are partners. I pro-
pose a 60-40 split, in her favor, of all revenues earned by employees after expenses; but she will keep all monies earned by her own labor, just
as it has always been.

She chews her lip and shifts her weight on my breakfast nook stool.
Her feet swing several inches from the floor. I suspect this deal will earn
me not so much as a nickel until we have employees working two hundred hours per week, and I suspect that will never happen, but I don't
care about the money. Why would I care about the money? She says
"Fifty-fifty or nothing," and I laugh.

It will be a classic partnership. Our skills complement each other.
From synergies spring profit. Raylene may be able to end her food
stamp life and never again dump her purse in search of nickels.

She leaps to her feet. "There," she says. "It's a deal."

"I'll have to file papers," I say. "You'll need to sign them."

She sags as if I have punched her. "I can't have that," she says.

"It's ordinary business," I say. "It protects us both."

She weighs this new part of the proposition. "I can't have that," she
repeats. "I guess we are busted."

"What are you talking about?"

Her fist pats her thigh. "Could we just make it your business? Keep
my name out of it?"

"We could, but you'd have to become a silent partner."

"I could not be silent."

"Just an expression."

"Well, all right then. Keep my name out of it. All the papers in your name and we are partners on a handshake."

The matter is settled. I walk her to the door. "What do you think of 'Raylene's Cleaning,'" I ask.

She freezes with her hand on the doorknob, and when she turns to me, even a blind man can see the panic in her face. I am having an attack of floaters—too much coffee. Dark dots occlude the center of my vision. Sometimes I think going blind at a single stroke would be easier. A bolt of lightning from God would suit me more than having my sight bleed away, the constant reminder of oncoming perpetual night.

"That's no way to keep my name out of it, Bob," she says. "We can't call it that. Not that."

"You've got a reputation. . . ." I am about to start my lecture on branding and goodwill.

"No, Bob. No. It's not me. It's James. Lee D.'s father. James Boncoeur. Don't ever call him Jimmy. He hates 'Jimmy.' James will come looking for me. I know he will. It's just a matter of time. I don't care what they say. Nothing stops James if he has a mind. He will. I cannot let him find me. When he gets out, he will come looking. I was careful when I came here, but James has his ways. Someone always knows someone who always knows someone and that person knows me. So it is just a matter of time. We can't call the business anything with 'Raylene.' It will cut the time it takes him to find me. My life is permanently temporary."

I ask if a restraining order will be a condition of his parole, and Raylene says, "You may know about checkbooks and taxes, but in my world restraining orders are nothing but PDC." She sees my puzzled look. "Pre-death certificates. Look, Bob, if you are to be my partner, you need to know how it will be. I will rabbit and never look back." And as if to persuade me of the seriousness of the situation, she turns, bends, and pulls her shirt up. She arches like a cat's back. Raylene wears no bra this day. The skin of her back is luminous as ever. I can make out the knuckles of her spine, where her ribs push at her skin, and I can see above the crowned two-headed falcon tattooed on her back a circle of six scars, each the size of a dime, the circle four inches in diameter, scars made with a cigarette. That much is plain.

"That's not the worst," she says, as she tucks her shirt into her pants, her back still to me. "It's Amy he wanted."

As she hurries down the steps and along my flagstone walk, she calls back to me, "You think of a name, Bob. Think of a name." The red truck roars to life. She pops the clutch, the rear wheels grab the street, and I think I hear her shout, "But keep me out of it."

The trees are leafy in May. Amy's birthday must be soon. Amy in May. I need to know the date, because if she is starting school in September, I want to buy her a fancy notebook. Maybe a backpack. The wind stirs the trees. There's just enough wind to make that leafy sound. The clear blue sky is dotted by a few clouds, huge and white; it's a child's-picture-book sky. I can look at the sky and see it as it is . . . plain as day.

I sit a long while on my cement steps, looking like the village idiot gazing up at Heaven. My neighbor waves to me as he walks across his lawn. I wave back at him. I think he nods, but I can't see until he is close. He wears boxy brown shoes and an undone yellow necktie. His name is Smith or Johnson or Jones. He is an ordinary guy who in an ordinary way comes across my driveway to me. He wipes his palms on his slacks before he shakes my hand. He tells me that in the coming weeks—he's not sure when they will start, contractors being what they are—a crew of landscaping guys will be working on his front lawn. How's that for ordinary? "You may want to pull further into the driveway," he says. "I'll be sure they keep it clear, but what with trimming the trees and what all to make space for a small pine, you may want to pull your car all the way in. Keep it safe from woodchips or whatever." He points at the big oak set in the sidewalk between our places. Its roots buckle the pavement. It must be four or five feet around, an ordinary tree.

I thank him for the warning. We shake hands, and he says something trite about how we men have to do things to keep wives happy, how I must know how it is. We share a masculine chuckle at the futility of dissuading women from redecorating, or landscaping, or some other fool project. "I just wanted to give you the heads up," he says, and adds, "Likely not until fall. They want the sap receding." As he turns to go, as if it were an afterthought he turns back to me and says, "There's a zoning hearing. I need a variance." I tell him I can't imagine that will be a problem. "In a few years, the tree might cast shade on your property," he says. "I want you to know it all in advance." I thank him again as he nods affirmation and in his ordinary, decent way ambles back to his front door. He has a wife and teenage children. Two or three. I've never really noticed. It's not something I've needed to see.

He waves to me from his front steps, identical to mine, and as his screen door bangs shut, I think how *ordinary* is a good thing.

Those burn marks must have been deep to have never fully healed, made by more than a touch, and then I realize that since they are in a near-perfect circle, all six of them, the cigarette had to have been applied by someone who was being deliberate and could take his time. I spread my fingers. They were closer together than that, and I see how James must have restrained her while he did his work. Held or tied? It is much too horrible beneath the perfect blue sky and white clouds on this spring day to think about those details, but that's the problem with a practiced imagination; visions come, unbidden. I do not want to picture the circumstances, yet my imagination is relentless. My ordinary neighbor is planting a tree, but the little woman's back carries six evenly spaced burns deliberately and slowly applied with a cigarette. I can invent whole lives for checkout aisle employees and kids at the mall, but this act of cruelty baffles me.

Maybe what Jeanne had always insisted was true: Evil stalks us.

By summer's end, Amy and Lee D. call me "Mr. Bob." The Traveling Goodheart Circus arrives at my house about once a week, sometimes more. Amy discovers treasure after treasure among Irene's castoffs; Lee D. in a year or two may find the same in the crates labeled "Geoffrey." I plan a tetherball court on the backyard. Dig a hole, plant a pole, anchor it with cement. Even a blind man can manage it.

At the mall, I buy a folding playpen, though Raylene tells me he should be outgrowing such restraints. Lee D., however, adores his private space in the living room. Raylene makes no other comment, which I have come to understand is as close as she allows herself to expressing satisfaction.

Best Cleaners grows. We employ Amber, Heather, and Wendy. They are steady, and they work without strong supervision. These women are happy to have jobs, they are honest and become loyal. Where did Raylene find such women? I wonder, but Raylene says, "Good people are all over the place, Bob. All they require is a chance."

Establishing Heather with a set of regulars requires more effort than it should, but I make the phone calls to clients that need to hear a man's authoritative voice. Heather is black, and in this enlightened corner of the world where everyone gives lip service to hearty endorsements against racism, when a black woman approaches the silverware, people require a masculine word of reassurance. Heather, who has traveled this road many times, just says, "Thanks, Mr. Bob," and goes about her tasks. She is, by the way, faster at her work than even Raylene.

But early in July, we have to let Enid, a fourth girl, go. We hire Enid in the same way we hire everyone else, though I have no idea what that is. Enid fails to show up three times in two weeks, and after our pointed requests nevertheless seems incapable of making a phone call to alert us. One thing or another disrupts her life, her no-good husband, her boy, her car, her cramps. "Maybe she is running hard luck," I say, but Raylene says, "Cut her loose," and that is the end of the conversation between Best Cleaners' senior partners. I slip Enid a fifty-dollar bill from my own pocket when I fire her. She thanks me, folds the bill into a neat square, and slips it into her jeans. She has been at this crossroads before.

None of the women choose to work more than four days each week. These are mothers of young children. They need a few dollars and flexible hours. Raylene reserves her Wednesdays for the library, and while I do not know the details of the others' lives, I am sure they do something similar with their free weekday. They all want to be home by 3:30 P.M. when their kids arrive from school. In some businesses, that seems a liability; we take it to be the sign of a responsible person. I often worked at the office until six or seven in the evening, later in tax season. What good did it do me?

In summer, they make child-care arrangements. I gather there are ad hoc summer cooperative daycare centers—probably unlicensed, illegal, and therefore affordable—all over town.

In July's high heat, the girls dress lightly, and they are careless about themselves in front of me. They scratch when they itch. They work braless for comfort's sake, and they wear thin cotton shirts. House cleaning is no act of haute couture. Why not relax? The old man is invisible, anyway. Wendy and Amber have the same tattoo as Raylene. The same, but different. I make no apology for seeing what I see; I am sixty-three, I say and do nothing to make them uncomfortable, and if the girls notice my looking, they either do not mind or, perhaps, they enjoy my appreciation. I don't stare. With my eyes, anything at the center of my vision soon disappears.

We redefine a "good client" as someone who leaves the air-conditioning on for the cleaning girl. Some do; most don't. At thirty, Amber is oldest, her legs skinny and long. Her hair is short as mine. Wendy smiles easily and laughs too hard, and Heather is always first to appear in the morning, drinking more coffee than anyone else, black with two sugars. Like me.

Best Cleaners grows to have about thirty steady clients. Some come and go, but on average we do thirty addresses twice each month at an average of a hundred dollars each visit. The house keys hang on a Peg-Board in Geoff's room. The Peg-Board was Raylene's idea, the product of her frustration of trying to find a set of keys in a drawer. She divided the board into five columns, Monday through Friday, with yellow electrical tape, and with blue tape she lined four rows, one for each week of the month. Our Peg-Board calendar reveals at a glance what is what. Each set of keys is on a small chain attached to a small cardboard disk with the first initial of the employee who generally does the work. The address is on a bit of masking tape beneath the keys. When the girls have their emergencies—and they do—they cover each other. They pool their tips; no one squabbles over generous clients.

From time to time, Raylene drops in on the girls at work, as much to assist as to maintain quality control. The girls—which is what Raylene insists on calling them, so I develop the habit, too—enjoy her company. We pay by the hour after gauging how long a job should take, but we estimate on the generous side and embrace the point of view that a job done is done. That means an employee can finish early, garner the same paycheck, and skedaddle. So who'd resent a boss who grabs a wet mop to help?

When Wendy's boy comes down with chickenpox, the girls cover for her for three days. She does not miss a dollar. When she returns she cries a little as she says "Thanks," and when Heather's mother takes ill, Wendy can't do enough overtime for her.

One morning, as I walk past them on my way from the office upstairs to the kitchen, they stop talking. When I bend to take milk from the refrigerator, they burst into laughter. My T-shirt? My shorts? I will never know about what is funny, but the sound is pleasant, and when later I ask Raylene what that was about she says, "Never you mind, Bob. Girl talk."

I keep the books on a laptop spreadsheet, but by August I have to increase the font. When I drive, I take care of everything on my left while God protects my right. At the Stop-N-Go, I park far away from the other cars. A little extra walking is a good thing, right? I park on the white lines. If you've been cursing the old fart who takes up two spaces, that old fart would be me.

And one hot afternoon when the air in the house is superheated and dry as dust, I open Jeanne's drawer and the jewelry box. The missing cameo ring sits on top of everything else. The heft of the collection feels right again, too. I keep the drapes closed to keep down the heat.

Dust motes float in the ray of sunlight that slices through the space where the drapes meet. It is funny, the things I can see and the things I cannot. If the ring was not there before, now it is. So what? If the jewelry was pawned, the pieces have been redeemed. That which was taken is returned.

One August afternoon when the air is heavy with water sucked from the black earth, the corn outside town stands head high, on a day when tornadoes may be breeding somewhere as the thunder boomers mount and grow dark, Raylene finishes early and I ask her to stay with me in the office for a rundown on how we are doing. She stands in front of the fan and airs her armpits, flapping her elbows like a chicken. I tell her that our clients are paying on time. They are regular, good people who like us. They enclose thank you notes with the checks, a good sign. If Raylene wants, we can manage one more employee. She shakes her head.

"One more thing," I say, and I hand her her first dividend check.

"This is five hundred dollars," she says, amazed. "Are you playing with me, Bob, you old rascal? Five hundred? Really?" She does a little dance that makes me laugh.

"It could have been more." I can see her look of amazement. "I have held some back for the business. Emergencies. Bills. Things like that. If you need to draw, let me know."

The business account at the bank has our two names on it. That required a long conversation and two days before I could persuade her to sign the bank form, and she did so only after I asked what would happen to her money if I died, and only after I assured her no one but the government can force the bank to give up her name and address. A silent partner can be silent only so long.

She shakes her head and sits on the wooden captain's chair that Geoffrey used to study in when he was a high-school student. Her reality is changing. Who she is. What she does. Who she thinks she is. I look at the little woman, her red hair and blue kerchief, her bangs aflutter in the fan's breeze, her sponge yellow halter, her jeans shorts, her bare feet in open-toe, blue high-heel sneakers, and her scarlet toenail polish. She holds the check with two hands. Her feet don't reach the floor. It is not the air-conditioning that gives me goose bumps.

"You took the same?" Raylene asks suddenly.

"Of course," I lie.

"Damn, Bob. Damn." She jumps to her feet again and holds the check held out at arm's length in her two hands before her. "This is a fine thing."

That day when Raylene leaves me, at the door she tiptoes to kiss my cheek and asks, "Bob, isn't it time you told me what is wrong with your eyes?"

"What makes you think I have eye trouble?"

She has noticed my head bobbles as if I cannot keep her in focus when I look at her, and she tells me that I do not seem to look directly at her but off to one side or the other, but Raylene tells me that the give-away is the magnifying glass on the dining room table beside my book-stand. "That wasn't there when I first met you."

I explain macular degeneration to Raylene, as though it has any explanation that is sensible. I try to sound casual about it, as if it was a natural part of growing old, which is what my doctor wants me to believe. The brochure from my ophthalmologist shows a cheerful-looking woman on the cover. She is smiling; perpetual night is a mere inconvenience, no worse than nail fungus. I do not tell Raylene the pact I have made with myself for when I cannot see at all. I will do what I have to do. God will be my judge.

"That is too hard," she says. She abruptly spins on her heel and walks away across my lawn to her truck on the street, but then she quickly comes back up the walk. "Should you drive?" she asks.

"I am all right, so far." Her hands are deep in her back pockets and she peers at the floor near her feet, her posture whenever talk becomes serious. She chews her lip. I know her tics. She waits for me to speak, and I say "I promise I will tell you when I cannot drive."

She nods. "All right, then. But I will read to you," she says. "You can't read with no magnifying glass."

"It's not so bad," I say, but she will hear nothing about it.

So Raylene makes time to read to me almost every day for near thirty minutes at the day's end. Sometimes she picks up the kids before she arrives. She juggles her schedule to move my cleaning day to Wednesday mornings. Some days she brings the children so that after lunch they can make faster time to the library. They also visit on some Saturdays. Amy comes to rely on my cable television. Lee D. knows where I keep his cookies. He prefers animal crackers, but will indeed accept Ritz if I am out of stock. One day in August, the sirens wail when a twister snakes from the sky somewhere nearby, and shortly after the all clear sounds, Raylene telephones.

"You all right?" she asks.

"I'm just fine," I say. "You?"

"We're sitting pretty," the little mother says, and after another minute or two of small talk we hang up.

In the cooling evening, I sit on my cement front steps and think how nice it is to have someone who cares.

Shortly after Labor Day, as I make my way through Register 4 with my green leafy vegetables, animal crackers for Lee D., carrot cake muffins for Raylene and me, and what turns out to be five sacks of groceries filled with who knows what, none other than Beth Anne says, "How are you?"

I have attained visibility. I ask how her pregnancy is treating her, and she rolls her eyes. She tells me, "I call you 'Mr. Animal Crackers and Carrot Cake Muffin.'" She smiles and touches the piercing in her eyebrow. "You must like animal crackers a lot." I confess that I do, and she waves to me as I exit through the electric eye door.

As I drive home, the lane markers snake before my drusen-warped vision, I see the splendid world we inhabit. Just at the edge of town, cornfields stretch as far as anyone can see. A west wind carries the smell of growth and renewal, the rich smell of fecund life springing from black earth. If you drive just a little further into dairy country, you are among barns, Holsteins, and silos set like toys on rolling green hills. The trees in my neighborhood, oak and spruce, full and green, lower their arms to the ground, but with students returned to town, the sense of fall is in the air. In a matter of weeks, the leaves will turn crimson and orange and yellow and then brown.

I am at my car's open trunk retrieving my groceries when I notice the man sitting on my front steps. He is right in the middle of my three cement steps, second step, center. You can't go around him, by him, or over him. He drops a cigarette between his knees to the step and crushes it with his black boot as he stands to greet me at my own door. "You'd be Mr. Evans?" he says and tips his Expos baseball cap and runs a hand back over his scalp. He scoops a grocery package from my arms. He takes it from me easily.

"Can I help you?" I say.

He opens my unlocked house door, and when I do not invite him in, he places the grocery sack on the porch. "I am looking for someone," he says. "My wife, actually. A woman named Raylene Boncoeur. Well, she was my wife, once." He walks beside me back to my car. There's an unfamiliar Dodge pickup parked two doors down, the same diesel model as Jolene's, but black, and I am wondering how fast I can get to the base- ball bat when he says "James Boncoeur," and puts out his hand. "She may not be calling herself that, anymore. 'Boncoeur,' I mean. She might be calling herself Raylene Shaughnessy." I take his outstretched hand. His grip is gentle, even respectful. Under the black stubble on his throat, I see the tattooed cross on his neck set well above his shirt collar. I can't tell if the cross is wavy from my sight or if it is just amateurish work, maybe self-inflicted, the kind done with a Bic pen and a straight pin. The cross's arms aren't crooked enough to be a swastika, I can see that even with my sad, old eyes. "Shaughnessy was her name when we met? Her people are Scottish and something else I cannot recall. But mostly Aryan?" He makes statements that sound like questions. "She's a red-headed gal."

"Why would I know her?"

"She's got two children with her, sir. One of them is my boy? I'd like to see him? You can understand that, I am sure?" He lifts two sacks of groceries and I take the last one as he reaches up to close my car trunk. "I am on my way north tomorrow, so this is a long shot. There's a job waiting for me up in Marquette. An interview, anyways. Crew of a lake ship. But I do want to see my boy, if I can, before I ship out. You can un- derstand that." He chatters on about the opportunities in the Upper Peninsula, a place where a white man can still work with his hands and make a respectable living, provided he has regular habits. "It's close to my people," he says. "I am a white American, but from Canadian stock. 'Boncoeur.' That's French. Means 'good heart.' They speak French in parts of Canada. Did you know that?"

"Is that a fact?" I say.

As if we are old friends, we walk to the house. He asks me if I have something wrong with my vision, and I tell him that I do. "I thought for a minute you were giving me the evil eye," he says. "I am sorry for your trouble. No offense."

As we reach the steps again, my neighbor, the ordinary man, shouts a greeting and scoots over to tell me that the landscaping will begin the very next day. "They figure four weeks, but I am betting more." He de- scribes the flagstone walk, the hedges, the flowerbed, and the new pine tree he expects will grow so high it will blot out the sun.

"James Boncoeur," James Boncoeur says, wiggling his fingers, un- able to extend his hand with my groceries clutched to his chest. "That tree will look fine come Christmas."

"Pleased to meet you," my neighbor says. "Art Jones."

We hear more about Art Jones's plans. I have not exchanged this many words with Jones in fifteen years. We are three men of the world, we are, one blind old man without the strength to hold onto his groceries, one ordinary man with an ordinary name who is planting a tree, and one sadistic jailbird just out and intent on God alone knows what.

When he heads back, James Boncoeur says to me, "Nice fella," and without waiting for an invitation, this time he heads across my modest enclosed porch and through the front door and through my living room toward the kitchen as though we are old friends. He passes Lee D.'s folded playpen as if it were not there, and he places the grocery sacks on my breakfast nook table.

"See, now," he says, "my Raylene moves around some, and she sometimes works as a housecleaner. I heard you run a business like that." He shakes his head and smiles about how all he had to do was go to the library and on a computer there type into Google the telephone number a nice lady gave him. Google supplies a reverse telephone book, and the lady lived on the east side of the river, a better neighborhood. He just went door to door. "Ain't technology wonderful?" he says, and lowers his eyes when he adds, "All those young mothers needing work. You must get plenty, you old dog." He lightly punches my bicep. James and I are old buddies. "You haven't seen a short, red-headed woman? Maybe she dyed her hair? Maybe you didn't hire her, but she applied? This is Best Cleaners, am I right? Oh, you'd remember Raylene if you met her. She's a pistol."

I thank him for his help with the packages and ask him to wait while I go upstairs. "I'll check my records," I say. He puts his hands in the back pockets of his jeans the same way Raylene does, and I leave him standing there, just a good old boy in jeans with a Montreal Expos baseball cap, a black Dodge truck, a haircut called a mullet, and the heart of a Nazi. His hair is dyed bright yellow on the sides.

Upstairs, I find the bat. The heft feels fine. It's not three foot long, a kid's baseball bat, actually. I smack it into my left palm. It will do. Geoff played second base and was awful at the game. Could not judge a fly ball with a compass and an astrolabe. But his bat will do. I take a cut at the air; the swing pains my shoulder.

I flush the toilet so James will know why I have delayed. I want him off guard, but I have no plan. I finally understand why homeless men kill each other over trifles. When you have little, you defend it ferociously. It's not comic. It's not pathetic. It's the way we are made.

Since my neighbor saw James, an affable man in a jeans jacket with his arms full of my groceries, I will have to explain that the stranger who broke in intent on doing me harm terrorized me. After years of use, the stairs creak from weight in their centers, so I move to the edge where the old wood make less sound. They will ask how I got the drop on him. *You retrieved a baseball bat? How did you manage that, Mr. Evans?* I want to come down on him from behind, but that is chancy. I put the bat in my left hand and grip the smooth handrail with my right. How will I get behind him? If I don't brain him with the first blow, he'll have me. He's young; he's strong; he's quick. I am old and going blind, but not frail. Not yet. The trick is to swing low across his legs, get lucky, hit a knee, and only then his head. Just once. Maybe a light tap won't kill him.

I rush the kitchen from the base of the stairs. I swing. The bat meets only air.

James is gone.

My groceries are neatly set out on the table, canned goods beside fresh produce. The brown paper bags are neatly folded on the high stool. The lingering faint stench of tobacco floats in the air.

I open the door to the garage and tiptoe down the wooden steps, and then I slap the wall plate that is the electric garage door opener. I haven't worked the garage door in years. The pulleys and rusted springs creak as the door rises. The last of the day's light floods in under the rising door. Under a blue plastic tarp at the edge of my narrow driveway are two bags of cement mix, the future anchor to Lee D's and Amy's tetherball court. I hold the bat rigid against my leg. I slowly walk up the narrow driveway. I stop at the front of my car.

James's black truck is gone from the street.

I lift his cigarette butt from my front walk and find three others. Marlboros, I think. He must have sat a long time waiting for me. Where has he gone? Will he be back? I hear cicadas. Evening comes earlier this time of the year, though it is still warm.

I make a selfish, criminally self-serving decision, a wager with God, cheap for me, but dear for Raylene. I gamble that James spoke truth and is hurrying to the Upper Peninsula, and so I will say nothing.

I endure a bad week of worry, but my bet seems a winner. I pray that James Boncoeur joins the crew of a lake vessel, and when I hum "The Wreck of the *Edmund Fitzgerald*" I pray that the witch of November comes early.

Amy's class performs a Columbus Day recital. I never had the patience for these things when Geoffrey and Irene were children. A teacher calls me *grandfather*, but I do not correct her. She is right. I *am* a grandfather, just not Amy's.

Would Raylene move in with me? All I know is that she lives across the river near the railroad. It can't be much of a neighborhood; nothing over there is. I have space enough. Too much. Should James Boncoeur return, he will come straight here, so I am raising the stakes of my bet. But the little mother will risk anything for her children, and the school near my house is the best in town; at least it used to be.

When Wendy is late for work two days running, Raylene guesses she has morning sickness, and sure enough Wendy shares her news with the entire crew of Best Cleaners at the next morning shape-up. Heather takes away her coffee and fills a glass of milk, and Raylene says "Well, that's wonderful, Wendy," and hugs her. "You just tell us what you can or can't do. You need time, you tell us. Will that be all right?" Wendy is a big woman. Nordic maybe, with boat hips and shoulders. She must weigh twice what Raylene does.

Raylene creates our maternity policy on the fly. She comes to this stroke of managerial brilliance in front of the other two girls, and I tell you the effect is electrifying. It's not lost on me that more and more she talks about Best Cleaners as "us," a joint enterprise that includes our employees. In all my years at the doll company I have never seen anything like it. These women's only jobs have been exercises in mistrust, a presumption that they will do as little as possible for the most they can get, but here is Raylene, unmistakably in charge, but choosing to abandon her power to cultivate loyalty with kindness. How will Raylene look on the cover of *Forbes*?

One evening, Raylene and I sit on the cement steps at my front door. The fall night grows chilled quickly. We wear sweaters, but cold still clutches at my ribs. Stars hard as pins burn in a cloudless night. I think I see fireflies, but there are no fireflies at this time of the year. How could I see such a thing? The cells in my eyes discharge a final electrical impulse as they die, starved of blood. Or maybe the flashes are my imagination. What I can't see, I imagine. Like faith.

Raylene's whisper suddenly percolates from the darkness. "I've done bad in my time, Bob." I can hardly see her shape in the dim light. Her presence is a feeling more than a testimony of vision. Our voices float.

I say nothing; she repeats her confession.

"What of it?" I say. "Who hasn't?"

"You're a kind man, Bob, so you don't imagine the bad people can do. You just always trusted me, haven't you?"

"That's true," I say, and think of the cameo ring, the jewelry once taken and then restored.

"See now, Bob, that's plain foolishness. You don't know what I am capable of. I've done things that make me ashamed. Don't you ever suspicion me? Just a little?"

"Never," I lie.

"I've done terrible things, Bob. Terrible."

The moon is a silver cup in heaven's ink black dome. Raylene touches the back of my hand with her fingertips, as intimate a gesture as she knows, and then, to join her children at my TV before they leave, she slips through the dark open door, gently shutting it behind her. I think how my random act of kindness to the little mother in the checkout aisle has paid me a high dividend. On that day she told me that she could not be bought so cheap.

She never said she could not be bought.

I cross my legs, uncross them, cross them at the ankles, and lean my head back against the screen door. Was Raylene ever sold? If so, what of it? Who doesn't have a past? We live in the present. Even a blind man can see that.

The door cracks open. She is barefoot. She's quiet until she says, "Do you want me to read to you tonight?"

"Not tonight." We're working our way through *Oliver Twist*. Amy likes the parts with Fagin. Her head emerges. I turn to look in her direction, but I can't really see her, so I face the street more. "Bob," she says, "Tell me true. Why didn't you never try nothing funny with me?"

"I don't think of you that way," I lie.

I can hear her breathing not two feet behind me. "You are so full of shit," she says, and the door shuts with finality. I sit a while more in the night laughing to myself.

Comes mid-November, I fix on the idea of hosting Thanksgiving dinner for Raylene and the children, but the idea takes on life and grows. Why then not all of them, all their kids, their husbands if they have them, their boyfriends, anyone they really want? Why not? What else is money for? Best Cleaners has much to be thankful for.

One overcast afternoon when the clouds have been lead all day, after I've accomplished my routines, opened the mail, deposited checks, and made a few spot-check calls to keep customers happy, I scoot over to the Stop-N-Go. I like to shop earlier now that the light of day scatters by six. Night driving is just too much for me. In September, Dr. Feldman ordered me into the passenger seat; she gave me the names and numbers of two car services and the Visiting Nurse Association, but I never called them.

Beth Anne at the Stop-N-Go is waddling with child. She says, "Hey," and I imagine the future life of her kid, better than I'd have predicted last spring. I have my green leafy vegetables for my eyes, romaine lettuce, broccoli, and kale, which I despise. I unload my shopping cart: a dozen jumbo carrot cake muffins for Raylene and the girls, two boxes of animal crackers for Lee D. and Amy, and I add some green and blue plastic cups and those disposable plates, two jugs of apple cider, and since I can't resist it, a paper tablecloth with pilgrims, Indians, and turkeys. Jeanne had a wonderful recipe for cranberry sauce. I'll have to look it up. I'll need those wicker plate holders.

The feast is more than a week away. I have not yet so much as shared my idea with Raylene, but I am nothing if I am not all about planning. Why delay to the last minute? The murky daylight is closing down fast as a pinched candlewick as I drive home. I peer over the wheel. I bobble my head this way and that to see what I must see. If I trusted my eyes, I'd be driving between wavy lines, but that's an illusion I adjust for by driving straight. The road seems to uncurl as I crawl forward, slow and steady, my pace no problem as long as I stay off the highways.

Since Art Jones started his landscaping project, there's a backhoe on our front lawns, but I hate parking in the street; there's no telling who will come by at night. The worst part of driving anywhere is coming home. The Taurus barely fits into the driveway between our houses. I cannot manage driving the length to the rear and the garage, so I park off-center in the driveway. That creates the most space between my door and Art Jones's wall.

Tentative, fat raindrops spatter my windshield. The wind is rising. I am so intent on navigating the narrow space that I do not see the black Dodge diesel truck parked on the street up the block. But once I have parked the car and have managed to come to the rear of my car to open the trunk, I see where the truck's dome light shines on a driver in a baseball cap. He flicks a glowing cigarette out the window to the wet street, cracks open the door of his truck, steps down carefully to grind the cigarette under his boot, and strides toward me.

James Boncoeur, returned like a bad penny.

"Can I help you with that, Mr. Evans?" he says and without waiting for my answer he reaches past me and takes the heavy jugs of cider. He can carry them with one arm. "James Boncoeur?" he says, with that smooth lilt in his voice that makes a statement a question.

"I remember you," I say as we cross my front yard.

He says he is happy that I do. "Nothing worked out in Marquette," he says. "The deck is stacked against white men everywhere. The trick is to be in your own business, not work for someone else. That's why I admire you, Mr. Evans. I do. That cleaning business . . . ," he sucks his teeth, ". . . that is a working man's dream."

I unlock my door, we wipe our feet on the mat on my enclosed porch, and we make our way in past the baseball bat, through the living room, and beyond the folded, hidden, playpen. We pass through the dining room where Raylene once a month dismantles my chandelier and washes each bit of glass. In my kitchen I put my packages on the slim, red Formica table in the breakfast nook while James Boncoeur carefully places the cider jugs beneath the table.

"You'll recall I am looking for Raylene," he says. "And my boy? That would be Lee D."

"I do remember that," I say.

We hurry through the thickening rain to the car for the last of my groceries. James Boncoeur stands beside me like an old friend and notes that I must be planning a large party, all those groceries for just one man. Thunder rumbles. He gently closes the trunk and he lifts the final sack. We raise our collars to the rising wind.

We walk the length of the house once more, James prattling on about the Upper Peninsula and his unqualified conviction that this country is being taken over by forces that will end it. "The family, for example. Judges are dismantling the American family. A boy needs his father, wouldn't you say?"

I agree.

"So if you knew of my Raylene's whereabouts, you'd be obliged to tell me, wouldn't you?"

"Why don't you tell me what she looks like again?" I say. "Maybe she isn't using her name."

He considers me before saying, "Now, I hear over on the other side of the river, there is a cleaning girl named Raylene who works out of this address?" He places the last sack on the breakfast nook table. The animal crackers tumble from a bag onto the floor, but he bends to pick those up and seems to think nothing of the fact that a man in his sixties stocks up on children's cookies. "Both Mrs. Jorgensen and Mrs. Edwards, you know them?"

"I do."

He nods, happy I will not choose denial. "Both Mrs. Jorgensen and Mrs. Edwards, they say they have their homes cleaned by this Raylene each Monday. Mrs. Jorgensen in the morning, Mrs. Edwards in the afternoon. They pay Best Cleaners. Now that's you, isn't it? They say the service is terrific and that if I am looking for a girl to ask for Raylene. You are Best Cleaners. Now, that's right, isn't it?"

"It is," I say.

He nods. He is pleased by our progress.

"Then my Raylene might be your employee? Short woman? Reddish hair? Kind of jumpy. Green eyes. Quiet most of the time? Given to airs about herself?"

"I know her," I say. "Just started with us."

"Well all *right*, then. If you can supply me with her address, I can be on my way, and sorry for the trouble."

"I don't know her address," I say. "I am sorry to disappoint you."

He sits on my breakfast stool and pushes back the bill of his Expos hat with his thumb like a man who is resigned and tired of pursuing what he wants, knows he will have it, and simply is exhausted by unconscionable delays. "Mr. Evans, how can that be? I mean, a man like you? I respect you. All those business smarts. All those girls running around doing what you tell them. How is it you would not know her address?"

"James," I say. "May I call you James?"

He nods.

"Why do you root for a baseball team that no longer plays?"

He half-smiles at that. "A man stays true to his first love," he says.

I nod. I lower my voice as if we might be overheard. "James, I tell you this in confidence because we are men of certain convictions. This, my friend, is a cash business. I pay the girls folding money. They come and go, so cash has certain advantages." I put my milk in my refrigerator, coffee in the pantry.

Why do these guys so love that solemn bullshit tone? As if they were part of some cloying brotherhood that shared knowledge of a higher truth, when in fact they are clueless about what makes life worthwhile: the love of a good woman, children, building something that will remain after them. I'd get these students, always men, who intoned what they said to their own chests, chins lowered to their shirts, sure that Life was not a gift or a celebration but a joyless obstacle course. They enrolled in my finance classes to learn how to beat the system, but I taught that schemes were no substitute for plans. First they'd argued, then they dropped out, sure I was part of the guvmint-jew-nigger-media conspiracy that barred them from their dreams. But their dreams were little more than inarticulate testosterone-ridden crap about freedom, a word they twisted to mean the liberty to beat women, keep their kids ignorant, and long for a paradise that was no more than a vague vision of a four-wheel drive, a muddy road, and a six-pack of Old Milwaukee.

"Why, you dog, you!" he says, grinning broadly. "You don't pay no taxes, do you?"

"Not a red cent. It used to be a great country."

He tips his hat, and runs his hand back over his head. The mullet is growing back. He has a small clip on his hair at his neck. The tattoo of the cross on his throat jumps above his collar when he throws back his head to laugh. I've never noticed before, but one of his canine teeth is gold. "I admire that, sir. I do." He smoothes his hair and replaces his cap. "And Raylene?"

"I think I know where she lives," I say, "but I am damned if I know the address."

"That's not going to do," he says, and narrows his blue eyes.

"I can take you there," I say, and his face brightens.

"You will?"

"Why not?"

"That suits me, Mr. Evans. That suits me just fine. We'd best go before this storm worsens."

So he pulls up the satin collar of his Expos jacket, and I pull up the collar of my black nylon windbreaker. We head out into the night.

It's dark. This is no longer some shadow hour. It is dark as it gets. The wind and rain are mounting. In the upper boughs, the rain slaps leaves with genuine force. We stand in the shelter of my porch as I lock my house door. James will be happy to follow me in his truck. Since the truck is parked up the street beyond the oak that dominates the block, I will drive him to it. It's only a few doors down, but in this weather, "that makes sense," I say. We push open the screen door and sprint for my car in the narrow driveway.

As we run, I shout to him. "The driveway is too narrow for you to open the passenger side. Wait here! I'll back out!" When I get to the Taurus, I shout back to him, "James, can you clear those leaves from the rear window?" I say. "And with all the construction, if you could guide me as I back out of the driveway, I'd be grateful."

He nods. "I'll clear them leaves for you, Mr. Evans. Easy enough."

I shout my thanks and climb into my car. I start the engine. I can't see a thing. That's how I remember it. I see just shapes and light. I hold my left foot on the brake and slip the car into reverse. The car wants to move. I near stand on the brake. As the leaves clear from my rear window, I abruptly lift my left foot from the brake and with my right press the accelerator. If James shouts a warning, I don't hear it. The wind is pretty fierce. The leaves blow. I am just a confused old man going blind, and this is wind-driven rain in November.

Confused, blind old man that I am, I run over him three times.

By spring most of the mess is cleared up.

I have paid every dime required to repair and repaint the stucco side of Art Jones's house. I gouged an awful bad scar. That good, ordinary, easygoing man is a friend. I don't know why we never spoke. I like Myrtle, his wife, as well. Art's only worry was that the construction on his yard was the cause of the accident, but I reassured him this was not the case. "It was me," I said. "Too proud to stop driving." Myrtle confided in me that tongues in the neighborhood had waggled about the short young woman who visited the old geezer so often, so I gave her the details of my blindness, mentioned that Raylene and I had not only been business partners, but fibbed that Raylene had some training as a nurse. This satisfied Myrtle's curiosity about the comings and goings of the other women. People are saying "Hello" to me on the street, so I guess those waggling tongues have been stilled, and my status in the neighborhood has climbed.

James Boncoeur required a full hip replacement. They make artificial joints from titanium. James will walk forever with a cane and a limp. He spent weeks in the hospital and will continue to need physical therapy for a long while. I am truly glad he is not dead. Since his right leg will be two inches shorter than his left, even Amy can outrun him. No one has designed an artificial retina, though I gather there is some research, which if successful will be too late for me. But good luck to them, I say.

When the time came, Dr. Feldman offered a deposition that my eyesight was shot and that I'd been cautioned to drive only in emergencies, a shade away from her actual advice, but my lawyer and I chose not contradict her. They pulled my license after my former student also by deposition told the county prosecutor about the snowy night I nearly ran her down.

My insurance company accused me of negligence for not informing them of a substantive change in my driving ability, but I had a driver's license in my wallet and no mandated state eye test to establish my inability to drive had been administered, so we remained in a gray area of law. All I need do, my lawyer maintained, is claim that I had not realized my sight had deteriorated as much as it had, which made me guilty of bad judgment, which is not negligence. Dry macular degeneration is an insistent, insidious condition, but it's hard to identify the precise day I should have decided I was blind. "And look sorry," my lawyer said.

I do not know if I managed that. I did stare at my hands.

When the D.A. learned of James's prison record for abuse, and Mrs. Jorgensen and Mrs. Edwards verified that this ex-con drifter had made inquires about his former wife in violation of his parole, the D.A. was disinclined to prosecute me for much of anything. I claimed I was trying to drive to a police station for my own safety after being threatened for not revealing Raylene's whereabouts. I was not a criminal, just a befuddled, frightened, frail old man.

The mess that remains is the tort. James will sue, but my lawyer thinks he will be hard-pressed to find a jury to rule against a blind man. They will settle out of court for the limit to my liability on my car insurance. James will whine to whoever is willing to listen that the courts won't give an honest white man his day of justice, but James is just another jerk with a mullet and a baseball cap, from a team that no longer exists, no less. Last I heard, he has returned to his grandmother in Quebec Province. His chances of demonstrating financial damages diminish every day he enjoys Canadian healthcare.

Heather and then Amber pretty much run Best Cleaners. I've lost interest, though I keep the books for them and make sure they are paid regularly. I've given them both raises as they take on more responsibility. Our Wendy had a healthy girl, eight pounds, eleven ounces. Wendy continues to work for us now and then, our first call whenever we get a special job or someone is throwing a party or something like that. Oh, and Beth Anne at the Stop-N-Go had a boy, Frank Jr. The store manager handed out cigars. Best Cleaners continues to grow. When we hired Phyllis and Carmen I made Heather a 10-percent partner to keep her from striking out on her own, her 10 percent coming from my fifty. When Heather sees our receipts she says "It just doesn't seem possible, Mr. Bob." When our Yellow Pages ad came out, we had a party.

But in the eight months since I ran down James Boncoeur, I have not seen Raylene. I suppose she heard a man was making inquiries, and she made like a rabbit, just as she said she would. She could not know that James Boncoeur could no longer hurt her. I picture her running out into that stormy night, her children in her arms, throwing a few things into the truck, gunning the motor, popping the clutch, and vanishing into the Middle American night.

Winter for me was a long, slow plunge into darkness. The snow that fell in December was still on the ground in April. When I was not with my lawyer, once the girls had the shape-up and were gone for the day, I sat in the house by the sunny window, but maybe because of the season, but maybe because of my eyes, each day grew darker than the day before. Night gathered early, it seemed to me. Some days I held a book on my lap just for appearances, which is crazy. There was no one to see. I could not fool myself. The world went cold, and I'd find myself thinking I would soon have to make good my promise to myself to end everything before I slid into perpetual night.

But three days ago I received a picture postcard from the Meramec Caverns, Jesse James's hideout in Missouri. "We are OK," is all it said, printed with red crayon in letters an inch tall. No signature. I showed it to Myrtle. God bless the woman. "Look at that," she said, "the postmark is from South Bend. That's the home of Notre Dame, Bob. They play wonderful football, don't they? We went to South Bend years ago. They have this bell tower, but South Bend is nowhere near Missouri. . . ." and she prattled on in this vein quite a while until my kettle whistled and she refused tea, all the time my wondering how a postcard from Missouri was mailed from Indiana.

The tiny red-haired woman peering over the wheel of a diesel red pickup, hauling her children to the library to read to them, crisscrossing the country to escape a man she did not know could barely walk, saved by a man who could barely see, was emerging from the American night.

It's June. The sun shines longer each day. The trees are in bud, and I can tell that less because I can see, than because my eyes and nose itch with new pollen. When the breeze is from the west, you can smell the farms and fields just outside of town. When I lift my face skywards, I can feel the warmth of the sun.

So though I cannot see much except flashes of light and shadow—shapes that move toward me or move away—against advice, I have bought a bus ticket. I have told the doctor I am going east to New York City to visit my son, and she grudgingly has admitted that journey is worth some risk. I am actually carrying a white cane. It folds neatly on three hinges. Dr. Feldman insisted on the cane. She gave it to me. I've never unfolded it until today as I climbed aboard the Greyhound bus. It is early morning, not yet sunup. I damn near broke my neck on the bus steps.

What Dr. Feldman does not know is that I have not called my son in New York City. No. I am unsure I will. The bus travels on Interstate 80, which coincidentally passes right through South Bend, the home of the Fighting Irish. I will depart this bus for a day or two to make inquiries about a cleaning girl there. Her name may be Goodheart, or Boncoeur, or even Shaughnessy. My guess is to try the neighborhoods where faculty reside. Their homes are neat and liable to be filled with books. I owe Raylene a debt, and I have the cashier's check in my pocket for $4,237.56, her share of the business profits these months passed. It must be delivered. Just three days ago, she mailed a postcard from South Bend. She could have been passing through, but I think not. At least, I have to go and see.

The driver assists me to my seat, up front, only a row behind him. As the bus belches to life and accelerates from the terminal, the sudden movement carries my head to the seat. I hum the Notre Dame Fight Song. Lee D. will like to sing, *Shake down the thunder from the skies!* He'll need to learn the words.

And so we set out east into the light of the rising sun. Dawn spreads over my face. Finding Raylene will take some luck, but I have been a lucky man. I can see that.

Dirk Snigby's Guide to the Afterlife

ALL YOU NEED TO KNOW TO CHOOSE THE RIGHT HEAVEN

plus a five-star rating system for music, food, drink, and accommodations

by E. E. King

Dirk Snigby is an advertising copywriter. Some might say that given his profession, he has already sold his soul to the devil. So he does nothing so pedestrian in this story. Instead, he enters into a business agreement with the red fella. Apparently there is increasing competition for available souls, and Satan has engaged Dirk to write a Zagat-like guide to the afterlife. Every major religion is equally skewered—Dirk is an equal opportunity offender—and Dirk has some complications with his business partner. This story has the feel of Heaven Can Wait, Bedazzled, *and* Damn Yankees *rolled into one.*

This is the story of a man who was never at a loss. No, I lie; this is the story of a man who was usually at a loss.

Fifteen years ago Dirk had taken a job with Ideas Incorporated where he toiled without joy. Ensnared in a pair of golden (or more accurately bronze) handcuffs that kept him chained to nowhere.

His single attempt at altruism, Copy Writers Without Borders, was nothing but a sad joke.

No, this life was too ephemeral to matter. If there was an answer, it must be in the afterlife.

Ah, the afterlife . . . therein lay both the solution and the conundrum. There were too many options.

The Jews were out. As far as he could ascertain, they didn't even believe in an afterlife.

The Catholics . . . well, he liked the idea of confession, but there was a tad too much persecution and pederasty in their history to make for comfortable conviction.

There were just too many afterlives. How could he possibly be expected to choose correctly unless he had more knowledge?

Dirk returned home after a hard day of trying to figure out a way to make Ex-Lax sexy. "Buy Bowel Pal."

"Heaven . . . ," Dirk mused, "I must learn more about heaven."

Dirk entered his cheerless apartment.

Slumping onto the overstuffed couch, he listlessly punched the remote control on his television.

The picture was clear, the color bright.

This was especially surprising because Dirk Snigby had a black-and-white TV.

"Are you concerned about your future?" queried a darkly handsome man.

Dirk nodded.

"Do you wonder about the afterlife?"

Dirk, who had disregarded the colorful transformation of his hitherto black-and-white set, now snapped sharply to attention.

"We are offering," continued the handsome (if slightly smarmy) stranger, "a course that will provide you with the answers to just such questions. Enroll now and all this knowledge can be yours. After all, what have you got to lose, except your ignorance? You can register at www.whatsinafterlife.com."

Suddenly the color flashed off and was replaced by black-and-white static and snow.

"Gees," thought Dirk. "That's some connection!"

Dirk rose and slouched over to his laptop, his computer flashed into brilliant color.

Welcome Dirk, flashed on the screen.

Do you wonder about the meaning of life, or even if there is a meaning?

Yes, thought Dirk.

Well, wonder no longer. Simply press the "Yes" button flashing now. This Thursday a qualified instructor will be available to answer all your questions.

"That's tomorrow." Dirk, almost without volition, clicked "Yes."

We'll see you tomorrow night at 8:00 P.M. at Elysium College near you!

"I've never heard of Elysium College."

A map flashed onto the screen.

"How weird," Dirk puzzled. "I could have sworn that I knew every street in this neighborhood."

Thursday, the very next day, Dirk spent trying to entice the teen market to purchase denture cream.

Once home, he got in his car and followed his map. To his surprise, the street he had never noticed was just where the map said it would be.

Dirk pushed open the entryway and found himself at a door on which was posted a torn piece of notepaper; the words "Religion and Afterlife" were hastily scrawled on it.

Dirk entered and saw the very handsome (if slightly smarmy) stranger he had seen on TV.

"Come in, come in," said the stranger with a rather forced jollity. In person, the stranger was even more striking, though rather more haggard than he had appeared on TV.

"I am here to answer all your questions."

"I doubt that," reflected Dirk cynically.

"I know, you doubt that," continued the stranger. "I realize that you feel your questions about the afterlife cannot be easily answered."

They can't be answered at all, thought Dirk moodily. The only way to really answer them would be to be able to visit all the different afterlives, and then live to make my decision.

"I know," said the stranger tiredly. "It is the only way."

"What?" squeaked Dirk, alarmed into full attention for the first time in years. "I didn't say anything!"

"Well," continued the stranger smoothly, "I rather just assumed that you feel the need for personal experience. "We are prepared to offer you exactly what you want: a firsthand visit to not just one but multiple heavens."

"B-b-but," stuttered Dirk, "you could only do that if you were God or . . ." Dirk's sentence staggered lamely to a halt.

"Do I look like God to you?" asked the stranger wearily.

Dirk had to admit that he did not.

"Okay," said the stranger with a slight lift of his eyebrow. "No more beating around the bush then. Let me introduce myself: Lucifer."

"B-b-but," stammered Dirk once more, "even if I believed you, which I most certainly do not, what would be the point of trading my soul for a premature glimpse of Heaven?"

"I can give you my utmost assurance that the very last thing I want is your soul," said Lucifer. "Do you know how overcrowded Hell is these days?"

He haggardly raked a hand though his glossy, dark curls. Dirk noticed that he was graying at the temples.

"I thought it would be a lot more enjoyable," the Devil confessed. "At first, when Hell contained only a few thousand souls it was. Now, most people don't even try to get into Heaven and, if they do, they often go about it in very disturbing ways. I don't care what you've heard; blowing up people is not the way into Heaven. Neither is blowing up medical clinics. In fact, I think it'd be safe to say that usually bombs, guns, and killing don't make for easy access."

He gestured in irritated fatigue to his chest. "Then there's the *idea* of Hell. People have a lot of different notions of what a Heaven is, but Hell, it's always just a lot of people jammed together burning.

"I tell ya, it's hard to manage. What with overpopulation and global warming, Hell compares very favorably to New York or Tokyo on a hot day.

"Then there are the burning flames. I mean, how much pain can you feel when you're dead? One of the things about being dead is that you aren't very sensitive! Anyway," sighed Lucifer, "I don't mean to complain, but if I'd have known what it was going to be like, I'd have much, much rather served in Heaven.

"So," said Lucifer heartily, trying to revive his former slick persona, "whatdaya say? Would you, Dirk Snigby, like to be the first person ever on the face of this planet to traverse the afterlife and live to tell the tale?" The Devil forced an insincere grin and extended his hand. "Whatdaya say we shake on it?"

"Okay," said Dirk, "even if I play along, what's in it for you? I mean, if you're the Devil, you can't be doing this out of the goodness of your heart, right? Hell, you probably don't even have a heart."

Lucifer unconsciously racked his hand through his hair.

"Well," he replied, grinning a tad sheepishly, "I do want something in return, sort of a quid pro quo."

"A-ha!" smirked Dirk in triumph.

"It's not a bad deal," pleaded the Devil hastily. "Just hear me out."

Dirk folded his arms and fixed Lucifer with a dubious stare.

Lucifer sighed. "Look," he began, "it's hell being me. I mean it. I thought it would be entertaining, and in the beginning it had its rewards. But now it's every Tom, Dick, and Mohammed! Some of them are pretty snotty, too. They keep asking 'Where are the virgins? Where are the virgins!?' I tell them, 'Look, it's Hell. No virgins in Hell, okay?' But they just won't listen!

"Finally I figured it out. I give them virgins now, but they never get to have intercourse with them. That way I can present them to the next fanatic who comes down the pipeline. Of course, the virgins are about two thousand years old by now, so it's really not much of a temptation anyway."

"But what about burning them?" enquired Dirk.

"Have you ever been to the Middle East?" retorted Lucifer. "They're not joking when they say it's hotter than Hell."

"I still don't know what you want from me," said Dirk.

"Ahhhh, well, here's where you come in. I think if more people were sort of . . . encouraged to go to Heaven . . . you're an ad man. You know . . . make it sexy. Highlight the benefits and downplay the difficulty."

"So what exactly are you asking me to do?" asked Dirk impatiently.

"Well," said the Devil, nervously tugging at a forelock, "I'd like you to write . . . you know . . . sort of a *Zagat Guide* to the afterlife. Touch on the different kinds of Heavens. . . ."

"Let me get this straight," said Dirk incredulously. "You want me to write a *Zagat Guide* to the afterlife?"

"Well," replied Lucifer, "in a nutshell . . . yes."

Thus began Dirk Snigby's odyssey through the afterlife.

Dirk showed up at Ideas Incorporated on Monday, rather the worse for wear. He was unshaven, the odor of stale beer, cigarettes, and a wild variety of heavenly scents clinging to him. Marcus E. Crystal, his boss, eyed him with disapproval.

Dirk slunk into his cubical. Today's mission: "Fart Fix."

A voluptuous babe filled the screen; she had huge, luscious breasts that protruded at a gravity-defying angle. Her waist couldn't have spanned more than eleven inches. Her hips were perfectly rounded and ripe . . . but not too ripe. Her eyes were huge, blue, and full of the promise of hitherto unimagined sexual delights. Her lips were fuller than Angelina Jolie's.

She looked too good to be real. In fact, she was too good to be real. She was a cartoon. But what a cartoon! She was the kind of cartoon you wanted to hold down and ravish! This was one hot, hot, *hotttt* animated baby!

Her unreal lips parted. "I like hot men," she purred in furry, honey-smooth vibration. "Hot men, fast cars."

Dirk sighed. That night and for the rest of the week the vibration of the cartoon voice resonated through his dreams.

The cartoon was a hit. Absurdly enough, for the first time in his dubious career Dirk was a success. The hot animation was nicknamed "Bootsie."

Dirk came into work late Tuesday. He'd been up all night on a whirlwind jaunt to Hindu Heaven.

"Well," said Marcus J. Crystal, as Dirk snuck in at 10:30 A.M., "good of you to join us."

Marcus was seated in the main lobby with a rather unprepossessing female. She was tall—five eight or so—with stringy brown hair, and what might have been pretty hazel-green eyes were hidden behind black-rimmed glasses. She certainly wasn't ugly, just plain and slightly ill kempt.

"Let me introduce you to our rising star," pronounced Marcus unctuously.

"Pleased to meet you," said Dirk, who was not at all pleased. He'd rather hoped to slither under the radar today, slip into and out of his cubicle and maybe hack some order into his notes on Ganesh, the elephant-headed God of wisdom and prosperity.

Angelica inclined her head and extended her hand. "Pleased to meet you, too, Dirk," she purred.

Dirk started. It was *the voice!* She had supplied the plush rich tones of Bootsie. She was the voice that had entered his dreams.

"Pleased to meet you," repeated Dirk with considerably more conviction.

He clasped her hand warmly, allowing her velvet voice to encompass him. "Are you working here?"

"I only wish," said Marcus ruefully. "Our lovely Angelica is, alas, a freelancer."

He leered in what he believed to be an enticing manner. "Maybe you can convince her to come here full-time. We sure don't want this voice working for the competition. I invited Angelica over to see firsthand how one of our brightest minds . . ." Here he attempted to smile slickly at Dirk, but his smile went a tad rigid as he once again noted Dirk's unkempt appearance. "Brightest minds," he repeated frostily, "uses her voice to sell product." He pronounced the words *sell product* with a reverence most reserve for prayer.

The remainder of the morning passed quickly. Dirk was lamely penning an ad for weed killer: "Absolutely one-hundred-percent natural, pure, chemical-free poison. Kills bugs dead!"

"Well you can't kill them alive," cooed Angelica, perched casually on the arm of his chair while he worked. Her voice, filled with sex, heat, and lust, unnerved him.

"Yeah," he replied, "maybe I should say 'sends bugs to bug Heaven,' or 'returns bugs to a new incarnation.' "

Angelica eyed him speculatively.

God! thought Dirk. *This double life is getting to me. Get a grip boy, get a grip!*

"Well," said Dirk weakly, "I was just trying to make it more . . . uh . . . hey, it's lunchtime! Would you care to join me?"

"After all this talk about pure poison and reincarnated bugs, how can I resist?"

The week passed for Dirk in a whirlwind. Working at Ideas Incorporated, voyaging to a plethora of paradises and trying to court Angelica all at the same time was wearing him down.

As with most modern courtships, lunch was followed by dinner and a movie and then proceeded into the bedroom, as rapidly as night follows day.

"I'm Marlene Dietrich's voice trapped in Madeleine Albright's body," Angelica cooed, as they lay in bed together one Friday, cradled in each other's arms.

Dirk was missing his second scheduled trip to the Sunni afterlife.

"Angelica," said Dirk earnestly clasping her hands, "you're not that bad."

"Of course I'm not that bad," she purred, softly stroking his hand. "I'm in advertising, I exaggerate. What do you expect?"

"You're beautiful, really," Dirk said a bit awkwardly. He was unused to giving endearments, unschooled in the language of love.

Their conversation was interrupted rather precipitously by a postcard that flew through the transom, turned into the bedroom, and hit Dirk squarely in the nose.

"What the . . . !" exclaimed Angelica.

Dirk hastily glanced down. "It's from my boss."

"Marcus?"

"No my other boss, I . . . kind of . . . freelance."

He had looked at the note long enough to read, "This is the second time you've missed the Sunnis."

A second card found its way into the bedroom with the missive "Call me immediately. 1-800-IMP-EVIL."

"I have to call my boss," said Dirk, blindly reaching for his robe. "Excuse me for just a minute."

"That's quite some delivery service he's got," remarked Angelica as Dirk hastily pocketed the cards and closed the door behind him.

Lucifer answered the phone before it rang.

"It's not easy to arrange these trips you know," he whined. "I can't have you canceling like this. The Sunnis will think we're not seriously recruiting. We need to get moving on the publication. I don't have all eternity, you know."

"I'm sorry," replied Dirk, who was not feeling at all sorry, "but this schedule is just too much! I can't keep it up."

"Perhaps if you were less interested in keeping *it* up . . ." Lucifer let the sentence dangle menacingly.

"How do you know . . . ? Oh never mind," sighed Dirk resignedly. "My schedule is awful, brutal, actually. I'm not getting enough sleep. I have no time to write my guidebook. It's gotten so that I don't even remember if I was at work or in Heaven yesterday."

"Hmm," said Lucifer, checking his notes, "you were in Calvinist Heaven. A lot get in by that route.

"So," said Lucifer, with a return to the smooth, cajoling sales manner he affected whenever he wanted something, "how would you like to quit your day job? Work full-time for me? One hundred K a year, plus expenses."

Dirk was shocked into silence.

"Not enough?" asked the Devil. "Tell you what; let's make it an even hundred and fifty K, but no more missing deadlines! No pun intended."

"Done," replied Dirk quickly.

And thus began Dirk Snigby's new career.

ROMAN CATHOLICISM

Note: There are two wings to this Heaven; this visit deals only with the new wing.

This new wing has kinder, gentler requirements than the old wing. The entry requirements seem not terribly arduous, but are a trifle unclear.

In the new wing, Heaven is currently a "condition," not a "destination." It is "like a glorious garden."

You will be given a superb new body. You'll still be a "creature," but a really, really marvelous, splendid, perfect creature. In truth, everyone will look a lot like God. In spite of paternal resemblance, everybody will recognize each other. No mean feat!

There won't be any close friendships or marriages, however, because all and sundry will be entirely, exclusively, rhapsodic just to be near God, like a teenage girl getting a date with her favorite rock star. "We will neither marry nor be given in marriage, but live like angels in Heaven."

This author has but the merest acquaintance of angels in Heaven, but the scuttlebutt is that being single doesn't have a negative effect on their sex lives.

Limbo and Purgatory

Purgatory is now considered a "condition," rather than a place of transition. It is (in the new wing) at once "painful and joyful," hard luck for those early Christians who spent a hell of a long time burning there.

Limbo was originally proposed as a place between Heaven and Hell for the unbaptized, mostly infants and idiots, who had not had the time or brains to sin.

Limbo is now "generally conceived as an erroneous (but logical) answer to a wrong question." That's some wild logic, if you ask this visitor!

If this author was one of those infants or idiots who spent thousands of years wandering around Limbo before being allowed into Heaven and given a sultry new body, I would be rather peeved, to say the least. Luckily, being infants and idiots, they aren't smart enough to be angry. They have fabulous, unsullied bodies, but not too many brains. There is a hot competition between the Pentecostals and the Roman Catholics as to who can gather the most infants and idiots into their Heavens.

If you are a scientist or a mathematician, this is probably not the afterlife for you; not only do these people have a long history of opposing astronomy, evolution, and genetics, they also appear to be arithmetically challenged. "For there is one Person of the Father, another of the Son, and another of the Holy Ghost . . . the Father incomprehensible, the Son incomprehensible, and the Holy Ghost incomprehensible . . . yet, they are not three incomprehensibles, but One incomprehensible."

Sounds completely incomprehensible to this chronicler!

**** Music—From Gregorian chants to *The Messiah* and "Ave Maria" . . . if you like classical music, this is the place for you!

*** Food—It is "like" a fabulous banquet: good, but less filling than the real thing.

**** Drink—Catholics have a long history of viticulture, and it doesn't end with this life. The result is darn tasty.

**** Accommodations—It's "like" a fabulous garden.

*** Overall Rating (New Wing Only)

Later that night Dirk lay in bed with Angelica.

"You really could be lovely, you know," he said, playing with her admittedly stringy hair.

"Could be?" she queried softly. "Nice love talk!"

"No, truly . . . it didn't come out right," he protested. "I'm not used to this. I feel so completely at home with you. I can be myself for the first time in a long time, maybe forever."

"Forever's a long time."

"Longer than you know," muttered Dirk.

"Are you turning religious on me?" queried Angelica incredulously.

"Yes. I mean no . . . I mean yes . . . I just don't know which one yet."

"This wouldn't have anything to do with your mysterious new job, now, would it?"

Dirk lay quiet, hoping she would not continue this line of conversation.

"Just what is your new job?" she pursued.

"I'm kind of starting a new project for him, uh I mean them. I'm writing guidebooks."

"Guidebooks? To where?"

"You wouldn't believe me," he said miserably.

"Try me," she enticed, raising herself up on her elbows.

And so, for the second time that day, Dirk tried.

"I work for the Devil," he confessed.

"Most of us do, in one way or another; but are you doing the Devil's work? That's the important question."

"I don't know," Dirk admitted.

"Why don't you confide in me?" she coaxed.

"I'm trying," cried Dirk unhappily, "but Angelica, can't we just talk about something else for a while?"

"What do you want to talk about?" she asked amiably.

"Maybe us?"

"What about us?"

"Well I think I love you. I really trust you, sort of."

"High praise indeed!" she mocked.

"I'm no good at this," acknowledged Dirk. "I've never felt like this before. I feel I've known you all my life."

"Well, maybe you have," she replied, melting him as always with *the voice*.

The Dirk of two months ago would have scoffed, but with his recent forays into paradise and under the strain of repeatedly running into reincarnations, he had to admit that this was indeed a possibility.

"Do you believe you knew me in another life?" he queried.

"No," she replied, "I think maybe I have known you always in this one."

He rolled over to look into her naked eyes.

"I don't know how to tell you this," she purred, her dulcet tones dripping honey. "I'm sort of here to . . . to watch over you. I'm your guardian angel."

Dirk lay still.

"Hey," she cooed, "are you okay?"

"I don't know," Dirk admitted. "I feel stunned, I feel shell-shocked, I feel used. . . . Are you fucking me for my salvation? If you're an angel, why aren't you a lot more attractive?" continued Dirk bitterly, trying to wound her. "Is this the best you could do?"

"Would you have asked me out if I was gorgeous?" her voice, like liquid butterscotch, flowing into all the sharp corners of his being.

Ruefully, Dirk had to admit that he probably wouldn't have.

"So I'm *shtupping* an angel and working for Lucifer; my high-school aptitude test never pegged me for this!"

"Well," retorted Angelica sweetly, "I didn't exactly choose to be the guardian angel of advertising myself."

In spite of himself, Dirk was falling in love. Angelica was smart, funny, had a great sense of humor, a luscious voice, and loved sex.

"All Earth species have four things in common: they are born, eat, have sex, and die. The middle two are the most fun, and I intend to have as much as possible of both while I'm here."

Dirk liked her philosophy just fine.

Dirk hadn't really thought about what it would be like when Angelica and Lucifer met. But he was certainly not prepared for it when it happened.

He had just risen from bed when a knock at the door sounded.

"Just a minute," he told Angelica. Wrapping his robe about him, he opened the door to see Lucifer standing on his stoop, his newly submitted notes in hand.

A hiss sounded from behind him.

He had to hand it to Lucifer; he was one cool Devil.

Angelica, on the other hand, entirely lost it. Dirk had never seen her like this. Her mouth was open; he had either never noticed her canines before, or they had grown. From her throat issued a sound Dirk had only heard in horror movies, usually occurring when the undead claim their own.

"Youuuu," she hissed in undulcid tones.

"So," said Lucifer smoothly, "it's the guardian angel. How is sex these days?"

"Fiend!" Angelica hissed. "Satan!"

"At your service, madam." He bowed.

Dirk was unnerved for the second time in the same number of days.

Life was getting just too strange. It had been difficult enough learning that the girl he might be in love with was his guardian angel.

Now she was acting like some weird, possessed creature. Her canines were undeniably lengthening.

"I can see I have come at an inauspicious time," continued Lucifer silkily. "Sorry I intruded on your bit of Heaven. Maybe we could schedule something later this week, Dirk?"

"Sure," replied Dirk shakily.

Lucifer turned to depart.

All in all, mused Dirk, you had to give the Devil his due. He was certainly handling the situation better than Angelica.

"By the way." Lucifer turned at the doorway. "Does God know what you're up to?" He stepped out, closing the door softly behind him.

Inside Angelica was still hissing, although Dirk was relieved to notice that her canines appeared to have diminished.

Dirk had begun to wonder if, indeed, God *did* know what Angelica was up to. Thus are the seeds of doubt sown. Still, now did not appear to be a good time for further inquiry.

He noticed with relief that Angelica had resumed her normal exterior.

"By the way, just what Heaven are you an angel for?"

"Oh," she replied, waving her hand in a vague circular motion, "I kind of freelance. Not like 'the beautiful angel,' God always liked him best."

"If Lucifer was God's favorite," asked Dirk, "what does that make Christ?"

"Dead."

"I mean before, no, after that," stammered Dirk in confusion. "Isn't he God's favorite now?"

"Surely you've been to enough afterlives to know that it depends on where you go," replied Angelica.

It was Sunday. Dirk had taken the entire weekend off. "Look," began Dirk, "there's some stuff I just need to understand. I've been to a lot of Heavens and I have never seen any guardian angels."

"Of course not, silly," she said, affectionately ruffling his hair. "Many religions and cultures have guardian angels as part of their . . . not exactly theology . . . more like mythology. If you're born into one of them, you get a guardian angel assigned to you. We just sort of hang around, watch over our charges and try to keep them from getting into too much trouble."

"Then what?"

"Then what *what?*"

"I mean, what happens then?"

"Then, my mortal darling, you die."

"And?" prompted Dirk.

"You go where you go; you're seeing the options, aren't you?"

"Yes," persisted Dirk, "but who decides?"

"Well, you do; generally speaking, you go where you believe you belong."

"And you?"

"We get a new assignment."

"Don't you ever die?" asked Dirk.

"I'm an immortal being, my love," Angelica giggled coyly. "In your case, perhaps an immoral immortal."

"What's with the teeth?" Dirk inquired.

"I prefer not to discuss that," Angelica said huffily.

"Look, I need to know why my girlfriend, my guardian angel, seems to bear a decided resemblance to Dracula when she's upset."

"Oh well," pouted Angelica. "If you must you must, I suppose. It's part of the immortal packet. We can't blush or grow pale, because we don't have blood. We can't gasp in shock, since we don't have lungs. We aren't biological beings, but we still have feelings. In fact, we're very emotional. There needs to be some way to vent. Some of us have teeth that grow; some of us vanish, and some turn into frogs, cats, wolves, or bats. It explains a lot of your mythology, if you think about it."

"What about Lucifer?'

"What about him?" retorted Angelica bitterly. "You surely don't think Mr. Handsome would do anything as unattractive as growing teeth, do you? Oh no, not for God's pet. He just gets a very petite pair of horns; they're kind of cute actually. When he's really upset he grows a cloven hoof, but since he usually wears boots, you don't notice it.

"What all you humans, or at least you Western humans, don't appear to grasp, although it is clearly stated in your Bible, is that Satan is an angel, too. The most beautiful, God's favorite. He didn't go through any big physical change when he left Heaven. God made sure of that. God always liked him best, you know."

"So," inquired Dirk, attempting a diversion, "what's God like?"

"Busy."

"Does he know what you're up to?" Dirk persisted, although he felt on the verge of danger.

"Well, yes and no," Angelica replied.

"What do you mean yes *and* no? It seems to me it's more of a yes-*or*-no question."

"Well," growled Angelica, "it's yes to the general, no to the specific. God doesn't tell us *exactly* how to do our work. He just trusts it will get done. He's always been into free will you know."

"I had a nice childhood," began Lucifer over a lunch of cold *niçoise* salad and white wine. "Not childhood exactly, but creation; that's it, a good creation. I got along well with most of the other angels, all except Michael and Gabriel. Talk about stuffed wings!

"I was always an artistic angel. I liked to draw, design worlds, that sort of thing. It's a little known fact, but I designed the seahorse!" Lucifer modestly gazed down at his salad.

"Then God had a contest, open to all . . . design the future! I entered, of course. I thought it would be nice if all people loved each other and got along. I thought that no wars, hatred, or pollution would be a good thing, but noooo . . . I made the mistake of wanting credit."

"Working for God is like drawing for Disney: you do the work, he gets the credit *and* the residuals."

"Michael, on the other hand, wanted a lot of illness, pain, and hate; he called it free will. Of course he didn't want credit for that! So, he proffered it to God. Well, that's when all hell broke loose (if you'll pardon the expression). So, here I am, just trying to reduce my workload."

"I'm thinking we should leave out the Baptists," said Dirk. "That will only appeal to people who have really pathetic taste in music."

"Let's get the show on the road," Lucifer stated, after finishing up lunch with tiramisu. "The first edition comes out in a month; you need to be on talk shows *now!* I've got you booked on *Michael Guy Alright* this Sunday."

"*Michael Guy Alright!*" gasped Dirk. "Why, that's the biggest show on TV! How'd you manage that?"

The Devil spread his carefully manicured fingers. "I'm the Devil," he said. "I have connections. Fiends are very heavy into the industry. Haven't you watched TV lately? Surely you don't think that's God's work?!"

"You're on," said a voice, firm hands propelling him forward.

Dirk wavered uncertainly, reverential of the man who sat under the hot white light of an interior sun. Behind him was a painted turquoise blue sea framed by palm trees, giving lie to the poem, "Only God can make a tree."

"Please welcome Dirk Snigby," boomed Michael Guy Alright. Soon Dirk was seated opposite his host, Michael Guy Alright. "Dirk Snigby, author of the soon-to-be-released *Dirk Snigby's Guide to the Afterlife.*" Signs flashed "Applause," and the small studio audience obediently banged their hands together.

"Dirk," cooed Michael Guy Alright in the soothing tones generally reserved for idiots, invalids, infants, animals, and audiences, "you claim to have visited the 'borne from which no traveler returns' not just once but many times."

"Y-y-yes," stammered Dirk nervously. He could write good copy in his sleep, but this business of lights and live listeners made him fidgety. "I have been to Heaven . . . well, not just Heaven, many Heavens."

Michael Guy Alright frowned slightly. "Many Heavens? Surely there is just one."

"Well, no," said Dirk gaining confidence slightly. "After all, you couldn't expect a Buddhist to be happy in a Pentecostal Heaven, now could you? Or a Calvinist to be happy, well anywhere really, but especially not in a Hindu Heaven."

"Hmmm," mused Michael Guy Alright, sagely stroking his chin.

"I find," continued Dirk, gaining assurance, "that Heaven is pretty much what you make it. If you expect golden streets, the streets will shine; if you expect Jell-O with fruit, you shall have it in abundance."

"Jell-O?" Michael Guy Alright cocked a quizzical look at the camera.

"Yeah, Jell-O," sighed Dirk. "For some reason, the Mormons are very fond of it. I had a lot of it last week."

MORMONISM

The opportunity to enter this afterlife after death is a definite plus. However, drinking, smoking, fornication, or almost anything deemed "sinful" (although some might say pleasurable) is wrong.

Entrance requirements are very complicated, something like a New York City Co-op Board: You will go to Hell until baptized by a living Mormon.

You will be forever bonded with your family, a dubious delight.

Men can be bonded to multiple wives but not the reverse. Warning, this sometime leads to a bit of trouble in paradise.

Men who go in for Masonic-type rituals will feel completely at ease. You get neat costumes and arcane rituals.

Both sexes get special underwear. This may appeal to those who missed out on summer camp, but I should warn you it's neither comfortable nor attractive.

You learn a secret handshake so that God knows you belong in Heaven.

The afterlife is viewed as a series of steps leading to Godhood.
Not a religion for the lazy.
End destination: Godhood.

* **Food**—If you are partial to Jell-O molds that feature such
  exotic additions as shredded carrots, cucumbers, and canned
  vegetables, you'll love it! Ambrosia—Food of the Gods—is
  also popular. This visitor thought Jell-O with marshmallows,
  canned fruit, and whipped cream an acquired taste, probably
  better acquired before eternity.
* **Drink**—What can you say about Postum? Ersatz alcohol,
  such as Martinelli's sparkling cider and near beer is available,
  although the rigorously righteous avoid "even the appearance
  of sin."
** **Accommodations**—Incredibly clean, but tacky.
*** **Overall Rating**

Dirk's appearance on TV caused considerable discussion in religious and non-religious circles. The pious were outraged by the idea that there were multiple Heavens. The atheists were not much happier with Dirk's assertion that there was a God (or Gods) and a Heaven (or Heavens). As for the agnostics, they couldn't make up their minds.

It was shortly after this that Dirk began receiving fan mail . . . of a sort. Most of the notes stated, in a variety of languages and styles, that Dirk was undoubtedly deranged, irrefutably wrong, quite possibly the Antichrist, and indubitably going to Hell. Quite a few writers actually offered to send him there personally.

It appeared that Dirk had succeeded in accomplishing what no preceding figure in history had managed: unite all religious persuasions in a common goal: Kill Dirk.

"I don't get it," said Dirk mournfully after an evening's exertion with Angelica. "Why are they all so angry?"

"Silly," Angelica cooed, "you're challenging their beliefs."

"But I'm not," protested Dirk. "I'm affirming them! I'm saying there *is* a Heaven, and just like they've described! I'm just providing guidance for those who haven't chosen yet."

"At least half the fun of going to Heaven is knowing that all the others are going to Hell," explained Angelica sweetly.

Angelica had discovered and fallen in love with the 99-cent store.

"During creation, God sometimes had design competitions and let angels have some input. There was a lot of contention over humans. There were those who wanted iridescent, multicolored rainbows of people; instead, the vote narrowly came down on shades of beige and brown. Just look how badly that turned out! Then there were those who wanted humans to at least have colorful nails and hair. Women probably dye their hair and paint their nails due to an atavistic, precreation sense memory."

Although she was never explicit about it, Dirk was fairly sure that Angelica had voted with the colorful-but-losing side on the human question.

"I'm showing you what you were supposed to look like," Angelica said, proudly waving a garish hand of orange, pink, and green at Dirk.

On the whole, Dirk was rather glad that her side had lost, but he took care never to mention that aloud.

It was shortly after this that Dirk received his first letter bomb. This was to be followed by a computer bomb, a car bomb, and a bomb bomb, to say nothing of the wild-looking gentleman wearing a rather volatile vest of dynamite who attempted to embrace Dirk.

The letter bomb was more of a package, really. It arrived one morning neatly wrapped in brown paper and addressed innocuously enough, to "Mr. Dirk Snigby."

Considering that the majority of Dirk's mail lately had been addressed to "the Antichrist," "De Anti CHrIst," "The Devil's spawn," and "The Abortion that should have been," Dirk felt rather relieved.

He was just about to open it, thereby ensuring that his next visit to the afterlife would be permanent, when he was interrupted by Angelica emerging from the bedroom, her teeth lengthening to a degree that Dirk had never seen before.

She turned her attention to the box. As Angelica approached it, she inhaled deeply.

"Someone doesn't like you, Dirk," she hissed.

Dirk was still trying to figure out if the "someone" she was referring to was herself, when she laid a long-fingered hand over the packet. Immediately it began to writhe, fizzle, and hiss, a bit like an extremely disgruntled electric blanket. The wrapping curled off of the package and a bewildering assortment of wires disconnected themselves from a glinting metallic panel, leaving the bomb dismembered though still writhing on the floor. Dirk inhaled sharply.

The stench of burned wires and thwarted hatred filled the room. At least that is what Dirk assumed thwarted hatred would smell like.

ISLAM

Getting into Islamic Heaven is like getting into a university in many Asian countries. Elementary, junior high, and high school are really difficult, and only a select few make it into college. If you do get in, though, life is a party.

To get into this garden paradise you must:

- Pray five times a day on a regular schedule. It's no good trying to cut it down to three really long prayers, or one mammoth prayer session. It's five prayers at the right time of day, facing in the right direction (toward Mecca), or forget it, you'll be damned.
- You must be clean.
- You must fast one month of each year. It's not a really brutal fast, though. You don't get breakfast or lunch, but at dinner you can eat all the hummus you want.
- You must visit Mecca and Medina. Do not try to replace these with London and Paris; in fact, you cannot even replace them with similar destinations such as Barstow and Bakersfield. They won't accept it on Judgment Day.
- As for Judgment Day, it's going to be really, really scary, even for the good. You have no idea just how completely, terrifyingly scary it's going to be.
- You'd better not doubt that there is a God or that that God is the *one* God. If you do . . . damnation.
- You cannot take your own life. If you do . . . damnation. (This writer failed to meet any suicide bombers.)
- You have to wait for Judgment Day in your grave. If you are good, you will have a windowed casket with a garden view. If you are damned (which you probably are), you will have a transom Hell that blows hot air into the tomb. If you are buried in the Middle East or Indonesia, it's probably hot enough.

On the other hand, if you do get in, you lie around on couches and face other lucky Muslims, all decked out in silk robes of green and gold.

***** **Food**—The food is fantastic. There is a lot of fresh fruit (that led this writer to experience a touch of "Mahammad's Revenge"), but worry not, there's a lot of flesh and fowl as well. And speaking of flesh . . . there are the houris: these are incredibly hot virgins. They have black eyes, white skin, and are amorous. (I have been informed by excellent sources that they have regenerating hymens, so the fun never stops!)

***** **Drink**—They have a great wine. It's really pure and you can drink all night without getting obnoxious. Guess what else? No hangover. It's also served by really immoral—I mean immortal—youths.

** **Music**—Like wailing? Like Sting?

***** **Accommodations**—Gardens, couches, silk.

*** **Overall Rating**

Dirk returned late from the garden of paradise so richly described in the Qur'an. He was drunk, but not hungover. He was still wearing his silken robe, which hung off one shoulder at a rather jaunty angle.

Angelica was up and waiting. (Dirk doubted if she ever slept.)

"You've been hanging out with the houris, haven't you?" she snapped, her usually dulcet tones acid.

Dirk swayed. "Houri . . . ," he slurred staring at her with unfocused eyes, "beautiful maidens, beautiful as pearls, eyes black as . . . black. That's pretty funny," he snorted. "Yeah, eyes black as black. Skin white as white." He howled with laughter, patting Angelica lustily on her behind.

"And their breasts," he continued, apparently unaware of Angelica's narrowed eyes, "like melons, pearly white, firmer than ripe peaches, nibbles . . . nipples . . . nipples . . ." He sputtered to a halt.

"*Houris* indeed," Angelica scoffed. "*Ho*-rees is more like it."

"But they're all virgins," Dirk cried. "At least they *were* all virgins." He gave a lascivious smirk.

"Don't worry," Angelica said coldly. "They are still all virgins. The sluts all have regenerating hymen."

She sniffed sharply at him, obviously not enjoying the heady scents of Heaven. Angelica entered the bedroom, shutting the door inhospitably behind her.

It was shortly after this that Dirk received the computer bomb. His computer had been cleverly programmed to explode whenever the words, *God, Christ, Muhammad,* or *Mohammad* were typed into his system, thereby adroitly obscuring the hacker's religious affiliation, as well as ensuring that Dirk would be annihilated during an act of apostasy.

Due, perhaps, to the almost continual presence of spiritual, hence unnatural, vibrations in his apartment, this did not happen.

Indeed, Dirk was not at the computer, nor was the computer on, when it began to make the querulous, crackling noises normally produced only by quails.

Dirk looked at his whimpering, clucking machine. As he approached, it began to smoke.

Angelica entered hastily.

"Don't touch it!" she commanded. Ignoring her own advice, she crossed over to the gibbering machine and extended her hand toward the screen. The machine exploded in an impressive burst of flame, completely engulfing Angelica and producing a cloud of very black, acrid smoke.

The smoke cleared and Dirk, blinking back tears from his eyes, was greeted by Angelica looking none the worse for wear. In fact, as Dirk examined her, he realized she was looking considerably better. Her hair looked softer and more lustrous. Her glasses seem to have melted away, revealing lovely green eyes. Her mouth appeared lusher and her figure more curved and voluptuous.

"It's the electricity," she purred, noticing his scrutiny.

"It's present in the human heart you know, and angels find it . . . um . . . very . . . uh . . . refreshing. It's how we keep track of our charges. However, God never planned for so much interference—so much other electricity—when he designed the system. There's nothing like a good meltdown or a crash to give us angels a buzz." She sighed. A narrow pink tongue poked out and reminiscently licked her now rather voluptuous lips. She gave a positively postcoital smile.

When Lucifer dropped by to discuss the new, updated version of *Dirk Snigby's Guide to the Afterlife*, Dirk showed him the damage.

"I can guarantee this won't happen again, because your new system won't be tied into the Internet at all. You will be directly connected to the Outernet." Lucifer smiled.

As for the car bomb, it had been timed to go off when Dirk started the car. Due once again to supernatural interference, it exploded when placidly parked in a towaway zone. Dirk's only consolation was that it took the policeman, who was writing him a rather expensive ticket, with it.

Dirk had only gone a few steps, when a large, hairy man ran toward him shouting "God is great." The man was wearing a Bill Blass vest fashionably hung with dynamite.

Before he could embrace Dirk, however, Angelica emerged, seemingly out of nowhere, but actually out of the 99-cent store where she had been eagerly shopping for new nail polish colors. Miracles are so often easily explained.

She inserted herself gracefully between Dirk and his admirer. The last thing Dirk remembered seeing was a pair of exceptionally hairy eyebrows suspended in space. He awoke to find Angelica looking ravishing, if not ravenous.

RASTAFARIANISM

This afterlife has an extreme affirmative action policy. "The blacker the skin, the quicker you're in; the whiter the flesh, go somewhere else after death."

End destination: Ethiopia.

A little history: Ras Tafari was crowned the king of Ethiopia in 1930 and became the Emperor Haile Selassie, "Lord of Lords and King of Kings of Ethiopia, Conquering Lion of the Tribe of Judah, the Elect of God and the Light of the World." (If only Napoleon had had Haile Selassie's press agent. "Lord of Lords and King of Kings" makes "emperor" seem so pathetic somehow.)

The Rastafarians, in spite of vehement protests from Haile Selassie (who was and remained a staunch Christian), decided he was God and that Ethiopia will become paradise eventually.

Rastafarians believe that blacks are the Jews, Jamaica is Babylon, and that Emperor Haile Selassie is God. This may sound a bit confusing to the uninitiated, but this is much easier to understand when you consider that Rastafarians also believe that smoking massive amounts of ganja (marijuana) almost continually reveals the truth.

Smoking ganja is viewed as an act of affirmation and faith.

To be a good Rastafarian and candidate for Ethiopia, you must:

- Not drink milk, coffee, alcohol, or soft drinks.
- Not eat processed or tinned food.
- Not use synthetic fertilizers. (This is a very organic religion.)

You must:

- Have sex with an abundance of women, thus producing a lot of Rastafarianitos.
- Reflect on God while smoking lots of ganja.
- Be black.

Time seems to pass very slowly here, and I kept forgetting what I was about to say, but I'm certain it was really deep and spiritual . . . if only I could remember!

***** **Food**—It tasted *great!*
*** **Drink**—Water and juice, but it tasted *great!*
***** **Music**—Reggae, throbbing, beating, pulsing Reggae! I became one with the music! I experienced the music as color and light . . . and, boy can these people boogie!
*** **Accommodations**—Huts, but really nice, clean, all-natural huts. If you've had enough ganja it's all good.
*** **Overall Rating**

Angelica was not pleased. She was feeling thwarted that there had been no fresh electrical attempts on Dirk's life. Like an amphetamine addict craving her next high, Angelica was craving extreme doses of voltage.

Doubtless this was the reason that Dirk, returning home early one evening from a fleeting visit to the Seventh Day Adventist afterlife, found her hungrily chewing on an extension cord.

She took to blow-drying her hair in the bathtub and toasting bread in the shower, and she even began vacuuming the neighbor's pool.

Dirk awoke. "I have been bombed three times," he mused softly. "I'm immortal." Those were to be his last words.

Outside there was a noise too vast to be heard, the calm before a waterfall, the silence before a tsunami. In the quiet dawn a dozen faint lines of smoke rose, blossoming like gray flowers into huge mushrooms shapes.

Angelica had finally found her ultimate fix.

The air was a tangle of souls, souls heading toward Purgatory, souls heading toward judgment, souls heading toward Heaven and toward Hell.

Dirk, or perhaps it was only Dirk's soul, stood, or possibly hovered, beside Lucifer.

So, he thought desolately, once again I wrote copy for a product that's going out of business. He slowly looked about at the confusion of ghosts curling around him.

"Well," said Lucifer, unenthusiastically opening his roll book, "although this was not precisely the result I had in mind, at least you provided some much-needed information."

Dirk peered more closely at the writhing masses; each transparent arm clasped a slightly translucent copy of *Dirk Snigby's Guide to the Afterlife*. Dirk slowly smiled and said a silent prayer (if dead ad men can pray) for the next world that had Angelica as its guardian angel.

Mexico

by Perry Glasser

Kirk is a bum and Doralee knows it. But with no better prospects, she follows him to a small Mexican town where he hopes to make a major drug score. All goes according to plan until the arrival of a minor league baseball team. She sees an escape from her miserable predicament—if Kirk doesn't kill her or her baseball savior first. It is what life looks like when you cross Traffic and Bull Durham.

I

Here it was their second morning in Rocky Point, a town the Mexicans called Puerto Penasco, and what Doralee Jackson wanted more than anything else in the whole world was a nice place with a real shower, something with hot water where she could shampoo the grit out of her hair and not feel like she'd been rolling in dust for three weeks. And what Kirk was doing at 7 A.M., the sun no higher than its own width out of the ocean, still reddish but turning yellow-white, was running into the water up to maybe his knees, then running out when a wave brushed by him, and then running in again.

Kirk wasn't even his real name. He'd told her his real name was Alexander Dugan when they were someplace in Oklahoma, or maybe it was Texas, and he told that to her like he was letting her in on some great secret and she should feel grateful. All she could think was to ask herself what was she doing there in the front seat of a blue '78 Nova with the cattle stink blowing in the car window with a guy whose name was one thing but who wanted to be called another? "But you keep calling me Kirk," he'd said, " 'cause I'm a Kirk. No wussy Alex." And he reached under the seat to pop another can of Lone Star and then he'd squeezed her knee.

Kirk wore just his Levis—no socks, shoes, shirt, or underwear, she knew—and each time he ran into the water he went a little farther before he ran out, like a kid working up his courage for the plunge. With a warm can of Carta Blanca in her hands, Doralee sat on the Chevy's hood, her bare feet flat on the metal getting hot from the sun, and she looked at her own knobby toes, or watched the waves roll in and smooth over Kirk's footprints on the dark wet sand. Carta Blanca for breakfast was bad enough, but warm it tasted like piss. They hadn't eaten since lunch yesterday and the beer was making her fuzzy. She'd have taken a box of good American cornflakes, even. She'd eat them dry.

She liked the Mexican beach. It was a big, dirty, yellow crescent of a beach and they were right in the middle. When she looked to the left or right she had to squint, and way out at the ends of the crescent, haze from the ocean made it hard to see clear, but she knew there was more beach and little patches of grass and weeds. Hardly any people at all except for some Mexican kids that were poking around in the sand, off by a beat-up white house, looking for something they could steal, she bet. The salty wind that blustered and snatched at her hair carried their voices, the sound not much different from the birds she thought were pigeons until Kirk told her they were pelicans, stupid. Well, how could she know? It was the first time she'd seen the sea, just a big lake where you couldn't see the other shore.

In Mexico not two days and she already knew that Mexico was dumbass as a place could be. It was crazy weird how they let you drive right up on the sand. Nice, but all the cars and vans and campers leaked oil and in the sun that crap turned into tar, so when a body walked barefoot the gunk got all sticky on the soles of her feet. Yesterday, Kirk soaked a rag with gasoline and wiped her foot clean. She was amazed how easy it was. Kirk knew stuff like that.

"Are you going in the water or not?"

He didn't answer, but took another run, the water splashing up around him, his jeans dark where they were wet but light blue above the knees, and this time when he got in as high as his waist he lunged head first forward in a kind of half-assed dive and broke a wave. For a second he was invisible underwater and then he shot up, waving his skinny arms in the air, shaking his head so his long hair swirled wet, slapping around his face. A wave followed him in and his footprints were washed flat.

Water streamed off him. His feet were caked with the whiter dry sand of the beach. He wiped his face with his palm.

"I could do with some food. I'm hungry, Kirk."

"We'll eat. I told you, we'll eat. Let me dry off, then we'll walk through town and see what we can find. We out of cupcakes?"

"Had the last ones yesterday at lunch."

"Shit." He took his black T-shirt from the car's front seat and wiped his chest, then his arms, rubbing carefully at the spot where the faded tattoo of the Zig-Zag man was. His black hair was all matted, and when he rubbed his head with his T-shirt his hair didn't look any drier, but was strung out in thick, knotted strands, like the hair on a nigger in some Jamaican reggae band. He smoothed it back with his hands, two, three times, and then snapped it into a ponytail with a red rubber band.

"Gimme some of that." He took the beer from her, filled his mouth by leaning his head way back, then gargled and spit. "I figure two, three days, Dora. Two, three days, and someone around here will notice us, and we score some dope. Run it back across the border. Los Angeles, Las Vegas, maybe. We sell it, and we're all right. Do whatever we want, then."

"I don't know, Kirk. This place doesn't look right."

"I been wrong so far?"

"No." She had to admit it.

"I'm telling you, there's dope all over Mexico. That's all these greasers do. Brown heroin. Grass. Hell, we get lucky, someone will offer us coke. All we got to do is hang around until someone picks up on us and tries to sell us a couple of joints. We tell him we're in the market for a couple of kilos. Next day, we're out of this piss hole."

Rocky Point was a fishing village. When they'd first driven through the town she was struck by the posters on the corrugated metal sides of some of the buildings. Neither of them read Spanish, but the posters were red and showed a big face above a hammer and sickle. Wasn't communism illegal or something?

Kirk had picked the town because he wanted to swim in the ocean, and Rocky Point was close to the border, was on the Gulf of California, and on the map it looked like an itty-bitty drive south from Arizona that had turned into hours and hours over the goddamndest emptiest desert in all of God's creation, just sky and land, big brown humpbacked hills with nothing on them but lizards and sick little bushes, the car like an oven even at seventy miles an hour with the windows open.

They had been in Tucumcari, New Mexico, the night he picked the town right off a map. He could have thrown a dart.

Doralee kept her doubts to herself. Maybe he hadn't been wrong yet, but she wasn't convinced he was absolutely on the money much, either.

And she wanted him to be right. This was a shot, and she wasn't ready yet to give up on Kirk Dugan, even if his real name *was* wussy Alex.

In New Mexico, Kirk had had three hundred-dollar bills folded small, and he'd pried the heel off his left boot, put away the bills, and with the butt end of the Browning automatic tapped the heel back into place. Then they'd driven way the hell south and way the hell west, charging gas, and whatever they could buy to eat in truck stops or gas stations, on the MasterCard Kirk took off a guy in Oklahoma named William Krantz—driving day and night until they were in something called the Organ Pipe Monument in Arizona. A few miles from the border he stopped the car, got out to take a whizz, and then walked with her a dozen or so yards from the road. They were at the three-mile marker on the west side of the road. She'd never seen so many cactus—big things with arms just like in a picture book. And it was quiet, no sound of any kind, and she thought that was spooky for a place called Organ Pipe. Kirk told her to look around, remember what the spot looked like, and then he scratched an X on a big white rock. He lifted the rock: Two scorpions, little orange things with tails curled in the air, scuttled out. "Jesus fucking Christ!" Kirk yelled and dropped the rock. He stamped the scorpions. Lifted his foot and brought his boot down hard, again and again till they were so flat they were nothing but dust, and then he lifted the rock again, scraped a little depression in the spot under the rock, put the gun in the plastic wrap from a loaf of white bread, and left it under the rock. You don't want to go over the border with a gun, he explained, but whether that would matter if they were caught with a car full of marijuana was something she didn't ask him.

So here she was, her second day in Mexico. Kirk pulled his black boots on over his socks and then pushed his head into his shirt. He touched his jaw, made the kind of face that showed he knew he needed a shave, something he did every three days or so if they could find hot water and a bar of soap.

"The shirt'll dry on my back," he said. "What do you say? Let's look around. I'm starving."

Doralee smiled. He was the goddamndest thing to make her smile, except the times he scared her to death.

They locked up the car and walked up the hill into the town, which wasn't all that big. There was one straight street that ran along the cement docks from where fishing boats had already gone out, and the street stank like hell from the offal right there on the ground, the flies buzzing so loud you could hear the noise a hundred yards away. And behind that street were a bunch of little narrow streets that climbed the face of what could be a big hill or a small mountain—she didn't know what to call it, there was nothing like it back in Iowa—and those streets twisted and turned on each other so quick a body got lost faster than a rat in one of those mazes. They went up the hill, Kirk smoking and getting winded but trying not to let Doralee see that; but she could hear him wheeze and when he stopped two times to look in a store window she knew he was just catching his breath.

He smoked Marlboros, the red pack tucked into the waist of his jeans. He smoked all the time. She'd never known a man to smoke as much as Kirk, sometimes up in the middle of the night to smoke a cigarette and then right back to sleep. She'd wake from the stink or his movement and she'd see the orange glow of the tip in the darkness, and she'd watch that, just that, and never let on that she was awake. And then Kirk would fall back and go to sleep again and she had to lie in the darkness with the burning stale smell settling into her hair and lingering in her nose, and it would take a long time before she could sleep again.

They climbed the hill, but then the street turned and they couldn't go up the hill anymore, and the street took them back to the Coca-Cola sign. The third time that happened, Kirk picked a street that didn't go up, but seemed to run parallel to the shore line and the docks down below, and they passed a few closed restaurants that through the dark glass looked like luncheonettes. And then they got lucky—they could smell it before they saw it—they found a bakery. There were Christmas bells on the door.

The woman who came out of the back and stood behind the glass counter was as wide as she was tall, and she spoke no English but smiled a lot. She put one of each thing they pointed at on the countertop. There was no beer, so Kirk took a carton of milk and placed it with the rest of the food.

"How much?" Kirk said and waved his hand over the the three loaves and the milk that were on top of the counter.

The woman smiled.

"Dumbshit," Kirk said. "How much?" He raised his voice. "Pesos?"
"Si, si."

"Just give her some money. Lord, doesn't it smell great?" It did. The thick aroma made Doralee feel warm and good, and for the first time in two days she thought maybe things had a chance to work out.

"I don't want to get cheated."

"She's not going to cheat you."

"They all cheat you down here."

The woman was nodding her head, smiling. Doralee'd bet she thought they were married or something, honeymooning. She smiled back at the dark, fat woman.

"Damn," Kirk said, and he pulled a wrinkled bill, still wet, from his pocket and passed it over the counter. The fan in the corner whirred. They waited while the woman went to the back, heard her talking to someone, and then came back with a bunch of bills in her hand and a few coins. She put the bread in a sack. Kirk took the money and waited for Doralee to grab the bag and the milk, and they left the place, the little bells ringing when they went out the door. They walked maybe a half block, then sat on the curbstone, the bag between them.

The rolls were heavy, the crust hard, and when Doralee broke one, the very white inside steamed. It was delicious, and the milk was creamier than any kind she'd ever had from a carton back in Iowa. "This is great," she said. Her teeth savagely ripped into the bread.

"Look at this," Kirk said. He held the money out to her.

"What about it?"

"Fucking Monopoly money." He counted it. "We've got thirty pesos and some centavos. Red bills and blue bills and I don't know shit about these coins. Feel 'em. They feel like tin."

"Isn't this bread outrageous?"

"What the fuck am I going to do with a pile of play money?"

From across the street, two skinny boys watched them eat. They were maybe ten, Doralee thought. Shouldn't they be in school? They had jet-black hair and jet-black eyes, and their eyes were enormous.

"Look at those kids," she said, and swallowed a soft lump of the doughy bread. "They're cute."

Kirk flipped one of the coins. It hit the cobblestone street, making a thin sound. He picked up the coin. "It's about the size of a quarter," he said, "but it doesn't weigh as much. You think I could use it in a machine back home? You know, get a game of Donkey Kong with it or something? Cigarettes? Or you think the weight won't let it work?"

The two boys continued observing them. They weren't so cute, she decided. They were spooky. They didn't blink. Hardly moved. They ought to be in school. Learn something and clean up this shitty little town when they got older. She never saw a place so filthy. She shifted her weight. When one of the little boys tapped his friend's shoulder and they ran off down the street, she was glad, but then she got depressed. The feeling she'd had in the bakery was gone. This would never work out. A full belly helped, but this time Kirk was out of it. No town with kids running around on the street staring at them because they had food and money was going to cough up a dope dealer that would sell them anything worth anything. There was nothing in this town you could buy, much less sell.

"You listening to me?"

"I heard you."

"Well, what do you think?"

"I don't know. I guess you'd have to try it."

He snorted. "That's you all the time."

"What?"

"Never mind."

"What's that supposed to mean?"

"Drink your fucking milk."

The sun was higher and it was getting hot. Sweat trickled from under her arms and down her ribs. They finished their breakfast. She had to wait while Kirk smoked another cigarette. Some mornings when they'd been on the road she'd wake up to hear him coughing in the bathroom of the motel room—the room compliments of Mr. William Krantz. She thought he was likely to die. He'd spit into the toilet and then he'd piss, the door of the bathroom open, sounding like a horse passing water.

They walked down to the dock and some of the boats were already in. Kirk said these guys had it easy, a job that was done for the day so early in the morning. She saw it wasn't fish but shrimp they caught and they tried to sell it to them. "Dollars," the fishermen said. "Five dollars, eight pounds," and they smiled their greasy smiles. When Doralee and Kirk walked away, they sometimes ran after them, and one guy yelling "Ice! Ice!" put his hand on Kirk's shoulder, but Kirk spun around so fast the man got scared and went right back to the counter where, with little curled knives, they were cutting the shrimp apart, scraping stuff right off the wood into the street, and there must have been a million gulls flocking in, picking at the stuff with their beaks, pulling, and shredding the leavings. The smell was getting to her, but it was not so bad now that, with a full belly, the fuzziness from the beer was gone.

Back toward the car on the beach, they passed a street they had not noticed before, one that ran along the beach in the other direction, what seemed away from the cluster of buildings on the hillside, and Doralee said "Let's explore," and Kirk at first said no, and then seemed to think about it a minute and then shrugged his shoulders and said "Why not? Maybe this is where the dealers hang out."

The long, straight street was wider than the others, and it was paved with blacktop, not cobblestones. Kirk played with the Mexican coins still in his fist, jingling them, the sound funny to his ears, not like real money. Trees were on the street, tall, scraggly things that were not growing well, but still were honest-to-God trees, and then the street turned one way and then another, and they were practically walking on top of a seawall, the waves crashing into the abutment, covering huge black rocks slimy with algae at the wall's base and sending up a spray of seawater. And at the end of the street, through an open, black iron gate, were four buildings set in a square around what must have once been a fountain, though now it was dry and covered with the same brown dust that covered everything else in Rocky Point.

Kirk started to walk away, like they'd come to the end of the road. Looking out over the seawall they could see across the water, over to the curve of the beach where the Chevy reflected the bright sun from its windshield. He was like that, wanting to keep near things he knew, she'd learned, so Doralee had had to grab him by the hand and they walked all the way up to the place. Over the iron gate, in letters that once had been bright blue paint but were now so faded they were almost invisible on the pale brown wall, were the words LA HACIENDA. And as they got close enough to read those letters, Doralee saw that in the courtyard, parked in the shade beneath the second-story walkway, were several dust-covered cars with American license plates, mostly California, but one or two from Arizona.

"It's a motel," she said, sounding to herself a little like she'd just discovered a lost gold mine or something.

"Good guess," Kirk said. "Let's go back to the car."

"I want to stay here. We can get a room."

"We can't take a fucking room here. We're here to score dope. You want to spend that money on a fucking room?"

But she pulled him further into the courtyard past the gate—and pasted on a glass door to what had to be an office that could not have been seen from the street was the MasterCard symbol.

"I want to stay here, Kirk. You can be William Krantz."

"I told you, that card's getting too hot. Every day we hold it, it gets hotter."

"Then what good is it?"

"Maybe we can find some asshole give us a hundred dollars for it. It's near ten days, now. The number is out."

"Even in Mexico?"

He looked at the building, the stark shadows falling black over the courtyard. A housemaid pushed a cart loaded with clean linen along the second-story walkway. "Maybe not. I guess they get the word slower down here."

"Well then, why not?"

"We aren't going to meet any Mexicans here. Just grampas from California. It doesn't make sense."

"You think we'll meet a dealer on the beach?" She grabbed his arm and put her face up close. This was no time to be chicken. "I want a shower. I need a shower."

"Listen, two, three days, I swear it, we'll be going to Las Vegas. You ever been in Las Vegas? We'll have the stuff and we'll unload it in Las Vegas. Just hang on."

"Kirk, this is a fucking fishing village, not goddam Acapulco. Which one of them fishermen you figure is the cocaine dealer in disguise? There were any dope dealers in this fucking town, one or two of these places might have had a paint job once or twice the past twenty years. I want a goddam shower. Is that asking too much?"

"You're losing faith, babe. I'm telling you, everybody in Mexico deals dope."

"How do you know that? Just how do you know that?"

"This guy said."

"What guy? I've heard about this guy a lot now. Who was he?"

"Lower your voice. You want the whole world to hear you?"

"What guy?"

"Just a guy I knew."

"When? Where?"

"He was a guy."

She watched him chew his lip, then tap his teeth with his fingernail.

She had to say it. He scared the shit out of her, but not that much. "There was no guy, was there?"

"Sure there was."

"What was his name?"

"I forget. Just a guy."

He couldn't bullshit worth a damn. He wasn't going to say it, but she was sure now. There had never been a guy. It was a dream. Talk about your Mexico, your dope, your dealers, your smuggling, or your selling, and Kirk knew bubble fuck.

"All right. There was a guy. That's terrific. But I tell you, Kirk, I am not doing my business squatting over the fucking sand. You don't want to stay here, fine. You take me somewhere else. Anywhere you like. But I'm not spending another night in that car on the backseat, you hear?"

"You're changing," he said. His eyes were darker. "You weren't like this back in Iowa."

"Fuck you." She'd always been like this; he just didn't know it. The first time in her life she relaxed and allowed someone else to take charge, she was begging for a toilet.

He was smiling now. "You're changing, all right."

"Are we going to stay here, or not? 'Cause if you say not, I'm leaving."

"Just where you going to go? Tell me that."

"I'll hitch."

"You'll hitch. In Mexico. Through that fucking desert."

"I swear, I'll do it."

"You'll be raped and dead in twenty-four hours."

"I'll take my chances."

"I believe you would, babe. I believe you would." He took a cigarette and lighted it with the silver-turqoise butane lighter he'd shoplifted in a truck stop outside Amarillo. He inhaled deeply, closing his eyes. "Well, I guess Mr. William Krantz can spring for one or two more nights. He hasn't complained yet."

She started to hug him, then thought she'd better not. It would tell him something she didn't think was true anymore, something she was learning more and more, something she did not want him to know. She'd taken her chance, and here she was; and nothing was the way it was supposed to be, because Kirk Dugan was a lot more asshole than she had guessed. And the truer that got, then the closer she got to the notion that she had not been too bright herself to hook up with him, and that this fact had to be reckoned with. She'd never thought Doralee Jackson the smartest girl in Des Moines, but she sure as shit was not the dumbest—though it was starting to look that way. If she kept her eyes sharp, she'd see the way out. Keep her fingers crossed, mouth shut, and spread her legs only enough to keep him happy, because if he wasn't happy he'd as soon leave her as take her. So, where she had set out for a good time and a nice ride, now she would have to concentrate on getting out with her skin.

She was awful glad that gun was under a rock in Arizona.

II

When Doralee Jackson was nine years old her Momma one night gathered up her and her two younger brothers in her arms, ran them out of the house to a taxicab, and took them to the shelter where they lived for two whole months before Momma was sure enough the injunction she got from the judge would really and truly keep Poppa away. Doralee didn't miss Poppa one little bit, and she never told Momma or anybody else about the two times he'd come to her in the night when she was eight and explained exactly what good girls did and kept their mouths shut afterwards. Momma didn't miss Poppa much, neither. The swelling on her face went down and she turned into a downright pretty woman once she learned how to take care of her hair, got some clothes, and quit the beer.

The people from the shelter got them an apartment on the southeast side of Des Moines, what was called the Bottoms, and they must have given Momma some training, because Momma got a job first as a waitress and then as a cashier at the Denny's out near the interstate. Doralee didn't remember much about those times right after the shelter, just especially how she would be alone and had to take care of her brothers Jimmy and Daniel, making peanut butter sandwiches, and when she got to be a little older defrosting fried chicken TV dinners night after night. It wasn't so much taking care of the boys she remembered, but the being alone in the darkness waiting for Momma, the boys asleep, watching the black-and-white television that stood on the kitchen table, expecting any time that Poppa would show up at the front door and take them away. But he never did, and Doralee never learned just where he'd gone to; and that was just fine with her.

Momma slimmed down, and by the time Doralee was thirteen she understood why there were nights Momma didn't come home at all, or if she did come home made it in at three or four o'clock in the morning. She was having her time, and she was entitled to it, didn't Doralee think? Momma would ask her when they both had a cup of morning coffee in the half hour before Jimmy and Daniel got out of bed, Momma's lipstick leaving rings on the rim of the cup that later Doralee would have to scrub to get rid of. Momma told her about the truckers that came in to the restaurant and how nice some of them were, the southerners the most gentlemenlike, fellas who'd been to faraway places with names that sounded to Momma (and to Doralee) like places from a storybook. Iron City was Pittsburgh, Bean Town was Boston, and the Music City was Nashville, of course. And there were places that didn't have nicknames, like Des Moines, but sounded nice when you said or heard them (not like Des Moines, which didn't sound to Doralee or Momma like nothing at all). Joplin, Missouri. Wichita, Kansas. Bakersfield, California. And the cabs of some of the trucks in the little space behind the driver's seat were fixed up like little apartments, with stereos, a place to sleep, pictures on the wall, even. It was a wonder how those truckers got so much into so tiny a space.

A body might expect all of this to have gotten in the way of Doralee's schooling, but the fact of the matter was that it didn't make much difference at all. By the time she was in sixth grade Doralee knew that she and schooling could never have all that much to say to each other. She could read good enough, and she could do her arithmetic, but beyond that school somehow seemed not to be the main thing, though she had no idea what the main thing might be. They called her "Dumb Dora" of course, but she took that in stride because it came from the kids who didn't know much about real life, like how to cook what you bought at the 7-Eleven, what to do when your little brother burned his hand on the radiator, or how to give your momma just enough brandy when she had the cramps. *That* stuff never showed up on those tests where you had to fill in the itty-bitty circles with your pencil. She knew what she knew, and she suspected that if the tests had questions about things that mattered, she might do all right.

So she was fifteen when she made it to the ninth grade, a mite older than the other kids. It was hard to make friends. That was the year she got her first job, because she wanted a little money for makeup and some nicer clothes, and Jimmy was old enough to take care of himself and look after Daniel. Right after school she had to get on the bus and ride to the last stop on the line, practically in the cornfields, and then she had to walk a quarter mile to the shopping center where she clerked at Faith's Gift & Card Shoppe. They gave her fifteen hours a week at minimum, and the job was all right until the day in January when she got off the bus and it was snowing like hell and the wind chill was thirty below, and after she made the walk to the store, the manager, a pimply faced guy who'd had one year of college at Iowa State, gave her shit for being forty minutes late. She'd damned near frozen to death. But she didn't say anything to the jerk until she had another job, which she got in the spring, and then what she did was show up at the store and accidentally-on-purpose drop a box of those ugly little plates with the too-cute pictures of the kittens on them. Then she quit.

She had the job at the supermarket for nearly two years, putting a little money away each month in an account that Momma didn't know about, though she gave the rest of it to Momma just as Momma asked. The day she turned seventeen she went into the counselor at school and said she was ready to quit, and the counselor sort of shrugged his shoulders like that might not be such a bad idea. Momma thought it was all right, too. She went on mornings at the supermarket and looked for an afternoon job, and quick enough got one at the Burger King right near the South Ridge Mall.

She hated the stupid polyester uniform, and she had to cut her hair because she wouldn't wear a net on her head, but it was another twenty hours a week. She brought home french fries to reheat for Jimmy and Daniel—they were growing up pretty good and she didn't worry about them anymore, Jimmy good enough at varsity football there was a chance he might go to college, the coach said, if he didn't hurt himself, and Daniel getting along in junior high.

Momma seemed to be slowing down, a steady fellow that had lasted more than a year now, though Doralee had a hunch he was married someplace or other, because Momma clammed up about him whenever Doralee hinted around that. She waited six months and then announced to Momma that she was moving into her own place. She had five hundred dollars in that private account.

"I'm nearly eighteen," she said.

"You're a baby."

"I ain't never been a baby, ever."

That remark made Momma cry, something she did more and more lately. Doralee was sorry for that, but she couldn't help any, now could she?

But she hadn't been asking permission or for approval, and so, soon enough, she found an apartment on the third floor of a five-story walk-up. Two rooms that weren't much, but they were furnished, they wanted only a half-month's rent security, which would leave her some left over to get linens and plates and whatever, and the place was real close to the bus lines she needed to get to her two jobs. Doralee was not walking in any goddam blizzards anymore.

There had been boys, but they had not been important, what with her not having a lot of time on her hands to go out in some redneck's pickup and park by Gray's Lake or the Saylorville dam. She knew she didn't look like any damned Hawkeye cheerleader whose shit smelled like ice cream, but she was far from ugly. Her figure was all right, her belly flat, and it seemed to stay that way no matter what she ate. She might have asked for a little more on top, but she did all right with what she had.

Ricky Laughton took her out now and then, a boy she knew from when she was in high school, who one day when she still lived with Momma had walked through her checkout aisle and recognized her. He came back a day later to buy just a loaf of bread, and she knew right away he was sweet on her, because he could have gone through the speed aisle but instead waited on line with just the one loaf of bread under his arm. He'd take her bowling, they'd have some beers, and once he took her roller-skating, but after a little time with him they would run out of things to say, and she could predict that as soon as the conversation dried up he'd take her home and park a half block from the building where Momma lived, and then he'd try to kiss her. She'd let him, now and then, but she didn't get any feeling from it, and he never tried to do much else, which was fine with her.

Art Phillips tried to do more. He worked with her at the supermarket, and the very first time he was with her got himself so worked up she almost laughed. He was so serious, smelling of Aqua Velva and hair tonic, but still smelling green and wet as the lettuce and cukes he worked with all day long in produce, and he spent the whole Clint Eastwood movie fiddling with the buttons of her blouse, trying to jackknife his hand under her bra, and her all the time keeping her eyes straight ahead on the movie, making like she didn't even know his hand was wrapped like a snake around her neck. When he took her home she practically jumped out of the car before he could turn off the engine, ran into the building where she lived, and leaned against the door while she laughed.

He asked her out again, and the second time she played hard to get, not so much because she wasn't sure if she liked Arthur well enough, but because she had spent a week trying to figure out if she was a virgin or not.

Did what her father had done count?

So, the third time Arthur took her out—another movie, it was the only thing he could think of—after the movie he bought a six-pack and she let him take her north of the city, halfway to Fort Dodge. It was May, and it was warm. There was moonlight of sorts. They drank the beer, and she let him do it to her in the back seat of the car so she wouldn't have to wonder about it anymore. She liked it all right, and she did it with Arthur one more time to be sure, and while he was going at it she was thinking about the green, checked cafe curtains she had seen at Montgomery Ward that might go nice over the little window she had in her bathroom.

Two years passed. There were a few other boys, even one or two she could properly call a man; and while she gave herself away now and then, she kept a rein on it, too. She never took any of them to her place. That was hers, by God, she'd worked damned hard to get it, and no one was waltzing into a place that was hers until she was damned sure the fellow mattered.

She hoped for a man that offered a little excitement. Some part of Doralee still heard the music in those names of places that were far off, those places that Momma's truckers talked of. Tulsa. Yuba. Chino. Denver. Houston. Corpus Christi. Albuquerque. Doralee Jackson was mired in Des Moines, Iowa, the heart of the toolies, which wasn't the end of the earth, but you could throw a rock off the edge.

The jamokes she came across chewed tobacco and wore adjustable hats that said John Deere on the crown, and it seemed if she let them into her pants they all either disappeared or started right away talking about children and putting in one hundred fifty acres of soybeans, and did she want to settle down? Which she most certainly did not. She was not one of these fluff-brained beauties that thought of a man as something that would take care of her forever and ever. No, thank you very much, Doralee Jackson would damn well take care of herself. She wasn't good at much, but she was damned good at that.

She was nineteen when Kirk Dugan came into the Burger King and she was working the second register on the right. He ordered the chicken sandwich, a Dr Pepper, and the large fries, and she hardly looked up, would not have noticed him at all, except that when she gave him change for a five he said "I gave you a ten."

She checked the register—she was careful with money—and there was no way he had given her a ten-dollar bill. If he thought so, he was wrong. But she checked, then did a check of the register tape against the cash drawer, running totals, and told him he had given her a five.

He raised his voice the slightest bit, said he would call the manager, what did she think she was doing to him?

"Listen," she said and noticed his black hair, stubble of beard, and blue eyes, so, when she started out stern, despite herself her voice got soft, "I'll get you the manager if you want. His name is Duncan, but he's going to do what I just did, which is to check the receipts against the drawer, and I'm telling you, you gave me a five. Why don't you just sit down and enjoy your sandwich? There're other people waiting."

And that was when he smiled and muttered, "Shit, can't blame a man for trying," and she'd had to laugh when he walked away, looking more sorrowful than a dog in a drought.

She forgot about him, but two hours later when her shift was up and she was ready to leave, she stepped out in front and there he was, still sitting at a table, still sucking on the straw in the same Dr Pepper.

"You need a drive home?"

"The buses run."

"You don't have to be like that."

"I sure do," she said and went to the bus.

While she walked to the bus stop he drove a white Ford flatbed real slow right next to her, the window rolled down so he could talk, him leaning all the way across the seat not watching at all where he was going, the other cars coming around the truck honking their horns, but he didn't seem to mind. She noticed the truck had Illinois plates.

"You're not from around here," she said.

"How'd you know that?"

"I could tell."

At the bus stop he parked and she stood, waiting. She thought he was cute in a rough way. She wasn't at all scared.

"I'm just passing through town for a day or two. Made a delivery. My name's Kirk. Kirk Dugan. You're Doralee."

There was no sign of the bus. It was due in a minute. "You read my name tag."

"That's right. What's your last name?" The flatbed's bad idle made it rattle and cough. Kirk bent toward her and the door swung open. "I could take you home, Doralee."

The bus rumbled up to the stop, and the driver gave Kirk a blast of his horn. Doralee got on the bus, and the whole ride home kept herself from looking out the bus windows to see if the flatbed was following the bus, and when she got off she expected to see it, but it was not there. Walking up the three flights of steps to her place, she didn't know if she was relieved or disappointed.

A month or so later, about fifteen minutes before quitting time at the Burger King, Kirk Dugan showed up again, waiting on line at her register, even though the one next to hers was open and twice the girl said "Can I help someone?" He ordered just a Dr Pepper, smiled at her, and gave her the exact change. Never said a word except to order. At quitting time she walked into the parking lot, her uniform stinking of the smell of cooked beef, and she looked for the flatbed, but it wasn't there, so she started out for the bus stop and that was when she heard her name called. She hadn't seen him because he was in a blue Chevy Nova, slouched way down low in the seat. The Chevy had Iowa license plates. She went to the car.

"Remember me?" he asked.

"Fella from Illinois. Kirk Dugan," she said, and the minute she said his name she realized it was a mistake to do so, because then he knew she'd thought about him. He smiled broadly, knowingly. There wasn't any point then to stalling, so she went right around the car and got in. The front seat was covered in cigarette ashes and crumpled pieces of cellophane. He started the car, making the tires squeal just like she knew he would, and she directed him to her place.

They parked right in front of the walk-up where she lived and he asked if he could see her the next day, now that he knew where she lived.

"You just passing through?"

"Nope. I'll be here a bit this time. Got a job. Knew a fellow who knew a fellow, so here I am."

"Doing what?"

"Pump gas. A little mechanical work. Been in town couple of days, got this car, and the guy lets me bunk in this trailer they got out back, until I find a place, he says. How about it? You want to go for a ride with me tomorrow?"

"Ride where?" Doralee knew she was going to say yes, but not quite yet. She saw no harm in it, and the car did have Iowa plates.

"Well, I don't know. I was hoping you'd have some ideas about that. I don't know my way around here at all."

He looked so damned confident, she wanted to scream; but he was acting like a gentleman, so she said it would be all right if he called for her at 7:30, and he did, the next night. That first time together she let him put his hand in her pants after they kissed some, and in a week he was coming by for her at work every day at the end of her shift, and pretty soon she believed she was in love with him, not for anything he said or did, but just because he had a way about him that made her feel easy with him. He told her about his times in Illinois, how he had been in what he called a boy's school because when he was sixteen—he was twenty-four now—he had gotten caught with three other fellows in a car they had borrowed just to go for a ride, and that was where he had learned to do some mechanical work. It was where he had gotten the Zig-Zag man tatoo with a straight pin and a Bic pen. The Zig-Zag man was the trademark on a brand of rolling paper.

The night she took him up to her own place, he rolled two marijuana cigarettes, and she smoked one, and then they "got it on," which was what Kirk called making love, and it was terrific, the first time she ever got so far into it that afterwards she could not remember what had happened, only that she had been rocked and sweaty and exhausted and turned this way and that. His body was hard and lean, all strain and muscle, and his strong hands on her here and there knew just what to touch for how long and exactly how hard to press. She let him spend the night. It was strange to lie beside a man, strange but nice, and sometimes even after he was asleep she'd get the quakes and these little tingles, even though they'd stopped making love hours before. It made her smile, and she was amazed. While he slept, she rolled to her hip and touched his long, black hair, longer than her own, recalling how it had flared out about him, wild, as he had gripped her with his skinny arms. You could give yourself up to a man like that.

In the morning they made love again, but it wasn't as good, because he'd awakened her and started right in, and all she could think about was that she had to pee.

A week later he moved in with her. It was sort of understood.

Kirk knew things, things you could not learn from a book, and Doralee Jackson respected that kind of knowledge. If you're hard up for a drink, you pour hair tonic through white bread, and to check you put a match to it. If it burned red, don't drink it; burned blue, it was okay. She couldn't believe anyone would be that hard up for a drink, but it was good to know a trick or two. She'd watch him separate the seeds from a batch of marijuana, squeezing the stuff between his fingers because that was how to tell if it was good stuff or not. He also told her how if you needed to get high you could put a stick of Wrigley Spearmint gum in a banana and set that out in the sunlight for a few days, then chew the gum; but when she asked if they could try that, he said "What for? We've got some good grass." He'd traveled a lot, too, and could tell her how to get from any place to any place else, reciting the interstate roads and where they came together or went apart, like the whole country was his backyard to play in. She liked how sometimes they would go in a place and Kirk would get stared at for his hair, and he would stare right back, facing down the crackers, he called it, and she was glad to be stared at as the woman who was with him. Special. Different. She'd never known how much she needed that.

So, when after two months of living with Kirk Dugan he said to her one day that he was ready to take off, her heart caught, but then she nearly wept when he asked if she wanted to go along. She did. She did, indeed.

He laughed at her when she said she needed a few days to settle things, especially to say good-bye to Momma and the boys. "That shit just holds you down," he said, but she insisted, and she felt even better about him when Kirk said it was all right, a day or two more would make no never mind.

Doralee was sure Momma didn't believe her story about a job she got in Denver, but Momma gave her fifty dollars and said to be sure to call if she got into trouble and needed more. She seemed tired, tired in a way that had nothing to do with working long hours. Lying to Momma didn't sit well with her, but she took the money. Daniel gave her a big hug and she promised to send him picture postcards of wherever she went, and as soon as she got settled they could all come visit her. And Jimmy listened to her talking to Momma, and then late that night while Momma was drifting off asleep in the big old livingroom chair, Jimmy took Doralee to the kitchen and while he drank a whole quart of milk straight from the carton told her that she must have thought their Momma was awful stupid. Doralee told him she loved this fellow, Kirk, and Jimmy nodded his head, wiping the milk mustache from his upper lip, understanding especially the part about how she needed to get out, there was nothing here for her anymore, never was, how she was sick of taking care of herself and just wanted a rest, and while Kirk Dugan wasn't some hero out of a book, he was not the villain, either. "If he treats you bad," her brother the all-state tackle said, "you let me know." He hugged her then, and that was all there was to good-byes.

So when Doralee Jackson got into the blue '78 Chevy Nova with

Kirk Dugan way up in Iowa, she did not have many doubts, and if the truth was she did not have a pile of good reasons to go along, she did not have many reasons to stay behind. The doubts came quick enough, though, miles before they reached Mexico and the beach at Puerto Penasco, but by then it was too late, she'd taken her chance, and she had to ride it out.

III

The shower stall's blue tile was cracked and chipped from the floor to the ceiling, the grouting, brown and rotten, fell out in chunks, the double bed's springs squealed every time you rolled over, so that you woke up three, four times every night just from moving, and if you made love the damned thing made enough racket you expected every Mexican for two miles around to come by to peek through the raggedy cloth curtain that was nailed into the plaster and hung across the window that faced into the courtyard. The walls were a sickly yellow, the paint peeling, and right above the bed was a hole you could see clear through to the beams, a hole that looked to Doralee like a horse, or maybe a camel. Over the beat-up bureau was a mirror, and beside that was a lamp with a three-way bulb that only worked at the lowest illumination.

But Doralee Jackson liked the room. And she liked that Kirk made slow love to her that first night, good as old times. And, damn! How she liked that shower—rotten tiles, spiders, and all. The water was a miracle, hot as could be, so she came out with her skin tingling, and when she pinched her hair she'd washed with the motel's soap, her hair squeaked and she felt her scalp breathe.

They took their meals in a small restaurant just outside the motel's gate, one of the dark luncheonettes they had wandered past that first morning. Eggs for breakfast and a hamburger at night. Doralee wanted to try shrimp *Vera Cruzana*, or shrimp in butter and garlic, but she kept her mouth shut because they had to pay cash in the restaurant. They were out of cigarette and beer money, so Kirk cursed up a storm and then pried off his boot heel and took out one of the hundred-dollar bills. Getting the heel back on he stamped around the room like a man gone crazy with roaches. It made Doralee laugh, and when Kirk first looked up at her he glared angry, but then he laughed too. And the clerk in the motel office gave them change without batting an eyelash, but

Kirk threw the deadbolt lock on the door that night and pulled the bureau to block the entrance, convinced they'd have their throats slashed while they slept.

Doralee might have wanted a bathing suit, but her cutoffs and a T-shirt worked okay. She might have wanted some tanning oil for the long afternoons on the beach, but she could do without, her skin naturally darker than Kirk's. All they did was sleep, swim, eat, make love, and sleep some more.

Four days in Rocky Point, and it was clear that no one was going to sell them dope. It would take Kirk a little longer to see that, or at least admit to what was already obvious. Well, it wasn't a bad vacation, and she'd be all right if he'd give it up and they would either head back to the border or south, maybe to a place called Mazatlan, that Doralee had seen on the map, where they might have better luck. And if that didn't work, then Mexico City. Whatever it took.

The problem with men was you had to get them to think that everything was their own idea, and Kirk just didn't know how to admit he might have been wrong. He became cranky as a wet baby, hardly speaking to her at all.

Some time after noon on the fourth day, the sun so hot and white a body couldn't even lie out on the beach, Doralee was in the room. Kirk was who knew where—probably asking dark-eyed little boys who had nothing to eat where the cocaine dealers were. An awful clanking came from the courtyard. She lifted a corner of the maroon curtain and saw a battered old bus pull up beside the Chevy. The bus was the kind that hauled kids to school, but it was grayish blue, not a bright, proper yellow. Mexico. Nothing was right in Mexico.

The men that got off the bus all wore open-necked sport shirts and slacks, bright reds and blues or yellows that were startling in Mexico, where everything was sun-bleached to the same no-color, washed-out, dusty brown or gray. Each of them carried a duffel bag, and they laughed and cursed like men did when they liked each other and were having a good time. Mexicans, but there were three—the three who got off the bus last—taller than the others, paler, and no doubt about it, American boys. She saw them only a second, and then they walked toward the motel office, under the terrace in front of her door, and they were gone.

Later she was with Kirk out on the beach at a round concrete table that had an umbrella that probably once had been painted with colors but now was just metal colored. They drank beer. The tide was out. All along the beach gulls and pelicans picked at whatever had been left by the tide along the rocky shore.

"You know what's wrong with Mexico?" Kirk said. "You can't tell what's what. We were in the States, I would know what to do. Find a bar with a pool table, talk to a couple of people, and pretty soon we'd score and be gone. But fucking Mexico, man, fucking Mexico. I bet there's not a pool table in this town."

"Maybe we should head back."

"No way. We have to wait it out. They'll find us, soon enough. They'll find us. If I knew what was what, I'd find them, but I don't, so we'll wait."

"Maybe we should go south."

"South? What in fuck is south?"

"Other towns. Different people."

He chewed a thumbnail. "No. It'll be the same."

"You scared?" She stared out to sea, but felt his eyes on her.

"What's that supposed to mean?"

"Kirk, I'm bored. We're not *doing* anything."

"If you'd have done time, you'd have learned patience."

"You did time?"

"Easy time. I told you. The boy's school."

"That's not like jail."

"Shows what you know. Juvey hall could have been a fucking penitentiary."

One of the three American men she'd seen come off the bus was emerging through the archway of the cinder block wall that divided the motel from the beach, trudging across the sand. He carried a towel and he wore a proper bathing suit. He started going down to the water where some other people were clustered, people with children and coolers, fold-up chairs and fruit, but Doralee saw him notice her and Kirk, and he changed direction, easy as you please, coming toward them across the sand, taking confident strides with his long-muscled legs, his bare feet sinking in the white sand, his straw yellow hair falling over his eyes, a white country-boy smile big as the sky on his face. She kept her head tilted way back and her eyes open, the beer still cold enough in her throat, though she lost a bit that flowed over her chin and dripped to her T-shirt. She wished to God she had a bathing suit.

"Hi," he said, standing just outside the puddle of shade cast by the metal umbrella. "You folks are Americans."

"That's right," Kirk said.

"It's hot."

"Sure is," Kirk said.

"Why don't you sit down in the shade?" Doralee said, and Kirk looked at her sideways, his eyes squinted, but she made as though she was Dumb Dora and did not see him glance at her.

"Thanks, I think I will." He sat between them, closer to Dora than to Kirk, but not so close you had to think anything of it. "I'm Bobby Kelly." He held out his big hand to Kirk, the back of his hand all covered with fine, white hairs, the knuckles big and red, rough hands that had known work.

Kirk hesitated, then took Bobby Kelly's hand. "I'm Kirk Dugan. This here is Doralee."

"Doralee Jackson."

"Pleased."

Bobby Kelly was smiling at her, so hard she had to smile back. He was soft-spoken, and his voice had something in it she did not recognize, not southern or eastern, but something else that was maybe sorrow and made a girl want to take him home and keep him safe.

"You folks on vacation?" Bobby Kelly asked.

"Yupper."

"Staying at the Old Hacienda, huh?" He laughed at some private joke.

Doralee had said nothing since she'd asked him to sit and told Bobby Kelly her whole name, and she knew that if she spoke she risked Kirk's anger later on, but to hell with him. Four days. He didn't know how to make things happen.

"I'm from Iowa," she said.

"Is that right? I've got a cousin in Iowa. In Davenport."

"I know Davenport."

Kirk sniffed as he wiped his lips after draining the last of his beer and throwing the brown bottle onto the sand.

"I'm from Oregon."

"You on vacation?" Kirk asked.

"No." Bobby Kelly swung his legs around and under the table, settling in. He put his elbows on the table. He kept right on looking hard at Doralee while he spoke and she kept right on looking hard back at him. It was a contest. "I throw for the Penguins."

"What are the Penguins?" Doralee asked.

"The Puerto Penasco Penguins. Triple-A Mexican baseball club."

Kirk laughed, a mean little laugh that made Doralee want to reach

over and slap his face and pull his ears, but instead she said "How long
you been doing that?"

"Three years. I played for the University of Oregon, and then came
down here. I thought it might be a way to the bigs." His smile was almost an apology. "You know, American baseball."

Kirk took Doralee's still-half-full bottle from her and helped himself to a long swallow. "How the hell can you play for a Mexican baseball team?"

"They allow four gringos to a team. I write home about the Penguins, and my daddy laughs, says it isn't a decent name for a baseball
team, sounds like we all wear tuxedoes and waddle in the outfield. But
it's not bad ball, actually. Valenzuela once pitched in a league like this."

Doralee wondered who in Creation Valenzuela was, but she just
nodded her head, trying not to smile because her teeth were so crooked,
and she wondered just how wind-blown and ugly her hair might be.
This beautiful boy from Oregon who wrote letters home to his
daddy—imagine such a thing!—this boy looked like he drank milk at
every meal and breathed easy in the mornings.

She said "Sounds like fun."

"Well, I wouldn't go that far. It's not much fun anymore. I just want
to play a while, and I can do that here. Came down for one season, and
here I am in my third. The money isn't great, but I get to play."

"If there's no money in it, it's bullshit."

"Kirk, don't be such a downer."

"Shut up."

"I'll say what I please."

"You usually do."

"Hey, I'm sorry . . . ," Bobby Kelly began.

"No problem," Kirk said.

They were silent a minute, watching the ocean, listening to the
crash of the waves.

"I don't get to see many American girls down here. Thought I'd
come over to talk a few minutes. Practice is at four o'clock and I've got
just enough time for a quick dip." He smiled that big, good old boy
smile that made Doralee think of home. "You two are married, right?"

Kirk whooped, his head back and his long hair flying. Bobby Kelly's
hair was short, longest in front.

"No, we're not married," she said, and added softly when she was
sure Kirk was laughing so hard he wouldn't hear, "We're just traveling
together."

"I see," he said and then smiled even more broadly at her, not leering, but glad, Kirk so busy laughing a gut-buster that he couldn't notice, and for the first time Doralee wondered if Bobby Kelly was her ticket out of here.

Kirk wiped his eyes when he stopped laughing. "I used to play baseball myself," Kirk said. "Second base."

"That right?"

"Sure. In Illinois. At this school I was at for two years. Batted four twenty-two."

"Is that right?" Bobby Kelly said, and smiled even wider before he pursed his lips and nodded like a man that knew a secret. "Heavy hitter like you would probably like to come to the game tonight. Eight o'clock. I'm pitching. Get you two seats right behind our dugout. Freebies."

Doralee said "yes" before Kirk could say a word.

Bobby Kelly smiled and said that he had to be off, shook both their hands—his hand really was rough, but nice—and headed right back for the motel without taking his swim.

"What the hell did you ask that cracker over here for?"

"Why not?" Doralee said. "I thought maybe he'd know somebody who might sell dope," she tried, knowing just from having looked at Bobby Kelly that he would never in a million years know anybody like that. But Kirk chewed on that notion a second. She watched his eyes cloud and then get clear. So she added, "And he probably speaks Mexican."

Kirk said, "That asshole probably doesn't know shit."

"Maybe he does."

"Maybe." Kirk threw an empty bottle at a gull that fluttered up and then landed right back, undisturbed.

"So we'll go to the game?"

Kirk drummed his fingers on the table. He looked out to the ocean where the wind made whitecaps on the waves, so strong it brushed foam into the air. "Sure. Why not? We'll have to find out where the damn ballpark is."

"We can find out."

"I hate guys like that."

"Guys like what?"

"Like that. Like that guy. So dumb. He thought I was married to you."

"You want to swim?"

"I want to fuck."

"I want to swim. First."

Kirk smiled, and as she stood he reached to pat her ass.

The tide was coming in and even though it was hot as could be the wind made her feel cool. She walked out a bit, stepping carefully on the rocks ready to hurt you, so unlike Iowa lakefronts where soft bottom mud sucked at your feet, and she bent to splash herself with the water, cold and smelling of salt. Then, as a wave came at her, she jumped straight up and when she came down she let herself sink, bending her knees, pinching her nose closed. Beneath the surface she opened her eyes and saw motes of light glowing from the sun, bubbles rising around her, and she listened to the total silence, so abruptly different from above the surface, and then she heard a roaring which was her own blood in her ears. She stayed under as long as she could, then exploded up, straightening her legs.

On the concrete terrace before the room Kirk said, "You swim like a shit."

"I never learned to swim."

"Well, you swim like a shit."

" 'Bout as good as you play baseball."

"What in fuck does that mean?"

But she didn't have to answer because they were going into the room and on the floor they found a little white envelope with two tickets, and on the envelope in pencil was a map to the ballpark. Kirk picked it up and threw the envelope on the bureau. "Are you going to take a shower again?" he said, and from behind her put his hands on her hips, pulling her toward him.

In fact, she wanted to. But she had figured out she would have to spread her legs enough to keep him happy, he was too damned dangerously close to being unhappy. She wanted him to want to go south with her, score the dope, make the money, buy the good life, have the good times, but Kirk could never be that bold. He was a mean, petty little shit. But there was no way she could piss him off if she wanted to go to that baseball game. She knew diddley-shit about baseball, had never once in her whole life seen a game except on television, but now she wanted to see a baseball game more than anything. Bobby Kelly might be her chance.

It pissed her off. Kirk Dugan or Bobby Kelly. How did Doralee Jackson's life become a matter of this man or that? Damn! She'd fucked up this time.

She pulled Kirk's hands from her hips under her wet shirt and onto her breasts and leaned back against him.

"I know just what you like," he whispered in her ear. "I know you better than you know yourself, woman."

IV

Doralee Jackson was still in love with Kirk Dugan the day they left Des Moines, heading east because he wanted to show her Illinois where he had been raised. But in the car Kirk became silent, and before they got as far as Iowa City he all of a sudden twisted the wheel, bumped the Chevy over the grass divider of the interstate so hard her teeth rattled in her head, and told her that it would be better if they headed west. She loved him for that, the quickness of it, the unthinking swift willingness to allow events to take a course, and she was sure that afternoon that she was onto a good thing, because even as her jaw snapped together when the car bounced over the divider she thought of the men she had known who knew nothing of horizons and could never have done anything with less than a month to think, weighing chances and judging prospects, until they'd bled the joy from it, thinking a thing to death. So she was sure she was along for a good ride.

They went to Omaha where Kirk knew some people, and they stayed there in a small apartment above a hardware store on the east side near the Missouri River for a few days with Lee Harkin, a woman named Sherry Anne, and their six cats. Lee and Sherry Anne would be out in the day, and they had the place to themselves, making love on the sofa with the cats looking on, the sunlight strong in the windows, and Kirk so cocky that he left the window shades up, which embarassed her some until she realized it excited her, too. In the evening they would all smoke a little dope and then walk in the Old Town or down along the riverfront, the gray river clogged with rusted barges and cranes taller than the office buildings against the western sky.

She liked Sherry Anne all right; she was a washed-out blonde woman older than herself who must have been pretty once, but Lee Harkin frightened her a little. A big man going bald, he had small eyes and a lot of dark hair on his arms. Kirk and he did some business, and Kirk told her later he had expected to do more, but that never happened. One night Kirk argued with Lee Harkin—she didn't know what about—and the next day they were in the car so early in the morning she was half asleep, and all that day the car took them across Nebraska to Denver, Kirk not saying a word, just smoking one Marlboro after another, the Chevy filling with blue smoke, until late in the afternoon when the Rocky Mountains in front of them were like a wall that meant you couldn't go no further, Kirk punched the seat and said that Lee Harkin was a chickenshit son of a bitch, motherfucking asshole who'd lost whatever balls he might have ever had.

They didn't stay long in Denver, just a night and a day, and they slept in the car to save some money, something Doralee didn't mind a whole lot because Kirk was smart enough first thing in the morning to get to a roadside restaurant with a bathroom and what was a pretty good breakfast of eggs and home fries. He said he'd been in Denver lots of times, but he got lost on the highways trying to find Larimer Square. When they finally got there it was pretty good. He was sweet that day, standing by her as they walked in and out of the fine stores and she made believe she could afford the dresses and makeup, even in one place trying on this frilly red skirt with a white lace border that actually cost more than three hundred dollars. Another man might have gotten bored and antsy, but Kirk admired the clothes along with her, patient as could be, sitting in a chair near the try-on room sort of staring up at the ceiling and buffing his fingernails against his jeans.

They left Denver near four o'clock in the afternoon, and Doralee was all turned around, but they must have been heading south and east, because by eight o'clock they were in Kansas, and that was when Kirk pulled into the darkest part of a Stuckey's parking lot and told her to wait in the car, he'd be just a minute. Then he smashed the Chevy's interior light before he opened the car door, and with the motor running and the door left wide, he walked to where she could see him in the bright white light and saw he was carrying something heavy and black in his right hand just behind his leg. He came back five minutes later and, even by the dim green-and-amber glow of the dashboard, she could see the heat in his eyes and the sweat on his face. He threw a brown paper bag at her, slammed shut the door, and the Chevy hugged the darkness back out onto the road half a mile before he put the headlights on, pumping the accelerator the whole time.

"You should have told me," she said when they were finally out on the highway and he was watching the speedometer, making sure he stayed right on 55. "You didn't have no right to assume."

"Honest, Doralee, I'd have told you, except I was afraid you'd disapprove and leave me. I couldn't stand that."

Put that way, it was hard to argue with him, and she thought that maybe hell was loving a thief.

She said, "It's dangerous."

"What's the difference? We need money. This is easy."

"Where'd you get the gun?" It was on the seat between them, big and black, and when she asked the question Kirk moved it under the seat between his legs. He took a beer from the back seat, steered with his knee while he popped the Bud.

"Lee. That pussy wouldn't do no work, but he sold me the gun. Two hundred dollars."

"I don't like guns."

"You expect me to go into a place and ask them sweet as pie to give me what's in the register? And they'll do it, of course, 'cause I'm so pretty, right?"

"I don't like guns."

"You just count what's in that bag, hear?"

Two hundred and twenty-eight dollars. More than she was able to save in three months when she had worked at two jobs in Iowa. She told him.

He smiled, drained the last of the beer, and said "I figured it right, then. End of the day, dark enough that no one can eyeball the car, and the register's got the day's receipts in it. Pretty slick."

She kept her mouth shut. They did need money—you couldn't go any place without it—and when they made it to Wichita late that night, Kirk took her to the finest motel room she had ever imagined. Drapery on the windows, a terrace, real glasses, big gold towels, free movies on the color TV, satin border on the blanket, and plastic wrapped across the toilet so you were sure it was clean.

They walked across the road to a restaurant with tablecloths and hot rolls in a basket covered by a napkin. After dinner, the night cool and the stars out, she realized that she didn't mind much at all what Kirk did, as long as no one got hurt. If that made her a thief at heart and as guilty as he was, well, she would be stupid not to enjoy the fruits of his labor. But he should have told her, and she knew she wouldn't trust him anymore, couldn't, because he was sure to get them into all sorts of shit sooner or later. The first sign of trouble—and it had to come, you couldn't just walk into any place you wanted wherever you wanted and take money without some time, some place, having the roof fall in—the first sign, she'd be saying fare-thee-well.

She loved Kirk Dugan, right enough, but that wasn't the same as saying she was ready to give over her life to him, neither. Look at that sweet girl Sherry Anne, what did she have to show for her life with a thief except six cats in an Omaha apartment over a hardware store?

They drifted south and east a while. It got so that when Kirk told her it was time to stop someplace and make a withdrawal she got only a teensy nervous, sitting outside in the car, watching moths, expecting any second to hear the gun go off. But Kirk was a lucky man—she began to realize that, like Momma had said, better lucky than smart—and not once did the slightest thing go wrong.

A hundred and thirty-seven from a Missouri gas station, seventy-eight from a convenience store outside Tulsa. They'd sailed down the Will Rogers Turnpike and Doralee watched out the window at the country passing her by, and she was sad for her momma, who'd heard of all these places but would never get to see a one, and here she was, Doralee Jackson from Des Moines, going places. It was not bad. When they had a room she felt clean, and she was happy to wash her clothes and Kirk's in the motel sinks.

Whenever Kirk Dugan stole, that night they lived high, and he would come at her those nights like a bull in breeding season, two, three, and once four times, and afterwards he would lie across her exhausted, sweaty; and she would hold him, her fingers laced in his damp hair, as she wondered at the mysterious workings of men, one day cold and so far in themselves you thought they'd forgot your name, and another so filled with force it took her breath away, and how that had to have something to do with what they'd done and how strong they felt, but nothing at all with how they felt for a woman.

Driving west in Oklahoma, Interstate 40, Kirk pulled over into a rest area because the sun was in his eyes.

"Why don't you drive?"

"I don't know how."

He thought that was so damned funny, but this was a day he was most like the sweet boy who'd leaned over the seat of a white flatbed truck and followed her all the way to a bus stop, and so he right then and there decided he would teach her, there was so little to it.

They both laughed the two times the car stalled, and then he had her drive in circles and then in figure eights until she learned how much she had to press the brake and how much to turn the wheel, and then Kirk said to her "You ready for the highway?"

"Kirk, I can't do that with all those trucks and such."

"Nothing to it. You just keep her at fifty-five, point her, and go."

So he talked her into it, and she stayed in the right lane. The tires drifted onto the shoulder once, and she raised dust, but he just leaned toward her and almost daintily touched the wheel until they were straight on the road again. "You've got to do more than forty."

She was too scared and worried just with going straight to look at the dashboard, so she near wet her pants when he sidled next to her and with his left boot pushed down on her foot and the car speeded up.

"Stop that!"

"Just steer."

"God damn it, Kirk. God damn it."

But the car went faster and faster, and Doralee was in a sweat. He would get them both killed for sure, but pretty soon she liked the feel of it, how the car, a ton of machinery, responded to the slightest move she made on the wheel, or the brake, or the accelerator. She drove all the way to Weatherford, and they stopped there. It was something to know she could drive a car if she had to.

That night they were in this beer and pinball machine bar and Doralee was sitting beside him on a high stool getting more than a little cockeyed giddy on the beer and juke box country music. Kirk said to her "Sit tight. I'll be right back."

She thought he was going to the men's room, and he did, but when he came back he was wild-eyed and she knew he had done something.

"Let's go, Doralee," he said and took her elbow.

"I want to finish this beer."

"Let's go right *now!*"

He practically lifted her off the stool, and they went straight out to the car, drove right by the pretty motel where they had taken a room, and out onto the highway. That was how Mr. William Krantz lost his wallet and credit card, taking a leak in a Weatherford bar they said was a private club because it was a dry state. So private you joined at the door and then drank as much as anybody else.

He showed her what he'd gotten, and explained that the credit card might do them good for two weeks.

"What did you do to get it?"

"I took it."

"You hit him?"

"Not much."

"Damn it, Kirk. This is different."

"How's it different? I swear, I didn't hurt him much. He'll be fine. What in hell you worried about? Hey, I walked in and stood behind this guy until he got his pecker out and started to pee. You should have seen his face when I reach out and took his wallet. He must have thought he had some queer fiddling with his ass. He spins around, still pissing on the floor, and before he opens his mouth I hit him one good one in the belly. It was funny."

He charged a tank of gas, and she watched carefully to see how it was done, having never owned a credit card. Kirk Dugan certainly knew things.

They slept that night beside the road in the car, just over the Texas border. As she listened to Kirk breathing in the front seat and she lay curled up in the back, able to look up through the rear window at the stars over Texas, she knew that he was changing. Or she was. Whichever, it didn't matter. She was not so stupid that she believed he only had to hit him once. William Krantz must have taken a few hard shots, and Kirk Dugan, the sweet boy who'd leaned across a truck seat not giving a damn about traffic while he talked to her, must have given them to him good. She hadn't thought it was in him. Maybe it was that exact moment—it was hard to tell—but maybe it was that moment she became more wary of Kirk Dugan than in love with him.

The tedious, long roads of the Southwest were like nothing she'd ever seen. Mile after mile of oil rigs and sky. The ride made Kirk talkative, and she found out then his real name was Alex, Alexander Wilshire Dugan, and that he'd "borrowed" cars as a boy in Illinois and spent two years in a juvenile hall where he'd met Lee Harkin and a bunch of others he talked about, most of whom he'd lost track of, but he was sure they were doing fine. She had her doubts, but kept her mouth shut, gazing out the windows at cattle pens and railroad tracks and the flat land, endless flat land that ran forever brown and away. They saw a sign that said 150 miles to Amarillo, and they both could not believe they were still that far from any place—when did Texas end? So, when Kirk said they could kill time and drive all at once, she didn't even think much about what he suggested but unzipped his fly and went down on him right there in the car, in broad daylight at sixty miles an hour. It seemed sinful, she was hot and bored, but she took no pleasure in pleasing him, and so she was sure she was out of love with Kirk Dugan.

He told her she was a good girl, and that he wanted to do right by her.

The next day, headed west into New Mexico after a dull night in Amarillo, he told her he had this idea about running dope up from south of the border to Los Angeles, and that way they'd make a lot of money fast, and maybe they could stay put for a month or two, live high, and have a hell of a time. His eyes got bright and he slapped at the wheel, all excited about what he started to call his plan.

"What will we do with the money?"

"Damn, Doralee, you ask the dumbest questions."

"Well, you answer that one for me, then."

"Why, woman, we'll live it up."

"Like how?"

"We're talking about big money here. Maybe a few thousand dollars. Shit, can't you think of what you would do with a few thousand dollars?"

"I want to know what you'd do."

"We'll get a nice room someplace. Eat good food. Maybe buy some clothes. How's that? Sure. We'll go right back to Denver and get you that red dress. How'd you like that?"

"I'd like that fine. But I still don't know just what you want to do with so much money."

"Aw, shit. *Spend* it."

She'd wanted to hear him say something else. Anything else. But there he was with no imagination. And hell, she couldn't think of a damn thing, neither. What *did* people do with money? Maybe settle someplace, buy a business, a little card shop or something, and she caught herself, right then, it was a revelation, here she was thinking about not being on the move, just like the men she'd known back in Iowa that she'd thought were so damned lame with their heads and asses buried so deep in black Iowa dirt they'd never think to move. It was a revelation that she, Doralee Jackson, wanted a place that was hers and something to do there. Yes, it was Doralee that was changing, faster than Kirk Dugan might, or probably ever, could. They said that travel helped a person find herself. Well, she'd been traveling, and it had been one kick-ass journey, but already it was getting old. All Kirk Dugan was was lucky, and no one's luck held out forever; but she couldn't say to him, No thanks, drop me off here.

They'd been on the road three weeks.

When Bobby Kelly reared back, foot higher than his shoulder, and threw the ball, the ball sliced through the air and hit the catcher's mitt with a sound that let you know that ball had been *thrown*. Chunk! Doralee swore that it sizzled, hissing like the zipper on a winter coat as the ball traveled to the catcher.

You could see every bit of Bobby Kelly in that ball, him falling forward following his arm that had windmilled over his head, all that power right down to the fingers. How the catcher didn't get knocked on his ass was a wonder. It was special to be sitting right behind the dugout watching Bobby Kelly warm up right there on the third-base line, sitting in Bobby Kelly's seats.

The top of the dugout gritty with dust was painted a pale turqoise. Kirk Dugan sat way back in his wooden seat beside her, his boots pressed against the cyclone fence trying to make like he wasn't impressed.

They'd found the ballpark easily enough, had parked on a dirt field surrounding the place where everyone left their cars every which way so it was clear no one could leave until everyone left together. This was Mexico, and the common sense of a lined parking lot just could never occur to no greaser, Kirk said, what could you expect?

You would not have thought there were that many people in all of Puerto Penasco, men smoking cigars and swilling beer from bottles, women with babies in their arms, and what must have been a million children running loose. The field was no pretty patch of emerald grass like on television, but was scrubby and dusty in the infield, and nearly all dirt and pebbles in the outfield. There were no stands out there, just a scoreboard and a big old fence painted with advertisements in Mexican—mostly for beer but one for Coca-Cola—and there were big, tall lights on posts that lit the place like day. Moths fluttered at the lights, moths so big you could hear them pattering into the glass, and the night was warm and sticky, the air thick with the smell of frying grease and peppers.

They played some music on the PA system, everyone stood, and then Bobby Kelly and the rest of the team came out from the dugout, right out from under their feet, and before they started to loosen up and throw the ball around Bobby Kelly came over to the fence and said he was real glad they could make it, and when he smiled that American boy smile so filled with perfect teeth Doralee couldn't help herself and had to smile right back, crooked teeth and all. A fellow carried stuff up and down the aisles, and Bobby Kelly shouted in Mexican—which proved she was right, he could speak the lingo. Next thing she knew, she and Kirk each had in their hands a paper cone of ice and syrup. Raspberry for her and orange for Kirk. Cold and sweet, coating her throat, delicious. Kirk tried to give the guy some pesos for the treats, but he wouldn't take any, and Kirk bitched about that. Then Bobby Kelly said he had to go to work and he started to throw, and that was when Doralee got so impressed with the sound of a baseball.

Hissss-chunk!

"Look at these greasers," Kirk said. "They're so short no one's got a strike zone."

"What's a strike zone?"

"Boy, you are dumb," Kirk said, and he started explaining about knees and armpits, but Doralee was watching the men on the field who looked snappy in their uniforms, pin stripes on white flannel, blue lettering, and little caps, and she liked especially how the pants fit. Bobby Kelly had a great butt, and she wondered how she hadn't noticed that on the beach that afternoon, but she remembered it was his hands she was looking at then.

"Do you think he's any good?"

"We'll find out in a minute, I suppose."

"This is fun, Kirk."

He snorted. "Better than the motel room. Why don't they have any television in Mexico?"

She knew barely enough about baseball to follow what was going on, but once the game started she was pretty sure Bobby Kelly was doing all right. The first player he faced struck out, and the next two hit little dribbling shots that were picked up easily and thrown to first base. The Penguins trotted in and she could hear them chattering in the dugout.

"I thought he'd talk to us," she said.

"Nah. Pitcher's got to concentrate."

"He's doing good."

"He's doing all right. When I was a pitcher, I used to do all right."

"I thought you played second base."

"That, too. I played lots of sports. Basketball. Football."

Her brother played football and she knew what her brother and his friends looked like, so she just looked at skinny Kirk Dugan whose real name was Alex and she didn't say a word. He couldn't even bullshit in a straight line.

There wasn't too much excitement, it seemed to her, as the innings went on. Just once a Penguin walked to first base, and that was all that happened. Kirk leaned forward, intent on the game, and Doralee wondered just what her Momma would think of her girl now, sitting in the sticky night at a Mexican baseball game beside a robber, Doralee a friend of the pitcher for the home team. She was a long ways from home, she was.

"I tell you, they are throwing smoke," Kirk said. "That Bobby Kelly has a cannon in his sleeve."

What was smoke? "Well, I guess, but I wish something exciting would happen."

"Doralee, you are dumb as rocks, I swear. We've got us two no-hitters going and you want excitement."

"I knew that." She licked her fingers where the ices had melted.

Then Bobby Kelly was standing with the bat in his hands, and he let two pitches go by, but on the third he swung and *craaaack* hit the ball a good one. She stood automatically, just like everyone else; it wasn't something you thought to do, and her fingers gripped the fence. "Go, go," she heard Kirk yell. The ball sailed high up, past the lights, and then came down right into the center fielder's glove, right at the fence. There was a big sigh from the seats, like everyone let go their breath at the same time. Bobby Kelly was already to second base and he slapped his cap against his leg with disappointment, but came right on in to get his glove and start in pitching again just as though nothing had happened and he hadn't almost hit a home run.

Bobby Kelly threw and nobody hit the ball past the infield. Twice the ball was hit sharp right at him, but both times he sweet-as-you-please caught the ball and gently tossed it to the first baseman. People clapped. By God, she was friends with a star! Then one of the American fellows on the other team cracked the ball a good one down on the ground, and it looked as easy as the others had been, but before it got to the shortstop it hit one of the pebbles and bounced over the fellow's head into the outfield. The seventh inning, and he was the first man to get to first base. The noise was like to make you deaf.

"That wasn't good, huh?" she said.

"I'd say, Doralee. Bad luck, but that shithead should have got the ball anyway."

"You think?"

"Sure. You need reflexes good as mine to play this game."

Bobby Kelly seemed different, then. He walked around the pitcher's mound a few times, his face grim, and he picked dirt out of the bottom of his shoe. He dug a little hole with his toe, walked around a few times more, stood with his hands on his hips and looked to the outfield and the darkness beyond the fence, like he was talking to God or something, waiting for an explanation, while all the time a new batter was waiting for him to get started. Then he turned and tried to seem ready, but Doralee knew he wasn't.

He kept glancing over his shoulder at the fellow on first. That fellow had Bobby Kelly's chin on a string and was giving it a tug. Twice

Bobby Kelly threw to the first baseman, but there wasn't any heart in it. He threw to the batter, and it should have been a strike, and there was a hell of a groan from all the people in the stands while Bobby Kelly stood and stared at the umpire like the umpire was in on some dirty secret, the same secret that had made the ball hit a rock and sail into the outfield. But he pitched again, and this time the throw was so high the catcher had to jump up to keep the ball from getting past him.

The catcher walked the ball back to Bobby Kelly, taking his time before returning to home plate. Sweat shined on Bobby Kelly's face, and he kept wiping his brow with the sleeve of his shirt, tossing the ball into his glove three, four, five, six times before a pitch. The fellow on first would run a bit to second, then scramble right back, and you could see that Bobby Kelly was going to lose it. When Bobby Kelly threw it, Doralee couldn't hear any hiss on the ball.

He pitched one that hit the dirt and bounced past the catcher, and the runner hustled himself to second base, got there standing up and just grinned at Bobby Kelly. The greasers booed, but that didn't seem fair to Doralee, because while Bobby Kelly might be in trouble, it was no fault of his.

"Can he do that? Just run to second like that?"

"He sure can. I tell you, that boy is in deep shit, now."

And on the very next pitch the batter hit one way, way out to a spot no one could reach. A double. They put a "1" on the scoreboard.

The manager came out, stood a while talking to Bobby Kelly, and then Bobby Kelly walked slowly in, kicking dust, his glove hanging from his hand, his head low.

She'd have thought he was angry or at least sad, but just before he walked down the steps to the dugout he looked up at her and the damndest thing! He winked at her. He winked!

The Penguins lost. Three to nothing.

It was only a minute or two back to La Hacienda. Kirk left her in the room while he went out to hunt up a six-pack of Mexican brew, "That Carta Blanca shit ain't half bad," he said, and she stood on the terrace in the hot night and saw the team bus roll into the courtyard. She'd have thought the players would be down, but they were laughing and noisy as if they'd won. She tried to pick out Bobby Kelly, but couldn't because it was so dark, so she waited a bit, then went into the room to take a shower. Just as she was pulling her shirt over her head, there was a knock on the door—not like Kirk who never knocked—and she knew it was Bobby Kelly.

Dressed in regular clothes again, a red golf shirt with an alligator on it, he was with two other fellows, also Americans, also baseball players, and damn! they were handsome. Nice boys with pressed pants and neat little thin black belts around their waists. She wished to God she had some clothes besides jeans and T-shirts, but they didn't seem to mind at all, big grins on their faces, big bare arms coming out of their short sleeves down to their big wrists and hands.

"By heaven, Bobby, you were right. That *is* an American girl," one of them said, and you could tell he meant nothing mean by it from the way he said it, and the three of them laughed. Doralee found herself laughing too, standing in the doorway of the room, glad for the dark so they could not see that she blushed.

"Where's your hippie friend?" Bobby Kelly asked, and before she could answer turned to the other fellows and added, "I swear, this guy has a ponytail."

"Naah. Nobody but assholes wears a ponytail anymore."

And she looked, and looked again, because it was the fellow from the other team that had hit the ball, gone to first, and given Bobby Kelly all that trouble, and here they were togther, and they were friends. How could that be?

That was when they all heard Kirk Dugan's boots coming up the walk, and they heard him say from the darkness before they could see him, "What's going on?"

They were delighted to see Kirk had some beer, because they had some, too, along with some tequila down in one of the rooms, and since they were having a party just for gringos would he and his lady friend like to join them?

Doralee said "Sure we would" before Kirk could say a word—she wasn't about to let this chance pass her by—and that was how they wound up downstairs in a white-walled room with red curtains that must have been Bobby Kelly's place when the team was in Puerto Penasco.

Kirk whispered to her, "What the hell are we doing this for?" as they'd gone down the stairs, but he settled in once one of the baseball players rolled a monster joint big as a cigar and in a few minutes the place was foggy with the sweet smell of dope. They had a big ghetto blaster with tapes of American rock and roll music, and Doralee realized just how much she missed home. All the Chevy had was an AM radio that once they made it to Mexico got nothing but static or Mexican stations that played nothing worth hearing. Bobby Kelly's tapes were mellow, college boy music, and when Kirk asked if he had any country-western Bobby Kelly gave him a mournful smile as if to say he expected that from him and was sorry to have his expectations come true.

They tossed themselves about the room, on the bed or on the floor, a sweated cold beer in each person's hand, passing a bottle of Cuervo they either tilted straight up and gulped or poured a little into their beers. And the joint passed around the room, and then another. Pretty soon Doralee had herself a buzz and the tequila was making her sweat, but it was damned nice to hear American voices other than Kirk's again. Nice boys. Nice American boys.

Rick Johnson, who'd gotten a hit off Bobby Kelly, was from Wisconsin. He said that if Bobby Kelly had gotten some hitting from his team, there was no way they'd have beaten him and it was a shame he had to pitch for a team that gave him no help, and how in hell the scorer called that shot he himself had gotten a hit was a mystery to him. Best man on Rick Johnson's team, Rick Johnson said, was the Penguins' groundskeeper that couldn't rake off a damn rock. He said to Kirk, "You wouldn't score that a hit, would you?"

Kirk brightened up and said, "I thought it was an error."

Stan Foley who also pitched but hadn't that night was from Maryland. He said "No way. It was a clean hit, Kirk."

And Kirk had to say, "Maybe."

So Doralee could see what was what. They were putting Kirk in the middle, but in a way he'd never know it, baiting him, making him feel like a fool without knowing why, and Doralee figured that out because she was watching Bobby Kelly's big grin get wider and wider. These boys were so free and easy, it was a wonder. Liking each other, liking what they did, telling stories about where they came from and what they hoped to do. They drank beer and rolled another joint, and Bobby Kelly popped the tape on the box and put in another, mostly Bob Seger and the Silver Bullet Band, hot music that made the room hotter and Doralee could feel the sweat trickling down her back, making her T-shirt stick between her shoulder blades. She sat cross-legged, a bottle of beer on the floor next to her, and she was grinning as broad as Bobby Kelly.

Kirk told a story about how he once put a Cadillac engine in a Dodge, going into detail about just how it was done, and when he was finished Stan Foley looked him in the eye and said "Why in fuck would anybody *want* to do that?" and the baseball players right away started talking about fly-fishing, Rick Johnson saying there was no place like a

Wisconsin lake. Doralee saw Bobby Kelly punch Stan Foley in the leg when Stan Foley cut Kirk so short, and she saw that Kirk didn't see.

Bobby Kelly went to the bathroom and when he came back he sat on the floor between Doralee and Kirk, so she could hardly see Kirk at all.

"Do you dance?" he asked her, and she said she didn't.

The baseball players groaned at that, all saying of course she did, nice like, but she was just shy being the only girl at the party, wouldn't she try? She said she didn't know how, and Bobby Kelly said that he would teach her.

So they stood up, and Doralee Jackson from Des Moines, Iowa, who had never danced before, danced. "Just move with it," Bobby Kelly said, and the tequila, the marijuana, and the beer made it easy. She was swaying at first, and they all clapped when she gave a bump with her hips— Bob Seger screaming about that old time rock and roll. She bumped it again, raised her hands over her head, closed her eyes, and felt the sweat pop over her face, down her neck, on her chest and belly, her skin feeling like it was alive and moving on her, and when she opened her eyes all she saw was Bobby Kelly. This was dancing. They were moving like they were one person. The song ended, and Rick Johnson up and gave her a whirl, and then she was dancing with Rick Johnson and Stan Foley at the same time, and she felt like a queen, these big, handsome American boys giving her all this attention. The song ended, and she had to sit down to catch her breath, and she noticed Kirk still on the floor with his eyes clouded black and mean, his lips thin and tight, and she suspected she would catch all sorts of shit later, but she refused to care. They were in Mexico, where nothing made sense, least of all Kirk Dugan's big plans, and by God she would at least have a little fun.

Maybe Stan Foley had seen what Doralee had seen in Kirk's face, because when Doralee sat down he asked, "What are you folks doing down here, anyway?"

While Kirk answered him, Bobby Kelly's hand found Doralee's sweaty knee, patting it like, in time to the music, and she did not push his hand away. Kirk said, "Business. We're here on business."

That got the baseball players laughing again. Bobby Kelly asked what kind of business could anyone have in shitty Puerto Penasco? "If Mexcio had an armpit, we'd be breathing Right Guard."

"I got business," Kirk said. "I got business. And maybe you boys can help."

Stan Foley smiled and popped another beer. "How's that?"

"I want to score some grass, man."

"He wants to score some grass, man."

"The man says he wants to score some grass. How much you talking about?" Stan Foley said.

"Bulk. A couple of bricks."

"You're talking weight, huh?"

"That's right."

Doralee could see Bobby Kelly was holding in a laugh, and Rick Johnson was rolling on the bed like he was having a fit, but Kirk was so hungry after what he wanted he couldn't notice anything else.

Stan Foley went on. "How much money you got?"

"Enough."

"Well, shit, I don't know anything about that stuff."

Rick Johnson guffawed in a pillow when Kirk muttered "Bullshit" and flicked a bottle cap across the linoleum floor.

"Tell me," Stan Foley said, "Where'd you get the ink?"

Kirk's hand went to his tatoo. "This here? I got that in a jailhouse."

He said it slow for the effect, to show he was tough, but the baseball players kept grinning and looked at each other.

"I tell you what," Stan Foley said, "You come out with me for a walk to my car and maybe we'll talk a little business."

Kirk's little eyes narrowed even more, the temptation eating at him, and then you could see he yielded to it. "All right. But don't bullshit me."

"Have I ever lied to you?"

Stan Foley stood up and with some effort Kirk did, too. They went out into the night. A few minutes went by and Rick Johnson said he left something in his room, he'd be right back, and off he went.

Now Doralee was not so stupid that she didn't know what was going on, but the funny part was that Kirk did not. So she said to Bobby Kelly, "Does that fellow really sell dope?"

"No. Fact is, Stan got this marijuana from his sister when she was down here two weeks ago to visit. No problem passing customs going south. We don't fuck with the stuff much. Hell, we work here. Mexican jail is bad news."

She smiled, shaking her head still buzzing from Cuervo and music, her body still perspiring from dancing, like the beer itself was pushing out through her skin. It made her bold. "Well, are you going to kiss me or not?"

Bobby Kelly put his big warm hands around her waist and pulled her toward him. She opened her mouth and he opened his, their saliva and sweat making the kiss slippery, and her head spun with it, his hands so good on her, her leaning toward him, his hands moving on her belly and up under her shirt, a long slow kiss that took her breath away, but she was worried that Kirk might come back any second now, so she stopped him.

"What are you doing with that hippie asshole, anyway?"

"I don't know. I just don't know."

He kissed her again, this time teasing his tongue all along her upper lip before she parted her lips and his tongue explored inside her mouth. This was so good, so good. Her pants were getting wet. She kissed him back, hard, urgently, and he asked her if she wanted to do it right then, and she would have said yes, taken him right there on the floor, this big old American baseball pitcher from Oregon, but she said, "Kirk might come in. Later?"

And Bobby Kelly just smiled that big American smile. She didn't know if he meant it. It was something to think about, it was.

He went to the ghetto blaster and turned over the tape which had run out while they were kissing, and right then Stan Foley and Kirk and Rick Johnson came back in, so with her and Bobby Kelly at opposite sides of the room they looked as innocent as kids at a church picnic. Kirk was still scowling, but he looked puzzled. Stan Foley must have gone on with the lie, telling Kirk what he had to to keep him interested, but not enough to let Kirk believe he had found his deal. It would be easy to fool Kirk.

They partied. Drank more beer, smoked more dope, chased the beer with tequila—the second bottle, now. Bobby Kelly had had his taste, and now with the half promise of "later" was staying far away from her. What would it be like to have Bobby Kelly? Nice, but it would not happen. She watched that man in his red golf shirt and pressed pants that weren't so pressed anymore, and she hated his easy confidence. It wasn't going to happen. She was disappointed with him, working such cheap tricks to get her alone, thinking she'd be easy, and for sure eager to tell his buddies all about it later.

But Kirk Dugan wasn't for her, neither. She could do a lot better than that. She could dance now—there was nothing to it, you just up and let yourself go—and Kirk Dugan was so dumb he couldn't see past the nose on his face or think about any time more than next week. She felt sad for him. He was getting sloppy and loud, talking how he had done this and had done that, that these guys didn't know shit until they stepped in it.

"Aww, hippie. Cut it off," Rick Johnson said.

"Who're you calling a hippie, motherfucker?"

Rick Johnson got the giggles. "What kind of ponytail is that?"

Kirk touched his head. "You fuckers think you're so smart."

"I am too tired for this," Rick Johnson said, and without another word got up and left the room.

"Asshole," Kirk muttered.

"I think he's got a point," Bobby Kelly said, and when he said it Doralee sat up straight and took a deep breath. Here it was.

"What point is that?"

"That asshole ponytail, friend. That's bush league. Coming down to Mexico without knowing what you're doing, that's bush league. All that jailhouse shit, that's bush league. All talk."

"I'll tell you what's bush league. Playing baseball in this shithole. That's bush league."

"Hey, man," Stan Foley said. "It's baseball. What's better than playing baseball?"

"That's right," Bobby Kelly said, placing a beer to his lips.

"Lots of things. I do anything you guys can do with my eyes closed."

"Whee-hew!"

"You laughing? You laughing at me?"

Bobby Kelly nodded. "Why don't you name something?"

"Fighting."

Stan Foley laughed. "He's got you there, Bobby."

Bobby Kelly just smiled that big smile and glanced at Doralee. But she didn't smile back. It had felt good to kiss him and it had felt good to have his hands on her, but what he was about now made her less than human, some damned reward, a blue ribbon at the fair. Bobby Kelly wanted her not because of who she was, but as the sign that he had in some way gotten over Kirk Dugan.

"Tell you what, hippie boy. Fighting is out. I got to be on the bus tomorrow night and I wouldn't want to break my hand on your jaw."

"That's a pussy excuse if I ever heard one."

"But I'll take you on in anything else you want to try. Fair and square. Doralee here can be the judge."

Kirk looked at her. She looked right back. He was wondering. Well, let him wonder.

Kirk said, "You think I don't know what's what? I know what's what."

Bobby Kelly said, "You swim?"

"He swims great," Doralee said quick as she could, and Kirk looked at her suspiciously, then puffed up some. "Oh, Kirk tells me he's a fine swimmer." So she got him in, gave the push and nailed shut the door, and now she'd see how it would work.

Bobby Kelly said, "Stan, you remember our swimming contest?"

"I do."

"What we'll do, hippie boy, is swim out in the ocean next to each other, nice and easy like. Just right next to each other. And the first one to turn back is the loser. Nothing to it. No race. Just to see who's got the balls. You want to try that?"

Kirk looked at Doralee for a second, sipped his beer, and said softly, "You're on."

"Well, that's fine," Bobby Kelly said, and he gave his hand to Kirk to help him up. "Stan, you coming down to the beach with us?"

"You bet," Stan Foley said, but as soon as the four of them were out in the night heading for the concrete wall that separated La Hacienda from the broad crescent of sand, Stan Foley lost his legs, sat right down on the blacktop of the courtyard and said "Boys, I do believe I am drunk."

They all thought that was pretty funny, but they couldn't get Stan Foley to stand, tugging on his arm but him falling back on his ass, and so they left him there, a beer bottle in his hand, and just before they passed under the arch, Kirk turned and yelled, "You remember we got business tomorrow. You hear?" and they heard Stan Foley shout, "Yessir. Big business tomorrow," and he cackled with laughter.

Doralee walked between Kirk Dugan and Bobby Kelly, both of them with their arms around her waist like the three of them were old friends, the men's hips bumping hers, the sand sucking at her feet. She thought how stupid men were, trying to prove something that needed no proving, and she knew that they were going at it because somehow or other she had become the prize.

She didn't like that, and she didn't care for either of them thinking that she was some damned trophy, so she kept her mouth shut, saying to herself, let the damned fools do what they will. Doralee Jackson was done going along for rides just to see where she'd end up.

They got to the shoreline and Kirk threw his beer bottle into the black water.

"We just swim out and back?"

"You got it, hippie. First one to turn around is the asshole."

"Then I got no problem," Kirk said.

Doralee sat down on a small hill of sand, cold and damp in the dark.

It must have been four or five o'clock in the morning. She was sober. The breeze at her back chilled her, drying the perspiration from her T-shirt, and she drew her knees to her chest and locked her arms around her legs to make herself tight and warm. Gooseflesh rippled on her arms.

The moon was setting, a new moon, shining just the slightest bit of silver light, a hand's width above the black water smooth as an Iowa lake. By the color-bleeding moon she saw the two men undress, not saying a word now. They sat to slip off their shoes, then stood, and she heard the ghostly jingle of keys as they stepped from their pants and then took off their shirts. In the moon's light it was hard to tell one naked man from the other, the light reflected off the water making them two silhouettes, Kirk the more wiry of the two, but otherwise completely the same. Kirk's black hair was no different from Bobby Kelly's blond in the moon's light. Two American boys who had somehow arrived at this Mexican beach. She heard them say a few words, though she could not hear what, and then the two shapes walked beside each other down to the water lapping at the shore, and there was greenish sparkle about their ankles as they walked forward. She could still see them black against the silver streak of moonlight reflected on the surface when they were waist-deep, and then she lost sight of them.

But she heard the gentle sigh of a splash as they began to swim away from the shore, and she thought maybe she could see flashes of phosphorescence as they swam, and then she couldn't even see that, just the darkness of the Mexican night and the flat, smooth, glassy black surface of the sea.

She rubbed her hands against her bare arms trying to stay warm, and she wondered where the birds went to at night. Pelicans and gulls, did they make nests? Or bob around on the sea waiting for morning? A fistful of cold sand trickled through her fingers. The moon slowly sank beneath the water and the breeze at her back picked up, and then after a time behind her the sky turned pink and she watched her long shadow that went down right to the waterline get shorter. She peered out over the water and saw nothing, as she expected, felt the warming sun on her, and stood to see further, but she knew there was nothing out there anymore for her to see.

To her left was the pile of clothes. They were damp from the night air. She took the keys to the Chevy from Kirk's jeans and with the keys pried the heel off his left boot. Two hundred-dollar bills, neatly folded. She could drive the Chevy good enough, she thought, and she'd have that long drive north over the Mexican desert to get better at it. Or south. Why not? How could she get lost? There was just the one road and she would go any place she pleased, do anything she desired. She'd survive, and if she found the right place, she would do better than that. It wouldn't be easy, but nothing worth doing ever was.

She thought of the credit card, but decided there was no point in asking for more troubles, she would have enough. She wondered how the waves breaking on the shore—crashing in, flowing out, crashing in again—could sound so sorrowful and lonesome. A gull fluttered to the surface of the sea and floated lightly on the undulating surface, and she thought how she was the only person in the world who would ever know that beneath a white rock with a scratch on it in the Arizona desert a gun lay hidden, and that chances were that gun would rest undisturbed forever and forever.

The Adam Collection

by Therese Mageau

Dorothea Fisher never imagined herself ever talking to a cop, much less working for the police. But starving artists teaching at the local junior college have this strange compulsion to actually want to eat and pay the rent. Thus, no one is more surprised than Dorothea when she winds up as the police department's official sketch artist. What is even more surprising is that Dorothea has a true gift: she not only connects with victims and witnesses—bringing to life even the most fleeting glimpses of perpetrators—she has an almost extrasensory perception. Which is both a gift and gets her into trouble. Think of this as Murder She Wrote meets The Sixth Sense.

My name is Dorothea Fisher and I am thirty-four years old. Let me begin by asking if you know the poem "In An Artist's Studio" by Christina Rossetti? Please do not be put off by the seemingly academic thrust of the question. The poem itself is hardly worth knowing, but I bring it up because it helps to explain what has recently happened to me. My life, you see, has been reduced to terms easily explicated by second-rate verse.

The poem is about the relationship between a painter and his model, and I call to your attention line nine: "He [meaning the artist] feeds upon her face by day and night." And the last line: "Not as she is, but as she fills his dream." Try to ignore the sentimentality here and look at the meaning: in the process of making art there is, ultimately, no relationship between the model and the painter, or the model and her portrait, only the painter and the portrait. Actually, I don't think the poem even says that much, but I point out what should be there, so that I may tell my story.

I myself have been an artist, more specifically a painter, most specifically a portrait painter here in Minneapolis. Three years ago, in 1980, I went to work for a pretty but overweight woman named Sally who ran an "outfit" (as she termed it) called the Portrait Palace. Sally had the kind of silver blond–streaked hair that is very fashionable among the country club set, from which she found our clients. Mother-daughter combinations were quite popular, as were golden anniversary portraits commissioned by the couples' children. My clients told me I was very good at "catching just the right expression."

Lest you think I have spent my life painting the smiles of Philistines, before I worked at the Portrait Palace I taught art at the Minneapolis College of Art and Design and had fairly regular showings in galleries around the Twin Cities. I received my MFA from Bennington (oils and acrylics, some tempera) after spending years in high school and college (and countless years before that) playing the protégé.

So why then would someone with my serious background hand myself over to assembly-line painting. And why do I now find myself employed, or rather, most recently employed—I regret to say that I have been fired—by the Minneapolis Police Department? I have an answer, although I am not sure it will satisfy you.

I would like to say that I am only an above-average artist. That, I grant myself, is better than most, and I admit that my standards are higher than most, but the fact remains that I have never (nor is it likely that I will ever) challenged form in any way, nor have I improved much upon existing forms. I began to realize in graduate school that what I and others had always taken for talent became mere competence when placed next to other serious artists.

You'll notice that I said *began* to realize. I did not let myself fully recognize my limitations until many years later. For, what was I to do at the age of twenty-five, in the middle of obtaining a graduate degree, after spending my entire lifetime creating this identity of "artist," but to continue onward in that disguise until I could no longer bear the pretense?

It was a question of false pride, certainly. But also simple desire: I wanted to spend my life in art. But at the age of thirty-one I reached the point where conscience, doubt, enlightenment—call it what you will—won out. I remember very clearly the moment of epiphany: I was teaching an oil class at the art college. We were studying Vermeer's natural light. The room was dark and a slide of Vermeer's "Woman in Blue

Reading a Letter" illuminated the screen. I spoke for a few minutes, pointing out that although the window is off the canvas, we can know its exact dimensions from the light and shadows that fall across the woman's body and the room. I was silent after that as the students looked on and took notes. The classroom windows were open and a slight breeze filtered through and ruffled the screen, so that the woman seemed to tremble as she read the letter. Her smock threw off a Wedgwood blue light that washed the students' faces and tops of their heads. I was newly struck by the enormous beauty of the work and found myself lost—vanished—into the quiet and pensive world that Vermeer had created. "I" was no more. I was simply and utterly absorbed into the sensual moment of this Vermeer.

And then very suddenly, with the dull thud of defeat sounding in the pit of my stomach, I knew that my work would never inspire such surrender in anyone. I grew dizzy from the nausea I felt rising. As it was almost time, I dismissed the class and then I quit. Oh, I gave my proper notice and finished out the term, but every day in that building, every day in my studio made me feel like a man on a hunger strike being force-fed.

But to get back to the Rossetti poem (for I did bring it up with a purpose in mind): Do you see that the demands I made of my art were all wrong? I could not continue as an artist because my work could not "inspire," and yet, what did we learn from the reading of the Rossetti poem but that the true relationship in art is not between an artist and her audience (the "inspired") but between the artist and her work? This may seem embarrassingly self-evident to you, but it is both horrifying and amazing to me the amount of my life's time I have spent on work that I cannot look back on and call my own. It is not merely a lack of proprietary feeling: between me and my work there exists only dead space. When in Genesis it says "Let us make man in our image, after our likeness," we are being given a divine artistic imperative: the distance between the creator and the creation should be the exact dimensions of the creator's soul. I did not know this when I was younger. I know this now only by chance and my own obsession.

My story begins when I quit the Portrait Palace and was hired on at the Minneapolis Police Department as a crime artist. I did not particularly seek out this job, but when I saw the ad in the *Star Tribune*, I decided that three years of painting people with post-orthodontal smiles had been penance enough for my past sins of hubris. I was ready for a higher circle in hell.

As a part of the interview, I had to draw a face described to me by a policewoman, who was role-playing (as they say) a rape victim. My years as a teacher helped me some here, for learning to draw is, to a large degree, learning how to see, and the kinds of questions I would ask of my students to help them train their eyes were similar to the questions I asked of this woman.

But I had never drawn a face I had never seen. As I put my pencil to paper it felt as if the neurons connecting my hand to my brain had suddenly been severed. I felt as if I were being asked to change water into wine but without the aid of divine intervention. I grew strangely frightened; but as I drew and a face began to slowly appear on my sketch pad I felt an unexpected thrill. It was a mild miracle to me that I could draw a face—accurately and well—without a model in front of me or in my mind. It seemed almost apparitional, as if the face's life were not at all connected to the detective's words, but to some mysterious seepage out the end of my pencil.

The job was mine. I discovered, however, to my great disappointment that the majority of the work consisted of doing graphics for the department—recruitment advertisements, softball team posters, department picnic announcements. I sketched a few crime scenes as well, but the real work, the business of creating new faces, came in small bites. And each new face had to sustain me until the next.

Early March of that year, two of the detectives stopped by my office. I worked on the top floor of police headquarters, in the rafters really. It was a large, open area that had no ceiling—water pipes wrapped in cotton rags and ice cube–tray fluorescent lights hung suspended over my head—but did have a wall of northern-exposed windows. I had my work station set up in front of these, next to a wall lined with cartons full of old graphics and art work. I was alone up there, and I liked it that way.

One of the detectives, a Sergeant Anderson, was tall and overweight—a bloated kind of heaviness—with thick lips that never quite closed over his large, full set of teeth. Consequently, it always looked as if he were smiling, although I was never completely certain, and so I always had an idiotic half-smile on my face whenever I spoke to him. His partner, Detective Burns, was slight and bony and never smiled (except, it seemed, at me—with a touch of lasciviousness that I found endlessly irritating), possibly to hide his nicotine-stained teeth, which also happened to be remarkably crooked. I always found myself—unwittingly, mind you—staring at these men's mouths whenever I dealt with them. I couldn't tell you the color of their eyes.

With them was a young woman in her early twenties whose shoulder-length hair had been lightened with some sort of lemon-based product some time ago, for her scalp was a dark brown but the ends of her hair were caramel-colored and dry. She had a wide face: almond-shaped eyes set far apart, a broad nose, large pores, and spaces between her teeth. She spoke diffidently, with a flat Minnesota accent, looking down periodically at her right shoulder and shrugging. Her name was Joyce Calvin and she had observed a crime.

"Miss Calvin is a bank teller at Twin Cities National," Sergeant Anderson said, half-seating his girth on a stool across from the window. "She was held up this morning."

"Please sit down," I said, indicating a steel folding chair facing the window. I turned to Detective Burns. "You too."

"No thanks," he wheezed, leaning against my drafting table and upsetting its balance. I tried to hide my annoyance and turned to the young woman.

"Did you get a good look at his face?" I asked.

"I guess so," she said with a shrug. "I was pretty nervous. I mean, I've never been robbed before."

I nodded. "Was he wearing a disguise of any sort—sunglasses, ski mask, or something along a similar vein?"

"Uh, no, Miss Fisher," Anderson interrupted. "It was a clean look."

"If that's the case," I replied, "you must have a picture of him from the surveillance cameras."

"No, not quite," he said, clearing his throat. "It seems the surveillance system was down at the time."

He smiled, or at least I think he did, so I smiled back and said, "What a pity." I turned to the bank teller. "Joyce—may I call you that?—I would like you to begin by describing the customer right before the robber."

"Why?" she asked with a slight whine. "I don't remember who it was."

"Try. It will help you better remember the man in question."

"All right," she said, crossing her legs and looking distractedly out the window. "I think it was . . . oh yeah, it was a woman. I remember now because she was wearing this sort of peacock blue coat. I remember thinking that it was the exact same color as Lady Diana's when she was pregnant with William."

"Princess," said Detective Burns.

"Huh?" She looked over from the window.

"Princess. You said 'Lady' and she's 'Princess' now."

I glared up at him. He ran his tongue along his front teeth. "Now, Joyce," I resumed, turning away from Burns, "after the woman in the peacock blue coat stepped away from the window, what happened next?"

She looked down at the floor. "I remember that I kept him waiting a little bit because she had a cashier's check made up, and I was still processing the paper work. So, let's see . . ." She inclined her head slightly to the right and squinted. "Before I saw him I saw his coat."

"His coat?"

"Yeah. It was this mustard yellow and had these huge mother-of-pearl buttons."

This woman, I thought, should have worked for a coat designer, not a bank. "But then you look up," I coaxed.

"Yeah," she said, suddenly breaking into a wide smile. "And there was this crazy-looking guy standing in front of me."

"Do you mean crazy as in deranged?"

"No, crazy as in goofy. He looked sort of like a clown."

I glanced over at Sergeant Anderson and raised my eyebrows. He smiled and gave a slight shrug as if to say, *I think she's okay*. I picked up my sketch pad and charcoal pencil. "What was particularly clownish about him?"

"Well, first of all, his hair. It was blond, but this totally weird shade."

"Dyed?"

She shrugged. "Who knows? It was like straw—or come to think of it—it was the exact same color as his coat!"

I was a little taken aback by that description. "A well-coordinated bank robber," I said wryly.

"Definitely." She sat up straight now and gestured with her hands. "And it stuck straight up, like he put his finger in a light socket." She laughed and looked up at Detective Burns, who looked back at her with narrowing eyes.

"Describe the shape of the head," I continued. "Was it round, or oval, or more like a square?"

"Definitely oval," she said with a confident nod. "Really long."

I sketched an oval face with a shock of hair on top. "Like this?"

"Even longer."

I extended the chin and drew in a mouth. "How about this?"

"His mouth was huge!" she exclaimed.

"Huge?" I said doubtfully.

"I mean it," she insisted. "He had this huge clown's mouth. When he smiled—can you believe that? He smiled. Anyway, when he smiled it took up his whole face. Or it seemed like it did." Her words began to pick up speed. "And he had a big nose and these bushy yellow eyebrows that went up and down when he talked."

I sketched furiously as she spoke, slowing her down and having her repeat herself several times. I had no idea where I was going. I was afraid I was going to end up with Bozo on my sketch pad.

"What color were his eyes," I asked.

"You know," she said after a moment's pause, "I don't remember."

We sat together for another hour while I continued to sketch and clarify her descriptions. And the end of the session I showed her my draft.

"Hey, that's good," she said, nodding in approval. "That's really pretty good."

I looked down at what I had drawn, taking it in whole for the first time. The face was animated in both senses of the word: it looked like a cartoon, and yet its essence was not silly but deeply enlivening. I felt attached to all my crime composites, but this one tugged at me in a new place. When I looked at the face, I felt as if we were both in on the same joke.

Sergeant Anderson cleared his throat once more. "Her description matched the preliminary ones we got from the guards at the scene." He took the sketch out of my hands. "This will help. Good work, Miss Fisher."

I reclaimed the drawing. "Let me smooth this out. I'll get a final right down to you."

"You betcha," he said, smiling. He gestured to the bank teller. "Well, Miss Calvin, you've been a good witness. I'll show you the way out."

Burns lingered around my desk for a moment, but when I didn't look up he grunted a farewell and followed the other two. I began to furiously copy the sketch for the police, recreating the same face, which was destined for a "Wanted" poster, yet somehow not imbuing it with the same life that emanated from the first drawing. I slipped the original charcoal drawing into my portfolio and took it home with me that night after work.

That was, if I may use a hackneyed phrase (and why not? my life, after all, has been reduced to a cliché), the beginning of the end. When I arrived home, I placed the sketch on my drawing table, turned on the overhead lamp, and examined it. The face needed more color. I took out my chalks and began to shade. I worked first in red, bringing the blood to his cheeks, and mixing in a little silver, filling in his lips with an iridescent pink. I colored his hair and eyebrows the deep yellow of the heart of a dandelion. When I came to his eyes I paused to consider. They must be green, I thought, meaning not in real life (for I had forgotten about that), but there, in my picture. The composition begged for eyes the color of ripe avocado.

By the time I had finished my heart was pounding. It was not a particularly handsome face, but it was alive. It pulsed on the paper. I taped the drawing on the refrigerator while I made dinner. I brought it to the table while I ate. Afterwards, I taped it to the wall next to my bed.

I awoke in the middle of the night. I had been dreaming about the face, but now there was a body attached and it had a name: Adam. I arose immediately and drew the scene. He—Adam—sat cross-legged in the corner of an empty apartment, or, at least the room he was in was empty. I could not see into the adjoining room at the left, but a dusky yellow light filtered through its doorway, casting discrete shadows across his smooth torso, which, though the color of warm honey, seemed visibly cool to the touch. He was naked from the waist up, his back erect, his arms loosely resting in his lap, his long legs clad in surgeon's blue cotton drawstring pants. On the wall behind him hung a map of the world. In front of him on the floor were parchments of ancient Sanskrit manuscripts (or so I believed) preserved between sheaths of pressed tree bark. He was translating the manuscript, but was forbidden (somehow . . . I don't know) from saying any part of them aloud or he would lose the meaning. He sat reading, calm and silent.

I slept restively after that. Right before I awoke in the morning I dreamt he asked me if there was any milk left (there wasn't; I had used the last in my tea the night before). Upon rising I drew a picture of him at the refrigerator, one hand on the open door, one hand holding the empty milk carton, bent at the waist, searching. The lightbulb inside the refrigerator lit up his head and shoulders in a kind of oleo yellow light. The rest of his body was obscured by the dark of the morning.

In the ladies room that afternoon, I saw how he would sleep: on his stomach with a feather pillow crushed into a small ball under his head. He would use no blankets, only a white sheet that I would wind around his body like a mummy casing. I drew this scene with only a charcoal pencil, casting part of his body in deep shadow, as if the moon outside his window were half-hiding in a cloud.

Two nights later I had another silent dream about Adam. This time he stood in the middle of an open field. Snow—resembling the paper cutouts of children—fell in large, geometric shapes. It quietly covered his entire body until only glimpses of his neon yellow eyebrows showed through. He stood there as unmoving as a child's snowman, or an unfinished chalk sculpture abandoned by its maker.

As with all the other dreams, this too I drew. By the end of a month's time I had enough drawings to cover my walls. I soon began to leave them in my bureau drawers, inside the door of the medicine cabinet in the bathroom, taped to the television screen, in between random pages of books. At work I was more discreet, but there were sketches of Adam hidden there too, mostly in the bottoms of drawers and slid into the back pages of my sketch pads. My life had reached a point where I could not see—literally—anything but Adam.

A case in point: One afternoon I sat at my drawing table at work, shading in a picture of Adam reclining in a chair. A man's shadow suddenly darkened my sketch pad and I started. I twisted around on my stool to find Detective Burns looking over my shoulder. Somehow he had entered my office and crept up behind me (crept, I'm sure, the way a voyeur might approach a keyhole) without my taking notice. I casually leaned back and placed my elbow across the drawing. Burns was the kind of man who took down the license numbers of squad cards parked outside doughnut shops, then dropped them in conversation with the precinct captain. I didn't want to hear a lecture from him about doing personal work on taxpayer's time. I quickly asked him what he wanted.

He tried noticeably to see beyond my arm, then said, "I came to talk to you about this." He threw on my desk a composite sketch of a mugging suspect I had done the day before. I glanced at it, then looked up at Burns and asked, "What would you like to discuss?"

He rubbed his tongue along his front teeth, making high-pitched little sucking noises that made me recoil inside. He said, "The witness is complaining that this doesn't look like the suspect."

I examined the picture, then suppressed a smile. Without consciously trying to, I had incorporated certain characteristics of Adam into this other man's face. I creased my brow in feigned concern and said, "To what in particular does the witness object?"

"She says the face wasn't that long and his mouth wasn't that big."

I nodded and thought that in addition the hairline was probably more Adam than mugger. "Well," I replied, "I'll have to have another session with the witness then. I apologize for any inconvenience."

Burns grunted, then looked around my office. "You've been a little irresponsible lately, don't you think?" He absently picked up sketch pads and drawings that lay scattered around the room, then tossed them aside after quick glances.

"You'll have to be more specific if you'd like me to reply."

He shrugged and looked out the window at the courthouse across the way. "This isn't the first witness that's complained in the last month. And the poster for the cerebral palsy dinner-dance was late getting to the printers."

"I doubt that should be any concern of yours," I said, irritated.

"Maybe not," he replied, then added, looking at me, "but crime sketches are, and yours haven't been satisfactory lately."

I sighed. "Detective Burns," I said with deliberate and patronizing enunciation. "Composite drawing is not an exact science. It is an impressionable art, and the success of any drawing is at best serendipitous. An accurate sketch depends on a number of factors, over most of which I have no control."

Burns shrugged once more, flipped through a pile of loose drawings, then walked over to my desk and leaned on it. "Just know that I've got my eye on you, Miss Fisher."

I smiled. "I can't tell you what that means to me, Detective Burns."

He grunted and left and I resumed shading in my drawing of Adam, more amused than annoyed.

One night in May I had a particularly unnerving dream about Adam. He was sitting on a bar stool; I was sitting below him, looking up from a booth. He was laughing and his whole face caught the bar light (candlelight it seemed) and reflected back at me like some crazy kaleidoscope. I followed the movements of the colors as if hypnotized by a spinning prism. I awoke wet and breathless. I leapt up to draw the dream and then stopped short: I knew that bar. I could not, for the life of me, recall what bar it was, but I knew I had been there, and the familiarity of it unhinged me. The details from the dream were inadequate: there was only the stool, the booth, and the candlelight. But as I tried to sketch the scene, I was inexplicably disturbed by the fact that I knew this place. I found it impossible to continue with the drawing. I needed to find the bar.

It did not take me too long. I am not much of a drinker and have little use for most of the music that is played in bars. Consequently there are relatively few establishments that I patronize. The bar in which the dream took place was only a few blocks away from the art college, and it was unfortunately named Le Rive Gauche. I used to go there occasionally when I taught at the college, because, as I said, it was close by and they had a surprisingly civilized wine list. The food was unspeakably bad.

The bar itself sat in a horseshoe shape, just as one walked in the door. To the right was a large, wood-paneled room filled with red-and-black tables and chairs and a stage where music was performed in the evening. To the left of the bar was a row of booths.

It was a dark and rainy Sunday afternoon, and with the exception of a few old men and women sitting at the bar (there was a subsidized retirement high-rise down the block) the place was empty. I sat in the third booth—it seemed to best approximate where I had sat in my dream—pulled my sketch pad out of my bag and faced the bar. A waitress approached slowly from the other side where she had been chatting with the bartender. She was tall, very slim, and disarmingly attractive despite the paleness of her skin. Her round eyes were perfectly framed on top by a brush of black lashes and below by a ring of dark concentric circles. She held her mouth in a pout that called attention to itself in an indifferently sensual way.

"What would you like?" she asked in a deep, blurred voice. I could understand her well enough, but her words seemed fuzzy, as if her tongue was lined with lint.

I ordered a *blanc de blanc* that I was happy to see they still sold by the glass and set to work.

When she returned with the wine she lazily dropped a small square of napkin on the table and looked down at my sketch pad. "You at the art college?"

"In a way," I replied evasively, uninterested in explaining myself.

"I haven't seen you before," she continued.

"I haven't been in here for a long time," I said, pointedly craning my neck around her as I drew.

"Am I in your way?" She looked around at the bar. "Oh, sorry." She giggled, then stepped back and moved listlessly away.

I finished with the sketch rather quickly, pleased that the colors of the bar—black, brown, burnt red, vespers yellow—would offset rather spectacularly the colors of Adam's face. I had brought along a drawing of Adam—the original sketch that I had taken home—and pulled it out to examine in the light.

The waitress approached again.

"Hey," she said, looking over my shoulder. "That's Quinn."

"Quinn?" I repeated, the word flying out of my mouth like a hard ball of spit. "You know this man?"

She raised one eyebrow and sucked in her cheeks. "Yeah, I do," she said slowly. "The question is: How do *you* know him?"

I could feel myself blushing—something I never do—and I stammered (again, something I do not do), "Well, I don't actually."

She reexamined the portrait. "I find that hard to believe. This looks a lot like him, or"—she took the drawing out from under my hands—"what he looked like a few months ago when he punked out his hair."

I froze. You must understand: until this moment I had forgotten that this portrait had come from a composite drawing, or more to the point, a composite drawing of a man who had committed a crime. And at this same moment, this woman staring down at me with narrowed eyes was, I feared, suspecting me of some kind of undercover police work. My hands began to shake. I gripped the side of the table.

"I asked you before, how do you know him?" Her words had lost their fuzziness.

"I don't," I said, trying to keep my voice even. "I've seen him in here before and I liked the lines of his face so I decided to draw him. You say his name is Quinn?"

"Look," she said, her mouth turning small and hard. "I know Quinn fucks around, but I never thought any of his women would have the nerve to come in here."

My relief must have been palpable. Being mistaken for a mistress seemed far safer than being mistaken for a police informer. I smiled. "Miss. In all honesty, I have never met your friend, Quinn." I reached up and gently reclaimed the drawing. "I am not his lover. I paint for a living. I've seen him in here and I liked the shape of his face. I choose many of my subjects from public spaces. If I were his mistress, do you think I would be foolish enough to pull out his portrait in front of you?"

I could see her relax. She looked me over, smiled, and then laughed. "I'm sorry, but the guy is such a problem, I'm willing to suspect anybody." She sat down across from me. "Can I see the picture again?"

I handed it to her. She looked at it and giggled. "I remember when he did that to his hair. God, did he look stupid. Like a real clown."

With a swiftness that defied the slower workings of my brain, I suddenly felt overwhelmingly unhappy. And then I knew: Adam was no longer mine. In fact, he was never mine. I had believed I had created a new face, when in truth I had begat nothing. I felt the old nausea rise.

"I've got to show this to Casey," the waitress said, rising and taking the drawing over to the bar. I didn't have the time or presence of mind to stop her.

The bartender wiped his hands carefully on a towel, took the drawing from the waitress, and laid it on the bar. He was a tall, balding man in his late thirties, perhaps early forties, with a round, hard middle. His skin was pale and shiny, like a man who spent most of his daylight hours in darkness. His black mustache only served to offset further the appalling whiteness of his complexion. As he looked at the composite, his face, if possible, grew paler. His head jerked up and he asked the waitress something. She gestured in my direction and shrugged. He looked at me and when he realized I was gazing back, he nodded politely. He said something else to the waitress and then she returned to me. The bartender held on to the drawing. I suddenly felt very afraid.

"Casey wants you to come over to the bar," she said. "He wants to buy you a drink."

I shook my head and started packing my bag. "I'm afraid I don't have the time," I said, fumbling for my wallet. "But thank him for me. How much do I owe you?"

I looked up and the bartender was sitting across from me. He held the drawing in front of him. "I'm Harold Casey," he said, extending his right hand. "Everybody calls me Casey."

"Dorothea Fisher," I replied, then added unexpectedly, "Thea," a nickname I hadn't used since childhood. His hand was moist and fleshy. It felt like the hand of a dying person.

He turned to the waitress. "Linda, get Thea another glass of wine. So," he said, settling himself in the booth and holding up the drawing, "this is a pretty good picture you did here of Quinn. How did you come by it?" His voice was oddly effeminate; it seemed to emanate from somewhere behind his sinuses, with a barely perceptible Irish lilt giving a slight sway to the cadences of his sentences.

"As I told the waitress—Linda—" I inclined my head in her direction with what must have looked like a nervous twitch. "I'm a painter and I saw this man—Quinn, she tells me is his name—in here, and I thought he had an interesting face, so I drew it. I had no idea he was

Linda's boyfriend. She actually thought I might be his mistress!" I laughed to show him how uproarious the idea was.

The bartender laughed too, but not, I thought, in the same spirit. He placed the drawing back on the table and smoothed it with his damp, white, plump hands. I picked up the bar napkin and began to tear it into little squares. Linda came back with the wine and sat down next to the bartender. "It's a good likeness, isn't it, Casey?" she asked. "Except he looks so damned serious, like he was posing for a mug shot."

Casey stared at me. "That's exactly what I was thinking." He paused. I took a nervous sip of wine. Casey then picked up the sketch as if to reconsider it. "Funny you should draw this picture of Quinn, because he only had this particular hair style for one week in March."

"Right, right, that's when I saw him here," I said, my words bottlenecking at my mouth. "I happened to be in here then."

"Funny," he said, putting down the drawing and looking calmly at me. "I don't remember seeing you. Have you ever seen her, Linda?"

"Not until today."

"I must have come on your day off!" I said brightly, taking another gulp of wine. "So! It's been so nice meeting the both of you! I should come in here more often. I mean, just because I'm not at the college anymore doesn't mean I can't stop by. Okay, great. You keep that drawing and give it to your friend Quinn and tell him I think he has a great face." I was standing, my coat was on, my bag over my shoulder.

"Why don't you tell me yourself?" said a voice from behind.

I turned and faced the man who had spoken. His hair, cropped close to his scalp, his wisp of a mustache, his cheeks, his wide mouth, were all the color of the halo around a candle flame—not yellow, not white, transparent, yet visible—except that a flame's emanation will quiver, and this man's face was as still as a field of wheat under a windless sky. In the middle of this stillness, his eyes—the palest blue, small and round like necklace beads—floated restlessly in place. They quickly looked me over, then wandered over to the booth where, I could tell instantly, they saw the composite. He looked back at me, his pupils noticeably dilating.

"What the hell is that?" he rasped, his Irish accent, which I had detected when he first spoke, soft and lyrical, now sounding as hard as bullets.

My vision blurred. I grew dizzy and could not speak. I felt him grab my arm, hard, and heard him say, "That looks like the picture the police are circulating."

I heard Linda say, "Police? You mean this *is* a mug-shot?"

I heard Casey say, "I know. I haven't figured out what she's doing with it."

All the while I stood there, limp, staring into this man's face, searching vainly for the light source I had seen in my dreams.

You may have been worried for my safety—no need. I must tell you that my friend, Detective Burns, had followed me to the bar and I was liberated into his bony hands. It seems that he had been growing suspicious of me and found, after an unnecessarily thorough search of my office, all the Adam drawings I had hidden there. He was determined to discover my "connection" to this criminal. (For the curious: Quinn and the bartender were Irish Republic Army fugitives, now living incognito among the Irish of St. Paul and raising money through bank robbery and other means for their cause back home.) When Burns afterward searched my apartment and found all the other Adam drawings, he became further convinced of my involvement; but as I had not committed any crime (or rather, in Burns's view, they could not prove I had committed any), there were no charges pressed. For my "gross indiscretions," however, I was relieved of my job. But this I've already told you.

And now there is this: my one-woman show of "The Adam Collection" at the Twin Cities Contemporary Art Museum. Before you judge me, let me tell you how I arrived here. It seems a reporter for the *Star Tribune* discovered my involvement with the case and wrote an article about me, complete with the original drawing of Adam, for the front page of the Sunday edition. The article described me as an obsessive, eccentric neurotic—the Miss Havisham of the crime-art world. Let me quote you a line from it: "She sits here hourly in this world she has created, a world whose borders are defined by her fixation on one man, a man whose crime was a violent need to bring justice to his violent homeland." Have you ever felt so nauseated? The article attracted a ridiculous amount of attention, much of which was from galleries and art dealers wanting to see the drawings. I refused all offers, but when the Contemporary Art Museum called I finally acquiesced; I grew weary of being misportrayed.

Don't think that I am fooled. I know that most people come out of morbid curiosity. Some compliment me on the pieces, but their praise is nothing to me. I speak as little as possible about the exhibit. Still, I come here every day and I wander among the drawings, and I feel the eerie peace that comes when one surrenders to the horrible truth of one's life. It is not so much what is on the canvas that accounts for my serenity, but rather what lies beyond the picture frames. These portraits draw me not to them, but to their unseen windows, whose light has exacted its just cost.

Gone to Mum's
by Barry Simiana

"What can you say about a twenty-five-year-old girl who died?" With those words Erich Segal opened his tear-jerker novella Love Story, *and a film (and cultural) phenomenon was born. "Gone to Mum's" doesn't allow a dry eye in the room. Told from Ray's perspective, it is a most improbable love story, set among the orchards and migrant farm workers of rural Australia. He meets Kelly when she beats the crap out of him for trying to steal fruit from her farm stand. Ray and Kelly do fall in love, but their romance is anything but conventional. If* Love Story *taught us that love was never having to say you're sorry, "Mum's" reminds us that time doesn't heal wounds, it just covers them over with scar tissue.*

The sign said:

GONE TO MUM'S. BACK IN A DAY OR 2. LUV, KELLY.

We met on a property about ten minutes out of Gol Gol, a small town east of Mildura. She was a part of the traveling circus that moves about the country picking fruit and vegetables. I was on the run—running from my life, responsibility, you name it. Anonymity was my aim. A desire to withdraw from the world for a while.

Everson's Orchard was where we first struck each other (literally and figuratively). She was coming down a trail behind the orchard carrying three bags of oranges to top up a roadside stand. It was dusk, the sun slowly sinking in the west, as it does. I was intent on liberating some of those same bags from said stand, with no intention of putting money in the attached honesty box. Let's face it, honesty and I were not exactly friendly bedfellows. Anyway, I was loading two bags into the passenger side of my car, my back to the stand. Wasn't paying a lot of attention to my surroundings. There might not have been much in the way of morals about my person at the time, but I was still worried about some Goody-two-shoes coming along the road and actually catching me. Wasn't counting on anybody coming from the farm—had no inclination of anything bad happening until three kilos of oranges smacked me up the back of my head. Off balance, I tried to turn around and took another one to my face for my troubles. I went down to the ground. Rocks dug into my hands and knees. I think I broke a nail.

Stones crunched around me. My attacker was circling. I looked up, trying to visualize and plan a counterattack. In the half-light I saw her. Five foot four or so, long hair, darkish, maybe red, jeans cut off into shorts, loose T-shirt, maybe fifty kilos tops. Right. I could handle a chick. With the reflexes of a reasonably agile cat I got to my feet. Big mistake. A punch to my face, a kick to my head and I was down again. And the language! You would have thought the money was coming out of her pocket. In hindsight, I guess maybe it was. She got a bonus from the grower to look after the stall.

I was feeling pain, but I was not going to be beaten by some skinny chick on the side of the road in the middle of nowhere. I got up again, staying close to the car. I'd been in fights. Limit the room available to move. Old fighting stuff. Later I found out she'd done eighteen-odd months of an advanced self-defense course. Part of the curriculum: in-close unarmed combat. But at that particular time I wasn't privy to that little bit of information. I lunged, expecting to use my mass and muscle against her. Imagine my shock when the rain of punches and kicks fell upon me again, accompanied by abuse in at least three languages. Before long I was on the ground again, trying to protect my face from the beating.

The punches stopped. I was kneeling at the side of the road, blood soaking into my jeans at the knees and dripping from my hands. There was a cut above my left eye getting ready to spread a little claret over my face, and my lip was swelling. I could feel bruises forming on my ribs and legs, and an annoying feeling of nausea growing in my stomach. I sucked air into my chest, then felt the pain there getting worse. I looked around for the one-woman SAS squad. She was a dozen feet away, pacing back and forth, glaring at me all the time. In the growing gloom her eyes looked like they were red. Or maybe it was the film of blood now flowing over my eyes. She noticed me looking at her and the language came again, casting aspersions upon me, my parentage, my maleness, my humanity. I made to get up and she took three threatening steps toward me. Held my hands up. Peace. Truce. The words came out slurred, but she understood. She told me to perform deviant acts upon myself that would be impossible for all but the flexibly double-jointed. I slowly pushed myself up, carefully getting to my feet. I reached into my pocket and she tensed. I pulled out a ten-dollar note and held it out. She spat at me. I dropped the note on the ground and backed toward the car. She kept pace with me until I was at the driver's door. As quick as I could I got in and slammed the door shut, winding up the window and locking it. She yelled at me again but I couldn't hear. I could read her lips, though: *I ever see you again and I'll really hurt you, then call the police.*

The car started first kick. Caught first gear and put pedal to metal. Didn't look back, but I could feel her eyes boring into me. I ached. I bled. I was embarrassed. Beaten by a girl less than half my size.

A week later. Bruises have faded, cuts healed and I can face the world again. Bank account looks thin, though. The ten I'd dropped on the ground had been the last of its kind in my possession. Fortunately, the pick is on and it's a bumper year. Able bodies are needed all along the river from Mildura to Berri and beyond. After registering, I'm sent to Schoenberg's farm to pick oranges. Those that are good at it can make two hundred a day plus. Unless I improve after my first day I'll be lucky to take home twenty. Something else. Orange trees bite. Maybe that's why they're called blood oranges. Don't know.

I'm up top, picking from the higher branches. This is before the shakers made their presence known. Ever seen them? Mechanical arms reach out and grab the tree. Hydraulic motors take over, the machine shakes the shit out of the tree and all the fruit drops into a big catcher's mitt. This is before them, when humans still had control. The machines had little platforms that raised a person to pick up high, rather than have to use ladders. Old man Shoenberg had them built with the intent of selling some to other growers. Lost thousands.

Anyway, I'm picking up top filling buckets, then dropping the fruit down a chute where it gets sorted into a larger basket that gets picked up later by forklift. There's a girl below who picks the lower branches and another who picks out the damaged fruit. A guy called Kevin drives the thing. We kind of have to trust him, because it's his count that we get paid on. Kevin works for a wage. He doesn't do all that much. Makes the occasional comment. The girls chatter amongst themselves. I'm rarely spoken to directly. Might be because I'm the only person amongst the whole crew that isn't from the traveling circus. The people are friendly enough but there's a distance. I don't mind. I'm there to make a few bucks, not friends.

Worst thing about the picker is that there's absolutely no shade. Even though it's coming into autumn, there's still some sting in the sun. A canopy would get caught in the trees. Guess who didn't bring a hat on his little voyage of self-discovery. The water bottle's nearly dry. So's my throat. Eating oranges only makes my lips burn. I'm sweating, trying to keep up. The girls below are muttering under their breath, casting glances that are not friendly in my direction. They've got wide-brimmed straw hats and water bottles galore. They're professionals. I'm slowing them down. The slower we move, the less money we make. Like I said, Kevin's a salary man. Bastard.

It's inevitable. A careless hand coated with sweat and sap and juice. A hot, hot day, a rock in the road. You do the math. Instead of down the chute, a whole basket of fruit goes over the side. I'm moving right away, but I'm surprised at the lack of wailing and gnashing of teeth. Before I hit the down button on the picker, it starts. Swear words and threats so demonic they would chill the blood, but that's not what makes me freeze. It's the voice. I know that voice. It's her. The Godzilla from a week ago.

Guess what the first thing through my mind is. If your guess starts with "F" and sounds like firetruck then you're close. That night a week ago had been dark and my memory was a little vague. Add to that, I hadn't really paid attention when the crews were set. But that voice, dripping with pure evil, was one I was never going to forget. Christ. I'm dead. The lifter is heading down. I'm ready to leap over the side and be off, but I wait until it's down fully and the electrical interlock lets the gate swing open. If I run it's going to look suspicious. Better to wait and tough it out, or maybe bullshit my way through.

I'm on the ground. A large lady of unknown descent is waddling toward our machine. Everyone calls her Mother Maree and she acts like a mother to one and all. She doesn't look happy, as though accidents were somehow a failure on her part. I look around for any form of support and find none. Good old Kevin is leaning back in his seat sucking on a cigarette, casually looking around at not too much, a smirk on his face.

Great. I looked around again. From the other side of the machine I could hear muttering and curses. I came around and saw one of the girls sitting on the ground, oranges strewn around here and there, one perched neatly in the crushed crown of her straw hat. The other girl knelt close nearby, offering words of comfort. She looked up, saw me, and scowled. Two against me now, the tally growing. I wanted to casually split, but my inner voice—which had been relatively quiet of late—told me to straighten up, be a man. You got caught by surprise last time. Go apologize.

The girl sitting quietly didn't look up as I drew near. I said sorry, worried about the tremble in my voice. She said not to worry, some idiot always did it every year and it was probably her turn to have a hundred oranges rain down on her head. No biggie. I apologized again, trying to get it into her obviously hard head that I was truly sorry. She looked up at me. The orange rolled out of her hat, into the hands of the other girl. The sitting girl pushed back the brim of her hat and I found myself looking into the most perfect and beautiful set of green gray eyes I'd ever seen. I was caught, hypnotized like a bird trapped in a viper's gaze. Right at that time I thought what a way to go.

Mother Maree pushed past me and dropped to her knees. The marathon hundred-yard waddle had knocked the wind out of the woman but she still managed to talk. Kelly Kelly Kelly. She reached over and carefully took the hat off the girl, sitting it in her lap. Kelly's long red hair tumbled free. Gently Maree touched Kelly's head, probing and rubbing, brushing hair from her face, cooing questions asking did this hurt, did that hurt. Kelly quietly and patiently explained that she was fine, just a little shaken and who wouldn't be after the world's supply of oranges had just pummelled her? Mother Maree oohed and ahhed a little more, casting dark looks in my direction.

After twenty minutes of consolation and consultation, it was deemed safe for Kelly to resume work. People went back to their various machines and started picking. Mother Maree was helped to her feet and led back to her station. Maree was chief cook and bottle washer for the camp, a position she'd held for over a decade. She knew everyone. She tended the fires, looked after a lot of the washing, healed wounds, hounded the lazy and praised the hardworking, and tolerated the drinking of alcohol but hated drunkenness. Fraternizing between workers was fine if they were married or at worst engaged. Her own kids left the circus when they were old enough, all five holding down good jobs in

Sydney and Melbourne. Maree stayed with circus because it became her family.

Kelly got up and took her hat from her friend. She punched the crown back out, piled her hair back on top of her head and sat the hat back on. Kevin asked if we were ready to make another five or six dollars before knockoff. Fired up the machine and waited long enough for us to get back in position before starting off to the next tree. Less than a half hour later and the muttering came from below again. I was being careful and holding them back.

The day ended without further incident. We ended up a hundred and fifty kilos behind the next lowest team. That meant the girls had to help Maree clean up that night. I was exempt because I wasn't part of the circus. The decision didn't win me any friends. I headed off to the paddock where the cars were parked. As I drove away I caught sight of Kelly in the rearview. She stood there in my wake, arms folded across her chest, looking at me. My mind melted. She remembered.

On the way in the next day I was sweating, dreading the reaction of her telling everyone about our first meeting. But when I got there it was cool. No shouts or cries of derision. No bashings. We sucked back some coffee, chatted a bit then got stuck into it. The day went better. No stuff ups and we improved on our total, though still behind. Next day was better still. As our quota caught the rest of the crews', we all got a bit friendlier, chatted more. The scowls stopped and some grins appeared. Kelly wasn't looking at me so funny now and we were getting along. A week later, another orchard, and I got invited to pitch a tent with the gypsies. Would I like that? Do koalas shit in the forest? Thirty five Ks one way plus sixty dollars a week board. I'd save nearly a hundred dollars a week. I spent the equivalent of two weeks' pay on an impressive but impractical dome tent, a sleeping bag, and some camping gear. My site was at the far end of the camp, away from the fire, past the row of porta potties. Not the best view or aroma, but what do you want for nothing?

Strange, but I liked the feeling of being part of a group. At this stage of my life, in the mood I'd been in for the past year or so, the last thing I would have said I'd wanted was friends. My main reason for running was to get away from everyone, everything. I wanted to start somewhere fresh. Was this the place? I didn't know, but I was enjoying the feeling. I was a part of the circus now. I helped set it up and I helped pull it down. I'd become known by most and had been given a nickname: Loudmouth. I asked why and got told it was because I didn't say much. Others said it was because I didn't shut up when the singing started. I didn't care. We all ate together near Mother Maree's van, then sat around and talked and laughed and sang. I didn't talk much, but I listened. I reckoned that if I wrote down half of what I was hearing I'd have a pretty good book. Mother Maree still looked at me out of the corner of her eye—like she knew my secrets—but the look softened over time. One day she might smile at me. Then I'd know I was really in.

Days became better. We kept up and sometimes led the tally race. Kelly and the other girl—who I now knew was Lucy, despite her name being Leisa—worked well together. They moved around each other, swapping jobs without discussing it, as though they sensed the need for a change. The girls spent a lot of time together off work as well. I wondered if maybe they were a little more than just friends, then wondered if maybe I was just jealous. The casually laconic Kevin sat at his post, moving the machine up the rows and working my bucket. He said little, smoked lots, and wasn't that bad a bloke.

Kelly intrigued me. I've always been a sucker for redheads. They get me every time. And her eyes. One moment pale green like good Chinese jade, the next smoky gray. I knew it was a trick of the light, but it caught me as efficiently as a spider's web snares a bug. Every once in a while I caught her looking at me—though not as often as I looked at her—with that strange, puzzled look. To break the moment I looked away or pretended to drop something. I wondered every time if she'd put it together, but every time it went away. It seemed inevitable that she would make the connection and I would be running again, but I wanted to drag the wait out a bit longer.

We chatted on a regular basis. I listened to her talk about herself. It wasn't that she was self-absorbed but I spoke little about myself at the best of times. I learned by listening. We got friendly. I made her laugh. It was a nice laugh. I found out that my earlier worries about her orientation were so far wrong it wasn't funny. She was born in a small town called Orbost, just south of the New South Wales/Victoria border, up in the lower hills. Her mum still lived there. Kelly got to see her six or seven times a year when the seasons slowed down. Mum didn't agree with her daughter's choice of profession. Wished she'd gone on to uni and made something of herself, but agreed that being free and working in the open air would be good for a body. It beat being stuck in an office as a receptionist or working as a checkout chick at Woolies. Like most parents, she just wanted more for her child.

Kelly's dad died in 1979. Happy and healthy most of his life, career soldier who'd been to Vietnam. Fell over out front of the house one day while picking up the paper and never got up. Maybe that was what fired up the rebellious streak in his daughter. Regimented for most of his life. Told what to do, how to do it and when to do it, treated like a number for what? A pine box and a nice funeral.

I listened, answered when asked, dodged questions that hit too close to the wall around me. We spent more and more time together. We walked, talked, sat, ate. We had minutes, moments when nothing else mattered. Slices of time when only we existed. Then one day, as had happened a dozen times before, our hands touched. The briefest feeling of skin on skin and a jolt so hard it hurt, like a shock or something. Our eyes met and I was blinded, partly by the sun I suppose, because I was sort of facing in that direction—but something more. It was microseconds, washed away by the ubiquitous Kevin telling us to hang on as he spun the picker.

Our minutes turned to coffee breaks and lunch. And more. We moved through the riverland. Oranges gave way to grapes. Some wineries still preferred hand picking to mechanical harvesting. Work was good. So was life. Strawberries in the Adelaide hills, potatoes in southwestern Victoria. We kissed our first kiss standing under a tree watching the rain come down over a wheat field in the Wimmera. I had to hide the sudden change in the shape of my pants, but I don't remember getting soaked at all.

Our breaks became days and occasionally nights. We worked together, played together. It seemed natural, a growing thing, despite the pangs of fear inside me that she would remember that other night. In my mind I wondered if I'd found what I'd left my life to seek. Were my travels over? Maybe it was juvenile or naivete. Maybe it was fear and hope and want and joy and all those things poets and romantics go on about. Maybe it was love. Maybe it was real.

Work slowed a little. We took a break, headed north toward Coober Pedy and slept under the stars, watching the purple line between night and day race across the sky. She lay on her side, her back to me. I cuddled up as close as I could without being on the other side of her, on our double blow-up mattress that creaked and groaned whenever one of us moved. We laughed at the noises sometimes and made fart jokes, or compared the noises to those made by people we knew. I told her I loved her. She told me she knew and touched my thigh.

Contrary to popular belief, the desert isn't quiet. All manner of things go bump or slither or scratch in the night. Lizards prowl the shrubs and rocks. Snakes slither across sand. Somewhere off in the distance an animal cries out, followed by another as something becomes something else's supper. Frogs and toads cry for rain. As much background noise as back in civilization. But there was a pocket of silence that surrounded us as we lay beneath the stars on that creaky blow-up mattress. If the rational side of me had been in residence I might have stopped and rethought the situation—either made light of what I'd said or apologized and spoken of it no more. Unfortunately, Mr. Rational was unavailable for thoughts or comments. Perhaps that was our undoing.

The end came a month later. Christmas had passed. We'd exchanged small gifts, despite promises that we wouldn't. I gave her an antique locket I'd found in a secondhand shop. She gave me a car care kit, though it was becoming apparent that no care was going to save my car. My mistake was sending a card back home. People I didn't want to see found it and came looking for me. My old life was calling and I didn't want to go, but I was in the midst of becoming responsible again. A quandary. I told Kelly what was happening and why, and asked her to come. She said no.

Our last night together was spent under the stars on the fringe of the desert. Rain a few days earlier had brought forth flowers and grasses from the earth. The small creek was flowing and alive with frogs. Up above, the stars were subdued by a full moon, its light outshining anything else. We made love and held each other until the sky turned pink in the east. Not a lot was said those last few hours. Promises were made to keep in touch, visit whenever possible. Lovers for a moment, friends forever. A couple of hours later and she turned away as I drove east.

My return to the city was not full of fanfare. I barely caused a ripple. There were questions—some pleasant, some not. I was better than when I'd left. The doubts about my life and myself were gone, but now a new strangeness surrounded me. Something not right. A feeling that cloaked my shoulders. I returned to my work. Threw myself into it to try and shake this feeling and return to my old "normal" life. At best, I covered it in exhaustion and numbness.

Each to our word, Kelly and I kept in touch. Cards and letters, phone calls. We met up when our situations allowed us. Once in South

Queensland picking pineapples. Once in a blizzard in Smiggins. Eighteen months after I'd left she told me she was pregnant. Three months, though you wouldn't have known to look at her. The pregnancy had some effect on her. She seemed thinner, a little pale. She told me she wasn't a small bucket when I mentioned it, and to not worry because she was fine. I said that I knew what fine meant: fucked up, insecure, neurotic, and emotional. Barely evaded the punch aimed at my ear. I fussed and bothered about her the whole week, annoying the shit out of her in a good-natured way whilst dying inside because of her news.

Time doesn't heal wounds, it just covers them over with scar tissue. Underneath, it itches. Over time the cards and letters slowed. Never stopped. Just slowed. Birthdays, Christmas and Easter, other memorable reasons. Phone calls became occasional, then very. Visits almost nonexistent, and short when they were managed. I married and moved north. My time away from the city had spoiled me. I wanted away and settled for a beachside village. My wife gave birth to a son, a towheaded little rascal who was the image of his mother, with none of my traits but exactly like me. The marriage split a year later. Irreconcilable differences, looking for something in the other we didn't have in ourselves and not finding it. We're still friends. It's easier and better. Just wasn't meant to be.

A call out of the blue. Kelly was in the next village, been there about a week. Picking blueberries and bananas. Didn't like bananas. Kelly hated rats and snakes and some of the looks she got from some of the growers. We met up at a Chinese restaurant. Plastic Buddha on a shelf. Silk paintings of egrets on the walls. Lots of red and gold paint. Food was okay though.

To my eyes she'd barely changed. A little thinner maybe. Certainly a bit browner. She'd spent some time further north where it was beautiful one day and bloody hot the next. I met her daughter Mellissa. The same hypnotic eyes. Same deep, dark red hair. The cutest little lisp when she spoke. Fifteen minutes into dinner and she was on my lap feeding me fried wonton faster than I could chew and swallow. After discussion and much pleading by my new best friend, they lived in my spare room the seven weeks Kelly worked. Mornings we walked along the beach chasing ghost crabs and pretending to see sharks in the waves. Days we climbed rocks and searched rockpools for shells. Nights we played games and talked about nothing. Heaven in the front room of my beachside apartment.

If it was hard to part that long time ago, it was twice as hard this time. In a short time we'd grown close again. All the same promises to stay in touch made and vowed. I'd recently lost a family, gained one for a couple of months only to have them walk away again. So much I wanted to say. So much I wanted to do. I suppose I'd said it before and been let down gently. So instead I helped them pack. Pretended to take things out of the bags to prolong the waiting. I loaded the bags and then the girl into the car, a beat-up Volvo she picked up somewhere on the track. Mellissa hugged me tight and kissed my cheek. Kelly did the same. As they drove away, through the cloud of smoke belched from the exhaust, I caught sight of Kelly's eyes in the rear view. Something there made me wonder if I'd made another mistake. But it was too late. With a wave out the window they turned onto the street and were gone.

I stood on that spot for what could have been an hour, staring at the space where the car had stood. Looking at the impressions in the grass the soon-to-be-bald tires had made. My mind—old Mr. Rational— made one of his infrequent appearances to analyze that last look, work- ing hard to convince me that the only message sent had been *see you again real soon*. Daphne from down the back, the lovely old matriarch of our little block of units, came and took my arm and led me to her place for a quiet cup of tea. As I followed along the path I told Mr. Rational in no uncertain terms that I'd royally screwed up.

True to our word we kept in touch, both of us with renewed vigor. We exchanged photos of our kids, report cards when they got to school age. Postcards and letters, birthdays and holidays. Kelly took a year off work, grabbed Mellissa and went up to the cape, ending up in Marybor- ough picking mangoes to make enough money to get home. They stopped and stayed a couple of weeks. I had my boy at the same time. The kids played together as though they'd been friends forever. Kelly looked as wonderful as ever. A little on the thin side, some laugh lines around the eyes and a tendency to get tired around midnight. I was the same, except for the thin bit. We were getting older. She still looked beautiful to me.

It wasn't as hard to let go, the day they left. I knew we'd see each other again. We called and wrote and got e-mail. Mellissa stayed at my place with my boy Peter the next Easter. Peter went to Kelly's Septem- ber school holidays while I went to England. The best eight days of his life, he declared loudly and proudly. He told me how he was going to marry Mellissa when he got bigger and had a job. Puppy love at six. I wished him well because everyone needs a dream.

Coincidences are uncanny things. Unexpected. Surprising. A book I'd recently read spoke of coincidences being spiritual messages sent from the higher self and beings in the spiritual world. If a person took time to take notice, one could see the changes happening in life and follow them for the betterment of one's self. Or words to that effect. It lost me when it said that no one was truly responsible for their actions, that gods and demons and aliens made things happen. I moved to a new house. Bought a little cabin next beach up overlooking the water, six hundred feet from the sand.

The days were growing shorter, the nights cooler. Winter was approaching after a long, hot summer. A cold snap brought on by a strong southerly had me hunting for newspaper and matches to light the fire, pull the ratty blue beanbag up close and relax with a good book and a jug of Brown Beaver Ale on ice. I had a couple of photo albums nearby and leafed through as a nice little fuzz settled over my brain. Pictures of Kelly and Mellissa, then Mellissa on her own. Obviously Kelly had taken the photos, but I could still see her in every picture.

A knock on the door. I decided to ignore it because I was pretty comfortable where I was. Turned down the stereo in case the knocker was persistent. They were. Another knock followed by another. I wriggled around until I could drag myself up and went to the door. Mrs. Gould from number 38 was there. She had a letter for me, misdelivered again. I'm number 28. Happens all the time and not because people who write to me have terrible penmanship or anything. I think it's because I didn't give the postman a beer at Christmas. I think he holds it against me. I offer Mrs. Gould a coffee but she declines. Kids are home soon. Her eldest is a dreadful little shit who likes to peer into people's windows and call out at all hours. Treats his mother terribly, but she lets him get away with it, so who's really at fault? I thanked her as she turned and left, waited until she'd closed the gate before going back inside.

Couldn't get comfortable in the beanbag again. The sweet spot had gone, or maybe it was anticipation. I like letters. Getting them, not writing them. This one was a snip though. Handwriting gave it away. Thin and spidery on a reverse angle, like frenetic chicken scratchings. It had been redirected from my old house. Right enough, because I'd really only just finished moving a week or so before. The new owners of my old place had promised to pass on my mail for a while to save the fee the post office was going to charge. It was date-stamped eight days before, so they'd held onto it for a week. But something unnerved me. One of those feelings. My grandmother said it was a goose walking over her grave. Still don't quite have a handle on that one.

I looked at the envelope for a long time, long enough to empty the jug and wish I had another. Holding it up to the firelight told me that there was a piece of paper in there with writing on it. Armed with that information, I looked harder, trying to find some secret sign or rune or something. Man, I felt something. Don't know what, but the best way I can describe it is like I felt a disturbance in the force—thanks, George Lucas—and all was not well.

I sought fortification in the spirits—the liquid kind—so I got up again and poured another jug of the Canadian Brown Beaver. Excellent nerve tonic. Double shot each of the eight brown spirits over ice in a jug, topped up with orange juice. Try before you condemn. Unfortunately, I was only feeling more uptight. I steeled myself. Christ, it was only a letter, like a hundred I'd received in the past. Believe me, I'd handled enough bad news in this relationship. What more could she say?

I held it up again between thumb and forefinger. Good old Mr. Rational was back. I think he liked the alcohol. Open the bloody thing he said. Your paranoia is showing. I shook the envelope, but don't ask me why. It didn't explode and waves of anthrax didn't fall out. I felt marginally better.

My handy-dandy pocket knife slit the envelope open. Trembling—must have been the effects of the beavers—I pulled out the slip of paper and shook it open.

Dear Ray,

Pretty painless so far, but so is the beginning of your average tooth extraction.

Hope I haven't caught you at a bad time. Sorry I haven't been the best correspondent, but things have been a bit busy lately. We need to talk, or at least I do. I'd rather it be face-to-face than over the phone. Can you come visit? I understand if you can't, but if you can I'd appreciate it. Sorry to be so mysterious. Directions are easy. Go to the hot bread shop if you have troubles. See you soon.

Luv, Kelly.

I turned over the paper. Checked out the directions. No explosions or anything. I read it again, and again. Didn't seem to be any sort of code or anything. She just wanted to see me and talk. That intrigued me. Mr. Rational got duck-shoved by Mr. Hopeful. She wants you to come and visit. She wants to talk. *Why?* Who gives a shit. I was catching the fever. Rereading, it didn't seem like it was a drop everything and run deal, so I decided to go the next weekend. Make a holiday of it. I could finish a couple of projects and have a break. It all fell into place. Must have been kismet or something.

The weekend couldn't come quickly enough. I resisted the urge to call. Probably should have, in case she had a bloke staying over or something, but I had the feeling that wasn't going to be a problem anymore. Friday night and I had the car packed, fuelled, and ready to go. I was on the road by six thirty in the morning. Got flashed by a speed camera south of Kempsey, caught a nap at Hexham. Five hours getting through Sydney because nothing was where it used to be. Caught a dream run once I got past Wollongong. Had another couple of hours at Ulladulla. Good fish and chips and a snooze, then back in the saddle. Finally stopped at Pambula. Fifteen hours later. I was exhausted. Was a time when I'd drive to Adelaide for a steak sandwich just for fun. Half a day and I was finished.

Decided to grab a night's sleep and do the last couple of hundred in the morning. I couldn't see the sense in killing myself right here on the verge of a breakthrough. A good steak dinner, a vodka and orange, and I was out like a light.

Next morning I was up with the sun. I was buzzing. I ran downstairs in a pair of swimmers and jumped into the motel's pool. Forgot I was over five hundred miles south of my usual locale. The cold water stopped the breath in my lungs and I sank to the bottom, screaming silently into the water. Got out as fast as I could without snapping bits off, and ran back to my room and stood under a steaming shower until my blue bits regained their usual pinkish hue. Sufficiently thawed, I packed and left and headed south.

Four hours later, I was touring the bustling metropolis that was Orbost. Along the way I spotted a dozen places that would have been perfect for a picnic—by a creek where the local apex had set up a barbecue area. Near a pond filled with ducks. A swimming spot close to the beach that might have had to wait until summer but looked inviting all the same. The directions to the house were dead easy. Through town, past the church to the park, turn left then next right, up to the outboard motor mailbox, down the dirt road to the right, stop at the A-frame set-tlers' cottage. Knock before you enter and leave your shoes on the mat. Easy.

From where I was sitting the house seemed deserted. A few plant leaves moved in the softest of breezes and there was a hint of baking bread. Probably from the bakery I was supposed to ask directions at if I got lost. I got out and wandered around. Peeked over the fence. Hills hoist, a swing set, a bike. Grass was getting a bit long. Down the back I could see a couple of citrus trees. That touched my humor button. I'd kind of thought fruit would be the last thing Kelly would have close by. Further to the other side of the yard stood an old timber shed. Leaning to the left and to the back at the same time, but had that sort of symme-try that made you think of old John Williamson songs. A Weber with the top off and a plastic outdoor set. No people and no people noises.

I wandered around the front of the house, checking out the plants in the garden. Weeds. Nasturtiums. A daisy. Shoes on a welcome mat that was nearly worn through. The sign on the door. It was cross-stitched, framed behind glass. The sign said GONE TO MUM'S. BACK IN A DAY OR 2. LUV KELLY. Funny, for a moment there I could see Kelly sitting out the back, sausages on the Weber, Mellissa swinging or playing or some-thing, while her mother carefully stitched the words and the little house and the sun and all. When she got tired of it, no doubt she headed out to the shed and did twenty minutes on the speed bag to relax. My girl was a series of contradictions, but not in residence it seemed. Rang the bell and knocked just in case. Tried the knob as directed but it was locked. Cool. Tried to find "mums." The directions said try the bakery. Seemed like sound advice. I hit the car and turned around. Headed back to town. The lady at the bakery knew everybody, including Kelly and her mother. Even my fame had preceded me.

Took an hour, but I got my directions. A dozen rolls, a chocolate cake, and a croissant for the road, too. I stopped at a general store and got a bunch of roses for Kelly, white ones and a yellow tube rose for Mellissa. Back in the car and following the directions. Down to the park, left then right past the fire brigade and five houses down. Look for the satellite dish.

Found it in five minutes. English daisy garden that filled most of the front yard. I parked and sat for a minute. Should have got flowers for the mother. Potential big mistake. Damn. Never a store around when you need it. Time to go. Do or die. Get your ass out of the car and go knock on the door. What the hell are you waiting for, an invitation? It's in the mail. Get going! Mr. Rational and Mr. Hopeful working as a team for a change.

I steeled myself, picked up the flowers, and got out of the car. Walked through the garden on stepping stones made of timber, a tree cut in slices. Made it to the door with resolve intact. Paused for that moment and heard voices. My nerve went. I felt like a little kid on his first play date, all knock-kneed and sweaty palms. My throat was dry. Brain overheating. What was the problem? Either knock on the door or run like a baby and make a fool of yourself. Go to hell, Mr. Rational. Thanks for your assistance. The door opened. I nearly screamed. Dropped the tube rose. Three inches below my nose stood a lady, red hair fading, but the fire wasn't out yet. Gray green eyes behind glasses. She was looking up at me. May I help you, she said. Ever the clever conversationalist, I mumbled something that might have been English. I understood it. She leaned a little closer and begged my pardon. Mouth full of cotton, I tried again, working to say all the letters in all the words, except the silent ones. Hi. My name is Ray. I've come to see Kelly.

The expression on her face was amazing. All at once she seemed happy and about to cry at the same time. A tear welled up behind the glasses. She took my arm. Come inside. That old feeling hit me again. That disturbance in the force. I allowed myself to be led inside to a sitting room that had all the hallmarks of becoming the bridge of the starship Enterprise. A giant multimedia entertainment system took up one wall. CD, DVD, video, stereo, TV. The adjacent corner was wrapped around a new Imac setup, with full multimedia. Contrast the three china ducks on the walls, probably fifty years old or more. Antique porcelain chargers on the mantle, a cabinet filled with old cameras. And flowers. Hundreds of flowers.

I sat down in the most comfortable chair I'd ever seen or felt and declined a cup of coffee. Kelly's mum sat across from me and leaned forward, took my hands in hers.

"Kelly passed away Wednesday."

A bullet to the forehead would have been kinder, certainly less of a shock.

"Cervical cancer. Diagnosed a year ago. Too late."

She lowered her eyes, maybe to save me the sight of her tears, maybe to save her the sight of mine.

Nearly a hundred people turned up for the funeral. Mother Maree brought a dozen from the circus. We talked and cried and hugged each other like a family should in times like those. People whose lives Kelly had touched sent flowers and notes, money for Mellissa, sympathy and regrets. Mellissa stayed between her grandmother and me the whole time. Everyone remarked on how much she resembled her mother and that Kelly's spirit would always be with us and that a person never died until the last person that remembered them passed away. Mellissa stood quietly, her eyes wide and moist, holding my hand.

There was a memorial at Kelly's house. More words of comfort and condolence. People started to drift away in the afternoon. A few of Kelly's mum's friends helped clear away the debris. When the last of the helpers left, Kelly's mum went to lie down. I sat in the sitting room and flicked through a photo album that had been left for me. The pictures were at most two years old. I could see the changes in Kelly. I thought back to the times we'd been together. Always a little thinner, a little pale ("I'm not a little bucket!"). Should have known something was up. But she never said a word. I flicked through the pictures. Kelly and Mellissa at home, on holidays, on the road. Some with me and my boy, some of just the kids. Some of Kelly on her own, taken—from the look of it— without her knowledge. Despite her failing health, she still looked beautiful to me.

I sat with the album until the sun started to go down. Mellissa came in from her room. She pulled herself up onto my lap and gave me an envelope. "Mummy wrote you a letter," she said. The writing on it was Kelly's, no doubt about it. Spiky, reverse-angled chicken scratch. Mellissa asked if I'd read it to her. I agreed but only after I read it first.

I took the envelope from Mellissa's hand. Without warning she wrapped her arms around me and gave me a hug, squeezing hard around my neck. I hugged her back, scared I might hurt her but not wanting to stop. She let go and slipped down and went back to her room.

The flap was held down with a little sparkley tiger sticker. I didn't want to wreck it. That would have been wrong somehow. Out came the trusty Swiss army knife and I slit the envelope open, making sure the letter wasn't cut. Two pages came out. I unfolded them.

Hey. [Nothing like that personal touch.]
Gump was right. Life is like a box of chocolates.
You never know what you're gonna get. It was certainly a surprise to me.
If you're reading this then I guess you know what's happened. Mum would have filled in the details. She didn't know until about six months or so ago.

No one did but me. Didn't want anyone to know. Sorry. Maybe I made a mistake. Not the first one. Made a bigger one years ago. I heard what you said, that night. I pretended not to notice, and to shrug it off. It wasn't the right time for me. I should have made the time. 20/20 hindsight. I guess it hurt you, and I'm sorry. Something else. That night on the highway. Don't look surprised. I knew it was you. Couldn't miss that piece of shit you drove. Took guts to stay after the beating you took. And don't go all macho and say it didn't hurt. I worked you over pretty well. I felt pretty bad afterward, but I didn't think I'd see you again. Bit of a shock when you turned up in my crew. Thought about belting you again but decided to wait and see. Maybe the best move I did make back then.

If you're feeling bad for me now, don't. Things happen. John Lennon got it right. Life's what happens while you make other plans. It's been hard, but I've learned a lot about myself. I learned I was selfish, or maybe self-interested is better. I didn't think much about other people's feelings. So long as I got what I wanted. It's been a hard lesson to learn. Wish I'd tried sooner. Late might be better than never, but maybe not in this case. I need a favor. Mum can't look after Mel. She'll try and she'll do the best she can, but she's not rich, certainly not rich enough to raise another child, and she's not getting any younger. Mel's father hasn't been around since she was six months old. He's not on the paperwork. No one is. Yet. Mum's got the papers. Put your name in the father section. Mum agrees. No one will know. No one will fight it. Be her dad for me. Please.

I stopped reading, partly to take it all in, partly because I thought I was going to pass out. I felt like my heart was beating its way out of my chest. Shit. There was more.

I know it's a lot to ask and I understand if you say no. But there's no one else I trust. No one else I know will look after my baby and help her remember me. I don't want to brag but I don't think you'll forget me. Please say yes.

I had to stop again. The writing was getting blurry. Some sort of mist was getting in the way. Damn country air. Who knew what floated around in it. I waited for it to blow away or dry up or whatever. Waited in vain.

I should have told you how I felt. Now it's too late. Can't say the words now because it feels wrong, like I'm clutching at straws. But I guess the feelings are there. Even today. With all that's happened to us and between us. I hope you understand. Please think about what I've asked you. I don't do it lightly. Please love her as much as I know you loved me. Not much else to say. Good-bye? I love you? See you when I get back? If there's a tomorrow or another side, I'll see you there.

Luv, Kelly.

It's three weeks beyond Easter. Weather's cooling down. The kids saw their first humpback whale two days ago, maybe half a k out from the beach. Mellissa and my boy get along like they've been together forever. If anyone notices the glaring differences in their looks they don't say.

It's just been a year. Neither of the kids have taken notice of the photo albums that are lying around. Maybe it's because they're always lying around. Anyway, I promised I'd do this for you, and I think I have. I'd like to say happy anniversary, but I can't. The kids and I are going back to Orbost next week to see your mum. Another promise I made that day. I promised we'd spend the anniversary together. Sit and talk and remember. But right now, while the kids are chasing seagulls and the winds are picking up, as autumn fades to winter, all I can say is I miss you.

The Injunction

by Don Wallace

Combine two of America's favorite pastimes—football and lawsuits— and what do you get? A terrific story about a successful-but-not-big-time lawyer who is hired by his college roommate to handle his (supposedly) amicable divorce. The former roommate, Dante Sifranco, is an NFL star and Charlie Wickham loves being on the fringes of celebrity. But nothing is quite what it seems to be, and Charlie—to everyone's surprise, includ- ing his own—engineers a strategy that puts professional football and his own scalp directly into the crosshairs. Any Given Sunday *meets* The Verdict.

Charlie Wickham heard his intercom buzzer, but, up to his ears in a widow's will, trying to keep his head down until lunchtime, he didn't respond. If it was an important call, Gloria would buzz again.

"I'm sorry, Mrs. Wickham," he heard Gloria say in the front room of the law office. "Mr. Wickham must have stepped out."

He held his breath.

"Of course—I'll try again," said Gloria.

He cut in on the buzzer. "That's all right, I've got it." He picked up the phone. "Hi, darling. What's up?"

Jean sounded grouchy. "I think that secretary of yours is intention- ally not telling you of my calls. This is the second time I called this morning, Charlie. Are you coming home for lunch? I'll leave you a sandwich if you are, but Trudy Mason made me part of her foursome."

"Oh, don't bother. I'll go to the club." He tried to keep the relief out of his voice.

"Remember, nothing fried and no salt. By the way, I saw on the news this morning that your friend Sifranco is getting a divorce. I knew it wouldn't last."

"It lasted ten years."

"She just didn't fit in. Got to run, lover. Bye." Jean hung up.

Charlie heard laughter up front and checked his watch: ten fifteen. Shoving back his chair, he blew out the door and surprised Alf, his son and sometime associate, leaning on the counter and chatting with Gloria. "Just getting in?"

Alf cautiously straightened up. His long hair was wet, the shoulders of his corduroy jacket soaked dark. "I got a call at home from a client, Dad. Personal injury with a good chance to collect, against a supermarket chain. Slipped on a puddle and hurt his back."

"Is this your three-time drunk driver, or the PCP user?"

"Neither," Alf said, with wounded dignity. "He says he was straight." He glanced toward the back of the office, past the open doors of Warden, Bertleman, and young Prineas, the other lawyers who shared the building, and who were undoubtedly listening in.

Charlie turned to Gloria and hoped Alf would take the hint. "Well, Dante Sifranco's getting divorced."

"Who?" asked Alf.

Gloria knew, as he thought she would. She'd come to him from managing a social club in downtown Los Angeles. The club had closed, leaving Gloria with a ten-year-old daughter in private school and a taste for living well. During her interview they'd talked about the Lakers and the Raiders as much as anything else.

"That seven-year itch," Gloria said. "So, we know why he was traded to Philly. I bet they aren't happy that their quarterback has domestic issues."

"Who's this?" asked Alf. "Will the sports junkies please speak English?"

The phone rang. Gloria rolled away in her chair. Every five seconds she gave her head a toss to keep her long blond hair off the pad on which she took notes. She wore a jade green leather jacket over a fringed, red leotard top. How she carried it off, he couldn't say. Maybe her height—six feet in stockings (and she wore heels).

Looking at her while telling Alf about Dante Sifranco, he wondered how much longer it would be before he lost her. She was too good; he was just one man; he couldn't pay her what she was worth.

Without turning, Gloria raised a hand in the air and snapped her fingers. Then she rotated the hand like a periscope until the index finger was pointing at Charlie's office. He went in, shut the door, and picked up the phone. "Yes?"

"This is Mrs. Sifranco, Mr. Wickham," Gloria said, deadpan. "She would like you to handle her divorce."

Gloria got off the line with a firm click. "Hello, Cathy," he said. "I'm terribly sorry to hear the news. Of course I'll be glad to advise you in your choice of an attorney—but I'm afraid I don't do divorces."

There was a long pause. "Hi, Charlie," Cathy Sifranco said finally. "It's been a while, I know. Not much of a reunion. But what about the Evans divorce? And the Kunkels."

"Those were two of my oldest friends. And," he added quickly, "all parties agreed to an amicable settlement beforehand."

"Doesn't Dante count as an old friend?"

Astounded at her brazenness, he could only say, "Of course." The woman must be in shock.

"I know I'm not. I know you and Dante go way back. But we both want to do this quietly and calmly. And no one ever heard one word about the Evanses or the Kunkels." Cathy Sifranco breathed in and out. "The thing is, Charlie, I live in this town, too. And I want to go on living here, with my children. Dante, you know, he's not coming back. He likes Philadelphia."

Driving to the club, Charlie Wickham kept hearing that as a refrain: "Dante . . . he's not coming back." It was, of course, true. That went without saying. The boy had finally made it up the last rung to the top. Dante's trade to Philadelphia, perpetual contenders, after several years of not-quite-playoff seasons with the Raiders, had given Charlie a degree of personal satisfaction. Dante and Charlie had both played football for the same high school coach, old Bud Henle, twenty-two seasons apart. Charlie had witnessed Dante's high school heroics; as booster chairman, Charlie attended all Dante's banquets, where ground beef was disguised twelve different ways, and Dante won everything but the field hockey trophy. Charlie once even led a movement at the club to fill out thousands of newspaper ballots and elect Dante to a college regional all-star team. Dante went to the pros as a low draft pick, but hung on. One day, after half a dozen years as an understudy, his star began to rise. Charlie couldn't have been prouder than if Dante was his own son. When Dante was traded to the Raiders, then still in Los Angeles, Charlie had dreamed of running into him and being recognized. That was all he wanted: recognition as a friend, despite the age difference.

It happened sooner than he dreamed. At Coach Henle's advice, Dante came to Charlie when he and Cathy bought their first house in Riverknoll. For a while he and Dante lunched regularly at Little Joe's, down by the Los Angeles courthouse, where celebrities and their lawyers lingered over drinks and antipasto. Then forty-five, Charlie had filled out and looked the part of a once-active player. He was mistaken for a former professional by the head coach of the Raiders, by assistant coaches of the Browns and the Chargers, and by most of Dante's teammates when they were introduced. He met heroes of his own generation, met heroes from his father's generation, Norm Van Brocklin, Frank Gifford, Lem Barney, played liar's dice with Audie Murphy—when he was the only person besides the bartender who knew that the shaky Irish drunk with the freckles and pink ravaged skin was a former Hollywood star, a Congressional Medal of Honor winner, and killer of a hundred German soldiers. The life of the stars wasn't all fun and games.

Then, just like that, the Raiders had returned to Northern California. Not much Dante could do about that, although Cathy stayed put in Riverknoll, for the kids. And that was it for Dante and Charlie. The years with Dante at Little Joe's had been good ones, but now were in the past. He was all right with that. Even now, whenever he won a case, he reserved a table at Little Joe's and took his wife, his secretary, and lately his son, out for a celebration dinner.

Though he hadn't seen Dante for years, he wished him only the best. Dante had brought Riverknoll true recognition. Dante was going places, and he, Charlie, accepted the fact that he was a small-town lawyer. To be touched by passing greatness was enough for him; to perhaps have helped Dante, in his way, was payment enough. As for Cathy Sifranco, he felt for her, he did not condone Dante's behavior, and he worried about their two children, but he could not take her case.

At the club buffet he let himself be tempted by the prime rib before settling for the whitefish, green beans, one scoop of scalloped potatoes, and coleslaw without mayonnaise. He sat in the men's grill with the usual group of retirees and those whose offices, like his, were close enough to excuse a lunch visit.

"Charlie, you proposed Dante for membership here," Bill Marsh said. "Is it true he's chasing after some porno actress?"

"Hadn't heard," Charlie said.

The others went on:

"Sounds like him, doesn't it? At the July Fourth barbeque a few years ago he went off during the fireworks. That wife of his—"

"Jesus, remember how mad she was?"

"Nice piece herself, too."

"Who did he go off with? Was it a waitress?"

"Somebody's daughter."

"Who said it was a girl? He went off with a caddy."

Everybody laughed, Charlie included, though he was watching some tiny figures on the green slope below the tinted window. When he recognized Jean as one of the women, he had to stifle an impulse to wave. There had been signs all along, he realized, that the Sifranco marriage was in trouble. He just hadn't read the signs.

Jean and Trudy Mason got into a golf cart and drove off to the next tee. It occurred to him that when Dante divorced Cathy she would lose the right to come to the club. Only widows were allowed to retain their privileges, and even they had to pass a vote of the board of directors. He wondered how she would take it. He couldn't imagine Jean, for instance, without her golf and social life at the club. A good lawyer would be sure to get Cathy proper compensation for her loss of standing in the community.

The letter from Dante was cordial. "Dear Charlie," it read, "Cathy tells me that you won't take her case because of your friendship with me. That is exactly why Cathy and I want you to handle our divorce. We don't want any flashy lawyers making things difficult. We're sad to have to do this, but we have grown apart over the years. It is for the best."

Cathy Sifranco sat in the leather chair, smoking a beige cigarette, her platinum hair elaborately swirled, eyebrows finely drawn, makeup perfect; she hadn't let herself go at all. Her figure, even after two children, was girlish.

She smiled; one cheek dimpled. "See, I told you. We're still friends." Her mood was beyond comprehension.

"This does make things easier," he had to admit.

She seemed to think that settled the matter. Maybe it had. "Dante's a special person—to achieve the fullest expression of his talents he needs to feel free."

He found such talk demoralizing. Even the Kunkels, whose Germanic forbearance had given their divorce a grave dignity, broke down and wept that first day in his office.

"You see," said Cathy Sifranco, almost shyly. "I really do believe that we'll be back together in our old age."

Then he understood. Dante had her iced; she wouldn't know what had happened until he was long gone. That, more than anything, decided him. He'd see to it that she was well taken care of, for the day when the truth sank in and there were no more illusions worth clinging to. In a way, it would be an even greater service to Dante, by keeping him honest, allowing him to—how did she put it—"achieve the fullest expression of his talents," without cheapening his soul. He'd give Dante his clean break, and minimize the guilt he would surely feel someday. All so Dante could continue to feel free.

"I didn't marry a divorce lawyer," Jean said that evening. They were standing in the kitchen. Until he gave in to her request for a certain Persian rug for the living room, its floor would be bare and all the furniture slipcovered. So every night they had cocktails in the kitchen.

"They just want to get off cheap," said Jean. "And you're blinded by stardust."

"Not true," he said, aware that with two scotches under the belt he would have no arguments with Jean.

"It's the same old story. No wonder you've never made the money the rest of your classmates have. You're too easy," she pronounced slowly.

"Now, now." He scratched a flea bite on his ankle.

"Everybody takes advantage of you—the hospital, the Boy Scouts, the Children's Dental Foundation. Do you think you're the only lawyer in town who has a conscience? Don't the others owe anything?"

"A lot of them are too busy." It was such an old argument, he hardly had to present to keep up his end.

"Busy making money," she snapped. "While even your own son takes advantage of you. Oh, why did I marry such a pushover?"

Jean's small shoulders hunched together as she bowed her head and stroked the orange cat, Juice, who was eating cheese from the hors d'ouvres tray on the counter. Charlie put a hand around the back of

Jean's neck and massaged it gently. That's how they stood, him smiling into space, Jean rolling her head from side to side as he rubbed, and the cat purring—until the timer on the microwave oven went off.

Jean's eyes darkened. "I didn't have time to make dinner. These are frozen enchiladas."

It was an interesting settlement. There were no disagreements about community property. He and the lawyer the Philadelphia team had given Dante followed California law and split everything down the middle. House went to the mother, sportscar and investments to the father. There was a creative wrinkle, the team lawyer's idea: the alimony and child support payments would be assumed by the team as part of Dante's bonus. There were tax breaks in it this way, and Dante's real income wouldn't be affected.

Practices and preseason games had been going on throughout, and the decree was granted before the first regular game. Dante Sifranco played sparingly but well in a loss on the road. "Sifranco Sharp in Defeat," the *Riverknoll Sentinel* reported. The next week he threw a first-quarter interception, then watched from the bench as his replacement led the team to a fourth-quarter victory. In the late hours after the game Sifranco's sportscar was clocked speeding; during the routine stop a small amount of drugs was found on his female companion. "Dante Says Unaware of Drugs," the *Sentinel* reported, and indeed he was not charged; but by midweek he had been traded to the newest expansion franchise, the Virginia Rebels, who'd just lost their quarterback to a knee injury.

Cathy Sifranco called on the twentieth of September to say that her payments were two months late. Charlie called Dante's agent, but never got put through, so he drafted a letter to the Rebels outlining the terms of Dante's contract. He waited two weeks, then wrote again. He received a letter back: "Under the laws of this state we are under no obligation to the former wife of Dante Sifranco. Your argument seems to be with Philadelphia." Enclosed was a form releasing the Rebels from any claims. "Please sign and return."

Charlie tried phoning the attorney whose name was on the letter. His calls were not put through, nor were his messages returned.

Although he was under no obligation himself, he loaned Cathy Sifranco the amount of her mortgage payment; that month he barely made his own. In fact, he carried it on his credit cards.

When he began due diligence, finding out that the Virginia Rebels team was part of a shell corporation chartered in Delaware made his heart sink. Nevertheless, through the office of a Delaware attorney who needed some work done in California, Charlie filed suit against the Rebels. In November he flew to the East Coast, rented a car, drove to Delaware and stayed in a motel. To save money, he ate breakfast at McDonald's.

He arrived early and waited in the courthouse hall outside the chamber in which the case would be heard. Following his ritual of pre-trial warmups, he read from a tattered newsprint list that he carried in his wallet, "The Fourteen Most-Used Objections," given to him twenty-five years ago in law school by his evidence professor, Bart Wright. Nicknamed "The Fright," Wright was now retired to a part-time judgeship in Long Beach. Charlie saw him down at the pier once, fishing on a Sunday, like any other old man—and even then he'd almost been too afraid to say hello. When he'd shown him "The Fourteen Objections," though, Wright the Fright had actually glowed.

He became aware of four men watching him.

"Mr. Wickham?" asked one, smiling. He pointed to the list. "Refreshing your memory?"

"Mr. *Charles* Wickham?" asked another.

"Yes. What is it?" he asked impatiently.

The man slapped an envelope against his chest. "This is a suit charging you and your client with attempting to maliciously interfere with the normal business operations of a corporation in the state of Delaware."

"We'll settle for a million out of court," said a third attorney, winking. "Congratulations on hitting the big time."

In the courtroom the most junior Rebel attorney spoke: "We confess that this suit catches us unprepared, Your Honor. It involves the jurisdictions of three states and an unscrupulous contract that resembles tax evasion."

The judge granted a continuance of two weeks. After making plane and hotel reservations, Charlie took a midnight flight home. Instead of sleeping on the plane, he read over the Sifranco settlement for the twentieth time and came to the conclusion that a) it was legally binding, and b) he'd never collect. He was up against one of the largest East Coast law firms. They had deep pockets; he couldn't afford another continuance and plane flight. Already he was a month behind in his own work. The countersuit, which he would have to defend, would drain him to the last drop.

The plane got in at five thirty Friday morning. Over breakfast he explained some, but not the worst, of his conclusions. Jean fell into a foul silence.

"That's just great," she said.

"We'll get through. They'll soften."

"I bet you're next going to say I have to forget about getting that carpet for the living room," she said.

"This isn't the right time to be making any big purchases."

"Excuses. For years it's been one thing or another." Jean prowled around the kitchen counter, setting out four separate and individualized bowls of catfood—some with liver, some with dry and wet. She took a piece of bacon off Charlie's plate and crumbled it into Precious Pearl's portion.

Charlie could feel the fleas scrambling up his legs. "We're at the limit of all our charge cards already."

"I've told Kashikan that I'm getting it, and I won't have you embarrass me. I'm sick of your 'mistakes,' your weakness, your nagging me about money. This is all your fault—because you were so thrilled to be seen with some football player. Well, you've ruined my life enough as it is."

When he got to the office he discovered that his son had taken off in his absence and had gone surfing at Malibu.

He called Cathy Sifranco. At first friendly, her manner quickly cooled. "You mean to tell me that they're not going to pay? You're a lawyer; I'm paying you to make them pay."

"The situation is going to take time to untangle."

"It better not. I've got a thousand-dollar grocery bill at Morgan Farms. Not to mention I can lose the house if I miss another mortgage payment. That house is all I have."

Charlie hesitated; the next question represented a new low for him. "Maybe you could call Dante."

"I can talk to him after Sunday's game."

"You can? Ask him to put on a little pressure from his end."

"I can ask him, but as far as putting on pressure, he's got a whole new offense to learn, and they play the Raiders next weekend. That's a big game. He's already sent the kids and me tickets."

"He can send you tickets but he can't help on the mortgage? What's with him, anyway?" His anger was genuine. He also hoped to stir up Cathy a bit. She had to get through to Dante; that was their best, perhaps only, chance.

She spoke as if offended. "Dante says this whole thing is your way of trying to run up a big bill to stick me with." She paused, adding, "I told him that wasn't true."

Afterwards he sat staring at the Currier and Ives print on his office wall. He loved the *Flying Cloud*, the clipper ship. As he lit one of his low-tar cigarettes, a nervous tremor shook the ash off it. He stubbed it out, reached into his bottom drawer, and groped for the pack of what his son called "cancer sticks." He also found a handful of chocolate mints and ate them all.

"Hey, Charlie," said Gloria over the intercom. "High noon. Time for the first official belt of the weekend."

When he joined Gloria in the photocopy room, she peppered a Bloody Mary and handed it to him. She was wearing high boots, a long skirt, a striped blouse, and lots of gold chains.

"Got a date tonight?" he asked.

"Yeah. Another creep who thinks he can do Steve Martin imitations." Gloria tapped the pack of cigarettes in his shirt pocket with a carmine fingernail. He nodded, and lit one for her. "Mrs. Sifranco a pain?" she asked.

"At this rate I'll be running a law practice out of my car."

"Not a bad idea. This is L.A., after all."

Bertleman and young Prineas walked past the photocopy room, looked in with identically raised eyebrows, and went on out to lunch.

"What keeps you here?" he asked; then he decided that he wanted to get the question right, now that he'd put his foot in it. "I mean, things are slow. The pay isn't that good . . ."

Gloria took him seriously. "I get my jollies. Small is beautiful, as they say."

Alf stuck his head in the door. His hair was wet, but at least he was wearing a suit. "Welcome back, Dad. Going to the club for lunch?"

"Get back in there and go to work," Gloria said before he could reply. "No lunch until I get that memo, surf bum."

He listened to Alf's steps padding on the carpet. "Wish I could get him to obey me like that."

"He takes it from me 'cause I'm not his old man." Gloria sipped her drink and stared at its red ice. "He's okay, you know. Decent. Unlike some of these others, the guys I always seem to end up with."

"Well, why don't you get him and we'll all go to lunch."

"Celebrating?"

"Yeah. I'm breaking my diet before I'm too poor to. This might be my last chance."

They went to a restaurant and not the club, because Gloria was along: one of Jean's rules that he didn't like to think too much about. "So, how was Delaware?" Alf asked. He summarized. Alf exploded: "What a bunch of hoods! Why is this Dante above the law, anyway? Hey, the Rebels play the Raiders next week. Let's toss him in the can for non-compliance."

It irritated him that in three months Alf hadn't grasped the fundamentals of the case. "We can't touch him, that's why. The deal says the team pays."

"So arrest the team."

"Don't be silly. And Alf, you'll never learn a damn thing about law if your attitude is to throw everyone who crosses your path into jail. You mediate, you persuade, you conciliate."

"And how far has that gotten you? I say we put leg irons on the Rebel team. Like a chain gang." Alf thrust out his beard at Charlie and, holding the tip between thumb and forefinger, wiggled it at him.

Charlie saw red—literally. He clenched his fists and felt the blood in his forearms throb urgently around the bend of his elbows, felt his heart's recoil thumping at the base of the brain.

"Charlie," Gloria said.

"Hey, Dad, are you all right?"

Why, I almost struck him, he thought.

"You'd—just better—" He caught his breath, "start looking for another situation, you keep that up."

Gloria handed him a glass of ice water. "Charlie," she said softly. She laid a hand on his arm. To get his attention. "He's right, you know. Alf's right. They'll bleed you by making you come to them. They'll put you off with continuances. But they are coming to California. Next week. Up in Oakland."

"So?"

"Isn't there something you can do?"

"Serve Dante's boss a subpoena," Alf said promptly.

"Not enough," he said. "That can't hurt them."

"The publicity could."

"Charlie," Gloria said. "What *can* hurt them?"

He paused to look at her. She'd been with him for two years, and what he saw was a long, freckled face with lips slightly parted by buck-teeth. Huge eyes, blue, intense. What he'd always seen was a woman in her thirties, with no husband, and with a child. Striking, but not pretty. A woman with a past. This was a woman with a future. He looked at her, saw that she was right, and was simply afraid.

"I'm not paying you enough for this," he said to her. "Not for all the trouble you're causing."

"What about me? She makes more than me as it is," Alf said.

Gloria reached over and patted Alf's hand. "He pays you too much already."

Alf sat back in his chair. "No fair ganging up."

"I know a judge," Charlie said. When he had their attention he went on. "He'll give me an injunction if my reasoning is sound."

"What sort of injunction?"

"One stopping the Rebels from engaging in any business in California, so long as the debt is outstanding and there is reason to believe that payment is being unlawfully avoided."

"Business?" Alf asked. "Just business?"

"Dummy," Gloria said. "He means the game, of course."

"But with an entire firm of lawyers at their disposal, they'll have it overturned in no time," Alf objected.

Gloria watched Charlie as she spoke. "That's why we deliver it Friday afternoon. After the courts close for the weekend. Right?"

He nodded. She held his eyes for a moment longer than necessary.

"They could still call an extraordinary session," Alf pointed out. "And they will."

Charlie hunched over the table. "They'll have to argue before the same judge—my old evidence professor," he said. "The real problem is going to be serving the injunction in person to the right guy. We won't be getting a second chance, once they're on their guard."

To track down the owner of the Rebels, Gloria phoned their headquarters, announced that she led their booster club and wanted to greet the team, and got the name of the airport and time of the flight. It was coming in on Friday evening, so they booked a shuttle to Oakland that arrived a couple of hours before. Once they got in, Alf hung around the ticket counters until a baggage handler, well-tipped, gave him the gate number. Charlie had visited his old evidence professor that morning and had obtained the injunction; old Fright Wright made no comment other than to say, "I'll be off fishing on the Pierpoint Landing day boat

Saturday. That'll give you until a couple of hours after sunset—I won't be able to hold them off longer than that."

Early Friday evening was quiet, and the Oakland terminal felt sleepy. Charlie watched from a window as a chartered airbus unloaded passengers at a deserted corner of the airfield. About ten people were waiting inside the lobby; a dozen more lined the edge of the landing strip. There was a low chain-link fence separating the runway and baggage handling area from the deserted public roadway. Two policemen stood by to prevent anyone from getting too close, in this case within twenty-five feet. They were laughing at some fool in red long underwear, a cloth tail, pointed felt ears, and cat whiskers drawn on his cheeks in lipstick, who was prancing up and down alongside the tarmac, pounding on a drum, and waving a stuffed Johnny Reb. Next to him bounced a very tall blonde in a cheerleader's outfit, cowboy hat, and beaded, sequined cape hemmed in ostrich feathers. She held a sign: GO REBELS!

The players and coaches, nearly eighty in all, filed past without taking notice. Charlie searched among them for the team owner, superretailer Arthur Lash. He didn't see anyone who might be him, but then Charlie didn't know what Arthur Lash looked like, just that he was over sixty and had been divorced four times.

The last of the players were vanishing inside when Charlie saw the three limousines parked at the tail of the plane, on the side away from the terminal. The first of the three began pulling out, without lights, and the rest followed. Alf spotted them first. He and Gloria switched their attention to the cars, dancing frantically in their makeshift costumes, bending at the waist and calling, beating on the drum. Both policemen walked over and stood beside them.

The limousines were passing ten feet away when Gloria stuck out a leg and began high-kicking. She and Alf chanted a name. Charlie couldn't hear through the glass, but he knew what name it was: "Arthur Lash! Arthur Lash!"

The middle limousine pulled out of line and slowed. The tinted windows offered no view inside.

Alf did a handstand. Gloria danced a fast solo Charleston. The limousine stopped, idling. She blew several kisses, then danced right between the guards and up to the passenger window. Hands on her hips, she bent and kissed the glass. Charlie saw the red lipstick mouth left behind start to slide down. A man's head filled the space, a smiling man, who nodded at Gloria's question and thrust his lips up to be kissed. Instead she dropped an envelope in his lap.

Charlie watched until she'd danced safely back between the guards. Then he went into a phone booth, dialed the *Los Angeles Times*, got the sports editor, and said "This is Charlie Wickham; we met at Little Joe's once. Here's an exclusive for you. The Rebels–Raiders game has been halted by an injunction filed over the failure of owner Arthur Lash to make child support payments to the former wife of Dante Sifranco. A copy of the documents will be at the front desk of your paper in half an hour."

Saturday morning, Charlie lay in bed with a hangover and read the papers. The *Times* put it on page one and in sports, playing up the little-guy-versus-big-organization theme. They only used one line from the carefully written, five-page statement that Charlie had attached to the documents, and that came from the cover letter to the sports editor. "Attorney Wickham," went the story, "in defending the use of what some might call a grandstand play, stated, 'These [the Rebel organization] aren't good guys. Good guys don't skip child support payments. Good guys don't go out of their way to humiliate you.' Not the sort of remark that will go down in legal history, perhaps, but then Attorney Wickham says he isn't interested in fame, only in what is right."

Jean switched from channel to channel for the morning television news. One newscaster got it wrong and announced that the children were Arthur Lash's by Cathy Sifranco; when corrected on the air, she laughed brashly and said, 'Well, I thought maybe they traded the children, too."

Not long after, the telephone rang. Jean answered, covered the mouthpiece, and whispered, "Cathy Sifranco."

He took the phone into the bathroom and closed the door. "Charlie, how could you?" were her first words. "What have you done?"

"You hired yourself a lawyer. It's my job to get results." He could hear the television on at her place, loud.

"Well, Dante just called and he's real freaked out. This is just terrible for his career. You've got to—"

"Mrs. Sifranco," he interrupted. "Dante's career only concerns me insofar as he continues to contribute to the support of you and your children. My oath of ethics won't allow me to use any other basis for my decision."

"What about me? I'll never be able to live in this town after this."

"That's your decision."

He was in the shower for the first call from the Rebels. "Say I'll call back," he shouted to Jean. He dressed, put some papers in his briefcase, and kissed Jean on the forehead. "I'll be out until dinner. Nobody knows where I am."

She held onto his arm and stared at him. "Where are you going, lover?"

He discovered that he wasn't entirely comfortable being adored. "It's a secret." Jean's face fell. "To the office," he whispered.

Alone in his office, behind closed doors, Charlie watched a good college game on the little Sony while Gloria fielded the phone calls. Alf paced the empty halls deep in thought, stroking his beard and occasionally taking down a volume of *West's Annotated Codes* and skimming a case. He'd worn his best three-piece suit on his day off.

The intercom buzzed. "That was the senior partner of the law firm, Big Daddy," said Gloria. "Somebody pulled him off the golf course in Orlando and was he steamed."

"You explained of course that I'd be in at eight Monday morning."

"I did. I hope his pacemaker was working."

The intercom buzzed during halftime. Penn State was up by a field goal, Paterno a genius. "Can I show you the champagne and cheese basket and smoked salmon that just arrived? Compliments of the Rebels. Oh, and Jean just called to report that the wife of Mr. Lash has sent her roses."

"How many roses?"

"I don't know."

"Call back and find out."

The intercom buzzed. "Two dozen, in a Limoges vase."

"Better. Getting better."

He pulled out a pad and began to figure his expenses. He buzzed Gloria. "No interruptions please." He put away his pack of cancer sticks and lit a low-tar cigarette. He stared at *The Flying Cloud*. Fifty-two, he thought. Fifty-two years old and I've finally made it. He seemed to see his whole life before him, telescoped into sections: early years; difficult youth; the law; waiting for the call; time of trial; victory. What next? Years of glory. A celebrity practice. A reputation. All he'd have to do was appear in Arthur Lash's suite at the Beverly Hills Hilton, pause until people noticed him, then watch Arthur Lash come to him. In that one gesture the facts of his previous existence would be swept away. They would only know him as the man who'd taken on the Rebels and won. That's how legends were started.

He thought of how his life had become entwined with Dante Sifranco's; out of goodwill he'd boosted Dante for years, in exchange for just a touch of the hero's garment. Now, suddenly, when it seemed that Dante had risen to the top, he'd planted one foot on Dante's back and soared above him.

That's how it's done, he thought. You finally figured it out.

The intercom buzzed. "Excuse the interruption, Charlie," said Gloria. "It's the walking one-and-only himself. Give 'em hell."

He smiled at that—Gloria had known when he'd yield. She knew him, better than anyone, better even than . . . Jean. He picked up the phone. "Charlie Wickham here."

"Charlie?" asked a voice with a trace of a New Jersey accent. "Art Lash. My lawyers bill five hundred bucks an hour and this is what I get. They don't even tell me about any Sifranco woman—they say they didn't want to bother me. Well, now I'm bothered, right? Good and bothered. What do you want? Be frank."

"First the contract."

"That's fine. You got it. I'll sign on the dotted line. Give the broad her due. Now, what can I do for you? I've got a box here at the stadium, it's just me and the wife and a few friends, Hollywood people, entertainers, the press—why don't you and the wife come on up and join us for the game tomorrow? I feel I owe it to you, Charlie."

"About my expenses—"

"The same as my lawyers get. Bill in at five hundred per hour. Add on the expenses, everything. What else?"

"Well, I can't bring myself to deal with any of the attorneys handling your countersuit."

"You won't have to, Charlie. Those guys are all gone. Fired. The suit is dropped. We'll give you a paper on that. Why don't you come up to the Polo Lounge right now and we'll take care of everything. You'd be doing me a favor, you know. I'd very much like to meet you. Bring your wife and your kids, they can meet O.J. Simpson—joking! Not Mrs. Sifranco's kids, mind you. My wife doesn't understand where they fit in. That's dinner at the Polo Lounge at eight, cocktails at six. Sound all right?"

Charlie held his breath just for a moment before exhaling.

"Thanks, Art. I'll send the papers by associate and instruct him to pick up the check, the signatures, and your paper dropping the lawsuit. I'm afraid we can't make the dinner tonight. Too short notice to cancel our other engagements."

"Sorry to hear it, Charlie. You're coming to the game, though, aren't you?"

"No, I don't think so."

"You sure?"

"I'm afraid we can't."

"Gonna be a good one, you know."

"I've got my usual Sunday golf date with my wife. Long-standing thing. But I'll try to tune in during the fourth quarter. Oh, do thank Mrs. Lash for the roses. They were lovely."

"Roses? What roses?" Another voice muttered faintly in the background. "Oh, *roses*. Okay, Charlie. It's been a pleasure, right? No hard feelings, I hope."

"Good-bye, Art."

"Hey. Wait a minute." Arthur Lash struggled to control his anger. "I can be a good sport about this, and I'm the loser. Why can't you be a good sport about winning?"

He thought about that. It sounded like something Coach Henle would say. Something that he, Charlie, believed in.

"It wasn't much of a game to me," he said. "I'm a lawyer. When I want to think about sports, I read the sports page."

He gave Arthur Lash the consolation of being the first to hang up.

Turning to the pad on which he'd figured his expenses, he picked up a pen. Where his standard fee would be fifty dollars per hour, he wrote in five hundred. It looked fine. He'd always wanted to be paid like a New York lawyer, just once in his life.

When he entered the front room, Gloria stood up, smiling.

He bent across the counter top and kissed her on the forehead. "That's for pulling me through this," he said.

"Anytime, Charlie." Her eyes were shining.

"Way to go, Dad," shouted Alf from the photocopy room. There was a pop of a cork. "Be out in a minute." Liquid splashed on linoleum.

In a silence that grew comfortable in its complicity, the prospect of a different future kept him from what he had to say. Then he took hold of himself. Today he was strong; tomorrow would be another story.

"I'm going to be sorry to lose you," he said. She stopped smiling.

"Who says you have to lose me?" she asked, and brushed the hair off her face.

He cheated, and pretended to stare down the hall. His face stared back at him, reflected in the clear glass partition between the secretaries' desks and the lawyers' offices. He studied it. His tongue felt thick, his lips dry. "We both know I do." "I do."

Back in the photocopy room, Alf dropped some glasses with a great crash. "Don't worry," he shouted. "They're plastic."

"Well, I'm in no big hurry," she said. "You're not going to rush me out the door, are you?"

She propped her elbows on the counter, and put her face in her cupped palms of her hands. Her expression was open to interpretation.

This time he didn't look away. "I hope not," he said. "I hope it won't come to that." He watched her eyes begin to smile again; he was actually sorry not to be weaker. "But if I have to, I will."

"Here we are," called Alf.

Charlie turned. Alf came walking up the hallway, lightly on tiptoe, carrying three glasses of champagne. He was in a direct line with the reflection on the glass, and as Charlie watched, Alf's face gradually filled in the outlines of Charlie's own. He looked like a younger version of himself, in his youthful beard and autumn tweeds, of a different generation and time, the Charlie he might have become. There was something reckless about him, something selfish that would be unsatisfied with just one day and night of testing his limits. It was a vision better glimpsed than attained. It was all he would get. It was enough.

My Stunt Wife

by Michael Guerra

As her husband often says, "Marriage to a woman who's famous for her aerial off the Hoover Dam can be extremely difficult." Jesse is Hollywood's leading stuntwoman. And her ex-con husband, former badass that he is, takes enormous pride in his wife's career. In addition to being the Valley's top copier repair guy, he cooks, sews, and attends a stunt-spouse support group. But his therapist has the hots for him and his wife's producer wants to see more than a double-back-flip-scissor-kick. Ah, the joys of films where the most memorable lines tend to be, "Back off!" True Lies meets Woman of the Year.

Marriage to a woman who's famous for her aerial off the Hoover Dam can be extremely difficult. Between the pyrotechnics and the motorcycle crashes, it's a tough business just keeping her clothed. We're in L.A. for the premiere of her latest film, *Smoked*, and Jesse has already torn her dress. She insisted on a size seven when I knew the nine would have fit better across her shoulders—a husband knows a few things. The way she's cut, she does a whole lot better in spandex. Let's just say her wardrobe suffers the assault of her daily needs. "Hold still," I say, mending the sequins beneath her armpit. "I'm almost through."

She's seated next to me in the limo talking on the phone with her agent. She's up for the role as another sultry undercover spy. Her agent thinks parachuting from a flaming jetliner will boost her career. He thinks landing on the St. Louis Arch is a good idea.

Nobody's asked what an ex-con thinks. Nobody wants to discuss wind velocity at ten thousand feet. I did two years for insurance fraud, so what would I know about the landing details on a stainless steel surface? I'm no expert, but this parolee has cleaned a few sinks. They're slippery. Add a chute and a natural curve to the equation and you've got a recipe for disaster. "Do the math," I tell her. "The last person to try a stunt like this died."

Jesse holds her hand over the receiver and mouths the words, *Not now*, while I'm sizing up her C cup. She has no idea how vulnerable she is, how dangerously close I am to poking her with the needle.

"I have to go," Jesse says to her agent. "Evan's in one of his moods. I'll call you when we get back to New York."

After she hangs up, she touches my neck tracing the outline of my tattoo. "You're obsessing," she says.

I tie a thief's knot and bite off the thread. "I'm not the one holding my wrist," I say. "Look at you."

"It's fine," she says.

But it's not fine. It's swollen. She's been rubbing it for the last five minutes and I can tell it hurts. She suffers from premature arthritis due to the stress of an active lifestyle. Ever since the union lost its leverage thanks to NAFTA, the industry's been getting away with cheap Canadian imports. Safety standards are practically nonexistent. She does a simple crash-and-roll on a Harley and ends up spraining her wrist on dry asphalt because some hourly hack forgot the oily surface spraydown—and she wonders why I worry.

"I'm worried," I say.

She adjusts her slip and crosses her legs. She's all business now. "I'll have lines this time," she says, as if a speaking part is going to keep our insurance premiums from skyrocketing through the roof. I love her, but she isn't very practical. Last year she had our entire apartment remodeled around a biplane, circa 1927. It once belonged to one of the first female aviation pioneers. She picked it up at auction, and now it hangs from the rafters suspended above the new eight-burner stove. I mention fire codes and cloth-covered wings over an open flame and the next thing I know I'm being called reactionary. I'm spoiling the prospects of ownership. She says a plane by Pancho Barnes doesn't come along every day. I say, *Who the fuck is she?* and Jesse just shakes her head and gives me the look. Next thing I know her agent's on the phone, and then her stunt coordinator. They're like a gang. They all stick together, wear me down.

I can't win.

So she gets a plane, while my plans for a game room complete with a shooting range and a pool table gets all shot to hell. My therapist says Jesse is overcompensating because she's past her prime. She's thirty. This doesn't mean I'm ready to be a widower. My therapist says this doesn't mean I'm not a good person.

Jesse pins her platinum hair up off of her neck. "Now you're upset," she says.

"Not upset," I lie. That's what I do these days. I pretend everything is wonderful. Our marriage, our life together, the need to ride motorcycles beneath moving trucks—is all perfectly normal.

She holds the door handle, and at any moment I expect her to open it and jump. She does that sometimes. "You've been talking to Cindy," she says. "Haven't you?"

Jesse doesn't approve of my therapist. She sees my group, "Spouses of X-treme Occupations," as a bunch of miserable, self-loathing gossips, because once during a meeting at our place she overheard Cindy talk trash about SWAT being an "old boy's club." I won't defend Cindy's politics, but I do know this: You can only take the pros and cons of machine-washable flak jackets so far. Besides, Cindy's my therapist. Can I help it if her husband's a mercenary for this outfit based in Bogotá? Between kidnappings and government takeovers, he calls wanting to know what's for dinner. And although I have taught Cindy and a few of the girls from group how to play poker, we're in consensus—sometimes a spouse needs more than a Tuesday night with the girls in a smoke-filled room, no matter how many beers and five-dollar minimums are at stake.

"No," I say. "Cindy has nothing to do with us."

Jesse opens the sunroof. "Spare me," she says, before climbing out on the roof. "I know what you're up to, Evan." She's mad because earlier in the week I hinted at the fact that she hasn't taken a break in two years. And now, with a *Smoked* sequel in the works, Cindy says I need to be more assertive of my needs.

As she climbs out on the roof, I yell, "I simply suggested to my wife that we spend a few quiet weeks riding Harleys through South Dakota. Is it my fault you canceled?" In truth, she had a kidnapping sequence in a helicopter that ended up on the bottom of the Hudson. I was in the kitchen, bags packed, and I get the call: "Sorry, honey. I'm a little tied up right now."

"I was working," she yells over the noise. We're on the 405, and traffic is surprisingly light.

"You're always working. Now it's the Arch," I say, as she crawls across the roof. We're speeding along at seventy miles an hour when I grab for an ankle and hold onto her heel. "Can't we talk about this?"

"I signed a contract," Jesse says. "I'm *committed*."

She uses the "C" word, which I have to admit doesn't come up much in our relationship. Words like *compromise* and *accommodation*, which seem to come up often enough in group, rarely seem to lend themselves to the stunt world—especially free-falling from a jumbo jet. Still, Jesse isn't usually so emotional.

"What the fuck's your problem?" I ask.

"Let go," she says, kicking her heel into my face.

"What'd I do?" I'm bleeding now, and a bit self-conscious knowing the driver's been eyeing us since the airport.

"Sir?" he says into the rearview. "Should I pull over?"

"No," I tell him, wiping my lip. "She just needs some air."

Aerial acrobatics may be Jesse's specialty, but some nights before bed I just want to make love on the trampoline, like we used to. Some nights I just want to be her big hairy ape again. Can I help it if I'm happy with my day job? I fix copy machines, *so what?* I'm the best service rep in the New York metropolitan area two years running. You want accolades? Ask me about my seventeen awards. You want speed? I can replace drum rollers in less than three minutes. My work is more than a steady paycheck—it's security. And in this high-tech, globalized economy the odds on paper jams are staggering. People need my services. When I'm working, I do have confidence in what I do. I am a good person. Jesse, on the other hand, performs an aerial out of a thirty-story window, and afterwards, when the endorphin rush subsides, she's left with nothing but this huge wave of ambiguity that takes weeks for her to sort out. I've seen it. After the Hoover Dam, she wouldn't leave the apartment. I'd go to work in the morning and she'd still be hanging around, suspended from the ceiling, when I got home at six. And the things that we used to do together—the late night motorcycle rides across Central Park, or the occasional wheelie down Fifth Avenue—have become chores.

I've been there.

After I got out of jail, I didn't know what I was going to do. I was ready to go back to collecting insurance. Then I met Jesse. We were both stepping out in front of the same car for different reasons, and my whole life changed. The things I had once held sacred were no longer necessary. Sure, when we were first married, Jesse faked a slip on a wet floor for a measly insurance settlement. But looking back, I know she did it for me. She pawned a truly amazing flip into a salad bar for a month of free rent. We were broke at the time, and although it was technically my idea, we've carried that with us. We can't change the past, but at the same time I've tried to let her know she doesn't have to take every job that comes along. She doesn't have to jump off the Arch, afraid there may not be a next time, because in her line of work there may never be a next time.

Before we hit Century City, Jesse climbs back in the limo. Her hair is windblown, to say the least, and when I offer to comb it, she says "Don't." She sits away from me and turns on the TV. It reminds me of home. Some evenings, after a long day of barroom fights, she gets like this—all reticent and tense—where all she wants to do is lie on the couch and watch reruns of CHiPs. The trick is to ignore her, but when the driver pulls up to the marquee and the lights hit that little scar beneath her chin, it's everything I can do to keep from sticking my tongue in her mouth.

"Evan, don't," she says, pushing me away. This is my role now. My boys in 4C would kick my ass if they knew what I'd become. I look out the window, and there glaring at me are the names Lilith Graham and Sven Olfssen, the stars of *Smoked*, up in lights. It's typical. Jesse does most of the work, for a blurb in the back section of *Variety*. She gets one sentence: "Ms. Graham graciously acknowledges her 'indebtedness to her stunt coordinator, Jesse.'" It's truly an actor's world.

The driver opens the door and Jesse steps out onto the red carpet where three zit-faced teenagers with digital cameras immediately assault her. They're leaning over the ropes asking her to sign autographs. Two years ago the makers of a video game recreated her physique with computer-enhanced animation. They transformed her into the action hero Juice Balens. Now, in its third edition, she's idolized by gaming geeks nationwide. The risk-free environment of virtual reality is a definite plus, but I could do without teens groping my wife.

"Hey Juice! Show us your Turbo Slam!" one kid yells.

"In these heels?" Jesse says. "You've got to be kidding." Then, before the kid has time to make some smart-ass remark, Jesse hikes her dress and does a flip with a double kick level with the kid's face. I'm just glad she's wearing underwear.

With all the excitement, I hardly notice Sven Olfssen, the big Swede with the spiked blond hair, until a mob of young women rush past us trying to get him to sign their tits before he even has time to get out of the car. Still reeling from the recognition he gained from his last film, *I'll Die for You*, he's the man. Among his credits, he's a precision driver. He's one of the few actors to perform his own stunts.

The lights are flashing all around him as he approaches and I notice a smile on Jesse's face—the first all evening. "He's so gay," I say, letting her know the tan escort straddling Sven's elbow isn't fooling anyone.

Jesse squeezes my snake tattoo around the neck, and I tell her to go easy.

"Relax," she says.

But I can't. Not until the flash subsides and the little spots in my vision disappear. Inside, the usher leads us down the aisle. There's white linen on all the tables, and waiters, ready to take our drink orders, stand off to the side. There's a full orchestra in the middle of "Mood Indigo," and we're up front in the reserved section, standing next to Larry Leibowitz, the action film producer. He's wearing his trademark orange sunglasses and a bolo tie. Just looking at him, you'd never guess he's bankrolled over thirty films in his career, not to mention the night's private screening. This is his night, and as he kisses Jesse I notice his hand lingering on the small of her back a bit longer than it should, because he thinks he's earned the right.

"You remember Evan," Jesse says.

Leibowitz nods. We've met half a dozen times. Twice, on the set of *In Your Face*. "Kevin," he says, shaking my hand. "Nice meeting you."

"Likewise."

Sven Olfssen makes his way over and pats Jesse's shoulder, then turns to me. "Congratulations," he says. We've never met, and before I can introduce myself, he says in a thick accent "You must be proud." He says it like Jesse is my daughter, and I run my fingers across my scalp because he's looking down at the top of my head. It's thinning, I know. I'm going gray. "Yeah," I say. "I'm very proud."

Sven pulls away from the blonde attached to his elbow and leans in close to my ear. "Your wife's one badass motherfucker," he says.

"The baddest," I say, motioning for the waiter because I'm thirsty, and when he comes, Sven orders a Flaming Torpedo and I get a Rum and Coke. "Diet," I say, noticing Sven still hasn't introduced his date. "What are you drinking?" I ask her.

"Get her a glass of Gewürztraminer," Sven says, before telling her where to sit. "Bring the whole bottle." Then he turns to me and puts his arm around my shoulders like we're best buds. He's wearing a leather jacket over his tux and smells like Old Spice. He's a foot taller, but I figure I could take him if it came to that.

"What's this about the Arch?" I ask, because Jesse doesn't tell me anything.

He eyes my biceps. "How much you press?" he says.

When I tell him, he invites me to his gym. "You should talk to my trainer."

"I'll be sure and do that," I say.

When the waiter returns with our drinks, Sven goes off on his precision-driving skills, explaining how he's recently trained the NYPD. "It's practically a license to speed," he says, then sets his drink down on the nearest table. "If you have any trouble, just tell them Sven Olfssen said to 'Back off.'" It's the one line from *I'll Die for You*, the one line people will remember after he's dead.

It's so sad. I don't want to like Sven Olfssen or his flaming drink that is about to ignite the tablecloth, but there's something about the stunt world credo, something that should put me at ease when he says, "She can handle it."

"Will you excuse us?" Jesse says, taking my arm. She knows my concerned look, as I hers. She's telling me I better keep it together.

We all sit down in our seats and Leibowitz attempts to grab my hand over Jesse's lap, grappling for the chance to touch her some more. At the next table, Tommy "Cannonball" Bucco is fondling his date beneath the tablecloth. He's one of the shortest stunt coordinators in the business. During the late seventies, when *Fantasy Island* and Hervé— "Da plane, boss, da plane"—Villachaize was big time, Cannonball cornered the market as a double for anyone under four feet tall. If you had a small person in your act that required some dangerous stunt, you called Cannonball. Everybody knows Cannonball Bucco—except his date. She's of normal height, seems to be of normal sensibilities, and smitten by his abnormal confidence and charm. The only thing that comes to mind is *run! Get out. Before you're up late at night afraid to answer the phone.*

Leibowitz leans over again. "Hey. Don't worry," he says into my wife's tits. "This next picture will make both of you very comfortable."

"We are comfortable," I say, and Leibowitz looks at me for the first time.

"Good to hear it," he says, offering me a glass of wine.

"No thanks," I say, while Jesse finishes off her third glass, and wipes her chin. She's never been much of a drinker.

Sven's date is seated to my left and I strike up a conversation. I've seen her around. "You do movies?" I ask. She seems extremely bored, running her fork along the edge of the doily.

"A few," she says, naming a couple of porns that went straight to video. "*Fields of Cream* sounds familiar," I say, and between polite nods she sighs, then excuses herself from the table, leaving me with the floral arrangement. Alone.

Looking around the room it all starts making sense: Leibowitz. Sven Olfssen. Cannonball. They're all part of the act. Jesse has already signed up. A husband is always the last to know.

I take the red-eye back to New York and Cindy is waiting for me at JFK. We're headed toward baggage and she's crying. "Run away with me," she says. "I promise I'll never do anything too dangerous."

"Now you sound like Jesse," I tell her.

"Why is it you always seem to find your confidence with me?" she says.

"That hurts."

"What if I told you I'm through ironing flak jackets?"

"I'd tell you he would never notice."

She stops in front of the gift shop, and behind her shoulder there's a toy airplane spinning in circles on a string. "Do you think it's wrong to leave a note?" she says. "Should I have called instead?"

"You do what you do," I say.

The truth is Cindy and I are a lot alike. We both have trouble saying no, which is probably why we've only had sex once. We both knew it wasn't quite in keeping with the shrink's code of professional ethics, but exceptions have to be made. And it was before I'd met Jesse.

Years ago, Jesse and I agreed never to leave each other mad. We made a promise to ourselves. Call it superstitious. Irrational. Of course, we've had our differences like any couple. There were times when she's wanted me to throw her down a flight of stairs and I flat-out refused. And once when we were coming home from her mother's she wanted me to push her out of the car for old time's sake. But never in the seven years since we've been together have we left each other angry. And yet, after the band wrapped up the night with "Meet Me in St. Louis," I knew it was time to leave. When people like Cannonball start breaking the wineglasses and swinging from the chandeliers, it's time. Sven Olfssen mentioned something about Hooper's—this bar in West Hollywood that caters to the stunt crowd—and I declined. I can only take so many barroom brawls, and Jesse and I have reached our quota. The whole night came down to her holding her wrist against a glass of ice water. She insisted everything was good, and then, when she thought I wasn't looking, Leibowitz slipped her some pills. Some kind of prescription painkiller. I tell this to Cindy in front of the gift shop.

"Did you hear me? I left my husband," she says. But I'm watching the airplane spin in circles over her shoulder. I need sleep. I shouldn't have asked Jesse if she'd slept with Leibowitz. I shouldn't have questioned her about Sven.

"Look at me," Cindy says, holding my face in her hand. "Your wife has certain things she needs to work out. *On her own.*"

She wants me to hug her, and when I oblige I realize I could never be with a woman who doesn't work out at least six hours a day. She's too lumpy and short for my taste. But it's more than simply physical, because Jesse is more than a tight ass. She's complicated. She has issues, yes—any woman who uses the Hoover Dam as a springboard has issues—but for the sake of argument I tell Cindy a woman who can bench-press as much as me kind of turns me on.

"So it's over?" she says.

"I'm sorry," I say, trying to sound assertive. "I like a woman with a firm stomach. I like a belly with bounce."

"Fine. Call me later. After she's disappointed you again."

"No, Cindy. I can't."

All morning at work, I'm in a daze. I can't concentrate. At Johnson & Schumacher the kid in receiving has a picture of Juice Balens tacked to his cubicle, and when I crawl into the copier to take it apart, he asks if I have some kind of strange death wish before he pulls the plug for me. Jesse won't answer her phone. I've left voice mails, and nothing. It's not like her. At lunch, Hepler, my supervisor, tells me he just got a message from that kid. Seems I forgot to put the toner back in before I left. "You all right?" he asks, finishing the last of his pastrami. "Because you don't seem all right."

Hepler's like family. We met through my parole officer. I've known him almost as long as I've known my wife. Some Fridays he lets me leave early so I can catch an afternoon flight to L.A., or wherever Jesse happens to be shooting. I know he looks forward to the glossy photos of Jesse in spandex every Christmas, but he also cares.

"I need this job," I tell him.

"I know," he says, then tells me to take the rest of the afternoon off.

I hit the corner and take a cab past all the reminders of our life: the place on Broadway where Jesse once jumped from a bus; the little bakery shop on Forty-seventh where she once slammed me through the plateglass window for eating with my mouth open. Everywhere I go in the city reminds me of her, and when I walk in the front door I know she's been home because her Kawasaki is parked in the foyer. It's warm, and her flame-retardant suit on the floor is still smoldering. I'll never get over that smell, but I've learned not to get on her case about leaving burned clothes on the tile. I'm just glad she's back. "Jesse?" I say. "Honey? I'm home." My voice sounds thin as it echoes off the fifty-foot ceiling. In the living room the trampoline, the biplane, even the surface of the Jacuzzi are all perfectly still. There aren't any of her fingerprints on the new stainless steel fridge, but her clothes are strewn up the stairs and down the hall to the bedroom, and for a moment I get that sinking feeling, like maybe she's not alone. Upstairs, the bathroom mirrors over the sink are wet with condensation from a hot bath, and on the makeup counter next to the toilet is a note: "Are you cheating on me?"

An hour later Jesse calls. She's at Hooper's II in the village. I can tell because I hear Sven's voice over the karaoke singing the theme song to *Smokey and the Bandit*. I figure she's been drinking, hitting the Molotovs at a steady pace, when she tells me she hasn't touched the stuff since I spilled the merlot down the front of Leibowitz's white suit.

"It was an accident," I say, trying to explain, but she wants none of it.

"Maybe I should just settle down into gaming, like we talked about," she says.

"It's not the money, is it?"

"Evan. Don't make me choose. I can't help it."

I press the receiver up to my mouth. "Will you come home now?"

"Will you make me dinner?"

"Of course, baby. You know I will. Just come home."

Since the remodel I've become pretty handy in the kitchen. If there's one thing I can do better than Jesse, it's cook—and I want to surprise her. I want to have everything prepared when she gets home, so I do up my version of a steak fajita, something with white bread and plenty of onions. When the door rings I tell her it's open, and there standing in the service elevator is Cindy. She's wearing this yellow outfit I helped pick out a few months back. It's festive and sort of square at the shoulders to help hide her ass.

She reaches up to kiss my cheek. "You need to shave," she says. "I thought for sure you'd call."

"I haven't had a chance."

She steadies her hand against my shoulder and takes off her heels, looking at me in a way I've never noticed before, a way that doesn't lend itself to group. I start to say something while she pulls off her nylons and shoves them in my pocket, but before I get a word out, she's running her finger along the stainless steel island making her way around to the stove. "What's for dinner?" she says. "I'm starved."

She's drunk and staring at the Jacuzzi beneath the living room window.

"You can't stay," I tell her. "Jesse should be home any minute."

She turns on the jets and unzips her skirt. "That's too bad," she says, letting it fall to the floor. "I thought we might spend a nice quiet evening together."

"Look Cindy, this is no good," I say, as she unbuttons her blouse.

"Oh Evan, stop. You just want someone you can look after."

When Jesse appears in the doorway Cindy's naked in the hot tub while I'm dousing the flames in the kitchen. I can't say exactly where in the fight with Cindy—between the coaxing and the arguing—the steak caught fire. I'm not sure when the flames shot straight up and ignited the skin covering the biplane, or how the grease started dancing across the wings. All I know is our insurance company is going to be suspicious, and my parole officer will probably be paying me a visit. Then there's Cindy. She's letting me have it with the insults and a spiked heel. Her arms are flying off in every direction, as she clips me just below the left ear. I take another to the gut before she grabs her clothes and heads toward the elevator, her wet feet slapping across the tile. "You're nothing but a whipped house boy," she says before the elevator closes.

And I suppose I deserve that, because through all of this is Jesse. Cool and levelheaded Jesse who doesn't say a word as she opens the hall closet and pulls out the high-powered rifle. Smoke billows from the engine of the plane and flames begin to engulf the kitchen. All around me is this black smoke, with Jesse rummaging through the box of explosives on the closet floor. She finally grabs the three-pronged hook and the nylon rope.

"Wow," she says. "What was that?" She doesn't have to tell me to stand back while she breaks the kitchen window and clears the ledge of any loose shards. Her wrist is still swollen, but she takes my hand and I try to apologize.

"Save it," she says, helping me out onto the fire escape, because I'm useless now, coughing from the smoke, soot in my eyes.

"I didn't mean to hurt you," I say, as she shoots the hook across to the neighboring building. When it catches on the opposite fire escape she pulls the rope tight and ties it off to the banister. Without a word between us she throws me over her shoulder and takes the rope. If she decides to leave me, I'll understand. But through all of this, everything we've done, I have to believe it's what we do in the daily routine of our lives that makes us who we are. I have to believe that somehow Jesse has already forgiven me, because the whole time I'm on her back suspended between two buildings, sliding fourteen stories above the ground, she's whispering: "This is the reason I married you, you big stupid ape."

A.K.A.

by Gerald O. Ryan

Rudy met Desiree at the strip club. Well, he didn't actually "meet" her, but they did get close during her lap dance. And "Rudy," not surprisingly, wasn't really his name. He soon regretted lying to her, since something (not on a pay-for-play basis) was developing between them. But something wasn't straight—with any of them. And that could be deadly when so much money, drugs, and scamming made up the mix. A cross between Heist *and* Snake Eyes.

He thought she might actually like him. A little. Her hips ground into his during their lap dance, while Desiree looked into his eyes and whispered his name. The name he'd given her, anyway. "Rudy," she moaned into his ear. "Rudy" and her eyelids would close and she pulled herself into him. "Rudy."

When the bouncer wasn't looking, she would pull his hands up to cup her smallish breasts or put them around her whipcord waist. He could feel the taut muscles, like a steel coil wrapped in a smooth, sensual covering. She smiled when he stiffened and jerked his own hips upward. She seemed pleased at the hard-on that sprung to life between them. As a reward, she kissed his ear, darting her cherry tongue in and out, in and out.

He thought it wasn't just the twenties that she would stick demurely into her garter after each dance that kept her coming back. He thought she might actually like him.

He'd noticed her first thing when he and John had come to the Silver Slipper. They'd been on the job with MacInerney Construction for three days. It was Friday and they were ready for a break. If he had to look at one more section of pipe or another hard hat, even his meds wouldn't stop him from cracking and going off on someone. The Slipper was down the block from the motel and looked like a great place to start the weekend. He drove the pick-up. He wouldn't be drinking. His medication automatically made him the designated driver.

After stepping out of the dry ninety-degree summer day, the air conditioning made him shiver. He squinted as his eyes adjusted to the dimly lit tables. It was early and there weren't too many people yet. At either end of the bar, two girls on small stages went through routine motions, bumping and grinding mindlessly at the smiling clowns sitting at the bar. He laughed to himself. *Look who's calling someone else a clown.* Then he heard her voice.

"What's so funny, cowboy?"

Small, maybe five four, even in high heels, brown silky hair that hung in strands to her shoulders, clear brown eyes, a long nose offset by the fullest, reddest lips he could imagine. He stuttered a confused "N-n-uthin" as he stared into her eyes. It didn't register right away that she was topless. He never got past her sparkling, brown eyes.

"Well come on in and sit down. We'll see if we can't keep you smiling."

She took him by his hand and led him to a table in the corner, away from the other girls who were circling the door, looking for new friends. John and a big brunette were arm in arm, headed for the bar, while he was guided into a wide leather chair with a rounded back. Then she was sitting on his lap. Then he knew she was topless.

"What's your name, honey?"

Force of habit made him lie. "Rudy. Rudy Lake."

"Well, Rudy, I haven't seen you in here before. New in town? What do you do? Where you staying?"

He told her yes. He told her about the job. He told her where they were staying. She nodded all the while, never looking away from him. He felt like a small animal must feel as it was hypnotized by the slow dance of a cobra. But he didn't feel threatened, just mesmerized. The usual questions didn't sound mindless and routine to him. The way she talked to him and listened to him made her sound like she really was interested. He thought she might actually like him.

A waitress came by and asked if he wanted a drink and would he be buying one for the lady?

"Ginger ale for me, and whatever . . ." He looked at her and cocked his head.

"Desiree," she said. It was like a cool breeze inside his mind.

". . . whatever Desiree wants is fine with me."

"Not drinking, Rudy? You get stuck being the designated tonight?" He told her that he didn't drink anymore. Because of the medication.

"You got an ulcer or something, Rudy?"

"Or something."

She leaned over and whispered into his ear. "What's the matter with you honey?"

She looked at him funny when he told her the truth, then laughed.

"That's okay. We can still have a good time tonight. I kinda like that funny little smile of yours."

Yeah. He thought she might actually like him.

He sat in a back booth in the busy restaurant, dawdling over a late breakfast, always watching the door. Force of habit. He sat a bit straighter when he saw her walk in, laughing at something funny her friend had said. He recognized the other girl from last night, another "dancer." They sat down with two other girls and opened large plastic-covered menus. In an oversized long-sleeve shirt and jeans, Desiree looked like she might be from around here, or another small town just like it, off an interstate, where everybody knows everyone else, and secrets aren't secret.

He spent some time reading the newspaper, watching her from behind the sports section. Grainy black-and-white pictures of baseball players dissolved as he stared at them.

When he'd run low on twenties last night, and she wasn't devoting her attention to the other patrons as the floor boss at the Slipper directed, she still came to sit with him. Before she took her break outside on the wooden deck to smoke a cigarette and relax, she had motioned for him to come along. They sat on the railing and chatted, looking at the stars, ignoring the occasional blare of music that burst from inside the club whenever someone opened the door. They talked like old friends, remembering old times. Except that she was topless underneath a short silk kimono.

He kept waiting for the come-on, the proposition, but she just talked and talked about her friends, her family, the problem she was having with the air conditioner in her car. It had been a long time since he listened to a girl just talk. He'd opened up with her as well. Sort of. Mostly.

A shaved head poked out the door, followed by a heavily muscled torso. "Break's over, baby."

Desiree cringed a bit and edged closer to him, resting her arm on his. "I'll be right there, Dave," she said over her shoulder. Her boss gave him the once over and he did likewise. Desiree pushed him back against the railing of the patio. "You busy tomorrow, Rudy? We're all going down to the lake. You look like you could use some time on the water. Relax a little. Don't know why, but I kinda like you. You sorta remind me of my old high-school sweetheart. And he kinda reminded me of my daddy."

"I don't want to be your daddy, Desiree."

"Honey, I don't want you to either. I've had enough daddy and men who thought they could daddy me into the sack, and a lot worse." She hesitated. "I just kinda like you. You know?"

He was starting to feel bad about giving her an alias instead of his real name. Besides that one little misspeak, he'd been pretty straight up with her. Even more than with the shrink. Now he wanted her to know his real name, to hear her say it the way she'd whispered "Rudy." But if he told her, she would think he'd lied about everything else. He didn't want her to think that.

"You got a pen and paper? Let me give you my phone number, and if you want to, call me. We'll have a nice time. I'll make some sandwiches and we'll have a picnic. Okay?" The door opened again.

"Break's over, Desiree," the shaved head said, tapping at a nonexistent watch on his wrist. He tensed and moved toward the muscle-bound man. Desiree held onto his arm. "Easy, honey. He's just doing his job." She finished writing on the inside of a matchbook cover and reached up to give him a peck on the cheek. It felt friendly and he leaned against her. The side door next to the wooden deck burst open.

In a stretched rectangular square of light, he saw John being frog-walked between two of the bouncers, one of whom was bleeding from his nose and cursing, the other twisting John's hands and fingers in a police lock. John had fucked up again and was headed out back toward the dumpster for a thumping.

"Excuse me, Desiree. I've got to do something."

He hopped over the railing and moved quickly behind one of the bouncers, grabbing a handful of black ponytail while he took the bouncer's feet out from under him with a leg sweep. As the stunned man went down, he struck him with a fist to the temple. The bouncer lay there dazed. He looked up and saw Desiree watching in surprise.

John had spun around and struck the other man in the stomach, then straightened him up with a knee in the face. He pulled the heavy, black flashlight from the bouncer's belt and was getting ready to go to work on him when more of the club's security staff poured out the door.

"Rick-ee," John yelled. "Get in the truck. Let's get out of here."

He saw Desiree's wide eyes narrow as she heard John shout out the name. Not Rudy. Ricky. Running toward the truck, he looked over his shoulder and saw her staring at him from the deck. John gunned the truck, kicking gravel up from its back wheels into the faces of the security staff, preventing them from reading their license plate. They'd come even with the deck and Desiree. He'd motioned for John to stop.

"My name's Ricky," he'd shouted as he'd looked into her eyes. "Ricky Blake."

Plates banging on the table behind him made him realize he was reading the first line of the lead article on the sports page over and over again. Then he looked up from behind his paper to see her standing there, smiling. Smiling from her eyes. "May I join you? Ricky?"

He thought she might still like him.

Desiree slid in next to him in the booth and motioned for the waitress. "Coffee, rye toast, and a side of bacon, please."

"Same check?" the waitress asked as she wrote. She looked up at Ricky, who didn't speak, just nodded. They sat in silence for a moment. Ricky looked at her friends in the other booth.

"Won't your friends miss you?"

Desiree waved to them. The girl she came in with whispered to the others and they all turned to look him over.

Ricky shifted in his seat, not enjoying being on the receiving end of such scrutiny. "What are they so interested in?"

"Don't play dumb, Ricky. It doesn't look good on you. You aren't quite the sweet, lost soul you looked to be last night. You know, a little confused, a little down. Kinda like a lost dog I just wanted to take home and cuddle."

"I wasn't trying to bullshit you, Desiree. I wouldn't have told you my real name if I was. I like you. I like you a lot."

She shook her head. "What should I believe? Is Rick-ee your real name? What else is made up? All that stuff about your shrink? About what you do? I've heard lots of stories from lots of men. Been fooled and taken advantage of. But I really believed you, honey. You made me cry last night and I haven't cried about a man in years."

He started to answer her but stopped as the waitress brought her order. When she was gone, he took a plastic pill vial out of his shirt pocket and put it down on the table next to her coffee cup. She picked it up, read his name, the medication, and the dosage. While she read, he stirred sugar into his coffee and clinked the spoon inside the cup. She reached over and put her hand over his.

"Cut that out, honey." She left her hand on his. "So it says here you're Ricky Blake and you're taking some pretty heavy medicine. It says you had this filled at the hospital in Springfield. Some of what you said is the truth. But for a guy who's so tranqued up, for somebody who was so happy to get a boner last night, where'd you get the energy to jump over a railing and kick somebody's ass?"

He shrugged. "John was in trouble and, you know, instinct."

"Honey, Ralph and Bruce are no amateurs. They're actually pretty bad guys and I was happy to see them go down. But I think it was more than just instinct. I think you might've done that kinda thing before, that you're pretty good at it. I don't think you and your buddy John are the shit-kickin' pipe-layers you pretend to be. What's up, Ricky? Who are you?"

She still had her hand on his. The air conditioning came on and he felt her shiver. He put his arm around her and drew her in. She resisted for a second, then leaned into him. He put his face in her hair. The shampoo that she used made her smell like vacation.

"All right, I won't lie to you. I haven't always been a construction worker. Maybe I'm not just a construction worker right now. Maybe I can't really talk about it right now. Can you deal with that?"

She took her hand from his, but didn't move away. The clinking started again. How much did he really want to tell her? He liked her but wasn't sure he trusted her yet. Why had she taken such a shine to him? Why had he fallen for her? How would this affect what he and John had to do?

"Yeah, Ricky, I can deal with it. A girl who grew up on the wrong side of the tracks in a Texas oil town can handle about anything. Just as long as you're not a dope dealer or a murderer. That's why I left Odessa."

The clinking stopped.

———

The boat rocked back and forth, bumping the wooden pier. The sun burned through the tree line on the edge of the lake, popping over the hull, making him pull his cap down over closed eyes. Desiree slept next to him, her Lone Star earrings glittering in the sun. She turned against him, emitting occasional high squeaks from her throat as she dreamed. Without moving the rest of his body, he reached across his chest and rubbed his hand on her arm, releasing her from her dream but not waking her. He knew all about bad dreams.

The boat still smelled like sex. Ricky knew that if he wanted to, he could open his eyes and take in her strong dancer's legs and ass, her flat stomach, her lovely breasts and the small trimmed patch of hair between her legs. He felt himself stiffen, opened his eyes to look at her, then turned to fit himself spoon-fashion against her hip. She moved against him in her sleep and he became more aroused. He hadn't felt this good for a while. It was a fool's paradise, he knew.

Pretty soon, he'd have to start taking his meds again. Then it would take dynamite to get him up. *Might as well enjoy it while I can.* He rubbed the smooth skin of her tummy, then the side of her hips. He looked up to see that she was awake and watching him, smiling, pulling his face up to hers.

"Looks like I'm getting a lot more than I bargained for with you, cowboy."

After they'd made love again, they swam in the lake, enjoying the feel of the water on their naked bodies. They splashed each other like kids, chased and caught each other by turns, then kissed as they trod water. Desiree floated on her back, moving her hands ever so slightly to bring her slowly toward the pier. She pulled herself out of the water in one graceful motion and then toweled herself dry. Her hair fell forward as she bent over and wrapped it in the towel. Turning to him, she put her hands on her hips and moved one leg slightly in front of the other.

"Jesus, Desiree, cut it out. You look like a picture in the *Playboys* I used to read when I was a kid."

She laughed and turned, posing for him as she looked over her shoulder. He swam as fast as he could toward the pier. She squealed in mock terror as he climbed the metal ladder and raced toward her across the wooden planks. They kissed again and her eyes widened. "Oh Ricky, you gotta be kidding." He picked her up in his arms and walked back toward the boat. His cell phone rang.

He looked at the caller ID. He put Desiree down and talked as he walked away to the end of the pier. John's voice threw ice on any romantic inclinations he might have had. Not even a hello, how are you, having a good time? Strictly business.

"What'd you find out about the club? What does she know about Baldy? What'd you tell her about us?"

"I told her we were cops and I don't think she really knows anything about what they're up to."

"She thinks we're cops, huh?"

"Why shouldn't she? I showed her my old badge and ID, asked her some cop questions. Told her we were checking into some payoffs on the highway project. That seemed to make her feel better. That we were on the side of 'Truth, Justice, and the American Way,' and all."

Ricky sat down at the end of the pier and let his feet dangle off the edge, patting the water with his toes. Some minnows came over and tried to nibble at them. Holding the phone in the crook of his neck, he turned to watch Desiree wriggle into a snug pair of shorts. *When this is over, I wouldn't mind spending my time like this.* "What did you find out?"

"Nothing yet. Went out to the construction site and hung out for a while. Eddie MacInerney came out of the trailer and asked me what I was doing there. Told him I was waiting for his brother, Charlie, and fell asleep. That I wanted more overtime. That old mobile office trailer with the cardboard taped over the windows, I'm pretty sure that's our meth lab. With those rottweilers chained up outside, I couldn't get too close. I looked in the dumpster and found boxes and empty bottles from Vicks Inhalers, ether bottles, starting fluid, lye crystals, anhydrous ammonia. All the ingredients for cooking up a pile of crystal meth. If we were still DEA, we could make the case just on their garbage. Hold on a minute."

At the other end of the pier, Desiree was still toweling her hair. She looked at him with curious eyes. He waved and held up one finger, he'd only be a minute. John came back on.

"I'm outside the club, inside the fenced-in yard where Eddie parks his disposal trucks. Baldy just pulled up and I don't want him to see me or recognize the car. He came out to the construction office while I was leaving and gave me the once-over pretty good, but I don't think he made me. It's the garbage again, man. They just can't clean up after themselves without leaving a trail."

Last year, when he and John had still been real agents with the DEA, they'd stumbled on half a dozen citations and fines issued to MacInerney Disposal, Eddie's business, but paid for with checks from MacInerney Construction, Charlie's business. Toxic materials kept getting hauled from construction sites and put into landfills. Charlie's construction company was also fined for polluting local ponds and streams. Meth labs generated ten pounds of toxic waste for every pound of methamphetamine they manufactured.

They investigated a little further and found that Eddie and Charlie MacInerney were up to their trash-hauling, pipe-laying elbows in the drug business. Except for the little piece of bad luck that came up, Ricky and John probably would have made the collar and been promoted by now.

Desiree was sitting on a wooden bench at the end of the pier, staring intently into a small mirror as she applied her makeup. A bird trilled in the trees behind them. The water lapped against the wooden pylons. It was getting harder to remember his life as a cop with every passing day.

"You know, John, I figured out who Desiree reminds me of."

"Let me tell you, Einstein. She reminds you of Judy."

He and John had been getting close to an Ecstasy dealer when one of Ricky's informants had died. In his arms. Judy was a nice kid who'd gotten mixed up with the wrong people. He really liked her and told her he would pull her record, get her set up with a good job, help her get back in school. She was coming around pretty good when she decided to have one last, really good time. Jesus, he hated to think about her!

She'd been rolling on Ecstasy all night, she was dehydrated badly, and her internal body temperature must have been 105 degrees. She'd felt like she was burning up in his arms. John was on the phone with the paramedics when she started to convulse. When they got there, it was already too late.

Ricky jumped into his car and sped to the dealer's house in a rage, driving too fast in the rain. He didn't see the little girls dart out from between the parked cars in the parking lot until it was too late. When he closed his eyes, he still saw their pink party dresses, their yellow hair and white shoes sticking out from under a blanket.

John had driven his own car to the dealer's apartment. When he got there, Ricky sat on the curb in the parking lot, just looking at the two girls crumpled in a heap next his car. He didn't say anything when John asked him if he'd been up to the dealer's place yet. John left, and a few minutes later Ricky heard a single gunshot. Then John was next to him again as the ambulance and patrol cars pulled into the parking lot, emergency lights flickering.

Internal Affairs had cleared John on the shooting, but had some other questions for him. When John finally went back to the apartment, Detectives Carter and Dehmer were already there. They said they found only a body, and a gun in the dealer's hand. No ten thousand tabs of Ecstasy, no $450,000. And then there was that phone call made from the dealer's phone after the dealer had been killed, and the fifteen minutes John couldn't account for.

Based on Carter and Dehmers's allegations, John was suspended while the investigation continued. Ricky went on medical leave. He wasn't sleeping. When he did manage to, he woke up screaming. Yellow hair. Pink dresses. White shoes. The agency dropped them like hot potatoes when the parents of the little girls sued and kept showing up on the evening news. John and Ricky both lived under a cloud of suspicion and mistrust.

John found him a few months back in pretty bad shape. On his last visit to the shrink, Ricky lifted a prescription tablet and had been breaking scripts at a drugstore where he had an arrangement. Valium and vodka for breakfast, lunch, and dinner made him a real mess. John took him to his place and dried him out. When he was sober enough, John filled him in on the past few months he'd missed.

"No one else has tumbled to the EPA citations and the MacInerney brothers," John said. "Especially not Carter and Dehmer. They're dirty, Ricky, and they fucked me over. There's some serious money changing hands. Why not get what we deserve and screw the agency? They don't care about us. They just want us to go to jail or go away."

Ricky thought about it a little and started to pull his scruples out of his back pocket when John tossed a letter into his lap. "While you were climbing the walls in the back bedroom, this came for you."

It was from the Agency and the union, saying that his medical benefits were being terminated because of prescription irregularities and abuse. He'd crumpled the letter and thrown it back at John, who'd just swatted it away. "Oh yeah, and the MacInerneys? They fronted the money to the Ecstasy dealer got us into this mess." Ricky felt the dead weight of Judy in his arms. That had made up his mind.

Now here they were.

Ricky said good-bye to John, then thumbed the memory button on the cell phone to call Baldy at the Silver Slipper, to make sure he was there. The phone numbers rolled on the display as he searched for the club's number. Abruptly, he took his thumb off the button. There were two phone calls made while he was sleeping. *Made to whom?* He pushed the Send button and called the phone number.

With the phone held to his ear, he watched Desiree walk toward her old Chevy convertible and put her bags into the trunk.

"Coffee Corner. Best pie in town. How can I help you?"

Ricky hit the End button and dialed the second number.

"This is Dave."

Ricky moved the phone away from his ear and stared at it. Dave Haney. Baldy!

"Who's there? Ralphie, if that's you fucking around—"

Ricky put on his best East Indian accent. "Is Ravi there, please?"

"Who? There's no Ravi here. This is Dave. Who is this?"

"I'm so sorry. Wrong number."

He hung up as Desiree walked down the pier with a laundry bag in her hand. "Come on, honey. I got to get rolling or I'll be late for work."

"Desiree? Did you use my phone?"

She pulled him to the boat, put the opened bag in his hand, and picked up his scattered clothes from the deck where they had been hastily thrown.

"Sure, while you were sleeping. You looked so pleased and peaceful, I didn't want to wake you. I called work to let them know I'd be a little late. You don't mind, do you?"

Ricky knew the Slipper's phone number by heart. The number she'd called was Baldy's cell phone. Why not just call work? he thought. Probably doesn't mean anything. But she didn't mention the Coffee Corner. Now he had an itch to scratch where there wasn't an itch before.

"Ricky! Pay attention! You were gone again. C'mon, honey. *Andale!* Here. Help me put the top up. It looks like it's getting ready to rain."

He was still thinking as the Chevy wheeled away from the pier and back toward town. Rain was just starting to patter on the convertible's ragtop. Desiree drove fast. Houses zipped by. They cut through the parking lot of a redbrick apartment complex that looked too much like that other parking lot. The car skidded a little as she turned a corner. *Too fast!* His hands gripped the side of the bucket seats. "Slow down, goddammit!" His voice was husky and shaking. Desiree jerked at the tone in his voice and slowly let up on the gas.

At the motel, Ricky pointed to a parking space in front of his room. Desiree pulled the Chevy between the two yellow lines and put the shift lever in park.

"What's the matter, honey?"

Ricky just shook his head with his eyes closed. 'No more pink dresses, okay?" he whispered. "No more yellow hair and white shoes."

Desiree pulled his head onto her shoulder and stroked his hair. "Don't know what you're talking about, honey. Maybe you'll tell me later. But right now, you're all right, Ricky. No dresses or hair or shoes. You're all right. You're all right." It sounded like a lullaby. He felt the tension drain. He felt all right.

He must have dozed off for a while. He felt Desiree move her arm to sneak a look at her watch. He pushed himself upright in the seat. "Didn't mean to keep you, Desiree. It's just that I, well, I haven't been with . . . I haven't been with anyone in a while. I think all my feelings are right up under my skin. You know, I haven't been taking my meds."

"I should know that better than anyone, Ricky."

He blushed a little. "And that apartment. That parking lot. Whew, that parking lot. . . ."

"Not now, Ricky. We'll have plenty of time to talk about it tomorrow. I've got to get going. After the fracas last night at the club, you can't very well come by and finish up your story tonight."

Ricky started to think with the old cop side of his brain. *She trying to keep me away from there tonight?* He was ashamed for a moment, but habit pushed him on.

"If I could, I'd buy up every dance you had all night long. All of a sudden, I don't like the idea of you grinding on other guys' laps. You know, you could call in sick tonight. Here, I've got the number you called stored in memory right here on the phone."

He picked up the phone to dial. She grabbed it from his hand.

"Ricky, don't start talking like that. I don't have you pegged as some jealous moon doggie. I got you figured as someone who's bigger than that. I'm not wrong about you, am I?"

She wasn't going to make the call. "No, you're not wrong."

"I didn't think so or I wouldn't have come over to you in the restaurant this morning. Or taken you to the lake this afternoon." She threw the phone in the back seat and leaned over to kiss him. "Aside from being a little mysterious and a little loco, you're my kinda guy." She kissed him again, a little slower this time. "You're my fella now, right?"

"Yeah." Her Lone Star earrings sparkled as she nodded her head, wanting him to agree. He wasn't thinking with the cop side of his brain now.

"I don't want you to be jealous of those goons at the club, all right?"

"Hey, if you don't remember, I was one of those goons last night."

"No you weren't, Ricky. You had that funny little smile that reminded me of my first beau. You talked nice, acted nice, didn't grope me when I danced for you. Then you kicked ass on two bad guys who manhandled me once or twice. But I was a little hurt when I heard your partner call you by a different name."

Ricky winced and started to plead his case. She put her finger over his lips.

"But when you stopped the truck to tell me your name, a shiver went up and down my spine." She put her hand on his cheek. "All of a sudden, I kinda liked you."

"I thought you might of."

"You took my heart with you when you pulled out of that parking lot, Ricky. I would have come looking for you if I didn't see you in the restaurant. I don't want to say the words right now. I don't want you to say them yet either. Just forget about the club. It's just a job. Those guys mean nothing to me. You're a cop. You know what it's like to pretend, to be someone else for a little while." Ricky didn't look at her. "That's all I'm doing, just pretending. I want to be with you, Ricky. Do you want to be with me?"

She took his chin in her hand and turned his head toward her. It got quiet for a moment and Desiree drilled him with her eyes. The cop side was back, weighing her words against what he wanted to feel. A truck rumbled to a stop at the intersection next to the motel. The sound of the driver revving the engine to keep up the rpms filled the silence inside the car. The light changed and the driver ground through the gears as Ricky answered.

Ricky opened the door to the room and found John sitting on the edge of the bed, scratching at an old scar on his leg. He sat down in a motel chair next to a table that had seen better days and threw his keys next to his open shave kit and holstered pistol. John stopped his scratching.

"Saw you two smooching it up in the front seat of her car. You got Miz Desiree under control?"

He smiled back at John, not showing his teeth, and nodded. He fished inside his shave kit and found the pills, popped two in his mouth and reached for a stale glass of water on the table. "Under control," he mumbled through the pills.

"You real sure about that, are you?"

"What are you getting at, John?"

The phone rang and John answered it. They watched each other as John uh-huhed into the phone. He hung up and sat back down on the bed.

"That was my guy in Little Rock. It's happening tonight. At the Slipper."

Ricky spit the pills out onto the carpet. His stomach went queasy, excitement rolling over him in waves. He looked at John. "How?"

"Some folks coming over from Little Rock tonight with lots of money. They're picking up shit out of state rather than buying it locally or cooking it themselves. The Arkansas cops there have been cracking meth labs like crazy. That's the good news."

"And the bad news?" Ricky asked.

"I saw Carter and Dehmer at the coffee shop this afternoon. They are in town, sniffing around. I don't believe in coincidence. I think they're here for the same reasons we are."

Ricky showed a nasty smile. "So those lousy bastards are here for the money."

"And the dope." John held his head in an I-told-you-so posture. "You didn't really believe me when I told you I didn't take the dope and the money on that last deal, did you? Well, I won't deny it. I was thinking about it. Real hard. But those guys beat me to it. I knew they were rotten and I figured, why should they get rich? Why not me? Why not us?"

Ricky started to answer, but John wouldn't be interrupted. "But you screwed up, partner. And I had to spend some time holding you up. I don't regret it, but let's not blow it this time. Let's get what we deserve for a change."

"What do you think those guys know, John?"

"Not sure. When they know a deal's coming down, they bust in just like it's a real arrest. Usually have a snitch working for them on the inside. Then they make an offer. If they can swing it, they usually take a good chunk of the proceeds and offer protection on future deals. For a consideration. But they won't hesitate to pop these people if things get out of hand. We know that from personal experience, right?"

"You telling me that's what happened to the Ecstasy dealer?

John nodded. "Carter and Dehmer are real nervous around tweakers. Meth freaks get kind of twitchy, get funny ideas, make funny connections. And they're usually well armed. Modesta and his partner went down in that meth bust last year. Nobody wants to take chances anymore."

Ricky chewed his lower lip. "Are we out of business then?"

"No way, buddy. Just a little change in plans. My original idea was the same as theirs. Bust in, pretend to be the DEA, take the money and the dope, and—"

Ricky held up his hand. "Back up a sec. Take the dope? And do what with it, John?" Ricky's hand moved toward his gun.

"Settle down, Ricky. I was just thinking that the meth is worth half a million on the street. We wouldn't have to worry about medical benefits or pensions again. Sell the dope, take the money, make a few investments. You could put a real respectable down payment on that sailboat you were always talking to me about on stakeout."

Ricky walked over to the bed and stood next to John, rocking back and forth on his heels, bouncing slightly.

"So you want us to sell dope, huh? Cross the line, go all the way? Be the guys who make some other poor jerk hold a beautiful young girl in his arms while she dies? We'd be dealers, John. The *dealers!*" Ricky raised his outstretched arm in front of John's face, fist clenched.

Ricky didn't move as John got up slowly and took hold of his forearm, pulling it gently down to Ricky's side. John put his face close to his and spoke in low, even tones, the way he would to a skittish animal.

"You're right, man. I wasn't thinking. Well, I was, but I wasn't thinking right. We'll just take the money. Forget about the dope. Just the money, okay?"

Ricky's nose almost touched John's as he peered into his eyes, looking for the truth. John acted like he knew something that he wasn't telling. He wished he'd been able to beat John more often when they played poker. He never had.

"You being straight with me, John?"

"Fuck you, asshole! I've been your partner for five years. I'm the one who pulled you out of the gutter when little Ricky couldn't handle things. You don't want to believe me, that's fine. Fuck you!"

Ricky followed John as he walked away from him. "Hey, I'm sorry. I really am." He tugged at his sleeve like a child. "You just make me crazy sometimes with your constant scamming and playing all the angles. Tell me how we'll take this down."

"Shut up, Ricky. Just shut up and I'll tell you." Ricky knew that John would huff and puff for a little while, but he was mollified. He sat down on the bed and went over the details.

"We have to figure that Carter and Dehmer are here tonight because they know what's going down. The people from Little Rock won't bring the money into the Slipper right away. They'll wait for a call from inside telling them that everything is cool. That's when you and I pick up the garbage."

"Huh?"

"Let me ask you, if you were going to wait in a safe place in that parking lot, where would you be?"

Ricky smiled. "Behind the Dumpster. That's where they'll be, all right."

"We break into the yard next to the Slipper where Eddie keeps his disposal trucks and pull one into the Slipper's parking lot, right next to the Dumpster. Nobody will notice one extra truck parked outside the fence. We wait for the boys from Little Rock, and then take their money."

"Pretty slick. You talk like you've done this before. Gee, were you ever a cop?"

"And those garbage trucks are almost bulletproof in case anything gets dicey. Ricky, we can do this, right?"

"Yeah, it's not like it's the first bust we ever made. What about Carter and Dehmer? How much do you think they know?"

John hesitated and studied him, like he did when he grilled a suspect he already had the goods on.

"They know a lot more than I thought, buddy. As much as we do, if not more."

John rubbed his thumb and forefinger together.

"What aren't you telling me, John?"

John leaned back on the bed, then sat up abruptly.

"Nothing. Just my usual jumping at shadows." He raised his hand in the air for a high five. "We going to do this?"

Ricky swatted his hand. "Yeah. We're going to do this."

John busied himself on the bed with his map and notes. Ricky walked to the window and pulled back the drape. On the other side of the interstate, the sunset blazed at him in reds and yellows. He could just see the top of the letters spelling out Silver Slipper on a big lighted billboard. He closed the drape and got ready for work.

Sitting in the dark of the parking lot, Ricky watched the cat on top of the Dumpster move its hindquarters ever so slightly. It stalked the mouse nibbling at the spilled refuse next to the green metal container. Ready to pounce, the cat twitched its mouth showing white, pointed teeth in the darkness. He knew exactly how it felt. Calm and alert at the same time. Ready to rid the world of one more parasite.

John snored in the seat next to him. *Typical.* Ricky thought about waking him up so he could sleep, if for no other reason than to distance himself from the sweet, stale smell of rot that came from the back of the truck. But that wouldn't happen. There was too much streaming through his head to let him sleep.

I should have told her the truth. We're scamming the meth dealers. Carter and Dehmer are scamming the Agency. Christ, it gets complicated.

Pools of yellow light from the sodium arc lamps dotted the bumpy stone lot. Their pickup was parked at the far end of the lot. Desiree's Chevy and Carter and Dehmer's green Ford weren't far away. He heard someone miss a gear during a downshift. A truck with MACINERNEY CONSTRUCTION painted on its side pulled in followed by a rented yellow van. The MacInerney truck with Charlie and Eddie in the front seat pulled up next to the garbage truck where they hid. Crunching stone under its tires, the rental pulled through the parking lot, circled once, then backed in next to the Dumpster. Ricky put his hand over John's mouth and shook him slightly. "They're here."

John's eyes opened, and he was instantly awake. Ricky took his hand from his mouth and whispered, "Charlie and Eddie are in the truck next to us. The boys from Little Rock are parked on the other side of the Dumpster. I don't know how many people are really in either truck."

John nodded and they both lowered themselves in the front seat of the garbage truck. Charlie and Eddie got out of the truck. Eddie leaned back in and told someone to stay put. Two shorthaired, wide-shouldered men got out of the yellow van and came over to meet the MacInerneys. John lowered the passenger window while Ricky lowered the driver side window. John cursed the creaky handle.

A creak and a thump came from the back of the yellow van as if someone was shifting his weight to get more comfortable. Ricky saw the rear door of the MacInerney truck swing open and a shadow silently close the door and walk around the back of the Dumpster. "Oh shit, John. This could get hairy. Doesn't look like anybody trusts anybody on this deal." He watched as the MacInerneys greeted the two men.

"Buster. Billy. How are you?" Eddie asked. They all shook hands warily. "Hey, why don't you ask Fat Freddie to come out of the van? He's got to be pretty uncomfortable back there."

Buster and Billy looked at each other and nodded. Billy walked over and banged on the side of the van. "Come on out, Freddie." They all waited while thumping noises and an "Oh shit!" came from the inside of the van. A large man with long black hair came out carrying an attaché and an automatic pistol. "Okay, he's out," Billy said. "Now, how about you ask Baldy to come out from in back of the Dumpster. He's got to stink back there by now."

Eddie shrugged at Charlie. "Come on out, Dave. Let's all go inside and get this done. We're spending too much time out here trying to outsmart each other. You guys bring the money, we'll bring the meth."

Ricky watched Baldy come around the Dumpster, open it up, and pull two plastic garbage bags from inside. Keeping their distance and watching each other closely, the six men walked across the parking lot and into the back door of the Silver Slipper.

"What do you think, John? Do we go in?"

John shook his head. "Why don't we just wait a couple of minutes." He pointed out the window and Ricky saw Carter and Dehmer walking up to the same back door. It opened from the inside. Ricky caught his breath.

Framed in the light of the doorway was the prettiest girl he'd known for some time.

Ricky exhaled, letting his breath out slowly through pursed lips. John spoke to him in a low, level voice.

"Yeah, their usual MO is to have a pretty, well-informed snitch involved to let them know what's coming down."

Ricky leaned back in the seat, thinking, This is what he was keeping from me. With genuine concern, John reached over and put his hand on his back. "Hey, buddy? You going to be okay?"

With tender logic and tough love, Desiree had convinced him that the Slipper was no place for him tonight and the only place for her. He looked over at John, who had already figured his girlfriend out. Ricky put his hand to his chin and stared at the doorway.

John reached up to the cab's roof, pulled off the plastic covering of the interior light, and pulled out the bulb. He opened the door, jumped out, and motioned for Ricky to follow. Standing next to each other by the side of the truck, John whispered into his ear:

"Tough break, buddy. You thought she really liked you, didn't you?"

The money, the dope, the MacInerneys, the boys from Little Rock, and Desiree were all inside the club. Outside, Ricky and John watched the door. Thinking.

"What's the plan, Ricky?"

"We can't bust in on them and hope to get what we came for without causing a ruckus. We'll just have to bring everybody back outside."

"And we do that how?" asked John.

"Shouldn't be that hard. Go back to the truck and get a flare and the tire iron."

John hightailed it to the truck and rummaged under the seat for a bit, then came back to stand next to Ricky by the door. "Going to set the place on fire, are we?"

"No. Next best thing, though."

Ricky took the tire iron and stuck it in the doorjamb next to the lock, tensed, and wrenched the door open. Loud music poured out as they rushed in with guns drawn. Hugging the walls, they covered each other as they hurried down the dark hallway toward the stairwell at its end. Ricky pointed at the ceiling. John nodded, pulled off the flare's cover and struck it. Red flame and sulfur filled the hall as John held it under the sprinkler in the ceiling. For a moment, nothing happened.

Then water fountained from the fixture as alarms mixed with the loud thumping of the club music. The music stopped and the screaming started. Ricky opened the utility closet next to the stairwell and they both stepped inside, closing the door until just a crack allowed them to see the first rush of the club's patrons and nearly naked dancers burst through the door that led from the bar.

The door at the top of the stairs opened and footsteps pounded as Carter and Dehmer ran past them, looking scared and pissed. Mentally, Ricky tallied the hours on stakeout, the hours sweating informants, the hours falsifying reports to the Agency to pull this caper off. All going up in smoke, or what they thought was smoke.

Buster and Billy were next down the stairs, Buster carrying the attaché case with the money. Billy rushed past them in a panic. As Buster rounded the corner at the bottom of the stairs, Ricky opened the door and slammed his fist into Buster's face. John hit him in the back of the head with his pistol and then dragged him into the closet. While Ricky tightened a thick plastic tie around his wrists, John yelled "Shit" and bolted into the hall. Through the open door, Ricky saw the MacInerneys hustling outside with the plastic garbage bags full of dope slung over their shoulders. John was right behind them. John was going after the dope.

The crowd in the hall was thinning. Time to leave. As he opened the door, he bumped someone and found himself staring into a pair of beautiful brown eyes. She looked at him, then at the attaché, then at the doorway. Eddie MacInerney stuck his head back inside the doorway and yelled to her.

"Darlene, come on!"

Looking puzzled, Ricky reached out to touch her arm.

She shrugged, then smiled. "My name's Darlene, Ricky." Her eyes darted over his shoulder.

Ricky turned to see Baldy looking at him with a wicked grin as he raised the long black flashlight over his head. "Her name's Darlene, Ricky."

He tasted the metal in his fillings as he crumpled to the floor.

"You okay, buddy?"

The peculiar silhouette of a fireman's helmet loomed over him. He struggled to his feet and slumped against the wall as the fireman held him up. "Come on, let's get you outside."

The parking lot was full of flashing lights, red trucks, and black-and-whites from the local police force. Woozy, Ricky found himself seated in the back of an ambulance while a paramedic applied a compress to the wound over his brow. "You took a good wallop from something, pal. You've got the makings of a pretty good concussion. You stay put here for a bit. We've got a few people who got trampled and I've got to go see about them."

The paramedic ran off toward the building. Ricky waited until he went into the building, then got up and staggered away toward his truck. There was no sign of the MacInerneys' truck, the yellow rented van, Carter and Dehmer's Ford, or Desiree's Chevy anywhere in the parking lot. When he opened the door, he half expected to see John waiting for him. All he saw was an attaché case on the front seat. He collapsed behind the steering wheel and passed out.

When he came to, the parking lot was a little less full. Firemen were stowing gear back into their trucks. In the rearview mirror he saw policemen wandering the lot, shining their flashlights inside of parked cars. Time to boogie, he thought. Without turning on his lights, he eased the truck onto the highway and away from the Silver Slipper.

He circled the motel once to make sure no one had followed him. The door to their room stood ajar, lights off inside. With the attaché in one hand and his gun drawn in the other, he pushed open the door with its barrel. Not a sound. He lurched inside and flicked on the lights. No one home.

John's stuff was still on the other bed. He moved toward the bathroom with a slow quiet tread. John's shave kit was still open next to the bathroom sink. The shower curtains were pulled shut. Ricky tugged them back quickly and saw two empty, black garbage bags lying in the tub. His head began to pound.

In the other room, he collapsed onto the bed and stared at the attaché case. He pushed at it with his foot, then got up and opened it. Inside was about half the money that he figured should be there. And a boat brochure. Taking the money out to count it, he saw something sparkle in the corner of the case. He pulled the case closer and found a gold earring in the shape of a star. A Lone Star.

A steady gulf breeze bumped the sailboat against the dock as Ricky tied the *Desiree* to the cleats with heavy rope. It had been a good day and his freezer was full of the day's catch. Ernesto would be happy and so would the patrons in his restaurant. He jumped back on board and went to the cooler for a cold beer. Slumping onto the cushions in the well of the boat, he ran the cool aluminum can under the brim of his captain's hat and across his forehead, letting it linger on the scar above his brow. The headaches were fewer and the medic said they would stop soon. He took a long pull at the can.

Twiddling with the tuner on the radio, he found a slow song on a Spanish station. A lovely senorita sung to him in words he didn't understand, but he liked the sound of it. He liked it when women sang to him.

A meow from the dock demanded his attention. He looked up to see Rosalita stretching out one of her paws to him. He tapped on his stomach and then she was in his lap, purring and butting her head against his chin. "You're hungry, I suppose?" he asked as he scratched behind her ears. Without moving, he flipped open the cooler with his toe to reveal a plastic plate filled with pieces of choice filet. Rosalita jumped onto the edge of the cooler and proceeded to dine.

When she was done with her meal and her grooming, the cat jumped onto his lap, found a comfortable spot, lay down, and purred herself to sleep. Ricky petted Rosalita behind her ear and watched white clouds float across blue skies. His eyelids grew heavy. He pushed his hat over his eyes. His head lowered onto his chest and he dreamed.

She walked down the dock looking at the name on the stern of each of the boats until she came to the last slip. She looked at the name of the boat and at him. Asleep with the cat in his lap.

Rosalita jumped from his lap to meow at someone in greeting. He smelled the perfume and pushed back the brim of his hat. He looked up into the most beautiful brown eyes in the world. A pair of Lone Star earrings sparkled in the sunset.

"Hi sailor. Mind if I join you?"

He thought she really might like him.

The Door Beast Nine Vee Bee

by Ed Jesby

Not since HAL in 2001: A Space Odyssey *has a helper been so . . . independent. Set in the not-too-distant future in an urban environment where personal security is top-of-mind and homes are guarded by primitive creatures called Door Beasts, this is, well, a love story. Think* I, Robot *meets* Eternal Sunshine of the Spotless Mind.

I'm going to buy a Door Beast." Smith had decided that locks were too easy to open. A screen mail correspondence course could teach you to open even the most complicated of locks, but a Door Beast was a different thing. A Door Beast barred and unbarred doors. Of course, if it died you would have to break the door down. There would be no other way to slip the bar out of its channels. But a Door Beast would only open the door for people it had learned to recognize. It would not be cheap, and it was a strong statement in favor of the right to life. Every ovum must have a chance to develop. That went without saying. The Right Life Society, Inc., knew how to harvest eggs, how to fertilize them, and how to guide the life to its fulfilled function. The twentieth-century philosophers had shown the way. The great Aldous and the esteemed Bush had pointed out the path, and now no life was wasted.

Smith's auto-Car driver took him to the Right Life store. The driver's saved brain knew the map way to all Right Life locations, as if it remembered who had grown it.

Smith shivered. "It knows its *family* home." The mild obscenity brought him to attention as the car vapored into a parking slip and the door blossomed him out.

The woman who sat behind the reception desk at the Right Life store wore a white coverall with the insignia of the society on her flattened chest. The red circle of organism capped with its blue male arrow, supported by the pink cross of femininity was as familiar as the striated globe of Universal Communications, and he felt immediately at ease.

"I want to buy a Door Beast." Smith said the words easily, but the woman corrected him.

"You cannot *buy* a Door Beast, you can only be *responsible* for giving a saved life the privilege of fulfilling its function." She spoke the correcting words, but she was ready to perform the service he requested. She might have been a Sales Beast, but he could not be sure. Sales Beasts were very expensive. They could perform manifold functions, and they had to make choices among oodles of possibilities. Such ability to suffer ambiguity did not come cheap, and even the society itself sometimes found the expense too high.

The first few days would be hard. He would have to think of all the people he wished to let into his apartment. But it would not be so hard. There was really only Mary.

Mary had a key now. When they were going to spend the night together, Mary would often get to his apartment before he did, and she would make supper, or call up food. The first thing to do would be to show Mary to the Beast.

Smith's planning was interrupted by the woman's voice giving instructions. She handed him the necessary manuals as she spoke.

"Read these when you get back to your domicile." She smiled and spread her hands open with their palms up. "It is important that you pay particular attention to the "Care and Feeding of Door Beasts." Your Door Beast has a diet that has been designed just for it. You will be receiving a week's supply of containers of Beast Feed before you leave, and a weekly supply will be delivered to your domicile." She smiled again and pressed a button on her desk's console and the wall behind her opened to reveal his Beast for his first showing.

Smith wished there could be a choice of Beasts, but there was not. You got what was available. But the Beast she showed him was male. All Beasts—male or female—were neutered, but secondary characteristics were secondary characteristics, and his esthetic sense demanded the additional expense of clothing for the Beast.

The Beast was short, but it was wide. It had a wide face that was very short from the brow line to its receding chin. It was hairless and very clean. It smiled, and the woman lifted the speaking mechanism from her console. She spoke into it, but the voice that came out of the talkers was not hers. It was a powerfully unaccented voice. A voice whose tones could not be confused with human speech. A voice that spoke the truth.

"9v/b/rPo3zY." She paused, and the Beast opened its mouth wide to make room for its thick tongue to form words.

It said, "I hear and remember." She nodded and continued. "This is Smith. You are his. See him. He is giving you a door and a bar to lift. You will lift it for him. You will accept the seeing and words of the others he shows you; they and only they will you lift for—hear 9v/b/rPo3zY." The woman put the speaking tube into its slot and touched her console and the wall closed.

She continued speaking in her unaugmented voice. "A technician has been dispatched to install your bar. It will have been installed when you return to your domicile, but first you will have to practice the saying of your Door Beast's key. Repeat after me: nine-vee slash bee slash are pee oh three zeee why."

Smith was careful to get the meter right. He followed the rhythms faithfully, and she was satisfied after a few dozen repetitions of the key, and said: "I am giving you this." She held a small pink cube out to Smith. "Say the key correctly, and it will pulse and grow slightly warmer." She smiled as Smith took the flesh of his property's flesh from her, and made her openhanded gesture. "It would be well if you practiced. It will retain its efficacy for just twenty-four hours. Say the key to it."

Smith sounded the codons. He made no mistake, and the ham-warm cube shuddered. He had known it would. He prided himself on his ear. He wasn't a supervisor because he lacked the ability to use the words of control correctly.

The trip home was uneventful. His auto-Car had to use evasive speed only once where some crowd of unemployed fled from the pickers, but his car was a good one, and it easily outwitted the simple ambuscade set for the hapless.

Smith used his keys and saw that Right Life had proven that his distrust of standard locks was well founded. The technician had entered his apartment and mounted the shackles that would hold the bar in place against the door. He turned a slow circle and saw that the bar was propped in a corner near his compu-Meal. He went to it and lifted it away from the wall. It was heavy. It was massive. He picked it up and cranked his arms in a weightlifter's curl to feel the weight of his new-found security.

He was pleased, and remembered that he must read the manuals that the Right Life Society's salesperson had given him. But first he tuned a Chicken Kiev dinner out of the compu-Meal, and chose a Wodka Surprise from the drink-Menu. He laid the manuals next to his plate and read as he ate.

". . . Door Beast can speak and will learn to converse with you, but you must take care not to exceed its limitations. A Door Beast is not de-signed for complex activities. It has great difficulty making choices be-tween alternatives . . .

Smith sipped his Wodka drink and lifted his eyes to the view win-dow. The room lights dimmed, and the window's filmy opacity turned clear. He could see the city. The buildings spread to the horizon and marched beyond, a field of pilings for an infinitely wide causeway on which no roadway had been erected. "Each in place." He said the words as an antidote to the metaphor, and blinked his eyes widely to close the view.

". . . ambivalence is bad for a Beast." Smith read on, surprised to find that a well-cared-for Door Beast could live for more than a hun-dred years. He could leave it to his designees, but it would be returned to the society if he could make no provision for its continued service.

". . . the Beast will feed itself when its hunger program orders it. Elimination is a private act for a Door Beast. It rarely needs to eliminate the products of digestion, and will do so when necessary, and always in the absence of its employer. It can receive and consume human food, but the practice of feeding table scraps is . . ."

Smith's reading was interrupted by his see-Phone. He waggled his fingers, one, two, three, and the view window showed him Mary's face.

"John. Have you done it?"

"I said I would and I did." He was annoyed, but he was sure he spoke in neutral shadings. He *always* thought out his actions, and then acted when his plan was completely laid.

"I didn't mean you would not . . ." Mary hesitated and chose her words, ". . . complete your plan." She smiled her crooked smile, but she looked down in the way her management status training had taught her.

Smith responded. "It is well that you were impatient to know." He nodded. Mary needed the praiseful reinforcement. They were contracted pleasure partners, but they were not of the same rank. His Social Security number had no addendum.

Mary looked up and asked "Will I see you tomorrow?"

"Of course." Smith outlined his planning. "I am accepting delivery of my new Door Beast." He did not think his voice betrayed his pride, but the glow in Mary's eyes showed him she recognized his accomplishment. The manual entitled *The Care and Feeding of Your Door Beast* lay in his sight, and he picked it up. "But I must study my instructions. Come after eight, and I will introduce you to the Beast."

The workday was neither harder nor longer than usual. General Food's machines made vegetables and Smith gave instructions to the machines, and approved overlooker's corrections, but he waited for the summons from the society. He must be at home to be the first to say his Door Beast's codons. He practiced giving the syllables the tone and phrasing that made them strongly valid, and carried the practice cube everywhere he went. He even spoke to the cube under the wet shadows of the bulk of the potato fabricator where Clean Beasts waited to be shown the new fastenings of the access hatches. When he reached the final ". . . three zee why" he felt the worker Beasts' eyes on him. One—a small, dark, and hairy creature whose texture was unusual for a Clean Beast—went so far as to shake its head, and mumble "Wrong." Smith was not sure that it had spoken the word, but it was wagging its head from side to side, and he used the strongest pitch of command to say "Work change!" and yet it hung its head and did not strain forward to hear instructions, and its neck trembled with controlled tics that sketched the movements its muscles wished to make.

He did not let momentary dysfunction disturb him, and soon his Comm-Beeps private channel brought him the welcome news that *his* Beast had been delivered.

The package of clothing was tucked under his arm and Smith held his keys in his hand, but the door to his apartment had no lock stile and no doorknob. He leaned close to its new, solid surface and remembered the instruction in the manual: "Announce your presence." "It is I—Smith." He waited, and a second newly installed peephole, mounted low in the door, sprang open to show him a blue eye's wide iris. He stepped back to give his privately owned Beast a fuller view, and he was rewarded with the clatter of the bar being set aside.

The opening grew incrementally as his Beast scuttled backwards with small steps, clutching the door's edge in its stubby fingers. Smith put the useless keys into his shoulder pouch and nodded to the Beast, but thought better of his greeting, and said, "Hello. I am here." The Beast gazed at him, but it made no other response, and he continued, "It is I, Smith."

"I see Smith." The Beast stood as straight as it could, but its head only reached Smith's chest.

Smith bent to have a closer look and the Beast said "And I remember Smith. I am Smith's."

"Here are clothes I have bought." Smith held the package out, but the Beast did not reach for it. It shivered and tried to peer around Smith's bulky form. Its eyes turned back to the bar it had put aside, and Smith understood its agitation. He stepped farther into the room and the Beast swung the door into its frame, took a hurried step to the bar, and lifted it effortlessly into its place.

The Beast seated itself in the small chair the society had delivered. It slumped and its stomach bellied forward, but its legs were spread and it was still evidently male. Smith offered the package again.

"This is clothing I have bought." The Beast regarded him, but it made no move. "These are clothes I have for you to wear."

"Clothing." The Beast's pronunciation made separate syllables of the word and turned the "thi" into a diphthong.

Smith did not allow his exasperation to show. He picked up the manual and turned to the section thumb-indexed: "Vocabulary." He riffled pages until he found the construction: "'Garments' I have bought for you to wear."

The Beast rose straight out of the chair. Its leg muscles gathered and it popped up without leaning forward and held its arms out. "Garments." Smith lay the package across the Beast's arms, but it made no move.

"The cloth—the garments must be taken out of their wrapping." Smith shook his head, and retrieved the package. He ran his fingertip along the sealseam and lifted the polo shirt and shorts out. He held the shirt out. "This is for your upper body." He gave the red shirt to the Beast, but it did nothing, so he raised his arms. "Raise up." The command pitch in his voice motivated the Beast, and its arms lifted to mimic Smith's position. "Stay." Smith worked the shirt over the Beast's arms and around its torso and said, "Lower." The Beast lowered its arms, and tugged at the shirt's hem. "Nice." It smiled, and Smith was confused. It did not know how to dress. He riffled pages in the manual and found that "dress" equated with "attire."

"Attire your lower body in this . . ." Smith looked along the listings again. ". . . lower body *trouser* garment."

Smith studied the Beast sitting in its little chair. He had chosen the garments well. His Door Beast was quietly calm. Clothing—garments—absorbed the light and he was relieved from the nacreous reflections of its white skin.

"John." It was Mary's voice. The Beast did not move, and Smith turned pages in the manual quickly. It was easy. He spoke: "Open."

The Beast lifted the bar away from the door and pulled it open, and Mary entered. Smith was pleased. She was dressed in the garments he liked best. A loose skirt and a half-blouse that hung just under the hollow curve of her ribs.

"Oh, how nice!" Mary smiled at the Beast and it smiled back. "What's your name." The Beast did not answer and Smith said "It has no name. It is not of the level to have a name."

Mary looked at Smith out of the corner of her eye. "John." She turned her eyes back to the Beast who sat in his chair and looked up at her attentively. "It should have a name."

"I don't know if that is appropriate." Smith was impatient. He wanted to code Mary into the Beast while its first impression was fresh. He raised his voice. "Nine vee slash bee slash are pee oh three zeee why." The Beast stood and faced Smith and he went to Mary's side. "This is Mary. You will lift the bar I have given you for her."

"I hear and remember." Smith knew the words were the correct response, but the Beast went on. "Mary."

"Thank you." Smith was not sure if the courtesy was for himself or for the Beast, but Mary continued, "Nine vee bee."

"Nine vee bee." Smith was puzzled. "That is not . . ."

"That's his nickname." Mary smiled. "Nine vee bee. It's a short name for him." She turned to the Beast and rubbed his smooth pate. "Good nine vee bee." The Beast's muscles shuddered in ripples. "See, he likes his name." Mary turned to Smith and her blouse swung as she turned—and Smith smiled. "I guess so, but . . ."

"No but." Mary went to the compu-Meal. "I'm exited. This is wonderful." She studied the machine buttons. "Do you want a snack? I'm hungry."

"And a drink." Smith wanted to celebrate. "We could have real-champ. I have a bottle of ancient Andre in the box."

Mary pushed a button and dimpled, round, brown crackers emerged with a small pot of cheesy spread from the compu-Meal port. Smith found the twentieth-century champagne and worked at the brittle foil until he could grip the knurled plastic stopper. He twisted and pulled and the bottle's neck let a small surge of bubbles into the air.

"Here we are." Smith turned with the bottle and two glasses in his hand and found that Mary squatted close to the Door Beast. She held a cheesy covered cracker in her hand.

"You're not feeding it, are you?" He poured champagne.

"Just a snack." Mary stood and moved away from the Beast, and it turned its body to follow her with its eyes. "Nine vee bee should celebrate too."

"The instructions say that Door Beasts feed themselves from their own food supply." Smith handed Mary her glass. "Please don't do it again."

"I'll be good." Mary lifted her glass and touched it to Smith's. "Here's to us and Nine vee bee."

"Beasts do not have names." Smith did not drink. "They have codes—codons which let them accept orders."

"Don't be so business." Mary sipped her glass. "This is good."

"If you won't follow the rules . . ."

"Now, now."

He was not to be turned. "If you won't follow the rules, then I don't . . ."

Mary took Smith's hand and lifted it and the glass to his lips. He drank, and she smiled at him. "I'll be good."

When Smith awoke the next morning he had a small headache and Mary had gone. Her workday was longer than his, and she must have gone to her apartment to change her clothes and prepare for work. He slipped out of bed and saw that Nine vee bee was in its place. He shook his head in irritation. Beasts should not be called by pet names. Dogs and cats were once named; children still were, but not Beasts.

Beasts. Mary was pretty, and she was pleasant, but she did not have the intellectual capacity to understand the necessary hierarchy of the world. He put his thoughts aside and prepared for work.

There was a half-empty container of Beast food on the kitchen counter. Smith sniffed at its contents. It was not like human food. Its aroma was more like the smell of the lubricants used in the vegetable machines. The half-empty can was not right. Smith found the Beast manual and searched for enlightenment. He scanned quickly, and read: "Each container's unit of nourishment is precisely defined as the quantity a Door Beast will eat at one time. If the Beast does not finish the quantity packaged there may be three (3) reasons for its incompletion:

"1.   It is receiving a formulation intended for a larger Beast.

2.   It is misfunctioning because of illness.

3.   It has been fed unapproved food."

It was more than the small piece of cracker that Mary had fed the Beast. She must have given it more food this morning. Smith pushed the compu-Meals record key and saw that Mary had requested egg and bacon. He looked over to the Beast, and it turned and held him in its unreadable gaze.

"Have you eaten?" The Beast did not answer, and Smith tried again. "Did Mary give you food?"

"I have seen and I remember Mary." The Beast erected itself out of its chair and went to the door. It stood in front of the bar expectantly.

"No one is coming." Smith considered. "Sit. Wait." The Beast went to its chair and folded into it, and Smith went to it and squatted down in front of it. "Did Mary give you nourishment?" He could see that the Beast was trying to make sense out of his words, but he was not using the words that were in its vocabulary store. He stood and took the manual and opened it to the rogetlist. He found the word he wanted. "Mary feed?"

"I have seen and I remember Mary." Nine vee bee turned innocent eyes to Smith, and John gave up his interrogation. The Beast would not—could not—tell him what he wanted to know.

He had turned his see-Phone on without knowing he had done it, and it dialed Mary's work number.

"Mary." Smith wanted to be calm, but he blurted the words out. "Have you fed the Beast *human* food again?"

Mary looked down away from her see-Phone's lens, and when she looked up again she shook her head. "No. You told me not to, and I . . ." She stopped. "Yes. I did." Her eyes opened very wide. "It begged me."

"A Beast cannot beg."

"That shows how much you know."

Smith waved the see-Phone off and pressed on the do-not-answer key. He had had enough. He must calm himself and go to work.

By the time he had reached the vegetable factory his mind was made up. He would call the mate-Service, and he would find someone to make him feel better about the way Mary had failed her responsibility to him over the matter of the Door Beast.

There was no work that needed his immediate attention. Smith keyed in the commands that would bring him to the catalog of women who had applied for partners in pleasure contracts. He conditioned his search of the data banks so that all of the choices would be one rank lower than Mary and three below his status. There were suitable candidates in the vegetable factory. When Mary had insisted on changing her hair color Smith had joined in a temporary contract with one of them, but—somehow—he had gone back to his relationship with Mary. Smith sighed. He did not want to change, but she had left him no choice. She would not obey the necessary rules.

Wanda fit his needs. He checked her current status and found that she was not currently contracted. She was smaller than Mary, and she weighed fifteen pounds more, but Smith thought he needed a change from thinness. He wrote through to the personnel department, and used his supervisor's access number to find Wanda's current work location.

The Taste Choice Laboratory was a quiet place. Samples of vegetables in cooking pacs whirled out of the automat gates and found the taster assigned by the scheduling software.

He stood behind the glass inspection panel and approved, as Wanda cut into a pac and spread the blue-green neobroccoli onto a tray. She leaned over the fan of stalks and rounded her lips as she blew the rising steam away. She straightened and spoke into the face of her talk-Data terminal. Smith studied the work monitor's screen as words grew into phrases in its electron aspic.

"Good color. Florets are tight and close to real. Aroma weak." Smith looked away from the screen and saw that Wanda was carefully masticating a small piece of stem. "Texture fibrous. Taste inoffensive." He approved. The words she spoke would translate into codes that the Management Information Systems would digest with a minimum of effort. He would request a meeting this very evening.

The glass walls of the open reception atrium were were radiating scenes of the boardwalks of a once-upon-a-time city, alternating with the bright shoals of fish that trafficked in its now-time streets. The surf music turned softly from rhythmic waves to sibilant scales, and Smith wished building maintenance had chosen louder afternoon sounds to hide the chants of the food demonstrators in the plaza.

It was not too bad; he did not have to wait long, but he was not sure he approved of Wanda's garment. Her dress was the latest style. She wore the full, long-sleeved style that was made in the way the style-Mag screens called the "second trimester look." It was cut to cling and to roundly show a tummy mound, around the focus of the sewn-in umbilical hump.

Wanda walked in the posture recommended by her dress. Her hip points were thrust down into the pelvic sockets, and her legs were propelled by her thigh muscles. She does not precisely "waddle," thought Smith. It is a glide worn down by gravity's field.

"Pleasure, Smith." Wanda's hair was black, and for a second, Smith covered the dark-piled coiffure with Mary's natural, almost-blond hair.

"I am pleased to meet you," Smith answered formally. He did not like to use short-Speak. The locutions of the latest word styles sounded like the speech spoken into data screens, and rang with the command structures that motivated Beasts. Wanda smiled. It seemed she liked his formality. Her smile was perfect, her lips opened and turned up without a millimeter of difference to disturb the symmetry of her even teeth. "I am pleased, too." Wanda spoke very clearly. Her voice projected into the space around them, and though no one stared, Smith could feel the attention she provoked with her dress and tone.

"Would you like to visit?" Smith followed through; he was not sure, but he needed to continue.

Wanda was very impressed by Nine vee bee. But she walked close to the wall opposite its little chair, and it followed her with his eyes as if she was not a part of its life.

"You are success." The obedience to the latest produced a twinge in Smith's inguinal ring, but he did not let his distaste show.

"I prefer a Door Beast to locks. Smith looked at the beast. It gazed into space, but it was aware of Wanda in the way it sat away from the back of its chair.

Wanda waited. She expected to be introduced to the Door Beast. He hesitated. They had a *temporary* contract. Temporary did not mean a formal introduction to the Door Beast and certainly not full access.

Wanda had forgotten her stylish slump. She stood flat-footed, relaxed into soft appeal, and Smith forgot his reservations about full access. He remembered instead her listing of Shakti-sex under "Hobbies" on the data screen.

Smith sung the codons of the Beast's control words quickly. "Nine vee slash bee slash pee oh three zee why." The Beast faced him. He said the formula. "This is Wanda. You will lift the bar I have given you for her." Nine vee bee stared at Wanda, but he made no response. Smith repeated the command syllables and pointed at Wanda as he said the words for lifting the bar.

The Beast shivered, and its wide lips spread in a smile. It spoke. "I hear and remember." The words were correct, but the Beast went on, it said "Mary," and grinned more widely.

Smith blushed and put his hand on Wanda's shoulder. "No! This is *Wanda*. You will lift the bar I have given you for her."

"Wanda." Nine vee bee's thick-tongued repetition of the name raised the pitch of the final vowel and made the title somehow interrogative, but it continued, "I hear and remember." It walked heavily to its chair, its feet punching into the rug. It sat with its head turned to study the bar across its door, and spoke a word behind closed lips. Smith thought it mumbled "Mary," but he could not be sure. Wanda swayed close to him, and he could feel the muscles trained by her hobby's exercises, working on his outer thigh.

In the morning Smith sent Wanda away to her apartment in his auto-Car, and studied the Beast Manual for the commands that would erase permissions from its memory. The manual was not very precise. The procedure seemed to be too easy—too simply canceling to be effective, but he did not want to use his screen to get further explanation. He would have to call the Life Society's Help Line, and he remembered the title, "Responsibilities of a Beast Owner," glittering on a manual page, too clearly to ask for help. The cost would be high, and his request would be recorded. He read the instruction again, "Say three times . . ."

Smith sighed and called to the Beast. "Nine vee bee." It stood and faced him, but it made no attempt to come closer. He called out. "Nine vee slash bee slash are pee oh three zee why." The Beast stared. Its large eyes' pupils dilated with attention, and Smith continued, "Do not, do not, do not lift for Mary."

Nine vee bee grinned and said, "Mary." He turned and moved to the door more quickly than Smith had thought he could move. He grasped the bar, and swung it free and said, "I prefer Mary."

Smith could not believe he had heard the Beast correctly. He shouted "What?", but the Beast sidled backwards with the door firmly in its hands. It leaned around the open panel and swiveled its head back to Smith. "Not Mary?"

"Mary is not here. You are not to admit Mary." Smith shouted the name. "Not ever. Not ever again." The Beast ignored him. It was caught in the prescription of its bioconditioning. It swung the door closed, replaced the bar, and sat in its chair.

Smith frantically thumbed the manual's colored indices and found the section he wanted. He read: "Say three times—after saying the Beast's command codes—'Do not, Do not, Do not admit,' and the person you have designated will be removed from the Beast's Permission's List."

Smith turned to the section headed "Permissions List" and read: "The Beast's store of permissions may be accessed by asking 'Who may enter?' twice." He tried the words and the Beast said, "Smith always; Mary always; Wanda sometimes."

"What about Wanda?" Smith was too confused to ask the question in a validated form, but the Beast answered: "I prefer Mary. I am Smith's."

"You what?" Smith asked, but there was no answer. The words held no meaning for the Beast. Nine vee bee smiled at Smith and stood. Its head went back so that its weak jaw pointed upwards, but it kept its eyes on Smith. "Nine vee slash bee slash are pee oh three zee why." The codons spoken in its thick-tongued speech were not as clear as Smith's or the pink cube's, but the rhythm was precisely the singsong of command. It grinned. "Somehow," Smith thought, "it is proud of its knowledge." He stopped the thought. A Beast could not be proud. A Beast could not have knowledge.

His screen lit with the news that it was time for him to get ready to go to work, and he moved away from the Beast. He would call the society from his desk.

Smith let his auto-Car drive. His mind was too full to pay attention to the streets. He recalled stories of failed genetic programs. He had dismissed the stories. "They are just things people say." Smith said the words aloud, but then he thought, "But the Society would not allow . . ." He thought of the story of the supervisor who had found night-shift Beasts playing a game. A Beast would mouth a part of a word and the other Beasts would guess. They were impossible words, obscene words. The lead Beast had moved its lips: "Mo . . . ," and the Beasts would chorus—Smith steeled himself—"Mother." It was impossible. The man who told the story had done it so that his listeners would follow the movements of his lips and form the word in their minds, knowing that Beasts did not have mothers, or the concept of parents. They were created by process. And there were the stories of Beasts who had been so deconditioned by their operators that they had to be destroyed. To have that happen would be the end of Smith's career. He would be downgraded. He would be a clerk, and clerks were not very far from being unemployed.

Smith studied the protocols he had brought to his desk's screen. It seemed he had one hope, and only one. He could ask for an unbound tête-à-tête. Smith considered; the ask-for-information-only rule was supposed to keep his query totally private. He would speak to a person, or an Information Beast, and his conversation would not be recorded, but Right Life was one of the Fortune Five. The government's audit track programs were not admitted to the society's memory banks. Supervisors said that you could ask for private information-only service once, but the exchange's costs would be billed to your employment credits. The company would know you had used the service.

"What can I do?" Smith looked around. There was no one to hear his words, but the building's occupant monitoring software may have been activated by the tension in his voice. He shook his head in short tics, and the motion shook the Beast out of his memory. He could ask the questions in terms of that Beast, and try to reason his way to an explanation of Nine vee bee's behavior. It would be a quasiofficial query. General Food was one of the Five. But first he had to make a record of the Clean Beast's behavior. He should have entered the datum immediately, but the excitement of his Beast's delivery had driven the task from his mind. Smith spoke carefully into the screen's mouthpiece: "Beast assigned Access Clean Potato 13X yesterday instant—Beast decript—," he waited a brief, blinking moment, as the screen flickered and delivered the pictures of the cleaning crew. The Beast he wanted was there, and he transferred the dark and hairy creature's equipment number to the report window, and then spoke again. "Beast unfocused. Looked away during instruction. Unordered physical movement. Request unbound tête-à-tête, Right Life info-help." The screen jumped and spoke. "Calling Right Life unbound." His screen had a pleasant voice. It was androgynously bland, but he thought of it as a helpful young adult. He smiled and wondered where the word child had gone. Once, not too long ago, the screen could have been a bright and helpful boy.

A head and shoulders came onto his screen, and the *person* nodded to him. "Smith—Food Supervisor, Grade 5—you have a query?"

"You have seen and read my comments?" Smith smiled, and the personage glimmering in the screen nodded. "Yes."

"I was practicing codons for a Door Beast I have acquired, and one of the Clean Beasts heard the codons, and it seemed to become disoriented."

"This is not uncommon. Has the Beast shown other signs of dysfunction?" The figure seemed to dim on the screen, and Smith wondered if a tap had been put on his screen to assess his response.

"No, it is efficient." Smith considered, and went on: "This is a request for information only, so that if I have been inappropriate I may remedy my usage." He tapped at his screen's record key and said, "Was it my use of the codons that produced this behavior?"

"Such happenings are rare. Code overlaps are carefully monitored."

Smith waited, but no more information was offered, and he went on. "Are there any other causes possible?"

"This condition has been observed in Food Corporation Beasts in the past. Exposure to random human food pheromones and taste elements sometimes produces *temporary* behavior anomalies." The screen came back to full brightness, and the Right Life representative continued: "Do you wish to make a request for a Beast-fix?"

"No." Smith smiled again, but this time the Life-rep smiled back, and Smith was relieved. "No. You have described the condition as temporary, and I am only requesting information to improve my interface with tasks." He did not like the repetitious disclaimer, but he knew it was necessary.

"Then this request is fulfilled?" The Life-rep's shoulder shifted, and Smith pictured its forefinger poised above the End key.

"I have one more query." Smith chose his words carefully. "Can Beasts prefer one person to another? Can they accept commands more easily from one or the other human?"

"No. This condition is not possible. Behavior may indicate more or less compliance, but this is an artifact of *human* observation." The Life-rep looked down at its keyboard, and raised its eyes to say, "I repeat—is this request fulfilled?"

"Yes—request fulfilled." The screen folded back into the formations of Smith's report window, and a precis of his conversation had been appended to his Beast memorandum. He read the last line. "No action. No X-index. Index rep." It was all right. As yet, there was no access to his query, but other requests for the same species of information would raise the flag to start audit software tracking through his life. The record of Beast Purchase would be found, and his Beast would be tested.

"I wish I was home. Safe with my Beast." Smith whispered behind the shield of his hand. He was shaken by his involuntary words, but he did not want to analyze his statement. He bent to his work, and called production numbers to his screen. The corner call window opened, and a miniature of Wanda's face appeared in its glowing frame.

"John." Wanda had lovely green eyes. Their golden flecks were amplified by the electronic coloration when Smith let the call window expand to fill the screen. "Did you have a *nice* last night?" Smith looked around his office. There couldn't possibly be any one in his space.

"Don't be embarrassed." Wanda lowered her eyelashes, and unveiled her eyes slowly, and Smith cringed.

"I am not embarrassed." He leaned back from the screen so that his head would grow smaller in Wanda's view. "But I *am* busy."

"Playing tough to get?" Wanda bristled with proprietary knowledge of Smith's nature.

"That's 'hard to get.'" He leaned closer to the screen. "If you're going to use ancien-slang, get it right."

"Ooo! Aren't we irritable." Wanda blinked, and the reference to tears hardened Smith's resolve. "Are we meeting tonight?"

"I have exercise tonight." Smith lied. He wanted to have a relationship, but not this one. He would cancel the contract. He would . . .

Smith's running thoughts circled back upon themselves and broke against his screen. The colors dove away into a spiral, throwing shards of clouds across the map of the world. The screen's unflappable voice announced:

"Hurracano. Attention. Hurracano." The map dove into itself and closed on the coordinates of Smith's city. Smith held the leading edge of the storm in his eyes as it moved toward his location, and listened to the warning. "Greenhouse hurraca—central winds at one hundred and fifty five miles per hour. Approaching this area at twenty miles per hour. All nonessential personnel who have protected domiciles should evacuate to their residences immediately." Smith pushed at his terminal's keys and the screen said, "Smith, John you are unessential. Follow instructions."

Traffic was orderly. It could not be otherwise. The auto-Cars all obeyed. They would allow no driver but themselves to control their routes and speeds. Smith sat back and looked up at the sky. High above, the albedo curtains sent unwanted solar heat back into space, but it was not enough to keep the storm from the nourishing heat of the seas that had warmed for centuries under the remnant carbon molecules of burned forests and burned oil. The street duct covers had been raised, and files of the undomiciled unemployed moved thankfully into the tunnels under the earth. It was a grandmother of a storm that was coming.

Nine vee bee swung the door back before Smith called out. The Beast smiled broadly. It leaned out of the door, overcoming its programmed agoraphobia to point up at the sky's silver vault. "Outside bummer."

Smith smiled back at the Beast. "How do you know? The sky is fine—same color as it always is." He looked up to follow the Beast's gaze, and remembered historical references—songs—"Nothin' but Blue Skies . . ." Once the sky had been as blue as the quiet-Color of walls, but not since the seas had risen, and the North American Desert had grown.

"John." Smith's smile grew broader. It was Mary. He remembered their argument, but he knew that their contract was still in force, and that Mary would have been sent to his apartment. The Public Security Software tried to move people to the safest places, and it scheduled them with declared relationships in mind.

"How did you get in?" He looked at the Beast. It huddled in its chair as if it knew that Smith was displeased. "I told Nine vee—" He caught himself short. He was using the name that Mary had given Nine vee bee.

I told the Door Beast that it was not to . . ."

"I prefer Mary." The Beast stepped out of its chair and walked toward him on its stumpy legs. It stood facing him and turned a supplicating look up to his face. "I prefer Mary." It blew the percussive sound out, almost plaintive in its statement. Smith shook his head. He turned to Mary.

"You see what you've done." Smith was almost crying. "Beasts are not supposed to act like this." He stopped. "It would follow . . . if—"

"What would follow, John?" Mary regarded him with blue eyes set off with the natural fall of a lock of almost-blond hair. Her lips were curled in a smile that Smith could only think of as kind, and she looked at him as if she knew him.

"It would follow that Beasts are not any less than me or you." Smith turned to the Beast and said the formula. "Nine vee slash bee slash are pee oh three zee why." The Beast came to attention. He turned to Mary. "Say three times. 'Do not. Do not. Do not." Mary obeyed. Smith paused, he had waited for her questions, but since there were none, he went on, "Lift for Wanda."

"I hear, and remember." The Beast smiled. It turned its head and pulled its red polo shirt to a smoother lay. "No Wanda."

Mary giggled and Smith turned to face her. He wanted to be stern, but he said, "Let's put the view window on see-through, and watch the storm."

Some Pig

by Nancy Davidson

In a town of foodies, no one has more clout than the leading restaurant reviewer at London's leading newspaper. Ivor Chelling is The Man—in a metro-sexual, food-guy sort of way. A top graduate of the leading culinary institute, he took a very different path from his classmates and is at the top of his game. He reviews only those restaurants he wants to review; and he absolutely refuses to review The Rabid Boar, the creation of his arch-rival classmate, Petrov Pacinko. But competitive forces intervene, and Ivor is compelled to review the hated Pacinko's restaurant. Ivor becomes completely obsessed by The Rabid Board, losing all desire to do anything other than eat there. Think Big Night *meets* Obsession.

Ivor Chelling was unhappy about his latest assignment. Typically, he decided on his own which restaurants he would review—visiting each one several times, and sometimes even deciding after two visits not to review it at all. But his editor had insisted, demanded to the point of threatening his job (though Ivor knew that, with his popularity, that was an idle threat; but still he demanded in such a way that Ivor realized he would be made miserable forever if he refused), that he review The Rabid Boar.

Ivor had planned to give it a miss for a number of reasons—most of which were indefensible. The restaurant had been open a few months and Ivor had managed to avoid going. Though the restaurant was located in a quiet village about forty-five minutes outside of London, it was attracting considerable attention from city dwellers. In cases where a restaurant attracted considerable attention, Ivor often chose not to review it. He preferred to write for those who might never know about a place without his coverage—and, even more importantly, to write for those who lacked the wherewithal to visit the high-end establishments.

For him—for the reader of the *Daily Sundial* who was not likely to have the price of dinner for two to spare—for him, Ivor wanted to create a complete experience, to give him the feeling of having been to a restaurant, to the point where he would almost not be sure whether he had or had not been there himself. Perhaps not the feeling of being there and tasting, but the sense of the day after, when the experience would become a delightful and lasting memory; but it would be the memory of what you tell yourself, because, like pain, the pleasure of a new taste could not really be recalled in all its range and depth, could not truly be recreated by merely picturing or remembering or even describing the food.

With his reviews, Ivor Chelling hoped to render a visit to a restaurant superfluous—unnecessary. With his heightened senses, he could enjoy it more than his readers could, even if they could afford the price of dinner; and with his powers of perception he could process the experience, rendering it in perfect, delectable prose, more delicious than anything the best chef could hope to conjure up.

His delight in the bad review was even more palpable. There were so many more ways to describe what made a particular dish bad than what made it transcendent. It was easier to remember a particular tasteless combination of ingredients, or the stink of a bad piece of meat, the rank odor of a mussel that had turned. Though having to actually eat the bad food was not an experience he purposely sought out.

He had also heard through the twisted grapevine that the chef-owner was a classmate of his from culinary school—a classmate whom he considered his antithesis. This was the real reason that Ivor planned to avoid The Rabid Boar. He did not want to acknowledge the existence of Petrov Pacinko. They had not been rivals in school. That would imply that they had been equals—and Ivor would not give Pacinko the compliment of considering him his equal. Pacinko had been the class clown. He could not be taken seriously. He made a mockery of everything that Ivor held dear.

His idea of a final project for a pastry class was to cover an edible balloon made out of spun sugar with caramel and nuts, fill it with helium gas, and float it above the heads of hungry schoolchildren. Another time he had made bright green spinach-whipped cream and served it alongside a rib roast. Once he had conjured up brown hamburger jello with a layer of tomato-colored, catsup-flavored gelatin and claimed that it was a dessert. He proposed live chocolate ants that would march across the plate in a confectionary class, but was told he would be expelled if he attempted it.

Everything was a joke with Pacinko. For his thesis, he had begun with a live duck, slaughtered it, plucked away its feathers, removed its feet and beak, its gizzards and squiggly innards, and then thrown away everything that was normally considered palatable, instead sculpting the waste into a multilayered terrine, dyed red with beet root and purple with pomegranate, colored with the juice of asparagus and puree of butternut squash, surrounding it with a bright yellow mustard foam.

That the final result was inedible bothered Pacinko not at all. He laughed—the high-pitched laugh of a hyena—when he presented his final meal and did not mind at all that his judges, aware of the ingredients before them, would not even take one bite. He ate the entire conconction himself, licked his lips, and patted his stomach. Ivor didn't know how Petrov managed it without tossing.

If he couldn't cook, that would be one thing, and Ivor would not hold it against him. But Pacinko's technique was impeccable. He just refused to take the culinary arts seriously. He made a mockery of Ivor's calling. His offense against cuisine was insupportable and could not be forgiven.

There was some satisfaction for Ivor in Petrov Pacinko's dismissal from the school. But Pacinko was not one whit humiliated. He did what he always did when the results were announced. His reaction was consistent with his behavior throughout the year. He threw his fist into the air, whooped loudly as if he had just won a long-jump contest, and laughed his high, hysterical hyena laugh.

Ivor's intentions at cookery school had been called into question as well. Although he was a talented cook, he had no intention of ever working full-time in a restaurant. He acquitted himself well at his required internships and externships, had proved himself an asset at the grill or at the salad station, or wherever he was placed; but Ivor knew from the beginning that his destiny was to write about food. He was a writer. His subject was food. His teachers did not approve of his decision—they felt ill-used—but he had done what any self-respecting writer would do. He had learned as much about his chosen subject as he could. He had thought that the teachers would respect his decision.

"Greetings, chef!" Ivor had said with a smile one day in 1974, when his instructor approached him as he filled a *bain marie*. His smile quickly faded in response to the chef's grim expression.

"Ivor," he said.

"Yes, chef?"

"I have heard a disturbing rumor."

"A rumor?"

"Chef Outre tells me you don't plan to cook after graduation."

"That hasn't affected my performance in his kitchen! Does he have any complaints about my performance?"

"No, no. That's not in question. The question is: Why are you here? Why did you deceive us?"

"I . . . it was never—"

"Chelling's going to be a famous critic!" Petrov interjected from across the room.

"Shut up, Petrov."

"Chelling!"

"I've never made a secret of my intentions. I want to be a food writer."

"But then, why come here? This is not some namby-pamby French school for rich American dilettantes. This is a serious place to study culinary arts."

Petrov's hyena laugh exploded in the air.

"Do you mind!" Chelling shouted.

The chef turned his entire body toward Pacinko with a single, sudden, almost violent movement. "Excuse us, please."

"No problem," Petrov said, and continued his chopping.

"Could you please leave the room? Immediately."

"Okay, but let me just say that I find Chelling's aspirations to be admirable—to really study cooking before commenting on it—it's just brilliant, devoted, passionate. Really commendable."

"Get out!" Chelling shouted.

"Get ahold of yourself," the chef said.

"I'm sorry," Chelling said. "I'm not a joker. I'm not here to fool around." He continued mincing Valrhona dark chocolate. He looked up at the chef. "I never kept my plans a secret. I have always intended to be a writer."

The chef put his face in his hands and rubbed vigorously. "I can't believe someone with your talents would want to be such a verminous creature."

"I don't plan to be a restaurant reviewer!"

"What then?"

"A writer!"

"What will you write? Cookbooks?"

"I don't understand why this bothers you!"

"You're going to write . . . ," he sputtered the word, "*cookbooks?*"

"No. I don't know. Maybe. I want to write about food. Books about food. I'm not ashamed. Do you think I should be ashamed?"

"This is a cooking school—a place men come to train as chefs!"

"I'm sorry, I see it differently." Chelling put down his knife and looked directly into the chef's eyes. "What do you want me to do?"

The chef blew air through his lips in exasperation, threw his towel in the air, and left the room, the double doors flapping behind him.

Tears welled up in Ivor's eyes. Before he could wipe them with his towel, Petrov Pacinko came back in the kitchen, wielding a butcher knife.

"What's up with him?" Pacinko asked.

Ivor ignored him.

"I just want you to know you have my full support. I think it's great that you want to be a restaurant reviewer. We need educated reviewers. These amateurs who think they can come in and tell us—"

"I don't . . . want . . . to . . . be . . . a . . . restaurant reviewer!" Ivor said. "And I don't want your support." Ivor collected the shaved chocolate together and prepared to put it in a storage container. As much as he could not bear to be in the room with Pacinko, his instinct to take care of his ingredients, and not to waste, overruled his revulsion.

"I don't know what your problem is with me, man. I'm on your side. I've always been on your side. You're my kind of people, baby."

"I am not your kind of people, sir. I do not wish to be affiliated with you in any way. I do not appreciate your cavalier and contemptuous attitude."

"Cavalier? Contemptuous? Do I not love fine cuisine as much as you do? Do I not find the highest passion and meaning in preparing the best ingredients in the most loving way? How can you condemn me like this?"

"You, sir, are nothing but a clown, a joker! And I wish to have nothing to do with you." Ivor had scraped the final bits of chocolate into their container, then dated and stored them in the refrigerator. "In the future, I ask you to cease and desist any and all communication with me."

"I just want to help you, man."

"I would prefer if you would pretend that I didn't exist."

———

Ivor had been the chief restaurant reviewer for the *Daily Sundial* since 1998—this was his sixth year. Over the years he had a built a collection of friends and acquaintances among whom he selected dining partners each time he visited a restaurant for a review. Choosing the right group to accompany him to each restaurant was the hardest part of his job. He usually brought three guests, so that he would be able to taste as many dishes as possible.

Since The Rabid Boar served only a tasting menu, he needed only one guest. They would each eat the same menu. This meant he could invite Itty Cahors. She was one of his favorite guests—she could be counted on to be amusing, charming, and even insightful about what she tasted. Her fatal flaw—and the reason he often chose other companions—was an extreme inability to make a decision. Dinners were long enough without waiting for Itty to wade through the menu, imagine exactly what each dish was, order, regret, change her mind, and finally end up disappointed with her choice. It added to her anxiety that she had to order something different from whatever Ivor ordered. And she refused to let Ivor choose for her. But a tasting menu satisfied her curiosity and her need not to miss anything or make a mistake. Itty took her responsibility as a dinner guest very seriously.

Ivor found that he often had to train his guests to keep the discussion away from his life as a restaurant reviewer, and to prevent them from making the kinds of special requests they thought they deserved as guests of the reviewer. They seemed to miss the point that Ivor wanted a *normal* experience and wanted to attract no undue attention. If the service was great, that was wonderful—but only if it was the same great service that the staff gave to all their guests. Itty understood completely. She was a perfect guest, too, in that she didn't want to talk only about the food. If there were such a thing as a professional conversationalist, Itty would have been set for life.

In a way, Itty could be said to be someone who sang for her dinner. She was a talented artist, yet financially a complete failure. Whenever she did make some money by selling her pantyhose stocking sculptures, or when she got a grant for her parachute wall hangings, she inevitably blew the whole wad at once—spending in a frenzy that made up for her usual financial repression. Her spree always included a great, big, fabulous party with great food and music. Itty had a knack for entertaining: Her generosity was not forgotten by her friends during the rest of the year when she had no money. Itty could be counted on to be amusing, and so was always a welcome guest at any dinner party or any outing to try the newest hot spot.

Though Ivor pretended he wanted to be treated like everyone else, in fact, he had a *do you know who I am?* kind of chip on his shoulder. He walked into a room—particularly a dining room—and expected all heads to turn in recognition and admiration. He had abandoned the idea of disguises to aid his anonymity, after the first few months, claiming that he found the disguises to be uncomfortable, time-consuming, and ineffective. In truth, he wanted to be seen. He liked to have Itty on his arm when he entered a room. She was like a perfect little bird, small and diminutive, but striking in appearance.

"Hello, Itty," Ivor said. "Sorry to phone at the last minute, but I just found out about this place. Are you free for dinner tonight?"

Itty said she would rearrange her plans.

"I'll pick you up at seven," he said. "Dinner's at eight, but it's a bit of a drive. We'll have a driver, though."

Itty said she adored having a driver.

"Okay, then. I'll see you at seven." Ivor loved making plans with Itty. She never asked any questions, needed no explanations.

Ivor looked through his selection of black and gray suits and chose a charcoal gray one with a very light blue pinstripe. He hung the suit in the bathroom so it would steam as he showered, and weighed himself as he waited for the water to warm. He was just 168 pounds, down from last week's 169, and maintaining the loss of over twenty pounds that he had struggled so hard for over the past year. He found, contrary to what one might imagine, that by dining in restaurants all the time, he could lose weight rather than gain, because the food was so abundant it became almost unappetizing. He grew so used to the idea that there was always more food that he never felt tempted to overeat.

He found his equilibrium by tasting and considering, rather than gorging and finishing everything that was set before him. The loss of hair was another matter, and one about which he expected he could do little. After his shower, he slicked his thinning hair back with a little gel and brushed his teeth with the flavorless toothpaste he had found at the alternative apothecary in Barnes. He hated to have the taste of food ruined by chalky peppermint or cinnamon, so he was quite pleased to have found this alternative. Ivor carried his suit back into his bedroom, where he decided to match the suit with a light blue shirt that had a thin, lavender silk thread running through it and a jet blue tie. He was shorter and balder and blonder than he would have liked, but he thought he cut a dashing figure nonetheless.

Although Ivor had heard that the dining room was understated and unpretentious, he was not prepared for its simplicity. The room was square, low-ceilinged, and beige. There was a warmth to it, but that came mainly from the overheated thermostat. At 7:47, when Ivor and Itty made their entrance, the small restaurant wasn't even half full, and there was no turning of attention toward them. The people who were there were completely absorbed in their own parties, laughing with delight and amazement between bites.

Ivor and Itty were seated at a table not far from the front door, with a view of a waiter's station, in a hallway that ran alongside the main dining room. Ivor could see that there were better tables available. He thought about asking to be moved but decided he would see how the staff acquitted themselves from this awkward position. Next time, he would request a specific table. Itty settled into her seat and looked around.

"There's something special about this place," she said, a wide smile breaking across her tiny face.

"Really? Why do you say that?" Ivor asked.

"Look how happy everyone is." Itty never knew anything about a restaurant before Ivor took her, another benefit to having her as a companion. She was a blank slate. Her impressions were not informed by any outside sources.

"But don't you think the dining room is rather unimpressive?"

"You mean the decor? It's plain, but clean and comfortable. Not distracting. I like it."

Ivor nodded and looked around the room again, trying to memorize what he saw. Some of his colleagues, competitors, and precursors used hidden tape recorders to make a record of their impressions, but Ivor preferred not to. He preferred the filter of his memory, believing that his most important observations would be those that lasted until the next day—or at least until he got home and wrote his notes.

Two waiters approached in gray tunics, each bearing what looked like a whipped cream canister. "Welcome," one said, "before we begin the dinner service, the chef would like to offer you a palate cleanser, with your permission."

"Whatever pleases the chef," Ivor said wryly.

"If you would please extend your tongue," the waiter nearest to Itty said. Itty giggled and complied. "And you, sir," the other waiter said. When both of them had extended their tongues the waiters, acting in concert, sprayed icy cold foam in their mouths. "Now close your mouth as quickly as you can."

Ivor laughed to see tiny white puffs escape from Itty's nose. As he laughed, plumes of cold smoke escaped from his own mouth. Itty covered her mouth with her hand. Her shoulders shook with her giggles.

As Ivor relaxed and stopped laughing he noticed that his mouth was infused with the refreshing flavor of rosewater and lemon, with a slight tingling aftertaste of shiso.

"Did you taste that?"

"I tasted vanilla taffy and violet water," Itty said.

"Really?"

The waiter stood by, a hint of a smile on his otherwise stern mouth. "Did we have the same thing?" Ivor asked the waiter.

"Not exactly." Ivor bristled at the waiter's inconclusive answer.

"Not exactly?" Ivor said, mocking the waiter's accent. "What *eggs-actly* did we *haf?*"

"So zat's how it's going to be?" the waiter answered. He paused to let his displeasure with Ivor's attitude sink in. "The lady had an infusion of lavender and *yuzu* in a mint base. The gentleman had a Douglas fir and pine emulsion."

"No rosewater?"

The waiter shook his head, heavy with pity. Ivor didn't believe him for a moment. This was how revenge sounded. "Well, in any case, it was delightful, quite cleansing."

The waited nodded slightly. Perhaps all was forgiven and the meal could proceed.

"As you may know," the waiter began, "we have only a fixed menu here at The Rabid Boar and I am sure it will be delightful for you. We will bring you each course, one at a time, and if you like, for an additional 65 pounds we will pair with wines."

Ivor preferred to order his own wine, and had to be careful in any case not to imbibe too much. "Itty, would you like the wine pairing?" Itty froze like the quintessential deer in headlights—she had not thought she would be called upon to make a decision. Ivor immediately realized his mistake.

"The lady will have the wine pairings," he said definitively. It would give him a chance to evaluate their choices.

Itty clapped her hands like a little girl. "May we have some of that delicious-looking bread now?" she asked.

"Why certainly, madam. We usually bring it after the *amuse bouche*, but if you like . . ."

"Oh no, no," Itty said. "Please do what you usually do. I trust you implicitly," she said, putting her tiny little hand on the waiter's forearm. He looked as if he wanted to recoil, but Itty gazed up at him with her deep, beautiful kohl-rimmed eyes, and he could only smile.

"Here is the menu—for your in-fo-ma-si-on," he said, placing a sheet of almost translucent vellum with silver writing before them on the table. "Next we have the live clam with the jus de raspberry honey." The waiter slipped a small plate covered with lavender petals in front of Itty. Ivor watched her inhale deeply, as the waiter set another plate just like it in front of him. A thumb-size clam in its shell rested on a bed of white crystals—Ivor thought it must be salt—but "It's sugar!" Itty declared, having dipped her pinky in the pile. On top of the clam were the smallest cubes of gelatin Ivor had ever seen, topped with just the leaves of basil microgreens. Ivor raised the clam to his mouth, carefully pulled on the contents with his lips, and received the entire communion in his mouth. He tasted herbs and flowers, fish stock and pepper, heaven and earth, and finished with the briny taste of the sea and the ever so slightly resistant tug of chewy, toothsome clam. He looked over at Itty and saw her rapturous expression.

"I want another one," Ivor said.

"Me, too," Itty said.

"But we mustn't," Ivor said.

"No, we can't," Itty said.

Another waiter came now with two kinds of bread: a white baguette and a hearty whole-grain loaf and four kinds of butter. "These two are unpasteurized goat milk butter," he explained. "This one is with salt, and this one without. These two are cow's milk. This one is dusted with pink peppercorns, the other is mixed with pear blossom honey from Italy. Enjoy!" he said with a flourish.

Itty took a bit of each kind of butter and put it on her bread plate. Her eyes gleamed with excitement.

"I've never seen you like this before," Ivor said.

"I know," Itty said. "I've never felt like this before—at least not about a restaurant. We have to come back here!"

"We haven't even had the first course yet!"

"I know. But we must. Promise me you'll bring me here again." Itty grabbed his hand with a desperate intensity.

"Of course. Don't worry," Ivor said.

Itty took a deep breath and spread some unpasteurized goat butter thickly on a piece of baguette. "This is the best butter I've ever eaten," she said.

"Salted or unsalted?" Ivor asked.

She looked down at her plate. "They are both . . . so . . . good."

"Whoever invented pasteurization—did he realize he was ruining good dairy for us all?" Itty asked.

"That would be Pasteur. I don't think he meant any harm."

"I guess not. When I was little I thought that homogenization and pasteurization were miraculous signs of progress. I thought they made drinking milk possible."

"That's what they wanted little girls in America to believe."

"But it's not true, is it?"

"It's a bit controversial. Americans are afraid of bacteria. Europeans believe that some bacteria actually aid digestion and health."

"Stupid Americans!" Itty's lower lip trembled like a cliche. Ivor was terrified she might cry.

"Well, no worries, Itty," he quickly assured her. "You can have as much of this raw milk butter as you like!" Itty smiled again. "But there's a lot more food coming."

"You're right," Itty said. "But I might never have butter this good for the rest of my life."

"True," Ivor said.

The waiter came forward with another set of plates, still not the first course, but another *amuse bouche*. On each plate was a small bowl. In each miniature bowl there was what looked like custard. "Be sure to dip your spoon all the way to the bottom of the bowl, there are three layers," the waiter advised. Itty drew her spoon out of the bowl and examined the three different-colored layers: green, yellow, and red. "It looks like a traffic light!" Itty declared.

"Pea, pumpkin, and beet!" Ivor guessed.

"Mint, orange, and raspberry!" Itty countered.

"Shall we taste it and see?" Ivor asked.

"Yes, let's."

It seemed that they were both right.

Each layer seemed to capture the flavor of everything that grew on earth that had that color. The green tasted of pea, basil, mint, zucchini, lime, and green apple. The yellow layer of lemon, spaghetti squash, yellow beets, yellow carrots and low-acid tomatoes, golden delicious apples, wax beans and daisies. The red layer tasted like raspberries, strawberries, red potatoes, and winesap apples. It was too much and it was not enough. When Ivor had finished everything in the small bowl, he had the flavor of nutmeg on his tongue.

For the first time in the meal, Ivor allowed himself to think about the chef. (He hadn't confided to Itty his acquaintance with Petrov Pacinko.) It was hard for Ivor to believe that this remarkable meal had been prepared by that clown; and yet, the sense of humor and playfulness was so familiar. The difference was that Pacinko wasn't just being witty, every bite was magnificent.

Next came a confit of boneless frog's leg with pea shoot and squid ink risotto. Itty looked at it and wrinkled her nose. For the first time during the meal, she appeared doubtful as she looked at the black rice on her plate. "I trust this chef," she intoned and took a little bite. "Mmmm." Brave Ivor didn't hesitate. He took a spoonful that contained all of the ingredients and rolled it around on his tongue.

"Unbelieveable," he said. "I don't know how he does it."

"Do you know this chef?" Itty asked.

"Yes. No. Kind of. I don't know," Ivor answered. Dots of perspiration beaded on his forehead.

"Are you okay?"

"Yes. Fine." Ivor snapped. "I'm fine. What did you think of the frog's legs?"

Next, a thinly sliced, Asian-inspired, duck tongue salami appeared, surrounded by bits of barbecued pineapple, with a thick, sweet sauce flavored with star anise, cinnamon, ginger, and cloves. Each course was slightly larger than the last, each seemingly more bizarre, and each one better than the last. Then, an intermezzo of smoked melon—small dices of fruit with smoked salmon sorbet—and a toasted slice of bagel, the size of Ivor's thumbnail, decorated the savory iced confection.

When the fish course came—turbot in preserved lemon butter sauce with reconstructed soft shell crabs baked into a flat, Indonesian pancake—Ivor could barely speak. "I'm ruined," he said and covered his face with his hands.

"What's the matter?" Itty asked.

"I'll never have a meal this good again."

"You don't know that."

"Yes, I do. I can't imagine eating anything else for the rest of my life."

Itty touched Ivor's hand.

"I don't know what I'll do," he said.

"You'll forget."

"I'll forget the exact feeling, what it actually tastes like, but I'll never forget that I've never had anything like this before. I've tasted perfection. My quest is over. What will I do? What will become of me? You don't feel it?"

Itty continued to eat her fish. She took a sip of wine.

"Ivor, dear. I know this isn't what you want to hear, but I think you're overreacting. By tomorrow, you won't really remember what the food tasted like."

"How can you say that?"

"Because it's true. We've talked about this. You remember what you are going to say about it, you remember what it looked like and whether it was properly prepared, whether you liked it or not, but you can't actually call up a clear memory of the flavor. It's like pain. It grows vague. Quickly. Tomorrow you'll be happy with a grilled cheese sandwich."

"I won't."

"Ivor," Itty said, her hand on Ivor's hand, "it's just food."

"Just food? *Just food?* I thought you understood me!"

Itty sat back in her seat, as if she could disappear in the cushions. She looked down at her plate. She was so quiet it was almost as if she had stopped breathing.

Ivor stood up, threw his napkin on the carpet and stomped off in the direction of the kitchen. "Pacinko? Where are you!"

In the kitchen, Petrov Pacinko sat on a high stool, examining each plate as it returned from the dining room. As usual, there was not a speck on any plate. The headwaiter reported to him on comments from every table, and tonight paid especially close attention to Table eleven—Ivor's table.

Petrov jumped off his stool and went to greet Ivor. "It's so good to see you, young man, and I'm so glad you are enjoying my food."

Ivor had no room for gratitude. "Don't mock me," he said. "Do you know what you've done to me?" he shouted.

"Cooked and served you the best meal you've ever had in your life?"

"You've ruined me. You have ruined my life."

"Oh, Mr. Chelling. That's not possible. You have a great life. You are the chief restaurant critic for the best-read newspaper in England."

"Exactly what I swore I'd never do. I'm sure that's what you're thinking."

"Not at all. I never thought there was anything wrong with being a restaurant reviewer. Remember? I was on your side."

"I never wanted you on my side. You didn't even know what my side was."

"But tell me, what have I done to you?"

"You've destroyed my purpose. You've prepared a meal that can't be surpassed. I can't believe the flavors you put together. It should be awful."

"Oh, Ivor, I'm very flattered, but that can't be true. I'll tell you what. Come back tomorrow night and I'll make you a completely different menu, and I promise it will be even better than what you had tonight."

"I don't think you can do it."

"But you'll have to come here and find out. It's something to live for."

"I still hate you, Pacinko. I love your food, but I *hate* you."

"There, there, Ivor. It's not worth getting so worked up about. It's just food."

"I know you don't mean that. There's no way you could cook like this and not care about food."

"I'm not saying I don't care. I'm saying it's not all there is. Surely, you must agree with that. You must believe in love and family and friendship? What is food without those things?"

"Yeah, whatever. You know what I mean."

"I know what you mean, but I'm not sure you know what I mean."

"Shut up, Pacinko. This isn't what I wanted to discuss. I want to know how you do it."

"How I do it?"

"How you make food that's so witty with impossible combinations that defy all logic and manage to make it taste better than anything else on the planet. Where did you learn how to do this?"

"Why are you so angry?"

"I told you. I'm ruined. Not only is there no longer any reason for me to do my job, but I'm not even going to bear eating anymore. The thought of ingesting anything less . . . it's futile."

"Well, we went to school together. You know where I got my training."

"But you weren't cooking anything like this."

"How would you know? You never tasted anything I prepared."

"Because it was so ridiculous!"

"But I'm doing the same thing here."

"No you aren't. There may be an element of wackiness—but the technique, the execution, the presentation, the flavor—it's on a completely different level."

"Well, I should hope I would have matured in fifteen years. Haven't you developed your craft?"

"But . . ."

"A question, Ivor? Do you cook anymore?"

Ivor shook his head. "I can't. I eat out everyday, sometimes several times a day."

"Don't you miss it?" Petrov asked.

Ivor stormed out of the kitchen, letting the doors flap wildly behind him. Pacinko and the other cooks broke out in loud laughter. "That is one tightly wound dude," Smith the sous chef said.

"Someone needs to loosen his knickers," Thompson the dishwasher said.

Pacinko laughed loudest of all, but then he stopped abruptly. "Okay. That's enough. Let's put him behind us."

"Come on, Itty. We're going."

"What are you talking about Ivor? We still have three courses to go. Not including dessert!"

"We're leaving. Trust me."

"I don't understand. You loved the food!"

"It's personal. I'll explain later. Please, Itty. I need to leave now."

Itty reluctantly got up from her seat, looked around the room at the other diners. She picked up a copy of the menu, tucked it in her purse, and followed Ivor out to the waiting car.

The next week Ivor tried to return to life as usual. He had three first-time visits to new restaurants, two return visits, and two lunches to finalize some reviews he had already written. He avoided Itty, even when she called to see how he was. He filled his lunches and dinners with appointments with other companions. When the food was placed before him, he pushed it around on his plate, but he couldn't bring himself to eat anything. For the first time in his life he brought his tape recorder with him, and wrote his reviews based on the comments of his friends. He grew thinner. His pants slipped from his waist and he pulled his belt tighter, but he refused to weigh himself.

In the following week, Ivor made no reservations. He tried to write reviews of places he had visited the month before. He knew that his work was weak, but he couldn't bring himself to compromise the memory of his meal at The Rabid Boar. He lay on the sofa in his office, trying to imagine a way out of his predicament. He avoided the phone and ignored his editor's comments.

Finally, his editor demanded to know when he would have the review for The Rabid Boar. "I've only been there once," Ivor said, stalling. He wanted to go back—he was dying to go back—but he was afraid. The editor insisted that the review be delivered within three days. Ivor called Itty. She was no longer happy to hear from him.

"But you have to come with me," he pleaded with her on the phone. "I'll do anything you like. I know you're dying to go back there. Please, Itty. I need you."

Itty refused to talk to Ivor in the car. She spoke occasionally to the driver, and Ivor tried to respond, but she made it clear she wasn't speaking to him. It was a beautiful autumn evening, with a clear sky and visible stars, so Itty's bad mood was particularly out of character and abrasive to Ivor.

But as soon as she stepped inside The Rabid Boar, Itty's pilot light turned up to high. She looked at Ivor and smiled as if to say "I forgive you." This time they were seated in the main room, in an intimate corner near the fireplace. The waiter came over to greet them right away. "The chef would like to offer you a specially designed menu—"

Ivor interrupted him. "Would you please thank him very much, and let him know that we will take him up on that offer another time, but tonight we would like the complete and regular tasting menu." The waiter nodded and disappeared.

It was impossible not to be happy inside the belly of The Rabid Boar. Diners all around them were giggling. Burbling with joy at the surprising flavors, laughingly guessing at the ingredients in their food.

Ivor took Itty's hand. "Thank you," he said.

"It's my pleasure," Itty answered. "Really."

"I'm sorry about how I behaved."

"I know you are."

"So you forgive me."

"You know I do," Itty said.

"You are a very forgiving woman," Ivor said.

"Oh, I don't know about that. You haven't really tested me."

"Well, then, I hope never to test you."

"It's unlikely you will. But if you ever do, just get me a dozen of these clams and all will be forgiven."

Ivor nodded, pleased to see the clam nestled on a pile of rock sugar that had taken up so much room in his imagination since his last visit to The Rabid Boar. The meal continued smoothly, a recapitulation of the perfection that Ivor and Itty had experienced before—though this time Ivor was careful not to offend the waiter. If possible, it seemed their level of bliss exceeded that which they had experienced before. Though the element of suspense was removed and the food puzzles had been solved, Ivor and Itty were able to focus more on the elemental sublimity of the actual food. If Ivor had felt any doubt (and he hadn't), the second visit reinforced his assertion that this was the best meal he had ever eaten or was ever likely to find elsewhere.

When they reached the part of the meal that Ivor had interrupted last time, the waiter approached, as if with a special request. "The chef would like to present you with a special course—in addition to the regular menu—and he would be very grateful if you would accept." Ivor looked at Itty. "It would be our pleasure. Thank you. And please relay our appreciation to the chef."

What came next was not one, but two additional courses: The first was called "Serious Pig," crispy pork belly with tender sweetbreads and shaved Brussels spouts, surrounded by a puree of butternut squash, flavored with shaved licorice, grated at the table with a microplane. The second was called "Big Fat Duck," a tamarind-glazed, barbecued, chubby breast of duck removed from the bone, but surrounded by sweet, crisp, skin and stuffed with a graham cracker, pomegranate, oyster, and sausage stuffing. It was presented whole for the table to see, and then cut into one-inch-wide slices. The portions were relatively small, just enough to leave Ivor and Itty wanting more, not so much that they couldn't continue the meal. The final "entree," if such distinctions could be made, was a clear broth, slightly viscous, but almost without flavor, but with a hint of lemon aroma, in which floated a perfect specimen of poached lobster. Fluffy bits of scrambled egg drops, ultra-thin crinkled pieces of gold foil, fava beans, and baby asparagus floated on the surface of the broth.

The progression of dessert courses began with cracked coffee and cocoa beans in a hot white chocolate soup with a dollop of osetra caviar served in a light blue porcelain eggshell with shaved nutmeg on top. Next, there was a glazed chestnut with a liquid champagne center. The penultimate dessert was the most bewildering—a cheeseburger rendered in ice cream with a sweet, eggy brioche bun and agave honey–infused tomato confit standing in for catsup. Words failed them. Itty ate in stunned silence.

The final dessert course, before the chocolates and petit four, was a palate-cleansing beet and parsnip sorbet with a hint of green tea and lemongrass.

The meal ended not with a whimper but with a bang. Itty took a small bite of a square, flat chocolate truffle and felt a tingling in her mouth. She covered her mouth but could not contain her giggles. "Take one!" she said. Ivor dissolved one in his mouth, and felt it explode. "Pop rocks!" he announced.

Ivor kept his promise to Itty and stayed at the table for the entire meal, except once, when he asked her permission to visit the men's room. When the waiter brought Ivor's coat, as requested, he asked if Ivor and Itty would like to visit the chef. Ivor shook his head.

"No thank you," he said, "our waiting coach might turn into a pumpkin if we tarry another second, but please convey our thanks and congratulations to the chef. And tell him this: He is the Master."

In the car on the way home, Ivor did something he had never done in his life: He kissed Itty on the lips.

The next day Ivor lay in a stupor, unable to write or eat. He kept going over the meal in his mind, convinced more than ever that he was ruined. He called Itty and asked her to tell him everything she remembered about the meal. He shivered with pleasure at her recounting. At night, he lay in bed, rehearsing the courses over and over again in his head. He found he had no words adequate to describe what he had eaten. He felt the inevitable withdrawing of sensation; he could remember what the food was, what was in it, what it looked like, but he couldn't recapture or recreate the actual taste, what it felt like when the food touched his tongue, what the flavor actually was. He would recognize it if he tasted it again, but he couldn't relive the experience of eating at The Rabid Boar in his imagination.

Two more days passed and Ivor found that he was unable to write the required review. If he didn't turn it in he would be fired, his editor had warned. Ivor still believed it was an idle threat. He sent a note to the editor, explaining that he didn't think it was appropriate to review this restaurant. By the end of the day, Ivor received a note in return by special messenger. He was fired.

"Bitch!" Ivor screamed. And then he fainted.

Ivor was revived by his cleaning woman, Ida. She found him lying on the floor. "Mr. Chelling, what's the matter with you? You're all skin and bones! A man in your profession—haven't you been eating? It's scandalous." She knelt by him and, after forcing him to drink some water, pulled him up onto the sofa and tried to get him to eat some soup she found in the pantry. "No thank you, Ida. I'm fine. Just had a bit of a shock."

"When's the last time you eaten, Mr. Chelling? I knows you don't usually eat at home, what with all the restaurants, but you haven't been to any restaurants this week, have you?"

"How do you know that, Ida?"

"A cleaning woman can tell these things, Mr. Chelling. From the suits you haven't worn. And the shoes. And you always seem to be home these days. Even at lunchtime. And there ain't no pots or pans to clean, or even a dish. It's not like you. What's happening, sir? If you need me to get you some groceries, that's no problem. Be happy to do it."

"No thank you, Ida. That's very kind of you. I'm fine. I'll pick something up later. You go on home, now. I'm fine. I'll see you tomorrow."

As soon as she left, Ivor burst into tears. Her kindness—and the way that she knew him so well, as if she made her life's study his habits and behaviors—reminded him that he would soon have to live without her. Without his job, he wouldn't be able to afford a full-time maid, or even a part-time one. It wasn't like he would just be able to get another job on another paper. He would have the same problem wherever he went. The only meal worth eating was the one he ate at The Rabid Boar.

When Ivor woke the next morning he knew what he had to do. He would lease his flat in London—or even sell it so he'd have a bit of income—and move to East Bumbery, as close as possible to The Rabid Boar. He would eat there as often as he could, as long as his savings held out. A few times a week would probably be more than enough calories to sustain him. And then he would write a book about it. He had always meant to write about food, not as a restaurant critic, but as an essayist. This was his chance for a new beginning!

Ivor called the restaurant and asked the reservationist if he knew of any flats in the area. He told Ivor that one of the waiters was looking for a flatmate. Ivor cringed at the idea of sharing his personal space with someone else, particularly a stranger, and particularly a waiter, but he thought it might be a good idea, considering his circumstances. "Can I give you my mobile and ask him to ring me? He might prefer that to me calling him. Would that be alright?" The reservationists said that it would. "And while I have you, may I reserve a place for one for this evening?"

Although Ivor had budgeted for just two meals a week at The Rabid Boar, he found himself (oh, look, there I am! *Quel surprise!*) every day, lunch or dinner, in the dining room. Sometimes he visited Pacinko in the kitchen, sometimes he allowed the chef to create a special meal for him. Other times, when moodiness or despair overtook him—he still hadn't fully reconciled himself to the fact that the best restaurant in the world had his former nemesis at its helm—he left without finishing the meal and without talking to Petrov.

After a month of this—in some ways the happiest month of Ivor's life—Ivor ran out of money. During the day he wrote—anything and everything he thought of. He loved the liberation of not writing for publication. Of not writing about restaurants. Of not having to find a different way to describe the same bright red, relatively bland tuna, seared on the outside, raw on the inside. He had run out of superlatives long ago. He pondered the ephemeral nature of flavor, the elusiveness of taste. He wrote short stories and essays. Villanelles and sonnets. Even an ode to Petrov Pacinko's chestnut pudding.

Lately, Ivor had come to question his singleminded devotion to the topic of food. When a person didn't care about what they ate, it could affirmatively be said that such a person was missing out on the finer things in life, but a person who thought about food all the time, he realized now, could be considered to occupy an equally unhealthy opposite end of the spectrum. He was glad to finally have some perspective on his obsession.

In the meantime, however, he needed to find a way to make money. He shared a three-room flat with the waiter, Pierre, but the sublease of his flat in London was only enough to cover his most basic expenses. He sold a few articles, but soon realized that this was no way to make a living. His flatmate made more money in a week than he could earn in a month. Nonetheless, he continued to eat at The Rabid Boar, as often as he could, every week, using his credit cards to pay for his meals.

Then one evening: "I'm sorry, Mr. Chelling. Your credit card has been declined. Might you have another?"

Ivor's lip trembled and he prayed that he would not cry. "I'm afraid that's the last one," he said.

"Well, no worries, Mr. Chelling, it's on the house . . ."

"Thank you very much, Paul. Tell Pacinko I'll pay him back. And you, too. The tip, I mean. . . . Excuse me, won't you?"

Ivor ran out the door and all the way to the flat he shared with Pierre. He didn't stop running until he was inside and under the scratchy flannel blanket on his thin, bumpy mattress behind the shut and locked door. He lay there for days, tossing and turning, unable to get comfortable, but unwilling to leave the bed. He neither ate nor drank, save for occasional sips from the tea mug on the floor, which he could reach without getting out of bed. He hesitated to visit the toilet and vowed never to shower again. He had never been so miserable in his life, and yet he found some strange comfort in the cocoon of his cot.

On the third day, there was a harsh rapping on his bedroom door. It grew increasingly louder—now it was a furious banging—with each moment he did not respond. Finally, he screamed, "What the fuck do you want?" but it came out weak and barely audible.

"Ivor, open up. It's Pierre."

"I can't come to the door," Ivor said. "Just tell me what you want."

"I don't want anything," Pierre said, irritated. "Pacinko wants to know why you haven't been in the restaurant."

"Tell him I have found alternative means of sustenance." Surely Pacinko would know by now of his embarrassment with the rejected credit card.

"Well, he asked me to tell you that he wants you to come in. He needs to talk to you."

"Tell him I am indisposed."

"Can't I get you something, Ivor?"

"No thanks. I am quite self-sufficient."

"Let me know if you change your mind."

"Thank you, Pierre. You are quite considerate. But please do not give it another thought. Have a good evening."

The next day, after the lunch service, Pierre knocked on Ivor's door again. This time, Ivor came to the door in his dressing gown. If Pierre noticed his extreme pallor, the way the loose flesh hung about his jowls, the white paste collecting in the corner of his lips, the way his hair stuck to his head, the crystals of dried matter on his lashes, or the rank stench of the unwashed man, he did not betray it in his manner or in his words. Pierre looked directly at Ivor. In his outstretched hands was a large package wrapped in butcher paper. "Petrov asked me to give this to you."

Ivor looked at the package with disdain, as if Pierre had offered up to him a plate of steamed rattlesnake on a bed of steaming bull feces. "No. Thank you. I said . . ."

"Please just take it. I beg of you. Pacinko is my boss. And he insists—"

"Thank you, Pierre. I am sorry that you are in the middle." Ivor took the package, bent at the middle as if to bow to his roommate. "Excuse me," he said, as he walked out of his room, past Pierre to the window in the hall. He raised the casement up as high as it would go and hurled the package with great force so that it landed with a bang and a splat on the refuse bin below. Ivor pushed past Pierre, back into his room, and crawled under the covers. About a half hour later, when he heard the front door slam and was sure that Pierre was gone, he ran down to the bin and pulled the package out. He carried it up to his room, barely able to contain himself. It was all he could do not to rip open the paper and stick his tongue in while he was still on the stairs. In his room, he opened the paper and spread it on his bed like a makeshift tablecloth.

Almost without seeing what he was eating, Ivor attacked the food. He swallowed without chewing, ate without tasting, and before he could even make a significant dent in the care package, was doubled over with stomach pain. "What am I doing?" He said this out loud. "Not only am I talking to myself, but I'm eating like a wild animal." Ivor lay down again, his hands pressed against his aching stomach. He ignored the ringing phone—the machine would get it—but he rose again, wrapping the leftovers as well as he could and hiding the remnants under his bed.

He had never been so ashamed of himself. His stomach rumbling, his ears pounding with a loud, empty, white noise, Ivor drifted off into a fitful, uneasy slumber. He dreamed that he was preparing a banquet for the King (who bore an uncanny resemblance to Chef Outre from his cooking school), but he had failed to procure any food. Then he dreamed about his lumpy mattress, as if the food under his bed had expanded and was pressing against his back. Finally, he was awakened from the worst dream of all—he was butchering a horse, the single ingredient in an eight-course meal—by a loud knocking at his bedroom door.

Relieved to be freed from his nightmares, Ivor jumped out of bed and flung the door open without asking who it was. "Pacinko!" he said, and ran to get his dressing gown. He pressed the garment against his chest. "What are you doing here?"

"I've missed you at the restaurant. I wanted to talk to you."

"This isn't a very good time."

"I'm sorry. You never answered the phone. I left messages—"

"I can't talk."

"Ivor. You're not well. Can I get you a doctor?"

"I'm fine. Thank you. Please don't trouble yourself about me."

"I'm here to ask you a favor. Will you come see me? Tomorrow? At the restaurant? Please?"

Ivor shut the door without answering and returned to his bed.

Pacinko continued to make his pleas through the door, but Ivor stuffed cotton in his ears, put his pillow on top of his face, and hunkered down into his soiled burrow.

Ivor woke up the next morning intending never to return to The Rabid Boar, but his body overtook his mind. He showered, washing days of grime and decay from his bony body, massaged his ever-thinning hair, and dressed in one of his best cashmere sports coats. He walked slowly, unused to the sunlight and weak from malnutrition. When he arrived at the restaurant, he walked through the empty dining room to the kitchen.

"Where's Pacinko?" he asked quietly, as if he didn't want anyone, even the person to whom he was speaking, to hear him.

A busboy pointed out back.

Ivor went through the back door of the restaurant. He opened the wrought iron gate that led to the garden where Petrov planted his microgreens and microvegetables. Petrov opened the door and motioned for the former restaurant critic to enter, closing the door behind him. Ivor was careful not to trip over an ice-cream machine and a juicer that lay on the floor in the cluttered room.

"There's something I've been wanting to ask you—but I wasn't sure how to approach you."

Ivor looked over Petrov's head to a contraption that looked like a mini-guillotine.

"My sous chef is leaving."

"Peter?"

"He wants to cook in Spain."

Petrov shrugged. "What can you do?"

"What can I do for you? Do you want some names?"

"Well, actually. I was hoping you might help me. Yourself."

"What? You mean cook?"

"I'd like you to join my staff. I've been thinking about this for a long time. Ever since you left the paper, actually."

"Left?"

"You never told me what happened."

"I hope you aren't offering me a job out of pity!"

"What if I am?"

"I can't stand pity! I may be pitiful, but I don't want you to pity me."

"If it were a pity job, I'd have you scrubbing potatoes. I know you can cook. I need you. And I think it's a waste, you not cooking."

"But I haven't cooked professionally in decades!"

Petrov put his hands on Ivor's shoulders and kneaded them gently. Ivor felt a tremor in his knees. "It's in your muscles. Your muscles have memory." Petrov took Ivor's hands between his thumb and forefinger and turned them so that the palms faced up. "It's in your fingers. Look at these hands—they were made to cook!"

Ivor pulled his hands away and leaned against a vintage sno-cone machine. "Okay. Let's try it. If I'm terrible, you have to fire me."

"Fine. Can you start tomorrow? I promise to keep you well fed."

"Staff meals, right? Chicken wings and meatballs?"

"We don't do that here. You can eat whatever you want. I just hope seeing behind the curtain won't ruin the magic for you."

Ivor was prepping for dinner service one night when Petrov came up behind him. "In honor of your three-month anniversary at The Rabid Boar, I've invented a special dish for you! If you like it, I'll name it after you." Petrov placed a small plate of a beautifully arranged tower of braised meat, square half-inch cubes piled on top of each other like a small building, surrounded by a moat of red-purple blueberry-pomegranate sauce, on the counter in front of Ivor. Ivor stopped chopping and looked at the plate. He eyed the plate with suspicion.

"What is it?"

"I want you to guess."

"Of course you do." Ivor smiled weakly. "It looks like some kind of city bird—small-boned and gamey."

"Yes?" Pacinko said. "Go on."

"Pigeon? I noticed some fat ones out back—"

"No. But not a bad guess."

"Give me a hint."

"Okay." Pacinko pulled a long, blue-black feather from behind his back and held it up to the light in front of Ivor's face. A flicker of recognition crossed Ivor's eyes. His mouth formed a rigid straight line. He picked up his fork and plunged it into a piece of the bird, without toppling the tower.

Pacinko grabbed Ivor's fork arm. "Wait!"

"What?"

"It's crow!"

"I know," Ivor said, and then he placed the fowl on his tongue. "If you can cook crow, then I can eat it."

Pacinko let his hand rest on Ivor's shoulder for a moment, then he pulled a fork out of the pocket of his chef's jacket, stabbed a piece of meat and popped it in his mouth. "Good, isn't it?"

The Good Kid

by Brian Richmond

Marty had barely escaped the botched bank job. The cops were all over the place and all his accomplices were either in custody or dead. When he took refuge in the used record shop with the ratty-looking kid behind the counter, he knew his chances of escape were limited. And the kid was making sense. Even if he couldn't trust the kid, at least he could control him. Or so he thought. Inside Man crossed with Collateral.

His lungs aching, his heart pounding, Marty slipped through the doorway of a ratty-looking record shop. His buddies were dead or cuffed outside and the cops had the street closed off. Marty turned the sign hanging on the door to CLOSED, knowing as he did so that it was stupid. Like the cops were going to say "Oh look, a closed sign, we can't go in."

There was one guy behind the counter in the shop. Twenty-something, baggy clothes, one of those sixties-style haircuts that were back in fashion now.

"The bank, huh?" the kid said.

Marty pointed the Colt at him.

"Good idea," said the kid. "Shoot me. Make a big noise. With the cops outside looking for you."

"Back door?" Marty was breathless, running was not his thing. He lowered the gun. Damn thing felt heavy.

"Sure, like they haven't thought of that."

Christ, the kid was right. He was screwed and this guy knew it. Here he was, thirty years at this business, off and on, and Slim Shady here was telling him the way things were.

"That the cash?"

Marty had actually forgotten he was carrying the sack. He brought the gun up again. This guy was just too cool.

"For crissake, stop wavin' the goddamn gun around, okay? Jesus." He walked past Marty, peeked out into the street. "They're starting to search the shops both ends of the street. Working their way down. They know you're still around. At large . . ." He laughed at the sound of the jargon.

"Christ, I may just shoot you anyway, only thing'll shut you up . . ."

"Hey, why do that when you can get away with half the money?"

Half the money. There it was. Okay. Good. Now Marty felt a bit more at home. Now they were talking business.

"How 'bout I just put a gun to your head, take you hostage?"

"Oh, yeah, like in the movies. Look, you know that's crap. When'd you ever hear of that working? Think about it. I'm your dream come true. Crooked. Greedy. Willing to lie just to get the green. We can work something out here."

"You're pretty cool about this. For a civilian."

"Hey, I've been in trouble off and on since I was twelve. I've been inside. And anyway, so far, I haven't done a thing wrong. This is a win-win situation for me."

"So, Mr. Win-Win, what's the master plan?"

"Let me think, will ya? . . . You're a customer. . . . Naw, that's not it. You're a rep. That's it! You're a rep from one of the CD retailers. Hell, we've known each other for years. We were in here, shootin' the breeze, heard the commotion. . . . What's happening, officer, is everyone all right? Yeh, that's it. A rep."

"That's the brilliant plan?"

"It is a brilliant plan. I own this shop. I've known you for years. Who's gonna doubt me?"

"I don't know . . ."

"Look, they're just breezin' through all the businesses here, looking for something suspicious. Why should anybody think you're not who I say you are?" He paused. "Unless . . ."

"What?"

"The money. The gun. You've got to give them to me."

"No way."

" 'Kay. Fine. You're on your own."

"Look, your plan's as good as you say, they won't even look at me."

"They might, and if they do . . . plus, cops come in here, you're standing there tooled up and carrying all that cash, you'll be nervous. Uptight. Cops smell that stuff. You know they do."

"Why should I trust you?"

"You don't. I take the gun and the money, I stick them in the safe. Soon as the cops are gone, you get the gun and half the money."

"How do I know you'll give it back?"

" 'Cause I say I will. And how do I know you'll give me my cut? What? You're worried about takin' me in a fight if it comes to that? Huh? You scared of me? Look, you think I wanna slug it out with you, make a lot of noise, drop both of us in it? Still, it's your call. But, I'm not kiddin', you're still carrying when they come in here, you're on your own. We're runnin' outa time. . . ."

He was right. It was decision time. Marty didn't like it. He didn't like it one bit. He took out the automatic, ejected the round in the chamber. Removing the magazine, he handed the unloaded weapon to the kid, along with the money. The kid didn't really believe Marty would hand him the loaded gun, did he?

The kid smiled. "Fair enough. I'll put these in back. Also, I've got a briefcase in there and a business card from one of the sales guys calls here from time to time. You can show it to the cops if they ask. Just remember the name, though."

The kid took the money and the gun and went out through a door behind the counter. Marty didn't like this. He didn't like it one little bit. But the cops were working their way down the street, time was running out, and he didn't know what else to do.

Mr. Cool rummaged around in back. Marty heard the safe being opened, a pause, then it closing again, the spin of the tumblers. When the kid came back in he was carrying a little nickel-plated .22 in his hand.

"Surprise." The gun made a pathetic little crack but Marty felt his leg go numb and he dropped straight to the ground, like a jacket sliding off a hanger. He sat up, looked down, and saw a pool of blood begin to well out from his left thigh. It didn't hurt, still numb from the impact. The kid kept the gun on him.

"I knew it," Marty said. "I knew you were working some move, you little . . ."

"The only move I'm working is getting you out of here. Jesus, did you really think the cops were just going to take you at your word? That a business card would satisfy them?" He threw a white card onto Marty's lap. It said: Dave Cash, Impact Recordings.

"Remember that name. And keep your goddam wits about you, you could still get outa this mess."

The kid stood for a moment beside the door to the street, took a deep breath. His face became anxious, fearful. He opened the door and started shouting: "Help! Please! My friend's been shot! Officers."

Christ, Marty had to admit, the kid was good. The way he put his hands to the side of his head, he looked really shook up. Marty knew he'd better get in character, too.

A couple of cops burst in, guns drawn. They looked down at Marty who was now lying back on the floor, moaning, blood pooling beneath him.

"Get an ambulance!" one shouted to the other. "What happened here?"

The kid looked really shaken. "This guy burst in here, just after I heard the sirens. He . . . he shot Dave here. Then he told us if we didn't give him some time to get away before we called you guys, he'd get some of his buddies to come for us later on. I was too scared to get help, but Dave was getting worse."

"It's okay, it's okay. My partner's gettin' an ambulance. Now, where'd he go?"

The kid pointed. "Out back," and the cop ran off.

Marty opened his eyes. "Did you really have to shoot me?"

Kneeling beside him, the kid whispered. "You're a shooting victim now. Nobody's gonna ask you any questions. They'll load you in an ambulance and take you to the hospital. It's only a twenty-two round and it went straight through the flesh in your flabby old thigh, there. Good thing you don't work out. You go to the hospital, get it bandaged, get a shot of pain relief, then you sneak outa there. Disappear."

"They're gonna know you lied if I take off."

"Guess you didn't read the sign."

Marty twisted his head to look at the shop window. The backwards letters said: CLOSING DOWN SALE—LAST DAY.

The kid smiled. "I'm finished in this town. I owe money to some pretty heavy people. By the time you're making your break from the hospital, I'll be gone. I'm taking all the money, of course."

"So, you shot me in the leg and now you're gonna rip me off?"

"Uh-huh."

Marty smiled. "Thanks, kid. You earned it."

The kid smiled back. "It *is* a brilliant plan." He slipped Marty the .22. "Keep this outa sight. Just in case."

Two paramedics burst into the shop. "We'll take it from here."

Marty groaned and closed his eyes as they lifted him onto the stretcher. Just before they took him out to the ambulance, he managed to look toward the kid, give a sly wink, then he was gone.

The kid went back behind the counter of the shop and sat down. He took a deep breath. The old guy was a pro. He knew that the cops would have seen through him without the shooting. And he was willing to give up the money for freedom, if that was what it took.

From the back of the shop, the cop came in.

"Gone."

"Officer," the kid said, "I lied to you."

"What!"

"That guy, the one in the ambulance—he's the one you want."

You could have driven a bus into the cop's open mouth.

"He bust in here. I've a twenty-two, it's legal . . . you know, for robberies . . . I shot him in the leg but then he pointed this gun at me. Made me hand over mine. He gave me a bag and his own gun, told me to hide them in my safe, that some of his friends would come and get it later. That if I said anything . . . he still had my twenty-two, had it on me the whole time, that's why I was so scared." He buried his head in his hands.

"The money's here?"

"In my safe."

"Jesus . . ." The cop got on his radio, reported that the guy in the ambulance was the guy they wanted, told them he was armed with a .22.

Then the kid led him into the back room, opened the safe, showed him the automatic and the bag of cash. Of course, the cop didn't know that the bag was lighter than when it came in through the door.

"Goddam. Would you look at that."

"Officer, you won't let anything happen to me, will you?"

"Don't worry, you'll get protection. And there'll be a reward."

"A reward?" Yeah, like he didn't know.

"Big one. Apprehending an armed robber. Some bank staff were shot, they pay out big to get guys that do that. Plus, there'll be something for gettin' them their money back."

"A reward?" said the kid. "Imagine that. Imagine that."

———

In the ambulance, Marty breathed in the air through the mask they gave him. The siren wailed as they cut through the traffic. Best getaway car Marty'd ever had. Okay, he'd come out of it all empty-handed but, he had to admit it, without the kid, he wouldn't have gotten out at all.

You had to admire someone as smooth as that, able to think on his feet.

Yeah, thought Marty, he was a good kid.

A good kid.

Marty heard more sirens, coming closer.

Hey, imagine that. A police escort.

Blind Man in the Halls of Justice

by John Minichillo

Is justice really blind? For the man with the white-tipped cane serving on jury duty, it is more than an expression. And for the kid whose jury service is no respite from getting high, his new "friend" may be the easiest meal ticket he's seen in a while. But it soon becomes unclear who is using whom, when the blind man asks the kid to take him to the strip club where the defendant was arrested for providing more than just a lap dance. A Civil Action *meets* Scent of a Woman.

The lumbering city bus rounds a corner and starts down one of the steep hills of Tacoma. I get up from my seat and the driver touches then rides the brake. The weight of the bus and the sharp angle of descent makes moving to the exit a lurching progression of grabs for the handles along seat backs, until I'm secure in the well at the rear door. The driver sees me, but I pull the cord anyway and he heaves the bus nearly into the curb, everyone dips forward slightly, and the brakes let out a stuttered moan until the bus comes to a complete stop. Halfway down the hill I see the new jail construction project, and at the far end of it, my destination, the familiar courthouse. This is one of the oldest parts of Tacoma, with the requisite McDonald's, scattered lunch counters, dive bars, bail bond offices, the public library, and a leather and shoe repair shop. Further down the hill is the Puget Sound.

In the distance I can also see the Tacoma Dome and beyond it Mt. Rainier. So, the remote natural beauty of Washington state hasn't completely escaped this inner-city scene of limestone, iron bars, dated neon, grimed-over windows, and never enough parking. Without that mountain and the body of water, I could be at the center of any semimetropolis. Recently, Tacoma was named the most depressing place to live among cities of its size. I didn't actually read that, it wasn't in the paper or anything. Some Internet poll. Something I heard, probably bar talk, most likely from someone depressed. Whoever told me this, it was easy enough to believe. And I have also passed it along as truth.

But this is one of the rare, cloudless days when Mt. Rainier towers over the horizon and commands the eye. I've never been out there but I know it exists. People climb it. Al Gore climbed it. The sheer enormity of it, the nearly incomprehensible but undeniable reality of its reaching into the sky. Once I'm firmly landed on solid ground I stop and stare. The sky is regularly overcast, with the sidewalks always wet, but the occasional sighting of this mountain helps me endure the gray days, and I remain here. This is my home. An unexpected, clear, sunny morning like this one has sometimes brought me to tears. I'm so used to attributing the fragility of my emotions to the depressing Tacoma weather. But that wouldn't be the whole story. I smoked a joint before walking to the bus stop, so I'm feeling pretty high. I'm on my way to jury duty on this rare, sunny day, and I'm stopped in my tracks by the immense snowcovered beauty that pulls the eye.

I take out my keys and pocket change in anticipation of stepping through the metal detector and of being patted down by one of the courthouse cops. They can go through my pockets all they want, because I'm going to be on the other side of the docket for a change. After a quick once-over with the magnetic wand, I'm directed to a large room with rows of chairs where they check my ID, I sign in, and I'm given a yellow badge that says JUROR. I'm early, but there are others here watching a video of a woman behind a podium who talks about the importance of civic duty. Most everyone has a book and is occupied with reading. One woman talks while she keeps her hands busy knitting, with balls of yarn and extra needles in a tote bag on the seat next to her. Apparently, she has been through this before and she wants us all to know.

"Could take two weeks, could take three," she says. "I was our jury foreman last time. I nominated myself but was sorry for it. That kind of responsibility weighs on you."

The same letter that said not showing up could be a violation of the law also explained we'd be paid ten dollars per day. This is more than enough to buy lunch, but I also expect to smoke a joint every morning, and that's going to put me in the red. I don't have a job and I don't know how they got my name and address. I'm probably not at all the type of person they want serving on their juries, but here I am just the same.

A younger man asks about having his bus fare reimbursed, something I hadn't anticipated, and I follow him to a bursar's window in the main lobby. At this window, the only window of its kind, there's a line, not a long one, but the postures of those in it and the heated debate at the front make it clear the line is idle.

A woman wants to cash a check and he points to the sign that says no personal checks will be accepted. There's a post office just a few blocks away. But the woman refuses to budge and she keeps saying she'd written a check before. I'm still high and I turn around to take in the room, to watch the reactions of the people as they're patted down coming in from the streets.

A female cop has a blind man over to the side and she's trying to pull apart his walking cane with no success. He wears a suit, an overcoat, and a hat, and she feels his chest and shoulders then gives him back the stick. He asks her for directions to the room where prospective jurors are supposed to meet. She faces him toward the same hallway I'd just come from and she lets go of him with a gentle shove, like pushing a toy boat. He proceeds, but it's a large room and he misses the entrance to the hallway. He follows the wall to a corner and eventually doubles back toward the bursar's window where I wait. The lobby is vast, with brass and marble. Crowds coming and going. The kind of place that would be nearly impossible for a blind man to get his bearings in, like the inside of a cathedral with the pews taken out, the sounds of people walking and talking echo into a cavernous cacophony. I close my eyes and try to imagine it. The room feels smaller, but the sounds are bent and warped.

A man buying a latte from the café cart notices the blind man's trouble and he goes over to him, engages him in conversation, and points him toward the hall just as the female cop had done. This time the blind man moves in a straighter line, but I stop watching when the woman storms away, the line moves, and I take a single step forward. It gives the sense that there is progress, but then the next man in line takes the opposite approach, addressing his questions in too casual and circular a manner. The last person was trying to force her will on this teller and this one is trying to kill him with kindness. And though it's nearly the appointed time for us to be in the room with the other prospective jurors, I continue to wait, hoping that the line will once again move. I feel a tap on the side of my foot and I turn to see the blind man coming toward me. I catch him in a kind of hug as I step back, and I decide I'll have to give up being reimbursed, because this poor guy needs help.

"Room one thirty-six?" he says, hoping I'll either tell him it's right in front of him or that I'll lead him there. This is the same room where I'd signed in, and I offer my arm and say it's just where I'm headed. I'll be happy to lead.

The first thing I notice is that the walking-cane technique has changed. Where they used to strike the ground back and forth in a tick-tock rhythm, now there's some kind of polymer in the shape of a ball at the end of his stick, and he drags it on the floor ahead of us. I'm not about to let him run into anything, but he continues to do it.

Back in Room 136 there are more prospective jurors, an assortment of two-hundred-plus people, attentive, now that they're being addressed, books resting in their laps. The woman at the podium, the same podium and the same woman who was in the video, goes over procedures: the number to call if we get sick or stuck in traffic, and that sort of thing. I hate to be late because I don't like people staring at me any more than normal. My helping the blind man makes it okay. It's a good excuse for coming in late, because I'm doing a good deed, and though people stare, they're staring at him.

We've come in at the tail end of the presentation, so the woman at the podium is soon enough calling names and lining us up in groups. They can try to place us on a jury for two weeks before they're supposed to finally give up. The blind man and I are split into different groups. His is marched out the door and down the hall one way, and after a few minutes of standing around, my group is led down the hall in the opposite direction. The woman with the knitting needles has stuffed everything into a tote, and she says, mostly to herself: "I'd rather be dead than blind." I'm surprised by the idea. I can't quite comprehend what blindness might be like, the total blankness and the finality, but it's also supposed to have its advantages. Like better hearing and an enhanced sense of smell. No one responds to the woman, so she keeps talking: "I'd heard about a blind preacher once. Now that's something people would go to see."

The clerk takes our group into an anteroom between the main hallway and one of the courtrooms. There are thirty-five of us, and she hands out numbered cards that we're told to pin on. Everything is anonymous, but the numbers make it so the lawyers can identify us. This is the jury-selection process, and the lawyers from each side are going to question everyone in the group to see if we have biases that might keep us from being fair. So, with an air of solemnity the group is marched into the courtroom and we're all scrunched together in the pews. As soon as we're seated they ask us to rise again, and we repeat some kind of swearing in, at the end of which we say, "I do." Like some giant group wedding. The judge mutters a few things and we can see the guy is a blowhard and really puffed up with himself. And this isn't even a criminal trial.

There's a doctor, and he's asked to stand so that anyone who knows him can excuse themselves. A few get up at this point and leave, and I feel like I should do the same, but the lawyers ask each one "In what capacity do you know Dr. So-and-so?" I'm afraid the doctor might call me out on a lie, because this whole deal is serious and an obvious lie might get me into trouble.

But it isn't long before I'm asked to leave. The case is a malpractice suit and the plaintiff is also asked to stand, but nobody knows her. She's huge, with bags of fat hanging from her arms, her face sagging in a perpetual frown. The poor woman had undergone surgery on her bladder and was now suffering from urinary incontinence. I can't help myself, it's rude, and it's not even funny, but I find myself cracking up and trying to hold it in at the same time. A snort manages to escape while I hold my breath and I feel myself blushing. The image of her wearing an oversized diaper under her skirt flashes into my head and it's too late, there's nothing I can do but to let myself go and I laugh.

When they're through asking questions they call out fourteen numbers and tell those people to stay. They skipped over my number but took all the people to the right and left of me. I didn't really care at all about that fat woman or whether the doctor's insurance company should give her a jackpot for a lifetime of pissing herself. But them skipping over me like that made me want to get on a jury more than anything.

Back in Room 139, the blind man sits by himself while scattered groups of people talk the talk of strangers: "What kind of work do you do?" "What cases have you seen so far?"

I hear a man say, "I don't know if we're allowed to talk about that. Isn't it supposed to be confidential?"

And the woman with the knitting needles says: "You can talk about the case as long as the trial hasn't actually started. They'll explain it once you get picked."

I sit next to the blind man, but not right next to him, so there's an empty seat between us. "We weren't really introduced," I say. "I led you in here this morning." He says his name is Tom, and before long he tells me he's divorced, retired, and his son has passed away. I get the sense that Tom lives in a lonely old world with his memories, and I try to imagine what kinds of memories a blind man might have. Is everything always dark, even in his dreams?

"Were you born blind?" I ask.

"No," he says, "but I have no recollection of ever seeing."

He's been asked this so many times that it's his standard response. "Childhood illness. I was two."

"So sorry," I say, but it doesn't sound genuine, more the way we say it when there's nothing else to be said.

"I got better," he says—his standard joke—and I force a laugh.

Soon enough the woman is back at the podium and she's lining up those of us who are left. We're brought to another wing of the large building. This time it is a criminal case and there's a man and a woman accused of selling crack. The questioning sticks to a few common themes: How we feel about cops; only they don't say "cops" but "police"; what are our views on drugs; do we think marijuana should be legal, that kind of thing. All the African Americans tell stories about being harassed by the cops, sometimes at night, without provocation or probable cause. Situations are described that would be deemed excessive by most and downright terrifying to people like the knitting lady, who is knitting now, and the judge doesn't seem to mind, nor do the lawyers from either side ask her any questions. People who look perfectly clean-cut admit marijuana should be legal, and I imagine that if they ask me this, to be able to say it in a room full of strangers, in the presence of the police and standing smack dab in the middle of institutional power—it would be liberating, like letting go of a heavy burden. But I also notice that one of the cops faces the jury and pays careful attention to what people say. Anyone who isn't white is stricken from the jury by the prosecutor, and so are those who are most vocal in their laxity toward drugs.

The blind man is also stricken. He admits he's not open-minded when it comes to drugs. In the course of questioning he brings up his son, the one he told me had passed away, only the language he uses now is stronger. "My son was *slain*," he says. "Just a few blocks from this courthouse." And there's tension in the room, the sound of ticking knitting needles slows then becomes still. But the lawyer for the defense pursues the matter until the blind man is weeping and telling the room his son was killed in a drug deal. Drugs had taken his son away from him and he didn't think he could ever be fair to someone who had been accused of selling them.

In the quiet that follows, the blind man is led out of the room by the policeman, even before the lawyers use their strikes. The judge can also strike jurors at his discretion, and the lawyers will try to get him to do this in order not to use up their own, by cornering us into admitting our biases.

I'm glad the cop is gone, especially since I'm asked to stand and they start in with their questions. But I'm not able to admit that I smoke pot, which isn't the same question they'd asked the others. They were asked did they think it should be legal, and I'm asked did I like to smoke it. Have I ever smoked it? I lie both times. It seems that everyone knows I'm lying but there's no way they can prove it. Then the prosecutor asks if I've ever been arrested and I answer in a way no one else had. I say, "I prefer not to say."

They can make me talk if they want; I'm under oath, and this has all been explained. They can take me into another room with the judge and question me privately, should they choose to do so. But all the tales of police brutality and the proclamations lamenting the legal status of marijuana have taken too much time. The lawyers decide not to pursue my story and they move on. At first I'm sure I'm going to get struck, but too many people have already been removed and I've at least demonstrated I was paying attention when the rules of the game were explained. So, while everyone else is asked to leave, I'm left in the court with a few of the others, including the knitting lady, and we're given the speech about not talking to anyone about the case, not even our spouses or close family members. We're given a rough estimate of how long the trial might last, we're dismissed for lunch, and we're told to return to this same courtroom the next morning at 9:00 A.M. sharp.

I follow some of the people from the group up to the courthouse commissary on the penthouse level. When the doors open to another of the drab municipal hallways I see the blind man slowly moving along the wall. He says, "Hello. Can someone direct me? I need assistance." And he uses a booming voice, though the hallway is short. Everyone walks past him without a word. I tell myself they'd seen me with him and they're expecting me to come to his aid, since I had once before. I want to believe they wouldn't act that way if I weren't here.

I take his arm and reassure him that I can lead him, and he senses that I know him but he doesn't recognize my voice, so we go through the introductions again: "I helped you this morning." I expect he must rely on the goodwill of others so often that I was just part of the morning landscape, like going through the security checkpoint. "Not the cop," I say for clarification.

"Are you going in?" he asks. And he adds before I can answer, "I'd like to buy your lunch."

"That's not necessary," I say, which is a way of letting him know I don't expect it from him but I'm also open to accepting this hospitality.

The commissary has a line, but it moves quickly as people select wrapped sandwiches, salads, fruit, or they name something off the menu board for the short-order cook. Behind the register is another blind man, and he doesn't wear sunglasses like my blind man, but I can tell by his posture, the way he stares straight ahead, and the way he takes money from customers, that he's blind too. He asks everyone which bills are which and he peels them out flat on his palm before he places each in the register. He feels his way along the compartments, returns the correct change, and gives out numbered plastic place cards for orders that the cook will bring. He calls everything by their numbers, so a cheeseburger order might be a number six with fries, hold the pickle.

Tom whispers, "Is he blind?" and I wonder what it is that gives him away. It would seem the way he asks about the bills, but I think maybe that isn't it—that it has more to do with the quality of his voice when he shouts out orders, not unlike the way Tom called for help in the hallway just moments ago. We each take a tray and push it along the counter as I describe all the items for Tom and tell him what's on the menu board. I'm hungry, and the smell of burgers frying increases my desire for food; but talking about it and trying to be honest about what's laid out in front of us makes it all sound less appetizing.

"There are watery greens that look like they've sat out under the hot lights all morning," I say. "This pudding looks good, and the butterscotch seems fresher than the chocolate."

He passes on most everything but agrees to an apple and some coleslaw. I'm not high anymore, but reality has left the room, because I'm now the go-between for two blind men in a money transaction. Tom takes bills from his wallet, and I can tell by the way he's folded them that he's got a system. He hands them to me, asking just to be sure, "Is that a twenty?" The blind cashier asks what we've got and I put in an order for a couple of cheeseburgers. He shouts out the number sixes and he asks about the bill I've given him. He gives me the change and I tell Tom what each bill is as he folds them in his own way. And he feels each of the coins before putting them in his pocket.

"Anywhere you want to sit?" I ask.

"Is there a window?" he says. "Let's sit by the window."

I guide him to a chair that faces the window and I wonder if maybe he can feel the daylight on his skin. The clouds have rolled in since this morning, but I know from the direction of this window that on a clear day we'd have a nice view of Mt. Rainier.

"Were you placed on that jury?" he asks. "The one with the two drug dealers?"

"I didn't think they'd put me on it," I say, "but they did."

"But you're not biased like I am," he says. Then he pauses and looks down at his food. If he could look, that is. His head is slumped over, so that at first I think he's saying grace but I decide he's remembering his son.

"I'm sorry about your loss," I say, and as soon as I say it I feel stupid, because he's apparently lost a lot: his son, his wife, his eyes. And if he isn't thinking about his son he might be thinking I meant any of these losses, which might be an awkward thing to say out of the blue.

But he answers: "We were trying to get him off it, but you know how it is."

And suddenly I really do feel awkward. It's just an expression, but what if he's saying I know because *I* know?

"The thing is," he says. "I really want to get on one of these juries. I've been through three sessions this morning and I'm beginning to think no one's going to pick me."

"Because of your disability? I don't see how that would make a difference. I thought Justice was blind."

He either doesn't get the joke or he chooses to ignore it. "I heard one of the judges talking about it with the lawyers. They were saying some of the evidence was visual and they didn't think I could get the full weight of their arguments."

"Each of the lawyers is allowed so many strikes, and some of them are freebies," I say. "So even if they are discriminating they won't have to admit it."

"No, I don't suppose they would."

"Most people try to get out of it," I say. "They feel like they've got better things to do."

"But it's important, right? It's our civic duty."

"Sure," I say, and I'm thinking I'm going to stand up to the system. Those crack dealers are going to get off and I won't give in, no matter how much the other jurors fight me. I imagine the knitting lady pointing her needle at me and telling me to go to hell. I smile, knowing they can't make me vote anyone guilty. I don't have a job or anything to get back to, and I'm also glad the blind man has no idea what I'm thinking.

When I see the blind man again he recognizes my voice and he asks if I've got time for lunch. In line, Tom asks about the case but I change the subject. There are too many people around, some who are on the same jury with me, and we were warned not to talk.

"They finally placed me on one," he says, speaking too loudly.

When we're seated we lean close to each other and talk in hushed tones. I tell him how the cops had gone to this seedy motel and posed as drug buyers. I was surprised at how young the cops looked and how inconspicuous. One apologized for wearing street clothes in court, but he said he'd just come from a stakeout. He looked just like someone I might meet at a bar and smoke pot with in a back alley. I needed to be more careful.

"I don't trust them," I say. "There were drugs there. Drugs were being sold. But I'm not sure they nabbed the right people.

"They seem to be represented by a public defender," I say. "He hasn't said anything and he never follows up on the questioning of the prosecutor. They've all been cops on the stand so far, and you'd think he'd try to discredit them. I mean, they went looking for trouble, right? They went down there looking to arrest some people. It's entrapment."

"You must know a lot about the law," he says.

"Just what I know from TV," I say, and I wonder if it's rude to bring up.

"I guess I don't watch those kinds of shows," he says.

I reach across the table and place my hand on his. It's the first time I've touched him when I wasn't leading him around. "Tell me about your trial. What's it about?"

"Have you heard of this Kitty Kat Club?" he says. "Supposedly, it's a stripper place."

"Doesn't surprise me," I say. "With a name like that."

"Anyway, these cops went down there . . ."

"Looking for trouble?"

"And apparently there was some inappropriate touching going on."

"Prostitution?"

"I'm not sure yet," he says. "That's what I'm trying to figure out."

"What have the other jurors said?" I ask.

"We haven't had a chance to talk," he says. "We're just supposed to listen to both sides and then we talk about it together at the end."

"Deliberation."

"And then we vote on it," he says.

"Have they mentioned which law was broken?"

"Some statute," he says. "Sounded like algebra."

"We should keep each other informed," I whisper.

I'd felt I'd be able to do my part by pushing back on the war on drugs, but now it seemed the blind man had landed himself on a more interesting case. I want to get a look at the girl, this stripper dressed up for court and sitting as proper as if she was in church. Strippers always have money, so she's probably got some nice duds. And I know the judge and all the male jurors will imagine her peeling off her clothes and dancing around naked to the music. I don't have that kind of money, but hearing about it makes me want to go down to this Kitty Kat Club.

Instead I go to the Overnite Motel, where the supposed crack deal had taken place. They'd asked us not to go to the scene of the crime or to try to do detective work. On the bus ride out, there are few riders left as I approach this rundown section of highway. There's a used auto parts shop with a kind of junkyard around it. There's a closed, condemned, and boarded-up junior high school. There's an overpass that crosses the highway near a neighborhood of cheaply built apartment buildings— over to the closed school, with graffiti on the school and cement barriers along both sides of the overpass.

At the Overnite I see cars coming and going. A few men stand in the open doors of their rooms, looking out. Women loiter along the frontage road like prostitutes, only they aren't dressed for the part. I walk past them and they proposition me. It's drugs they're peddling and not sex. I say "No thanks," just like they'd told us to do at a different junior high in a better part of town, where these kinds of encounters were more remote and not nearly as menacing. But I want to give these women money; they seem so desperate for it. I want to make things right for them, at least for a while. But then I can't help thinking there are undercover cops on the scene, watching and waiting.

The place is nothing at all like I'd imagined, and I know this trip is going to help me when the time comes to deliberate. I'll be able to say to the knitting lady, "I've been by that place, and it seems to me . . ." Because one of the things that hasn't been made clear by the cops' testimony is how busy the intersection is and how many people are always in the vicinity. Why were the cops' descriptions so general? The undercover cop said both defendants sold the crack rock in question, taken into evidence and referred to as Item A. The supplier was in the motel room with a stash, while the woman was his runner. She took the twenty-dollar bill to him, they made a handoff, and she came back down with Item A. There was testimony about the lab work, how the bag of cocaine had been sealed and double-sealed, testing positive in the field and also in the lab. But there hadn't been any testimony about what the woman was wearing, or what room the man had been in. How could they be sure they'd gotten the right supplier and the right runner? Because it seemed they could have handcuffed just about anyone out here and called them guilty.

In the office I ask about room rates and the manager looks me up and down.

"You want to stay here?" he says.

"Thought I might," I say, but I'm wondering if he thinks I'm one of the cops. I don't belong and it's obvious.

"Cheapest price," he says, but when he gives the actual quotes, which include hourly rates, they don't seem so great.

I thank him and turn to leave as he says, "We got HBO."

The blind man asks what a lap dance is. His trial has reached the deliberation phase and it sounds a lot like mine. Cops giving testimony, the judge reading from the law books, and, in the girl's case, that meant deciding whether or not "inappropriate touching" had occurred beyond a reasonable doubt. I'm used to the way the blind man feels around on his tray for his food. The way he sticks his finger in his cup to feel the level and temperature of his coffee. He mostly eats cheeseburgers and if I meet him on his way up to the commissary he'll buy me one too.

"A lap dance," I say, "is when the girl sort of strips while she's sitting on your lap. She gyrates. She rubs herself on you. It simulates sex, but you've got your clothes on. Some of the girls are real athletic. Some will do a headstand and stuff it in your face. That's what I've heard."

"Without touching?" the blind man wants to know.

"She gets naked, but she rubs against you where you've got clothes on. She rubs on your lap."

He lowers his voice to a whisper and leans toward me. "I guess I still don't understand. Stuffs what in your face?"

"Not always. Just the more acrobatic ones. Sometimes there's a pole."

"A stripper pole," he says. "They've said something about it."

"And if she's upside down . . ."

"Yes . . ."

"And she's naked . . ."

"I think I get it."

"You might get a good look at what she's got down there. You might even get a whiff."

"But that's not why this girl was arrested?" he asks.

"I can't say for sure, because I didn't hear the testimony," I say. "But it sounds like she was brushing against the men somehow, maybe rubbing herself on their faces."

"With all that activity," the blind man says, "and if she's naked. That might just happen by accident. Especially if she's well endowed. One of the men explained to me she was well endowed."

"It would make a reasonable defense," you say. "But everyone here is guilty. We're all guilty, and the stripper is, too. She did it for tips."

"So, why's that illegal?" he asks. "It's not prostitution."

"We don't get to make the laws," I say. "The judge explained all that. We just decide guilt or innocence."

"Then what's the point?" he says. "I understand the idea behind a jury, the history on which it's based. I went to school same as the next guy. But like you said, if they're guilty why are we going through the motions?"

"That's why I'm fighting it," I tell him. "I ain't about to send two people to jail over a twenty-dollar crack rock. They can't make me."

This quiets him and I remember how his son died. He says, "If you're biased, you don't belong on that jury."

"I don't have to tell them everything about me," I say. "I don't get to make the laws, but I can still believe in things."

"You think this girl . . . you think they should just drop it?"

"What do you think?"

"I think I need to go down there," he says. "I need to see what it's like. I need a lap dance."

I struggle over whether to smoke a joint before going to the blind man's apartment. He'll notice it with his keen, blind man's sense of smell. But he probably already knows I'm a druggie, so I don't care. I'm going to need to be high to really enjoy this club and let myself go. I want to be the good-time boy. So I smoke a fat joint, wait a while, then roll up and smoke another. I've always been shy around girls, but I want it right in my face. I want to try to touch her.

I'm running late, but feeling good and high by the time I get off the bus on the other side of town. I ring the bell and he buzzes me in. The blind man's place is small, to the point that it feels claustrophobic. I suspect there's never anyone else who comes to visit, but the place is presentable. It's tidy. There's the aroma of warm food, and everything looks worn—the curtains, the couch, the carpet, the TV, even the walls. There are dirt smudges about four feet high along the length of the hallway, and I imagine this must be from his feeling his way along. His cane is folded up and sitting on the coffee table. He's wearing one of his suits, only there's a white carnation in the lapel. His hair is slicked back so stiff I can count the ridges that would exactly match the teeth of his comb. He smiles, pats the inside pocket of his jacket, and says "I got us a lot of one-dollar bills, just like you said." He reaches into the pocket and holds out a wad. I've let him know, repeatedly, that I don't have a job. Work comes around occasionally, but something always fucks it up. I say the wrong thing to the boss, I don't have a ride to the work site; or I'll reach a point where I just can't get myself out of bed.

"Thanks," I say, I hope not too enthusiastically, and I instinctively start to count the bills.

"It's one hundred," he says. "You said you might have to give up a dollar per minute, with the girls always wanting tips. I mean, I know they take their time undressing, but I tried to imagine how long it might take. A song takes four or five minutes. I thought if we liked it we might stay a few hours. It's better to have too much, don't you think?"

He shows me, after handing me this wad, that he also has a wad, and while, at first, one hundred dollars apiece seems like a lot, I decide if I play it right I can make it home with some of this money to spare. But I'm also hoping for a lap dance of my own, so it isn't inconceivable, depending on how things go, that we could both spend one hundred dollars in no time flat.

"That's just for tips," he says. "I can charge the cover, our drinks, and lap dances or anything else I want on my credit card, right?"

"Most men don't want those charges on their statement," I say.

He hands me his wad of bills and says, "Check this?"

I flip through and it's mostly ones but there are fives, tens, and twenties in the stack too. I think he must know this because they're in ascending order. So maybe this is a test of whether he can trust me. I fail immediately, peeling off three or four twenties and stuffing them in my sock. He can't really keep track of what's here, and I shuffle the rest so the larger bills are mixed with the ones. When he hands out the occasional five, ten, or twenty, it's going to make the girls that much more attracted to us. What he doesn't know can't hurt him, and he's apparently looking forward to throwing money around, so why not?

He asks if I'm hungry, and I am, but I remember his habit of sticking his fingers in his food. I'm sure it's like that for anything that he's cooked, the same fingers that run these dirty walls, and I say, "Already ate."

"Let's do this," he says, and he's excited. I suppose it's a combination of having a friend, getting out of the apartment, and the prospect of being with naked women—but if I were in his position it would be too much. He calls a cab, asks for a driver by name, and we walk down to the street to wait.

I argue with the other jurors just as I knew I would. There's one in particular I fight with most, one of the men who had nominated himself for foreman but was beaten out by the knitting lady, a man who says we should go ahead and vote them guilty and all go home.

I say, "The defense lawyer made a good point in his closing remarks. None of the cops' money turned up. How can they be charged with selling without the plant money?"

"We've been over that," he says. "Have you been listening? The judge explained it."

"Can we really convict two people with just one crack rock?"

"They were both involved in the crime," he says. "It was a business they were running out of that motel room."

"But the cops searched the motel room and found nothing," I say. "We don't even know the room number. How can we be sure they got the right guy?"

"The undercover guy saw them. He saw it all."

"He saw what he *thinks* was a hand off," I say. "But did he see the crack rock leave the room? Did he see Item A pass from hand to hand?"

"It's reasonable to assume, based on what the cops described, that the cocaine was handed off."

"But beyond a reasonable doubt?" I say.

"It's a reasonable assumption."

"And how many other people were at the scene? How come we haven't heard about that? Who else was in that parking lot? Can we be sure this isn't a case of mistaken identity?"

"I think you're biased," he says. "I could tell it by the way you were ogling the cocaine in that baggy. You're some kind of druggie and you're going to rig this trial. You act like you've been down to that motel before, too. I think you should remove yourself from the jury and let one of the alternates take over."

"I think *you're* biased," I say. "I'll remove myself if you remove yourself. Let both alternates take over."

"I'm not quitting," he says. "I've put too much time in to just quit. We've discussed it, but you won't listen to anything our side has to say. You've been tuning us out. I wouldn't be surprised if you were on drugs right now."

"I'm not even going to dignify that with a response," I say. "Let's just vote. We're obviously split. And you're not going to be able to convince me that a speck of cocaine is enough to lock two people away in prison for God knows how long."

"It's not for us to decide," he says. "They broke the law. They knew they were breaking the law. They have to pay."

The Kitty Kat Club, like all such establishments, draws us in with a trick of light. The neon sign is shaped like a cat girl in heat and her perched rear moves back and forth while her tail and torso are still. Inside the door we're met by two versions of hypermasculinity. The owner sits at a table with a cashbox in front of him. He's an enormous, flabby, balding globe of a creature who seems unaware of the revulsion his girth might inspire—because in this club, his small universe, the girls come up to him and touch him on the arm or the shoulder, they lean into him, and they whisper in his ear. He wears gold and diamonds, he laughs, he smiles, and he looks at the two of us with disapproval.

"Tell him he can't touch the girls," he says to me as if the blind man can't hear.

"He won't touch anyone," I say.

The second hypermale is of the muscular version, pumped up and angry, a bouncer just waiting for something to happen that will require him to throw his might around. He's also balding, but he's tan and wearing a baseball cap.

"I don't even think he's really blind," the muscle guy says and that gets the owner to give us a more scrupulous look.

"If he's faking," the owner says, "the two of you are out of here."

"He's really blind," I say. "He really is."

The blind man produces his credit card, the fat man swipes it, the blind man signs the wrong side of the receipt, the fat man takes it anyway, and the muscle guy steps out of our way.

On this the third day of our deliberation the judge has grown tired of our unwillingness to agree on a verdict. The clerk says that he is considering polling the jury, which amounts to asking us individually how we find the defendants, but for now we will have to continue to talk it out. The jury room has grown smaller with each passing day. We leave the coffee on, though no one drinks any, the taste of it increasingly bitter as the minutes pass slowly. We've polled ourselves countless times and are hopelessly split. I know that the hardest thing for the knitting lady is that, in her capacity as foreman, she feels she can't just sit and knit, as some of us might sit and read a book, or doodle, or even put a head down on the table in disgust, because there are those who have decided the crackheads are guilty and need to be removed from society, while the rest of us want more proof, a better accounting from the cops, and something else unnamed. Maybe it's an acknowledgment that we're guilty too—or a desire to help—or maybe what we feel most is a disappointment at witnessing the system in motion—with its boiling down lives, its lack of awareness, its inability to understand, to hope, to forgive. So the knitting lady says, "Should we go over it again? Is there anything we're leaving out?" Our deliberation had reached a point where we didn't know what we were arguing, and even the knitting lady was referring to the defendants as crackheads.

"What is keeping the crackheads from being guilty and what is keeping them from being innocent?"

But this suggestion only musters audible groans from the group. We have a fundamental difference in the way we see the case. There are those who feel the crackheads are the victims of entrapment, and those who don't even see entrapment as an issue, since the law was broken and the means of reeling them in inconsequential. There are those who feel the crackheads are guilty, but the evidence against them is sketchy. They might be swayed if police did their jobs. Then there are those, like the blind man, who have a deep hatred of drug abusers and don't see them as human.

To my surprise the youngest members of the jury are of this type. They hadn't yet begun to think for themselves, and here they are deciding the next few years of other people's lives. They resented that the two awaiting our decision hadn't demonstrated the will to just say no. We represent a political rift, the liberals and the conservatives, those who've tried drugs and those who won't admit it. And I'm growing tired of waiting. I'm wishing I'd gotten on the blind man's jury, the case with the stripper. I'm convinced the crackheads really did it, that they knew they'd end up in jail, that they'd probably just gotten out of jail, anyway.

And even if our jury's hung, they'll retry them and find them guilty somewhere down the road, the cops better able to describe what transpired next time and the prosecutor more practiced in her arguments. I thought I was fighting the system, but now it's about me and them, the other people on this jury who don't think like me and also don't like me, and there's plenty of fight left in them, too. They'd be just as pleased to lock me up and I'm feeling them winning. I don't care about the trial anymore or any of it but I just want to get on the bus and go home. And the clerk is ordering pizzas which means they plan on keeping us here through dinner.

Inside the Kitty Kat Club I lead the blind man to the edge of the stage, where we sit and the performer crawls across the floor until she's in front of us. The music is loud and it takes time for my eyes to adjust to the disorienting lights, with the whole place dark, except for areas where spotlights are dropped, with the stage the brightest part of the room. There are poles on both sides of the stage with seating that wraps around and a catwalk that leads to the parted, black curtains that front the hallway to the dressing rooms.

The girl is topless and she sits back and slips out of her thong so she's completely naked, except for stockings and a garter belt where she stuffs the bills the men hand over. Her hips hump the air in a slow circular way and I stare at the toned muscles in her ass; but she looks right at the blind man with the fuck-me-look that would have me handing over the large bills in his wad. He seems aware of where we are sitting, the thumping bass of the dance music, and he maybe even knows there's a naked woman writhing around in front of us, but he cannot react with the same sense of awe as myself and all the other losers parked on stools around the edge of the stage. Then she crawls right up to him and removes his sunglasses. He smiles at this, aware for sure now, and she strokes both his cheeks with the backs of her long fingers. He reaches out instinctively, but she dodges his touch.

She wears his glasses, and laughter can be heard in the room, the blind man also aware that he's got something to do with it. She jerks her hips quickly with her open thighs just a few feet from him. And as I watch both his and her reaction, it seems, for just a second, that he sees what she's showing him, that he's looking right at it, and that he has full comprehension. Soon afterwards she takes the bill he holds out, guiding his hand along the inside of her leg and up to where she folds it over with the rest of her money hanging from her garter belt. She puts the glasses back on him and he returns to just staring out, the dumb gaze of the blind, while all the rest of us know exactly where to look.

The blind man asks if there's somewhere we can sit and talk, so I lead us to one of the tables near the back. There's a row of booths along the far wall where lap dances are taking place, and I listen to the blind man but I'm looking at the stage and at these booths. I'm trying to decide which girl I might like to have on my lap, and I expect the blind man will want me to pick one out for him, too. I decide looks don't matter so much for him, but for me that's the number-one thing. A homely girl might be more appreciative and would give him a really nice ride, but after a few songs I see that's not necessarily the case. The best-looking ones seem to get propositioned more for dances, but they're also not walking the floor, while the other girls will come right up and ask, and they get plenty of guys who go ahead and say yes. Two come up to us while we're talking, first asking me, then indicating the blind man and saying "Does he want one?"

The blind man looks at me, that is to say he turns his face in my direction, and he says, "I don't know. Do I want her to give me a lap dance, friend?"

So he wants to know what I think of the girl, and he's asking if I think she'll do.

"No thanks," I say. "We're just talking."

"Well, there's a two-drink minimum," the girl says, and we give her our order.

When the second girl comes by, I say no thanks again, and this time I add "We're still working on our drinks. We're just talking right now, is all."

I ask about his trial, and we both want to know if we can figure out which girl she is. The well-endowed part doesn't really help, though it rules out one or two.

"Her name is Carrie Johnson," he says and this is so surprising it makes me sit up straight and look. I hadn't expected he'd know her actual name, but it makes sense, since she's been accused of a crime and it's part of a public trial. But I can't just ask for her, since all the girls go by stage names.

"Can you tell me anything else?" I ask, but he shakes his head. How does a blind man know to shake his head I wonder. They must teach them that in blind school, growing up. They must have classes in that sort of thing.

"She's the one I want," he says. "Ask if she'll give me a lap dance."

But it's not that easy. First of all the jury he's on has been just as hung as mine, so his trial is still going on, and the accused giving him a lap dance would be highly inappropriate and possibly illegal. And this is what I'm turning over in my mind when he says "I need to know how she dances. I need to feel it for myself."

"What if they think we're cops?" I say.

"I'm the blind juror," he says. "So I can't be a cop. She's going to recognize me."

I really hadn't expected this from the blind man. It's a side of him I hadn't seen. I didn't think a blind man would try to take advantage of another's misfortunes in that way. He *wants* her to know who he is. He's trying to get this dance as a bribe.

I take my drink and walk back toward the door. The owner and the bouncer can sense right away I have something to say and they're on guard.

"My blind friend wants a lap dance from a girl who works here named Carrie. I figured the girls would get upset if I asked for her by name, so I came straight to you two. I wanted to be up front about it. He knows her and he's asking for her. Is that okay, or do you want us to leave?"

The bouncer takes a step forward so that he's in my space and he says "You know it ain't cool. How does he know her?"

And it occurs to me that maybe this bouncer and Carrie have some kind of relationship, but as soon as the fat owner waves him off I realize the macho behavior is just his job. The fat man puts the cash box under his arm and he stands and puts his other arm around me, leaning close so I can hear him over the music. "I can arrange it," he says, "but only in the V.I.P. room, and the blind man pays double."

"What about me?" I want to know.

"You wait out here," he says. "You want a lap dance, you get yours in one of the booths."

I don't like the sound of this, because I'm curious to know which girl is the one. I wanted to be able to watch her dancing on the blind man and I wanted to see the look on Tom's face when he felt a female body for what must be the first time in years. And since he's blind he can't really care if we watch. To him it's all the same, whether he's in a V.I.P. room or a room full of perverts. And then my instinct to protect him kicks in. If they take him back into some room while I wait out here, how will I know they won't do something to him? Who's to say they won't trick him out of his money?

But when I present the owner's message to the blind man he's pleased, and one of the girls who I'm sure isn't Carrie Johnson comes up to him, takes him by the hand, and leads him onto the stage, across the catwalk, through the part in the curtain, and down the hall into the lighted recesses of the building. This brings cheers from all the men seated around the stage, because they know precisely what it means, and I'm left slumped in my chair. One of the homely girls comes back by, so I order another drink with the blind man's money, a double.

When the girl leads the blind man back across the stage to the table where I wait, there's no applause, but a sense of awe. He sits next to me and a few of the men seated around the stage take their eyes from the stripper show to stare at us, probably wondering if the blind man is made of money. I'm also wondering what went on, what it cost him— and I'm feeling left out. Didn't I get something for bringing him here? Whatever he spent to go back there, shouldn't I get something like that, too? He reaches for his drink, which is still sitting on the table right where he left it, but I already drank it. Did he meet the girl? Did she recognize him? What did she do—was there prostitution? The questions fight in my head, but I play it cool. I don't know what's appropriate at this point. He'd brought me here, or at least asked me to bring him. He couldn't just sit silently forever. Sooner or later he's going to have to say something. But then I decide he's probably used to sitting quietly. So I say, "Is she guilty?"

"I'm pleased to report it."

"Are you going to vote against her?"

"Haven't decided."

"Did you make any promises?"

"She knew who I was," he says. "And she knew what she was doing. She knew what it might mean. So that's an unspoken promise, isn't it? And I didn't exactly stop her." He's rubbing it in and acting glib.

A meanness rises in me and I say "She felt pity. Because, what possible pleasure could a blind man get unless there's some inappropriate touching? The rest of us could really go for something like that, but we don't need it as bad. I can watch and let my imagination run wild. But you don't really have an imagination. Not like we do. You can't play master with the things you see."

"I see a lot," he says. "It's different, it's not what *you* call seeing, but I can project with the third eye."

"Your blind man's eye."

"I don't need *sight*."

"I can't fathom it," I say. "If it weren't for seeing the girls, this place would mean nothing to me. And if it weren't for seeing the mountain every now and then . . ."

"Mt. Rainier?"

"That mountain is sixty miles off but we can still see it," I tell him. "Can you imagine? It's that far away but it's so big it takes up a piece of the sky."

"Like the moon?"

"Not like the moon, because it's on the ground. It *is* the ground."

"I know how big it is," he says.

"I don't mean like a number in some almanac. It's beyond reason. It's so big I can barely believe it's real."

"But I know how big it is," he says. "I've climbed it."

"*You've* climbed Mt. Rainier?"

"I had a guide," he says. "I went up with a group. It takes three days. It's a day to hike to the base camp. Then you wake up in the middle of the night to make your run for the peak. You're up there maybe an hour and you have to turn around and head back, so as not to get caught by night. It gets extremely cold once the sun goes down, and you don't want to be up there."

"So why'd you do it?" I say. Then I answer: "I know why. It's the old joke, right? *Because it was there.*"

"For the view," he says. "It's unparalleled."

"But what did you see?"

He gets up from the table, feels his way until he's behind me, and he covers my eyes with both hands. "Can you see it?" he says.

The pounding bass of the dance music and the smoke of the room are all I can think about. There's a gap in his fingers and one of the homely girls dances naked around a pole at the edge of the stage. I close my eyes and really concentrate. I try to imagine walking through snow with no sight for a day and a half. Uphill and steep. Sweating from the climb, but my face and feet frozen. He stands behind me until I'm re-

laxed with my eyes closed and he sits back down. I'm sure of his movement, though I can't see him or hear him.

"You made it," he says. "You're on top of the mountain."

I feel a smile creep across my face as I look down at the earth
through closed eyelids. "I can see it," I say. "It's really something."

We sit at the table without talking, both of us blind. We sit for a
long time.

With the pizzas eaten, the boxes stacked in the middle of the table, and
the smell of tomato sauce permeating the room, we are tired of talking,
tired of being held here, and we wait for the judge to give up on us, to
accept our hung jury status and to send us home for good. One of the
young women who nominated the knitting lady as our foreman says to
me "I think it's really great what you've been doing." She's pretty, but I
haven't really paid enough attention to her. I'd thought she was too
young, and on top of that she'd taken a hard stand against the crackheads. We'd all stopped talking some time ago, but now that she'd broken the silence everyone hears her and listens for my response.

"What do you mean?" I say.

"With the blind man," she says. "I've seen you together. Is he a
friend of yours?"

"No," I say, "I mean yes. We weren't friends, but I suppose we are
now. He needed help getting around. I couldn't stand and watch. No
one was helping him." And as I say this I look across the table at some of
the same people who'd ignored the blind man when he'd asked for their
help. The man who had fought me hardest is looking down at his hands.
He says, "It's the law," but it's as if he doesn't believe it himself, as if he's
given up fighting too, and they're all prepared to vote 'not guilty' for
the sake of going home, but also as a way of ditching the guilt that is
creeping around the room, not the guilt of sending anyone to jail, but
guilt from not helping the blind man. They felt it, but forgot about him
as soon as I came along and they were relieved. It was easy for them.

And just like that, it's all over. The judge calls us into the courtroom,
polls us, and we're free to go home. I walk with the girl down the corridor and we wait by the elevator.

"It's been kind of you," the girl says and she's smiling, a smile that
includes her eyes.

"It was only what anyone would do," I say.

We walk out past the metal detectors and down the hill to the bus
terminal. There's a new performing arts center and a garden with esca-

lators, waterfalls, and fountains. The pigeons love it. The homeless love it. We ride the escalator together, the girl is in front of me, but twisted around to talk. For an instant, between a six-story parking garage and an office building, I get a glimpse of the mountain.

"Look," I say, and she knows what I'm saying but turns too slowly to see.

"Oh," she says, in disappointment.

"Would you ever climb it?" I ask.

"I don't know," she says, "I suppose."

"It takes three days or something," I say. "And people die."

"In the crevices," she says.

"You step into a hole you can't see in the snow, you're buried alive, and no one sees you again." The girl turns around instinctively and we're on solid pavement.

Small crowds loiter then huddle at the corner as each new bus approaches. She and I wait for different busses and I wonder if I should follow her home, if maybe that's what she wants. We're still talking. No substance, but we can talk.

There's a man at the pay phone and he has a computer the size of a briefcase, with the phone set into a cradle. He types but looks upset. It seemed like a stereotype maybe, a frustrated deaf guy. Weren't they always getting frustrated? So I go over, not so much to impress the girl as out of curiosity.

He indicates I should talk to the operator, and she explains that his computer can synthesize a voice and also has voice recognition, so he can type and converse on the LED screen. I'm really taken by the voice of this operator. She sounds sexy and she must be really caring, working for the deaf and all. I watch and I wave as my girl gets on a bus and rolls away. I knew her name was Jaime, because we wore name tags, but she's gone and I'm stuck talking at the pay phone. The deaf guy wears a straw hat and doesn't seem so well off. His shirt and shorts are wrinkled, soiled, worn. Then the operator starts to tell me about him. She says he had been a musician in the sixties and had gone deaf onstage one night.

"All at once?" I ask.

"In an instant," she says. "He wrote that song 'I Like Bread and Butter.'"

"It's an Appleby's commercial," I say.

"I haven't seen it," she says.

"One of them," I say. "Appleby's. Shoney's. Chili's. I can't tell them apart."

"Don't tell him," she says.

"Tell him what?"

"About his song."

"He can't hear me."

"You could type it."

"But you don't think I should? I'll type to him that I really liked it, that I liked that song when I was growing up."

"That would be fine," she says.

The Piano

by Janet Neipris

Grandmother's piano was big, black, shiny, and completely off-limits to us kids. In fact, it was off-limits to everyone. But there it sat, in the middle of the parlor, the center of our lives, representing potential more than accomplishment or fulfillment. I'd be damned if I was going to let it sit there unused. That piano became a metaphor for our lives as it was passed down to my generation and then to my children's. Steel Magnolias has a fling with Terms of Endearment.

My grandmother's piano was big and black and shiny, and stood behind the French glass doors that led to her front parlor. The keys themselves were genuine ivory, made from the tusk of an African elephant, and paid for fifty cents down and fifty cents a week to the Ivers and Pond Company on Atlantic Avenue in Boston in the year nineteen forty-three. I know, because I delivered the payment every week, the coins hot in the pocket of my dress.

The piano was bought by my grandmother, Sally Dennis, and my grandfather, A.G. Dennis, tailor for the United States Army, First Service Command, and famous for having once altered General Patton's jacket. The piano was clearly acquired by my grandparents as a symbol of their stature in this new country. The way I understood it, every good family had a piano.

Our family lived in a brown three-decker house, on a street with other three-decker houses, with back porches and cellar doors, stairways lit by stained glass windows, and kids calling "Olly Olly Oxen

Free" across fences. Ours was a house of distinction, however, located next to the lady who sold gravestones.

In the normal course of humiliations, this location was no great liability; the stones sat and we sat and the piano sat. But once a year, on Memorial Day, with four cemeteries at the end of the street, our neighborhood became the center of that time and place I grew up in.

Early on the morning of Memorial Day, the lady who sold gravestones, Mrs. Garlanaux, would set out her wreaths and flower baskets, which she bought from a man in a pickup truck who came around the day before. Her two sons, Alex and Billy (one turned out a lawyer, so I heard, and the other sells Japanese scissors to hairdressers), would dust off the monument display, including my favorite, the two hearts intertwined in a salmon-colored stone, as the bands gathered on the corner of Walk Hill Street, shining their instruments and warming up.

First the soldiers assembled: the American Legion; the Veterans of Foreign War; the Francis Langford Post; the Sons of Italy; followed by the Boy Scouts; the band from St. Angela's; the Red Cross; the Fire Department—and anyone who had *anyone* buried at the end of that street, which was practically everyone. Women and children and soldiers and policemen and dogs, all preparing to step to the tune of John Philip Sousa. These were patriotic days, between the wings of two wars.

My cousins and I watched the parade from the roof of our house, sneaking up to the attic and out the window. My grandmother, old "Eagle Eye Sally," would discover us halfway through the parade and shoo us off with her broom, but by this time we were ready to march anyway.

We lived right off Blue Hill Avenue, the main thoroughfare, which led to the Blue Hills. There was actually only one hill, but it was very large and quite blue, and on a clear day you could see it from downtown Boston.

In this same neighborhood once lived "little Lennie Bernstein," who, we were told, practiced on his piano every day, "And now look at him, on his way to fame and fortune in New York City." Listen, I was willing to sacrifice anything—my cat Betty, my prize collection of aggies, including my Servian shooter, in order to play my grandmother's piano, press my hot fingers to those keys, and make a sound beyond the walls of Walk Hill Street; but my grandmother was determined that the piano be kept in first-class, pristine condition, which meant no one should play it. And so it remained untouched, but not in my dreams.

In the popular movies of the day, Dick Haymes and Fred Astaire were songwriters, knocking on doors and selling tunes the world had been waiting for, like "My Blue Heaven." They get rich, get the girl, lose the girl, and after moderate anguish, win back the girl, vowing never to ever let her go again. They played pianos, made music, and how I longed to be just like them, sitting under the make-believe stars of the Oriental Theatre on a Saturday afternoon with my brother Howie.

When I asked my mother recently why the piano was forbidden, she denied it was ever prohibited, and said I was making up these stories again.

Every Friday afternoon my mother and her sister Fanny religiously polished the piano. Have rags, will travel; and, dutiful daughters that they were, they did. Up they climbed to the third floor, considered the prized flat because it had the most light and was therefore closer to God. They climbed to where Grandma Sally held court, ringing her cowbell brought from the "old country," calling her two daughters into service. Over the years, the more the piano was polished, the more it shone, and in its silence its potential virtues escalated.

"Did you ever see such a thing of beauty?" my grandmother would ask. My grandmother, in retrospect, was a lesser Keats. "You can see your face in that piano." Your face? Your entire soul.

The more I looked, my nose pressed against the panes of glass on the door that led to the room where the piano stood, the more obsessed I became. My plan was to get to the piano secretly, without permission. It would be like getting past the Gates of Heaven without stopping to see St. Peter.

Clearly, to a girl of my imagination, a plan of outlandish proportions in order to play that piano was not unseemly. The thing was to get Grandma Sally out of the house, which she guarded like the Statue of Liberty guards the harbor of New York.

She left for only one of five reasons: to go to the doctor; the Dover Street Public Baths; shopping; an unexpected disaster, which was entirely unpredictable and therefore undependable; or to guard our sidewalk during the Memorial Day parade. My plan was to be sick with something that was "going around" on the morning of Memorial Day.

So, in the spring of my thirteenth year, the year one lilac finally grew miraculously on the lilac tree in our backyard, I waited for the annual hit of whooping cough. And in early May, as luck would have it, my best friend Lorna came down with it. A week later, Mike, the shoemaker's son, caught the most dreadful case, which put me past due, I figured, on Memorial Day.

On that morning of Memorial Day my mother discovered me still in bed, after the band had started. I had practiced the "whoop" for months and was easily believed. W.C. was proclaimed and I was kept in bed, "poor thing," juices at my side, while the longest parade on record passed in the streets below. It was red-white-and-blue-forever time, and the locally based armed forces, "the Boys," were out in large numbers, marching to "The Halls of Montezuma."

I climbed the back hall stairs to the top apartment, through my grandmother's kitchen, past the white enamel table, down the hall past the telephone table, the black phone receiver hanging in its hook, past faded sepia photos of ancestors, opened the French doors to the parlor, and lifted the cabbage rose slipcover, sewn from remnants to "protect" the piano in the winter from the damp, and in the summer from dust and pestilence.

After placing my hands in position on the keys, I played the first note, a C, followed by the second, an F, then an A flat, a C, another C, then B flat, A flat, C again, and so on. Can I tell you, on that Memorial Day morning, the piano played far sweeter than all my imaginings.

So, with the sounds of bands marching up the street, I went from song to song, every melody I'd ever heard, and each one, like magic and by "ear," came onto the piano. That is the only way I can describe it.

"Santa Lucia," "How Are Things in Glocca Morra," tumbled into the "Miami Beach Rumba," and on to "I'll Be Seeing You," then songs with girls' names, songs about states, songs about moons, singing and playing the piano—"Oh, it's only a paper moon . . ." I played as if in a trance, unaware the parade music had ended.

I heard my grandmother coming up the stairs between "Goodnight Irene" and "I'm Always Chasing Rainbows." By the time my she reached the top stair, it was too late. There was no route of escape, just the one door out into the long corridor where her footsteps already sounded.

"Who's here? Who's in here?" she called. "Lilly?"

Then she opened the glass doors and there I was, trapped in my own undoing. From then on I knew nothing would ever be the same again.

"Let me see your hands!" my grandmother demanded. "Aha! Dirty! Just as I thought! Look at that! Banging on the piano without washing your hands."

"No, I can play. I can play anything," I insisted.

"I thought you were sick," she challenged, her eyes now on fire. "Full of germs."

"I said that so I could come upstairs when you were out and try the piano."

"A liar, then, is what I have for a granddaughter."

"No, I'm telling the truth," I pleaded to heaven's blocked ears.

I begged her not to tell my parents, and she agreed to spare them the grief of this serious defect in my character. I would bear the burden of guilt alone. The Christian martyrs never met my grandmother, but if they had, it would have improved even *their* style.

Four years later, with our secret still well kept, and a scholarship to college, I left the house on Walk Hill Street, never to return again, except for occasional holidays, and finally, my grandmother's funeral.

In the summers I worked as a counselor at a girls' camp in Maine, organizing the Annual Show which the campers wrote, and spent the season rehearsing. At college I majored in English, managed through biology and economics, was vice president of the literary club, and got to introduce Robert Frost the night he came to read.

But I never quite got over that piano which remained beyond my reach and for years represented to me a place I couldn't get to—call it love, call it home, the place where, as Frost said, when you go there they have to take you in.

The case was not reopened until years later, and then in a very strange manner.

When Grandma Sally died, my mother and aunt decided to sell the house. My mother, since widowed and remarried, now lived in Florida with her new husband, Charlie, who was in real estate. Charlie agreed my mother should stay in Boston a few weeks to go through the house and Grandma Sally's belongings, while he minded his business, which was boomeranging through every orange grove and inlet. On the first day after the sorting my mother phoned.

"We're cleaning out the house, Lillian, and oh what we're finding, and I don't know what we'll do with it all. Your brother's taking the samovar, and Aunt Fanny and I want to know, would you like Grandma's piano, including, of course, the adjustable piano stool?"

Hope, like the plague bacillus, may be silent, but it never dies for those things just beyond our grasp. After so many years, I had given up on the piano, and had gone to other battlefields. I was married, a mother, waiting the birth of our second child, and trying to write my first novel, a love story.

It's probably true that the place of our childhood is the only one we can always manage to reach down into, easy as a cookie jar. I went the next day to see the piano, climbed up the back stairs with my mother, those same back stairs I had walked up so many Friday afternoons. The stairs appeared newly scrubbed in the early morning light. My grandmother would have liked that.

When my mother opened the doors to the parlor and lifted the green-and-rose cloth, the piano was as I remembered, black and shiny, with "Ivers and Pond" printed in gold lettering across the front.

Sitting on the stool, which squeaked, my hands shaking, I played with one finger, "Twinkle, twinkle little star," then humming the rest of the song, "how I wonder what you are."

"It's a bit off," said my mother. "It needs tuning."

"Of course I'll get it tuned," this treasure, this relic, this monument.

"I know a tuner, a Mr. Willis, the tops," my mother offered. "Mr. Willis is an artist of pitch and resonance."

"Fine."

I took out my ruler and measured the dimensions, touching the keyboard, but not pressing, not believing it was really mine.

My husband and I had recently bought a splendid Victorian house near Brookline Village where he worked as an architect. It had a study on the first floor, and we had been planning to build bookcases along the wall. We could now measure the bookshelves to fit exactly around the piano.

It was finally determined that the piano would have to go out the front sun parlor window, and be hoisted over the side of the house, down three stories and around an overgrown maple tree. The estimate for this job by the cheapest "We do it cheaply" movers, the Kilroy Brothers, was six hundred dollars. Considering the difficulties, I was convinced it was a bargain.

The date for the move was agreed upon. This left enough time for a carpenter to build in the finest pecan bookcases. Then, on the appointed morning, I met the Kilroy Brothers in front of my grandmother's house, where they were already busy cutting back part of the maple tree. That done, I went with them to the third floor, where my mother and aunt were overseeing the operation. They could not, I must add, remember how the piano had gotten up there in the first place.

The movers insisted the slipcover be removed so they could get a better grip. My mother and aunt were staunch to the last, instructing the movers how best "not" to scratch the wood when fastening the ropes. Once the piano was tied up and the sun parlor window removed, the movers were ready to lift the "baby," as they referred to it, over the side of the house.

With my mother and aunt shouting down directions, and with me in the street below, my eyes shut from the moment I saw the first tip of black come out the window, the movers shouted things like, "A little to the right. . . ." and then "A little to the left!" and "*Hold it!*" and finally "Watch out, lady, anchors aweigh!" The "baby" was home.

I opened my eyes as they swung "her" up and into their truck; then, joyfully, I led the way in my blue Buick Skylark to the final resting place. They moved the piano into my house with no trouble.

"Looks perfect to me," said one of the movers, out of breath. "It's a nice piano," the other offered.

"It was my grandmother's," I told them.

"Looks brand new," the out-of-breath one said.

"Well, it practically is," I assured him.

After the movers left I sat down at that piano and played my absolute heart out.

The next day I made an appointment with the piano tuner, who would come the following week. In the meantime, I bought some special polish for the finish, which I intended to keep up in due respect, but without obsession. Then, I bought a piano light, made arrangements for our daughter to start lessons, and began a needlepoint cushion for the stool. The piano had become, in effect, the focal point of our lives, an unexpected gift in our middle age.

I was home for the piano tuner when he came. Mr. Willis, eighty if he was a day, arrived carrying his instruments in a black leather satchel, and dressed for the job in a starched white shirt and yellow bow tie.

"That's some piano you got here."

"Ivers and Pond," I told him in case he'd missed it.

"Nice cabinetry."

"Solid cherry wood," I proclaimed.

"Well maintained."

"Polished every day."

"Care's important. Take care of what you've got," he warned.

I agreed.

"Of course, you can't tell a book by its cover," he said as he lifted the cover.

"No."

"Sometimes you get this flashy exterior in order to hide something."

Well, I assured him this piano had nothing to hide, and in its day was the best. Of course, every day is a new day, is what he told me, his head now lost in the piano's recesses.

"We'll just take a look here and see what's here," he said, his ear against the sounding board, touching the first note, and me, by his side, anxiously awaiting any sign of approval.

"And so, if you'd leave me to my own devices," he uttered, without raising his head. I had been dismissed.

From the kitchen, where I made myself a cup of coffee, I could hear him.

"Aha . . . aha . . . ahm . . . aha . . . aha . . . ahm . . ." As he went up the scale note by note.

Then "A . . . ha . . . A . . . ha . . . aaaa," and then he called me from the other room.

"Missus, if you please."

"Yes, sir, yes, yes, yes," I stuttered, my heart beating as I walked across the hall separating us.

"It seems you have a problem here."

"This piano's in mint condition," I threw back at my accuser. "You can see."

He shook his head.

"I spent six hundred and fifty dollars to move it," I told him.

"It's a big piano," he continued.

In those days they made them big.

I was getting irritated. "This piano was hardly used."

"Aha! Aha, aha, aha!"

"Certainly not abused," I assured him, getting angrier. "Human hands hardly touched this piano, Mr. Willis," I said, suddenly taking stock of the hair in his ears and protruding from his nostrils.

"I believe it," he retorted.

We were shouting at each other now. He took a handkerchief out of his pocket and wiped the back of his neck, adjusting the piano stool and sitting down.

"So what's your problem here?" I challenged.

He scratched the back of his pants, which I noticed were rumpled and in need of a good press.

"Your problem, my dear woman, is that you have yourself a rotten piano."

Mr. Willis began packing his bag, carefully wiping off each tool.

There was something very final in this act, as if it were the doctor sewing up the case. Inoperable.

"Stop," I said, which stopped nothing.

"You say this piano was never used," he continued, oblivious to the meaning of things, this stranger whose breath smelled like cabbages, who had no right in my house in the first place.

"A piano is made to be used," he proclaimed, never looking at me. "Why else construct an instrument of this potential to make a sound which no one will hear? A man would have to be a fool."

"It was my grandmother's piano," I told him.

"You see," he said, closing his bag, making certain it was latched. It was clear he was a person who valued preciseness, who took care of what was his. ". . . a piano depends on atmospheric conditions."

"No one's put this piano out in the rain," I argued. "It's been covered in summer. And here, look inside," I entreated him. " We've kept a little bag of mothballs in it." My mother had sewn the cheesecloth bags herself.

"Wouldn't help," he explained. "A piano, you understand, is a thing which has to be played."

He was telling me to understand. I, who had stood, nose pressed against the panes of those French doors so many times, hands scrubbed clean and ready, wanting.

"You have to keep a piano at the proper pitch," he continued, "which is, give or take, A4440, meaning four hundred and forty beats per second. A piano which stands idle over a period of years, has what we call a pinblock. This pinblock, which holds the pins in place, is plain and simple responsible for the pitch of the piano. Then you add expansion and contraction, dryness, dampness, and who knows what, and one day, *boom*. Then, you could stand on your head; it will never again hold the pins in place, because now it is warped, or maybe even worse, rotted, which seems to be the case here. Rotted through and through."

"In addition, and also," he added for good measure, "Your crown has relaxed, making the action sluggish and without vitality. You then factor in the humidity extremes, which are part of a piano's life, which have affected, sad to say, your wool bushings. You protected the piano from moths, it's true, but you forgot the humidity."

"How much will this cost to repair?" I inquired, readying myself for the blow.

"Repairs?" Mr. Willis was in no hurry, repeating my question. Age had conferred on him a power that comes of particular certainties gained from noting the sun actually rising each morning and never failing to go down.

"Fix," I said, my teeth tight. I could hardly breathe.

"Fix, my dear woman, is not possible with this machine. It's gone beyond repair. Look for yourself. Gone. Go ahead and look." I didn't, fearing he might push me in. He and I were now enemies, after all.

"The whole thing is gone," he repeated.

I was blinded by his words, deafened by the steadied bulk of him. Everything was bright, white, stilled.

"With pianos, it can be as with anything: If you don't use it, you don't hear it when it makes a little complaint. Then one year leads to another, and it gets like some marriages, so far gone you don't know where it went off; so how could you know where to start?"

Mr. Willis straightened himself up. "My advice? Toss it out and begin again, and this time—play your piano. A piano that nobody plays, who can know what it's saying inside all those years?"

He paused, and then perhaps sensing my distress, he said, "It's only a piano."

I was silent.

"It's only a piano . . . it's only a piano . . . it's only a piano" reverberated in my head.

"You don't understand," I said, and began to weep.

The next week my husband and I drove into Boston to the largest piano store on Boylston Street and bought a new piano, the best in the store, for fifteen hundred dollars down and one hundred and sixty-five dollars a month.

In the end, we gave my grandmother's piano to the Home for the Aged, where they were happy to have any tune. And when friends and family and children would visit us, I would point to the room where the new piano stood and shout—more like a command, my husband insists, than a request—"Play."

Waltzing Matilda

by Russell Bittner

Susan was in a rush to get to her meeting; a major deal was at stake. And the damn cops chose that morning to enforce the HOV restrictions on the Brooklyn Bridge. With but a moment's hesitation, Susan asked the man in black leather just getting on the pedestrian walkway if he wanted a lift across. That was her first mistake. Terrifying, eerie, and all too possible, this is a story of obsession and torture in the cyber age. Natural Born Killers meet the Hitchhiker.

Susan slowly eased down the charcoal-tinted window of her Ford Explorer SUV for effect. She wanted the officer to enjoy the full impact of her face, eyes, hair, neck, and hint of cleavage through a lacy bra. She wanted him to take it all in very slowly—like catnip—one sprig at a time.

"No transit allowed without a minimum of two passengers," he said matter-of-factly, even if his eyes lingered unofficially over the lace.

"Officer, *please*. I'm already late. I've *got* to be on the other side in fifteen minutes."

"Sorry, lady. No exceptions." His voice snapped back to attention, taking with it his eyes. He began to wave her quite officially out of the lane and back onto Tillary Street for access to the BQE. Her vehicle had just become another errant cow; and he, a horseless cowboy with a herd to move.

"But where . . . ? How . . . ?"

"Triboro Bridge. Closest access point for Manhattan-bound, single-passenger vehicles at this hour."

"The *Triboro*? But that's miles from where . . . ! I'll never . . ."

"Move it, lady. Or park it and wait until ten o'clock. Nobody goes over with less than two passengers before ten."

Susan had miscalculated. Not once, but twice. She'd miscalculated in not taking the subway or a taxi. Now she'd miscalculated a second time in assuming she could negotiate her way across the bridge during HOV-only hours. Two miscalculations on a day she could ill afford to make any mistake at all. She absolutely *had* to be at Temple Street in twenty-five minutes, or her prospect would likely walk. No wiggle room. No margin of error for logjams or traffic bottlenecks of any kind. Her prospect didn't know her, had never met her face-to-face, had not yet given her the chance to imprint herself and her cleavage in his mind. Her prospect had simply designated a meeting time and place by telephone. If she failed to appear at exactly nine o'clock, her prospect would walk. They always did.

Susan felt a bead of perspiration drop from her armpit into the seam of her dress. Oh, God, now *that!* she thought. She squeezed her arm against her chest wall like an ink blotter. She glanced down at her dress to see if the single bead of perspiration had left a mark. Instinctively, she lowered her head and sniffed. Good. No stain, no odor. She glanced at her watch. Twenty-three minutes to nine. A bit of chaff formed at the corner of her mouth, and she snatched it away between two fingers. *Jesus*, she thought. *Get a grip, girl.*

The officer stood in front of her vehicle, hands on hips. She wasn't moving out of her lane fast enough to please him, and the line of cars forming behind hers was turning sullen. No one dared honk—not with a cop standing by. But the subtle revving of a car engine was an acceptable way to chide one recalcitrant cow without also running the risk of offending a cop. Several now began to turn up the RPMs in unison.

Just as Susan was about to swing out and away from the bridge, the image of a man entered her peripheral vision. He was apparently headed toward the pedestrian walkway in the direction of Manhattan. His pace was neither desultory nor hasty. Susan first noticed the predominance of leather. And his shoes badly needed a shine. She didn't particularly like black leather on men, but it was a question of fashion, not an instinctive dislike. She really needed more time to observe and think. But the officer was waving her on, and the line of cars behind her was getting downright restless.

Susan lowered her window. "Excuse me?" she shouted over the roar of car engines behind her. The man didn't turn his head in any particu-

lar direction, yet he appeared to register her shout as a signal to him and
him alone. Louder: "Over here." This time, he turned his head directly
toward her vehicle. She leaned her head out the window at a coy angle
and let her hair cascade across the door handle. Then, without reflection: "Going my way?"

The man squinted at her, but otherwise remained expressionless.
"S'pose it depends which way you're going."

Susan didn't know whether this was an attempt at wit, or just stupid.
She decided to ignore the gambit. "Look, I've got to get across this
bridge and into Manhattan in twenty minutes. They won't let me across
unless there are two of us in the car. Can I interest you in a ride to the
other side?"

This time, just the slightest smile formed on the man's lips. "To the
other side? You mean, to the wild side?"

The line of cars behind Susan's was edging up on her rear bumper.
The revving was becoming an angry chorus. The police officer rapped
his knuckles against the hood of her vehicle and indicated the direction
in which he wished her to move *now*. A bead of perspiration fell from
Susan's other armpit. She glanced at her wristwatch: 8:40 A.M.

"C'mon, guy, I can't afford to quibble. If you're interested, jump
in." In spite of her best efforts to remain calm and in command, the
man detected an edginess creeping into her voice. He liked that. He
also noted the familiar "guy"—not exactly a word that fit well in this
woman's mouth. A woman already of a certain age, he thought, and
likely just a certain age for fun.

"Well, now. Maybe if you ask me *very* nicely." He toyed with her as
he might have toyed with an older sister—if he'd had one—laying down
a bit of sexual undertone in order to bring into bolder relief the clash of
cymbals of an opposite-sex sibling rivalry.

At that moment the officer abruptly pulled a memo book out of his
hip pocket and marched up to the driver's window. "Okay, lady.
Enough's enough. I gave you a chance. Now you can discuss it on your
lunch hour with the judge."

Susan put on her most contrite face. "Officer, I'm sorry. This young
man and I were just agreeing to share a ride over the bridge."

The cop looked the man up and down. "All right. Then let's get a
move on." He put the memo book back in his hip pocket and perfunc-
torily pounded the hood of Susan's SUV as if to prompt it forward.
Susan—exasperated, but with no more time or room to negotiate—
turned her full attention to the man standing alongside her vehicle.

"*Please*. Pretty please. With a cherry on top."

The man smiled and skipped around to the passenger's side of the SUV. He put his hand on the front door handle and attempted to open the door, but found it locked. Susan hastily looked for the universal power lock and threw it, but by that time he had already moved to the back door, which he opened and entered.

"No, no, I didn't mean that you should sit in the back. I just didn't realize . . ." Susan attempted.

"No problem. I like it here just fine." He signaled to her with a flick of his wrist and forefinger. "Drive on."

Susan felt slightly nettled at his quip. But with time running out, she settled for irony. "Certainly, sir."

They drove straight on in silence. She caught just a hint of cologne—Aramis or something, she wasn't quite sure—and cracked her window. Traffic was heavy, bumper to bumper, and the going was slow. She glanced at her wristwatch: 8:45.

She felt a nervous tingle rise up in her from no place in particular, then noticed that both of her armpits had grown warm and damp. Still, she could detect no odor as she bent her head down to sniff first one and then the other. Her deodorant was clearly doing its job, even on over-drive. Or maybe it was just the Aramis doing double duty.

When she looked up again, she glanced in the rearview mirror and saw the man smiling oddly at the back of her head. "Don't worry," he said. "You smell just fine back here."

Susan began to feel something vaguely unsettling, as if there were some other bad smell she could not identify or get rid of, and which insisted upon muddling her other five senses. At the same time, the man had started to hum and softly mouth the words over and over to a song she registered as something out of a far-distant past, absurdly out of season, and which grated upon her nerves like the sound of a steel circular file being forced to expand a round hole:

> *I'm dreaming of a w-h-i-t-e Christmas,*
> *just like the ones I used to know . . .*

She settled upon talk as a means to clear the air and kill the tune. "You live in Brooklyn, work in Manhattan?" she asked.

"Uh-huh."

"Walk to work and back every day over the bridge?"

"Walk on the wild side."

She ignored the comment. "Nice. Must be a good stress reliever at the end of the day. Always the Manhattan Bridge, or sometimes the Brooklyn Bridge?"

"Yeah. Stress reliever." He chuckled. "Nothing to relieve stress like a walk over the bridge." He didn't offer any further information about his preferred bridge of transit.

"It sure beats driving."

"Then why do you drive?" The man had a way of saying things that seemed to put Susan off balance. She felt as if his questions and answers were uneven cobblestones in a street she was trying to walk in high heels. And yet she wasn't sure whether it was intention on his part, or simply a matter of social awkwardness.

"These windows are cool. I guess you can see out, but they can't see in, right?" he asked.

Speaking of windows, finally a window of opportunity to get the conversation back on a lighter track, Susan thought, and she threw this one wide open. "Yeah," she said. "Exactly that. Sometimes I make faces at people as I drive by, and they have no idea. It's a game I play by myself when I'm bored or lonely."

"Like one-way mirrors, right? The kind they have in casinos on the ceiling and probably in lots of motel rooms. The guy at the front desk takes your money and gives you your room key. Then he smiles politely, wishes you a most pleasant and restful evening, and goes around back to a false wall. On the other side of this wall, he's got a one-way mirror looking directly over your bed or into your shower stall."

The slightly unsettled feeling Susan had noticed earlier was gradually giving way to queasiness. "I don't know. I guess I never really thought about it." Looking for a way to detour the conversation, she had stumbled, giving the man just enough of an opening to squirm through.

"Never thought about it? By the way, do you play with yourself only when you're bored or lonely, or other times, too?"

The queasiness of seconds earlier now became vertigo. Susan fixed her gaze on the rear bumper of the car in front of her so as not to let her eyes catch sight of the drop to the water of the East River far below. Beads of perspiration under both arms were becoming rivulets. For the first time that morning she could smell herself. She glanced at her watch, but failed to register the hour. She studied the speedometer, and noted that the needle lurched only occasionally from zero to five as her foot danced back and forth from gas to brake pedal. She looked out her driver's-side window and across at the Brooklyn Bridge, then refocused on the Statue of Liberty beyond. Like a satellite guidance system triangulating between three points, her brain quickly calculated that she was not yet even halfway across the Manhattan Bridge.

She looked again at her watch: 8:48. She'd never get across this bridge and onto Canal Street in twelve minutes unless there was a sudden change in the flow of traffic. She was going to miss her appointment, miss her sale, maybe even lose her job. She'd have to give up the SUV, give up her apartment in the Heights, move out to Bensonhurst or Grave's End, for God's sake, or to some nameless corner of Queens. She'd be shunned by her friends, disowned by her family. Only her pet iguana would agree, begrudgingly, to stay with her. And now she had this creep to deal with.

Why, God damn it, hadn't she taken the subway or a taxi this morning, she thought to herself. *Why?* Because an SUV, like a Rolex or an American Express Platinum card, or maybe even just a Cross pen if you can't afford a Mont Blanc, makes a success statement to a prospect. This, the sum total of the wit and wisdom of her sales manager.

She heard a clicking sound and realized that the man was playing with the child's lock on the door directly behind her, trying to pry it open with something hard and metallic that kept slipping out of the locking mechanism. She couldn't see the metallic object in the man's hand, however much she angled her head to look through the rearview mirror. She reached out and rotated the automatic side mirror adjustment mechanism in an attempt to see the man and his metallic mystery thing. She realized that she could not see back in through the tinted windows, however, and promptly abandoned the effort.

In desperation she said "The switch is up *here*. I'll pop the lock if you like. You think you might have more luck walking?" she asked optimistically.

"Walk on the wild side, baby. Walk, walk. Wild, wild. Wild and weird, wonderful world, baby." The man's tone became abruptly stentorian and reverberated throughout the confines of the SUV as if in a canyon. "Don't touch a fucking thing! Just keep driving."

Feeling unsettled, then queasy and finally vertiginous, she was now descending into delirium. Her SUV was moving forward in the center lane a yard or two at a time and directly behind a sanitation truck whose stench penetrated her vehicle's air circulation system and entered the SUV without the possibility of exit. To either side, she felt squeezed in by a pair of dirty and rusting yellow school buses, a din emerging from within each that was matched in its ugliness only by the jeers of the schoolchildren as they pressed their faces up against the bus's greasy, fingerprinted windows and looked down upon the roof of her SUV. One of them actually put his mouth up to the quarter opening the window would allow and spit down onto the sunroof. Susan noted how the glob of spit stuck hard to the fiberglass. Behind her, and practically riding up on her rear bumper, was a cement truck. Although it was a bright morning, the truck's headlights were on high beam, and they stared through the tinted glass of her rear window like two angry electric eels.

Without warning of any kind, the man reached up under her and released a lever, so that the vertical half of her seat lost its brake and fell back into a semireclining position. With his other hand, he then took hold of a fistful of her hair, and pulled her head back hard against the head restraint. Her arms were taut, and it was with her fingertips only that she was able to manage the steering wheel.

"Got children?" he asked.

"No."

"Married?"

"No."

"A boyfriend or a girlfriend?"

"Yes. Uh . . . a boyfriend."

"Then I guess that means you get horny, right? But stay tight. Horny and tight, everything right. That's what little girls are made of."

The man plunged a blade into the leather top of the armrest between the two front seats. Susan realized what the metallic object was that he'd been using to tease the rear child's lock up and down. It was a stiletto with a retractable blade. The grip, seemingly of ivory, was the body of an absurdly buxom woman dressed in a kind of toga. Two transparent glass beads posed as nipples. She stood upright, her legs slightly apart, sandals peeking out from under the hem of her toga, each one resting on the twin quillons of the stiletto's cross-guard. What Susan could not see was the trigger mechanism tucked up somewhere between the woman's legs. What she *could* see quite clearly was the figurine's ivory breasts and glass nipples, pointing directly up at her, the blade deep into the leather of the armrest.

In a panic, Susan reached out to unlock her door, but the mechanism didn't respond. She realized that the man had jammed or broken the power lock system with his knife. They were both locked inside. Doors locked, windows up and locked. To all appearances, just a quiet, gray Beetle crawling forward in stops and starts somewhere on a bridge over a river, moving on over that river with the steel and glass canyons of lower Manhattan in the foreground and off to the left, a bright early winter sun reflecting hard back off the same steel and glass, but whose rays were muted as they passed through the tint of the windshield of this quiet, gray Beetle crawling its way to the island of Manhattan.

As if by instinct, some fight-or-flight kind of thing, she stretched her neck out and put her nose and mouth to the little bit of horizontal relief she'd facilitated moments earlier in her attempt to rid the SUV of the suffocating combination of Aramis, garbage, and her own disintegrating antiperspirant. It was like a last, desperate gulp of breath before the vortex sucked her down. Eddies of fear and repulsion pressed in from both sides as the indefatigable, insatiable, unrelenting, deafening, blinding, blasting centripetal force claimed her, staked her, nailed her feet fast to the floorboards.

"Let's see just how tight, how firm we are, whaddya say, doll?" As he pronounced the words "tight" and "firm," he squeezed her hair tighter and pulled her head back harder against the head restraint.

Another sound escaped involuntarily from Susan's throat, this one more like a gurgle. "Please, mister . . ." He appeared to like that. Addressing a man easily ten years her junior with "mister." He appeared to like that a lot. The implied deference of it. And that she understood their respective positions.

"No, lady. *Please* is how you asked me to get into your car, remember? With the cherry on top? We're already done with *please*. Very soon, we'll be moving on to *thank you, thank you*."

"What is it you want? I've got money. Not much. But I've also got an ATM card. We can find a machine just as soon as we get across the bridge."

The man narrowed his eyes. "Do I look poor to you? Do I look like I want your money? Do I look like I *need* your fucking money? ATM cards are for bankers and other losers. I don't deal in plastic. No, what I want is your chips."

Susan didn't understand where he was going with this. Chips? What did he mean by chips? Was this some kind of code, or slang, or street talk she'd never heard before on the fine, cobbled streets of Brooklyn Heights? Or was this his own private invention? "My *chips?*"

"Yeah. Like in a casino. With one-way mirrors. Chips."

Susan held onto the steering wheel with one set of fingertips, un-buckled her seat belt, and reached over to her purse with the other hand, both arms taut and splayed out like those of a starfish clinging hard to the face of a rock on which the surf is crashing, only the suction cups at the very tips of its arms released and allowed to explore other sources of nourishment and retreat. She snapped her purse open and began to rummage around inside, but she had no idea what she was looking for or even what she was *supposed* to look for. In the meantime, the man's grip on her hair remained relentless, and she was beginning to feel the strain in her neck muscles.

"Here, let me make this easier for you." He used the fingers of his free hand like a zipper to pop the buttons on the front of her dress from neckline to waste in one motion. The material fell back against her softly rounded, yet respectfully muscular shoulders, exposing her breasts inside of a lacy push-up bra. A silver St. Christopher medal danced briefly at the end of a chain and came to rest on the bridge of that bra.

"Nice set of *chips*," the man said nonchalantly.

Susan gasped. The world outside her SUV became like a glutinous, whirling soup in her brain. She no longer perceived the vehicles in front, behind, or to either side of hers as solid objects. Even the bridge and skyline began to melt and dissolve into one viscid mass. She was only vaguely aware that the man's hand had left her dress and moved to the stiletto, which he withdrew in one smooth motion from the leather armrest. That vague awareness turned to ion-charged recognition, however, when she saw the dagger directly before her eyes, the blade pointing indecently southward at her crotch. The man cupped the ivory grip with four fingers while his gloved thumb massaged the figurine's back. Susan grasped in the same instant that only action would divert this man from whatever sick little sideshow he had in mind for her. For both of them. Her eyes refocused past the figurine to the dashboard, then to the windshield and to the vehicles surrounding her own. She could stomp on the gas pedal and smash into the car in front of her. Or she could hit the brake pedal without warning and hope that the car be-hind hers would slam into her rear.

Either way, she'd get the attention of someone outside, she hoped . . . blindly, irrationally, against all of the evidence, against all of the history of this city, in which screams of violation and degradation tended to get lost in the shuffle.

As if he could discern Susan's intentions, the man suddenly rotated the stiletto up to a horizontal position, and brought the tip of the blade directly to Susan's bottom lip. "Don't even *think* of parking here!" he hissed into her ear.

Susan wanted to crumple up in the seat and give herself over to childlike grief. But the man continued to hold the tip of the stiletto against her trembling lip.

The man smiled. "Move into the right-hand lane." She put her blinker on and gradually edged her SUV over to the right-hand lane, as ordered. She could clearly see the East River below. "Put the emergency lights on." She complied. "In thirty seconds, you're going to come to a complete stop and turn off the engine." The man began to count backwards from thirty. When he reached zero, Susan complied and turned off the engine. "Give me the keys." She withdrew the key from the ignition and handed him her entire set of house, work, and car keys.

The man reinserted the stiletto into the gash in the leather armrest. Susan strained out of the corner of her eye to see him take the key ring between thumb and forefinger, then raise his still-gloved hand to his mouth. He grasped the lip of the glove with his teeth and pulled it back over the keys and off his hand, then took the leather ball of inside-out glove and keys and pushed it into the pocket of his jacket. His now un-gloved hand reached out and withdrew the stiletto once again from the armrest. At a glance, Susan took in the long, spindly fingers, like raven's claws, nails bitten back almost to the quick, cuticles red and white and raw like fresh-cooked lobster meat.

"Now, let's take that stroll on the wild side."

Susan's only plan of escape had just been dashed almost at the point of conception, and her mind was blank. She was entirely at his command. They both knew it. And the bile born of helplessness and fear rose up from her stomach and settled on the back of her tongue. "Please, mister . . . please don't hurt me."

"Don't you listen?" he shouted. "I told you already: We're already way past *please*. If I hear it one more time, I may just have to . . . *excise* it." With this, he jerked the tip of the blade across her lower lip. Susan felt the sharp point, but it didn't penetrate. No taste of blood.

"P-l-e-a-s-e-c-t-o-m-y," he hissed again in her ear.

The man removed his stiletto to a point six inches in front of Susan's nose and positioned it on an imaginary vertical axis. At the same time, he reached up under the figurine's robe with his pinky and pressed the trigger mechanism. The blade retracted with a snap. With his left hand, he continued his grip on Susan's hair, but gently pushed her head forward from the restraint. With the thumb and index finger of his right hand, he grasped the robed figurine by either side.

"Now, may I present Matilda?"

Susan stared at the figurine, but made no sound or motion.

"Be polite to Matilda, God damn it, or she won't be polite to you!"

Susan was entirely nonplused. "But, what does she . . . do you . . . want me to do?"

"Be po*lite*, I said. That means introductions all around. Be friendly. Offer her some libations."

Susan inhaled deeply. "Hello, Matilda. My name is Susan. Can I offer you anything (she gulped) to drink?"

Quite ironically and singsong: "That was very good. Matilda is happy now."

"And I'm . . . I'm happy . . . to know that Matilda is happy."

"Do you know Matilda's favorite thing? I mean second favorite, really, after cutting and slashing and stabbing?"

Susan tried in vain to suppress an involuntary whimper. Her eyes began to tear. "No, what is Matilda's second-favorite thing?"

"Matilda likes to go waltzing." The man snorted. "Yeah, really. Waltzing!"

Susan attempted a smile through her tears. "Waltzing Matilda."

"But first things first. And right now, Matilda is thirsty."

"Huh?"

"Be po*lite!* Offer her something to drink!"

"But I don't *have* anything to offer. Not here in the car."

"You *do!* You have a milk bar, and dispensers." The man pointed with the figurine in the direction of Susan's breasts.

The suggestion hit home. "Oh, my God . . ."

"*Do* it. Matilda wants to drink, God damn it!"

In quiet surrender, Susan unsnapped her bra. Her breasts fell gently forward as she squeezed her eyes shut. A couple of tears fell from the corners of her eyes onto her torn dress, darkly stained around the armpits. The man thirstily moved the figurine toward paydirt. As he did so, however, he drew the tips of his fingers as far back as possible so that he was holding the piece almost exclusively by the folds of its ivory toga. Susan felt the hard contours of the figurine touch her skin. It was not cold, but rather warm. And clammy. As the figurine had been in the man's hand for some time already, this fact did not strike her as odd. What *did* momentarily impress her was that she felt none of his skin against hers. He was touching her in a semiprivate place, but through the medium of a robed, female figurine, under whose ivory dress there lodged a single stiletto blade. Neither the skin of his fingers nor the blade of the stiletto touched her; the only contact he sought was between her warm, soft, human breasts and the warm, hard, somewhat clammy ivory breasts of the figurine.

The man nestled the figurine under one of her nipples and began to make slurping sounds. This pantomime continued for perhaps a minute, during which Susan's mind began to turn as if on a potter's wheel, drifting through a dense fog between successive scenes. She first saw herself as a child, holding her favorite doll up to her own flat chest to let it suckle. Next, she saw herself in early puberty, bending down and pushing just the sprout of a breast up to her own mouth to taste the sensation of lips on nipple. Next, she saw herself as a young teenager, her first boyfriend struggling clumsily to claim the prize of an early conquest. Next, her breasts now fully developed, prom night, her senior year in high school. The low cut of her gray, velvet dress held them for display, like two soft, milky-white mollusks peeking out over the mantle edge of their shells.

The eyes of grown men—of male teachers and of the dean and even of the school principal—drawn to them very much against their responsible, *paternal*, adult will. (It was delicious, this power to attract older men; she suddenly had no use for her young date with his white carnations and Clearasil-covered acne.) Next, she heard her own among a chorus of girls' giggles, her freshman year in college, an evening with a bong, two or three or four classmates—she didn't really remember—naked and silly and self-conscious, lying in bed, nobody wanting to initiate, nobody wanting to terminate, and the strangely mixed sensation of others' hard nipples against her own hard nipples, against her will, against their solid collective will, yet no one able or willing to defy the natural, sensuous pull of warm bodies mingling. Then she saw herself, the fully developed woman, with her fiancé, her breasts against his chest, both bodies heaving, both bodies lusting, both bodies searching for something beyond swells of fleshy pleasure and sufficiency.

The potter's wheel was slowing down. In her inner ear, her mind's ear, she thought she heard a click, a metallic swish and lock and then the sound of gears grinding to a halt. With eyes still tightly shut, she perceived just the slightest twinge of pain in one of her nipples.

She opened her eyes. The man had released the stiletto blade and was teasing her nipple with it.

"Oh, please. . . . Don't hurt me, please!"

"Matilda's happy now. Matilda wants to waltz."

"How . . . would . . . Matilda . . . like to waltz?"

"Barefoot."

"I don't understand."

And then it all came rolling out, like vomit or diarrhea. "No shit, you don't understand! None of you fucking Yuppie, SUV, Roto-Rooter scumbags understand. This is payback, little darlin'. The rest of us out there? The ones you don't see, because your fucking SUV, big-ass driver's seats are too far off the ground, your noses too far up in the air, or up some other fucking Yuppie, SUV, Roto-Rooter, scumbag's asshole to even take a glance. This is payback. Three cherries on the slot machine. I'm taking the whole bundle home with me. Then I'm gonna spread the wealth. Robin-fucking-Hood they call me." Here the man paused and took a breath to regain his composure and his command. "But first, a little fun."

"Then it *is* about money. Perhaps we can come . . . to some arrangement."

"Oh, yeah. We can come all right, doll. But I don't know about any *arrangement*. You're not really in a position to *arrange*, now are you? I'm the composer here. I write the composition. You just feed me data. Oh, and by the way, feel free to come whenever the spirit moves."

Susan deliberately ignored the implications of his last order. "What kind of 'data'?"

"Well now, I think we're getting the hang of this. A real feedback loop. Straight questions to straight orders. No detours by way of *please, please, please,* or *help me, help me, help me.* You learn fast for a Yuppie bitch. 'Data'? Like, for instance: Wha'd *you* lose on 9/11? Your cherry? No, I think we know that *that* little Pop-Tart had already been plucked long ago. Money? Doubt it. Probably made some the very same day. Quick little investment in a weapons-producing gig, something like that."

"I don't invest. I don't make enough money to invest. I just sell real estate. Small parcels of land and buildings."

His sympathy for this brief, self-serving defense lasted the space of two blinks. "But more to the point: *Who'd* you lose on 9/11, huh? Friends? Family? Not likely. Oh, yeah. There *were* a few hundred of your kind inside, wasn't there now? A few hundred who got the big, crocodile tears on CNN, their mugs still looking out from the front pages of the *Times* like Little Orphan Annie's. But the fact is, most of the people who tried to get down and out the service entrance that day were nameless, fucking robots. Back-office people. Green-cardless, working paperless, minimum wage GEDers. And let's not forget the few hundred coppers and fire jocks stupid enough to be in the wrong place at the wrong time, and not get the fuck out. All because some fucking, white-collar, maverick engineer had never considered—at least never thought to inform their sorry, blue-collar asses—that when jet fuel ignites at two thousand degrees Fahrenheit and the stacks of paper begin to burn and burn and burn, everything—and I mean *everything*—comes down. Sooner, rather than later. And that you don't send a bunch of dumb, obedient, cheerful, thrifty and kind, blue-collar yellow jackets, each carrying over eighty pounds of gear, *up* the fire escape to a blind, stupid, inhuman death, so that you can then play out their heroes' hand over the coming weeks and months to keep people from asking the harder, more embarrassing questions."

"I'm sorry, truly sorry, about those people."

"Yeah, I'll bet. I'll even bet you have your very own souvenir surgical mask, right? Hangs right there on the wall with some newspaper clippings from the day after. Whaddya call that, a *montage* or something? I'll bet you got all weepy-eyed putting it together, hanging it on your bedroom wall. Got some votive candles burning in front, right? Your big boyfriend comes over, you have a nice little glass of chardonnay while he looks over your artwork. You get naked, then have a little more chardonnay while he looks over *that* artwork. And then you start getting all rabbitlike, him looking at you, the two of you looking at your montage. At the total fucking destruction. At melted steel girders and the spoiled meat products buried underneath."

"That's not me you're talking about. Not me or anyone I know." Susan, for perhaps the first time in her life, began to think outside of herself. "But . . . you? Did *you* lose anyone or anything? I mean, like someone close?"

"I lost a fucking dead-end job, that's all. I lost my way back over the bridge. But then I got entrepreneurial. And I walk the bridge daily to remind myself. You know that word, I'll bet, 'entrepreneurial.' Or maybe you don't. You sell real estate, right?"

"I'm happy for you. But then, why . . . *this?*"

He sensed that she was getting a bit too cozy. "Okay, doll. This feedback loop has clearly crashed. You're really a nosy bitch, you know? *And* boring. All I know, all *you* need to understand right now is that Matilda is running out of patience. Listen carefully and see if you get this now: Matilda likes to dance in her bare feet. She likes to feel the floor under her bare feet."

"But your kni . . . your Matilda is wearing sandals. Ivory sandals. How can she dance in her bare feet?"

"Bare feet, bare floor. It makes no difference to Matilda. She just likes it bare. *Naked*. You with me *now?*"

Susan's understanding of the man's off-ramp way of thinking had gained exponentially in the twenty minutes they'd spent together in her vehicle. Soon, she realized, they would require no further words to complete the transaction of command and obey. Her only wish was to remain alive and, if at all possible, unharmed.

Her vehicle was at a standstill. The emergency lights blinked on and off. Other vehicles behind hers moved quietly around to the lane directly to her left and passed by, not one of them stopping to offer assistance. Faces appeared through half-open windows. Glared. Searched briefly for information or entertainment. Found none.

Susan leaned forward, reached up first to one shoulder, then to the other, and pushed her dress down to her waist. Her bra fell to her lap. Several buttons sprang out, hit the dashboard, and bounced back to the floor. As she reached the juncture of waist and hip, just an inch below her navel, she hesitated and slowly turned her head in the man's direction.

"Bare floor." He stopped her pivot short. "Those are the rules. Barefoot or bare floor."

Susan turned back toward the windshield and stared straight ahead into unfocused emptiness. She hooked her thumbs inside her dress and pantyhose as she kicked off one shoe, then pushed the other off with the toes of her now shoeless foot. Using her feet for leverage, she pushed her hips up and off the driver's seat and slid her dress and pantyhose down over her thighs, her knees, her ankles, and let them drop off. She continued to stare straight ahead, awaiting the man's next order.

Holding the stiletto in a vertical position, the man moved it from one breast to the other, then very slowly down toward Susan's crotch. He inserted the point just inside the elastic waistband of her panties, pulled them out to expose her pubic triangle, and held the elastic band in suspension.

"*Bare* floor."

The command was clear, even before he'd spoken the words. But

Susan had wanted, needed, demanded, in her own turn, this further order from him.

As she had with her dress and pantyhose, she placed her thumbs alongside the twin buttresses of her pelvic girdle, inside her panties, and pushed them down and off. They now lay on the floor of the SUV, together with her shoes, dress, and pantyhose.

The man abruptly retracted the blade of the stiletto, and Susan gasped. Was this a retreat? Was he finished? Had it merely been a bizarre game of strip poker in which he controlled the outcome of every hand by dint of his weapon and the subterfuge of jammed door and window locks? For one brief interlude in what seemed to her like time out of joint, she noticed the morning sun reflecting off some of the skyscrapers in lower Manhattan. Just beyond the tint of her windshield, the reflected sun shown brilliantly back toward the bridge, her SUV, and Red Hook. As it had *that* day, but for the charcoal gray filter of buildings collapsing and going back up, literally in smoke.

With the blade retracted, the man again began to move his stiletto back and forth across her pelvis. After a series of horizontal swipes, he stopped and paused directly over her vulva. He dropped the piece slowly down until the stiletto's very hard, very male-contoured cross-guard made contact with Susan's very soft, lightly down-covered upper thighs. The figurine's sandals rested in the crook of Susan's legs, and its glass-bead nipples stared directly at the upper horizontal line of her pubis. Still, Susan noticed, the man allowed absolutely no contact between his skin and hers.

She parted her legs an inch or two. The man continued fanning the figurine a bit more persistently. Susan closed her eyes tightly and opened her legs until one knee touched the median armrest, the other, the driver's door. She felt hot and damp all over, but it was the hotness and dampness of fear. She could again smell herself as the odor of her body in distress filled the SUV.

A snap, followed by a metallic swish, and Susan knew the blade was out once again. The muscles of her inner thighs trembled violently as she felt an overwhelming desire to snap her legs shut and blunt the anticipated thrust of cold, hard instrument into her liquid soft, most tender parts. Just as suddenly, however, the nerves of those same inner thighs sensed a blow to the driver's seat, while her eardrums simultaneously registered how the blade first ripped, then penetrated, the seat-leather just in front of her vulva. The man's gloved knuckles inadvertently and almost imperceptibly grazed her pubic hair as he yanked his hand away.

"Now, drive on."

As precipitously as the delirium had overtaken Susan, it left her. She was in the driver's seat, naked, sitting in front of a fully clothed stranger. A stiletto stood upright between her legs. The scene was grotesque, absurd, yet somehow definable and manageable within its own peculiar context. She was still alive. She was not wounded. He had not physically violated her with any organ or any instrument. The only part of her body he'd even touched was her hair—and that, through a gloved hand.

Manhattan was less than half a bridge away.

She conjured up an imperative voice: "Give me the keys. The car won't move without my keys." The man reached into his pocket and withdrew the ball of inverted glove and keys. He held the whole lot out to her as he clumsily peeled back the leather with his own free hand to reveal her key ring. She took it, found the car key, inserted the key into the ignition, and turned the engine over. It started immediately. She turned off the emergency light blinker and slipped the transmission into drive.

The SUV moved forward and joined the procession of morning commuter traffic into Manhattan. There was a more even flow now, and she thought she might be able to reach the end of the bridge and entrance into Center Street in a few, short minutes. What would happen to her and the man and her SUV once they reached Manhattan was anybody's guess. But that curiosity was at this moment entirely in the future conditional tense. She simply drove forward, eventually easing again into the center lane so as not to have to see the water below.

From what seemed to be all directions at once, she heard the sound of police sirens. She checked her rearview mirror, but saw nothing. The man let go of her hair. She leaned forward and checked both of her side mirrors. Still nothing. She wondered whether the sirens were just wishful thinking and in *her* ears only.

"Keep driving," he commanded as he dropped to the floor behind the driver's seat.

They were real sirens. The man's reaction was clear evidence of their reality. Susan never had found the scream of police sirens more comforting than in this instance.

Still, she could see nothing through any of her mirrors. Although the windows of her SUV were up tight and locked, the wailing of police sirens was becoming almost deafening. Sound, but no sight.

Just as she moved her foot to the brake to slow down and eventually stop her SUV, two police cars raced past either side of her. The Doppler effect of their quick retreat worked as much on her spirits as it did on her eardrums. And what had just welled up in her eyes as warm tears of gratitude abruptly spilled over in cold tears of despair.

The man raised himself slowly from the floor, once again grabbed a clump of hair on the back of her head, leaned forward, and whispered in her ear: "Wild and wonderful! NYC's finest! Wizards on the warpath of death and destruction! I'm *really* sorry—aren't you?—they couldn't stop and pass the time of day. But, you know?—I'm in kind of a hurry myself. So *you* would have had to do the talking for both of us. And you don't really seem to be in the mood for talking just now. You strike me as more of an action girl than a talk girl, anyway."

As if she'd entered the wake of a speedboat, Susan noted, even through the distorting cataracts of tears filling her eyes, that the lane before her was clear of all traffic. She accelerated sharply in a head-strong wish to sprint off the last couple of hundred yards of the bridge, maybe even to crash her SUV into the tower just short of the island of Manhattan, only seconds away.

"Slow down, action girl."

She obeyed. The SUV passed under the bridge's tower and rolled onto the ramp on the hard granite of Manhattan. "*Mommie,*" she said to herself quietly for perhaps the first time in twenty years.

"Move to the curb right over there, action girl." The man indicated with his right hand, once again gloved, the spot at which he wanted her to stop. She obeyed, pulled up to the curb, and stopped the SUV. She stared straight ahead, hands clenching the wheel, feet flat on the floor.

And then in singsong: "I think it's time to say 'thank you,' for all your com-pan-y." Susan nodded her head, but said nothing. "M-I-C . . . 'C'? Because we've *see*n your cookies and your batter. K-E-Y . . . 'Y'? Because we *love* the sight and sound and smell of you while you're bak-ing. M-O-U-S-Eeeeeeeee."

The man reached down between her legs with his gloved hand, careful not to touch any intimate part of her, grabbed hold of the stiletto, and paused. As they had once before, Susan's thighs began to quiver. She closed her eyes hard, and two new pools of tears emptied themselves from between her lids and streamed down her cheeks, over her breasts, and down to her thighs. Whatever had not been absorbed by her skin in its fast waterfall from cheek to groin disappeared into the grotto of her pubis. She did not see but she could very much sense the presence of the black gloved hand poised over the stiletto standing sentry between her legs. The muscles of her inner thighs screamed out to snap shut, but she couldn't obey their command. Not while the ivory-robed sentry with her sharp, steel bayonet stood guard just an inch in front of Susan's exposed vulva, holding her legs splayed as if with invisible traction restraints.

The gloved hand, slowly and deliberately, withdrew the blade from the leather seat that had been its sheath. The gash, the wound in the leather, did not close as the blade came out. The gloved hand pinched the sides of it together like a pair of soft and swollen labia, and gently pressed each lip down. Once again the snap and swish, and Susan knew that he had retracted the blade. But to what end?

"Before she goes, Matilda would like to request a little souvenir to remember you by."

Susan kept her eyes shut, but forced herself to ask the question she knew he was waiting to hear. "What would Matilda like as a souvenir?"

"Matilda likes soft things. Not too wet and not too dry. Not too clean and not too dirty. Not too new and not too old. You're a smart action girl. Get smart and active."

Word games and riddles had never been Susan's forte. But thirty minutes with the man had supercharged her mental batteries with his own very peculiar kind of current, and it was as if his thoughts and language had become hers by some sort of mystical, electrical transfusion. She reached down to the floor, picked up her panties, and offered them to his outstretched glove. He balled them up and put them in his pocket.

"Now, I believe, we've come to 'thank you,' don't you, Matilda? I believe that Susan would like to show her gratitude for this quite fun-filled interborough field trip we've shared today."

Susan's extraordinary effort to put a voice and sound behind her words resulted only in a hoarse whisper: "Thank you, Matilda."

"No, no, no!" the man said. "You've got to smile and open your eyes and *look* at Matilda when you speak to her! Don't you yet understand the meaning of the word 'courteous,' after all of the lessons I've set for you today?"

Susan slowly and mechanically opened her eyes to see directly in front of her face the glass-bead nipples of the toga-clad figurine. Once again, and with excruciating difficulty: "Thank you, Matilda."

The man withdrew the figurine with a swipe and placed it in the inside pocket of his black leather jacket. "Well, I hate to eat and run. But duty calls." He put his gloved hand on the door handle to open the rear door. The handle moved up and down, but the door would not open. He pulled the stiletto back out of his pocket, released the blade with its usual snap, then put the tip into the child's lock and pried out the stub of a wooden pencil.

To the back of Susan's head: "You should *never* let children play in the car without first setting the child's lock and checking around for sharp objects. No, no, no!"

This time he reached out to the door handle and opened the door easily. Sunlight flooded into the SUV in the three seconds it took him to exit the vehicle, shut the door, and vanish.

Susan sat motionless in the driver's seat. She heard the ticking of the SUV's clock and looked up at the console: 9:20. Every muscle in her body felt as if it had been strained to the breaking point. She gave in to her exhaustion and collapsed onto the steering wheel. At the same moment, her urethral sphincter emptied her bladder onto the driver's seat.

In the same period of time, the man had walked quickly to the subway stop and had there descended to track level and taken the first train back to the other side of the East River.

Once in Brooklyn, he stepped out at the York Street station in Vinegar Hill, close to the Brooklyn Navy Yard. He saluted briskly in the direction of the yard, then walked west the three short blocks to his apartment on Plymouth Street, climbed to the top floor of his four-story walk-up, and pulled out his door key. On the door hung a hand-lettered cardboard sign—his little nod to the glories of American history—which read: THE ROCK.

He opened the door and stepped in. He then closed and locked the door, turned on his PC, and emptied his pockets. He opened the bottom drawer of his dresser and threw Susan's panties in with the dozens of others he'd *retired* from the sport. (The man liked to think of his collection of panties like a collection of athletes' jerseys: the really good ones were pinned to a clothesline that spanned the hypotenuse of his one-room apartment from corner to corner; second-best got retired into the bottom drawer of his dresser; the not-so-good ones simply got dropped into a Dempsey Dumpster. Sometimes the women had urinated in them, even before he'd persuaded those same women to take them off. In that case, he didn't bother to take their panties home as souvenirs, and he knew the women wouldn't keep them, either. "Some evidence is just born to die on the vine," was how he summed it up.)

One pair in particular, however, a single pair of very sheer cotton, pale emerald green in color, with a couple of dark green pythons stitched into the seams and disappearing into the crotch, he'd actually framed behind matte glass and hung at the head of his bed. As he prepared his little digital Eucharist, he genuflected soberly before the emerald green and made the sign of the cross with his own thumb on his own forehead.

He picked up the figurine and twisted the cross-guard. Out fell a tiny diskette. With lint-free paper and a can of Radio Shack's own anti-static spray, he carefully cleaned the glass bead nipples. With a flash-light, he then looked up inside the figurine past the blade and its release spring to inspect the connections between glass bead lenses and the tiny digital TV camera. All good and intact. He hooked the figurine up to a recharger and verified the connection and the flow of current. (When the connection was secure and the juice flowed, the glass bead nipples signaled the injection of current with a beep and a steady green glow.)

He next slipped the diskette into its tiny player. His PC had completed its warm-up exercises and invited him to log on. He did so with his own password, "Pilgrim," and awaited a further invitation to log on to the Net. The pop-up appeared on his screen and he completed the instruction set. Within seconds he was on, through his high-speed DSL connection, courtesy of a pal at Verizon, off of whose truck enough spare fiber and backhoe loaders had fallen to get him hooked up to the trunk line that ran through Pratt Institute. In exchange, the pal got "sweetheart" access to his video library for life.

He then went to www.9/11Gold.com and scrolled down to the click buttons for "Members," "Guests," and "Producers." He clicked the third button and typed in his other password, "Entrepreneur," which gave him access to his account status, including number of visitors and subscribers current to the minute. The count was mounting impressively, now that he was able to supply live-action material on almost a daily basis, and the hundreds digit of the pop-up counter registered loggers-on, even as he watched it, in rapid succession. Forget the tens and singles digits; they spun round in a whir.

This, he knew, was not yet a peak hour for viewership. Most Japanese eyeballs were too heavy either from excessive drink or from over-work to have an interest at this hour. India—for whose 1.036 billion this would otherwise be prime time—had limited access because of the dipshits at the Indian telephone monopoly who kept all the really good stuff to themselves. Ditto for the entire Middle East, with its censor police—except, of course, for certain "privileged" clientele. In Europe, most folks were just finishing up a late lunch with a lover, or—lacking one—were on their way home to an early dinner with the wife and kiddies, and wouldn't be logging on en masse for another few hours. When they *did*, however, varoom! (He could say a lot, statistically speaking, about late-night German viewing habits in particular.)

But on the East Coast—ah, yes—just after morning meetings, millions of instant needs for gratification and a quick, refreshing dip into his Coney Island cyber-thrill spill would translate into a huge spike just over an hour from now and just before lunch. By four in the afternoon, between East Coast boredom-on-the-job and West Coast lunch breaks, he'd practically be able to smell the ozone burning off the servers in Brno. "More eyeballs on my chicks," he liked to muse, "than maggots on road kill." Another spike would follow morning meetings on the West Coast, and then on into the night.

By four o'clock in the morning, East Coast time, eyeballs had begun to dwindle. He was always slightly amused by the minispike, indicating intense and disproportionate interest from down under, but Australia's and New Zealand's exceptionally zealous populations just didn't matter enough to his Net business for him to get really excited.

He'd already had his ten millionth visitor in less than two months. Lifetime subscribers numbered in the hundreds. One-month and one-week subscribers, of course, were his bread and butter, and they numbered in the hundreds of thousands. He wondered whether this increase in traffic might be overtaxing the server, and made a mental note to have his pal Bohumil, at Česká Televize, run another check on it at the cyber hotel in Brno. "*Churn is the Enemy of Progress and Profit*" was the title of a presentation he'd once attended at an industry trade show in Las Vegas, and he'd made the title of that lecture his mantra. "People don't like to wait for their cyberfix," the man reckoned. "The Net is not the fucking post office," he now and again snapped at Bohumil, every time they came to loggerheads over the matter of further hard-Krona expenditures. It was the great cyberdilemma: Whether to upgrade for growth, or simply to cash out and move on to the next game in town.

Slow or not, customer retention was no longer the problem it had once been—now that he'd moved off the porn sites and onto www.9/11Gold.com, where visitors and members alike could buy almost anything even vaguely related to that second date of great American in-famy. He personally thought that some of the stuff was in bad taste, and he occasionally felt a twinge of remorse about many of the vendors whose digital—if not exactly *physical*—company he was forced to keep by the nature of the business. But those vendors liked to say: "To stare is human." God knows he'd seen more than his fair share of gawkers on and since 9/11.

Besides, in his mind at least, he was an artiste, not just a vendor or purveyor. He'd invented a whole new genre of Internet *cinéma vérité* he liked to call "scratch-'n'-sniff" films. "Nothing," he thought, "beats fear." He knew it was only a matter of time before the forward march of technology would allow him to install a tiny microphone in his Matilda in order to capture audio—i. e., sighs, murmurs, groans, weep-ing, pleading, begging for mommies elsewhere in the night. Still, noth-ing to compare with the *ultimate* sideshow: digital smell. In fact, he already had a pal at IFF, Inc. working on it for him. In exchange for "sweetheart" access, of course.

And then there was the money. It was all flowing into a bank account in the Cayman Islands, untouched by human hands (including, for the time being, his own), until the day he was ready to give up his passport and buy an island in the South Pacific. His own, entire, freaking island. He'd never again have to worry about wearing leather gloves, not in the South Pacific, that was for sure. He'd visited an educational Web site or two in his time, and he knew that the temperature never dropped below seventy degrees in the South Pacific. "Sure beats sweater weather," he often chuckled to himself, and also shared with anyone who cared to in-quire about his exit strategy.

He clicked around the content providers' section of 9/11Gold.com until everything was in place for him to encrypt and upload the video. Then he keystroked in a title for the trailer, laying down the dark brown letters with black borders against his favorite shade of pale, emerald green wallpaper: SUSAN'S CHOCOLATE CHIPPERS.

"Showtime!" he breathed to himself in imitation of Susan's hoarse whisper, as he clicked on "Upload." As the pop-up giving him the bit-rate at which he was transmitting appeared on his screen, he began to sing an old Woody Guthrie tune:

> *"Believe it or not, you won't find it so hot*
> *If you ain't got the do re mi."*

He figured he could cut, edit, label, and archive on the fly. Reduce the lot to five minutes, then repurpose the remainder for a rainy day. Maybe add some digital effects, new background, new players from other episodes. "Nothing like repurposing to goose the revenue stream," he sometimes mused to himself.

"Little darlin' Susie," he murmured to the still-vivid memory of her. "I'm gonna make you a worldwide starlet in less time than it'll take you to get back home here to Brooklyn and find yourself a fresh pair of panties!"

"Gray is nice," he murmured. He glanced reverently at the matte-glassed frame hanging over his bed. "But there ain't nothing, *nothing*, like emerald green."

The Equation

by J. Paul Cooper

Professor George Anderson had been striving for recognition—if not legitimacy—for years. And now he was going to get the chance to present his theory to a symposium of the leading physicists from around the world. By the end of the speech, they would either consider him a genius or just some idiot from Canada. Unfortunately for Professor Anderson, at the very same moment Irzak Sullar, president of the Thorzalene Planetary Council, had decided that the professor's discovery could threaten his planet's very existence. And of course, the president could not let the professor give that presentation. Galaxy Quest *meets* Men in Black.

P rofessor George Anderson hung up the phone and looked out his office window. He watched students walking across the campus, and wondered how the news he had just received would change their lives. He had finally been invited to present his research on light-speed travel at a prestigious science conference.

In one month, he would be standing in front of scientists from around the world at the conference in Los Angeles. By the end of the speech, they would either consider him a genius or an idiot from Canada.

He'd told himself a thousand times that it didn't matter what others thought, but he knew it wasn't true. He wanted to be recognized as the scientist who discovered light-speed travel. He wanted to be there when the first light-speed vessel left Earth's orbit to explore the galaxy and beyond.

Perhaps he could arrange for the first light-speed vessel to begin its historic voyage on a Tuesday at 8:15 P.M. It was 8:15 P.M. on a Tuesday evening when the theory first began to take shape in a karate class.

Sensei Johnson was talking about how to deliver devastating power with a reverse punch. Even if you were running toward your opponent, your feet had to make contact with the floor, but only for the instant when the fist started moving toward the target. Shoulder muscles had to be tense enough to produce power but fluid enough to allow lightning-fast delivery of the technique. It was all about balance and flow, using the natural movement of the body to transfer kinetic energy to the target.

Professor Anderson was convinced that light-speed travel involved plotting a course so that a vessel continued moving through one planet's gravitational field to the next in a constant slingshot action. The vessel would be close enough to use the force of a planet's gravitational field, without being drawn toward the surface. Properly timed bursts of energy from a rocket or fusion engine would maintain the slingshot process, until the final destination was reached.

He looked at his watch and realized that he was going to be late for his next class. He grabbed his briefcase and rushed out of the office, slamming the door behind him.

When the professor arrived at the classroom, he was breathing heavily from running across campus. He walked over to the podium, grinning, and then he began laughing. He had no other way to express his emotions. Years of self-doubt had instantly faded away.

He took a moment to calm down before he addressed his students, because he always stuttered when he spoke too quickly. It was a simple case of letting the mouth catch up with the brain.

Professor Anderson relaxed and smiled at the confused students. "Just in case you think a case of insanity might get you out of writing your final exam, you're out of luck. I want to state for the record that I am perfectly sane."

Several students responded with nervous laughs, others stared in silence.

"Several years go I began developing a theory of light-speed travel, but no one was willing to listen. I've lost count of how many rejection letters have been mailed to me by the editors of academic journals around the world. A few minutes ago, that all changed. I have been invited to present my theory of light-speed travel at a science conference in Los Angeles."

Irzak Sullar, president of the Thorzalene Planetary Council, looked out the conference room window at the busy streets of the capitol city. In the distance she could see the Monument to the Ancestors at the gates of Thorzalene City Park. Naturally, the monument was a statue of a deep-space freighter captain. Thorzalene was not rich in natural resources, so its prosperity was due to the skills of the officers and crews of the intergalactic merchant fleet.

Now, because of one human's discovery, it appeared a new trade route would be opened to the planet Earth. The problem was, it threatened to draw trade away from Thorzalene.

The president glanced at her reflection in the window and wondered how a human would react to her appearance. Like other Thorzalenes, she had light gray skin, red eyes, and no exterior formation for auditory organs. White hair formed a triangle on her forehead, with the tip starting at the bridge of her nose. As it reached the top of her forehead, her hair became red and then became gray as it flowed over her shoulders. She held up her hands and tried to comprehend what it would be like to have two less digits on each.

The president turned to face her cabinet ministers, seated around a large, oval conference table of polished metal. "Are you absolutely sure that he knows?"

The Minister of Military Operations pointed a small device at the wall opposite the table, and a large screen appeared. On one side of the screen was an e-mail message sent by Professor Anderson to a colleague at another university. On the other side was the translation in Thorzalene: "I'll see you at the West Coast conference. The title of my presentation is 'A Theory of Light-Speed Travel.'"

"Normally," began the minister, "any mention of light-speed travel by humans is ignored. It's nothing but harmless speculation about the future. However, because of the potential impact that the development of light-speed travel might have on our planet, our long-range scanners are programmed to search for the Light-Speed Equation in all human electronic media. Our scanners have detected the Light-Speed Equation stored on Professor George Anderson's computer at the university where he teaches, and on the computer at his residence."

"We could destroy the data in his computers, but that won't solve our problem. He has the Light-Speed Equation memorized. If we are going to stop him from presenting the equation at the conference, we will have to take drastic action."

President Sullar looked over at the Minister of Science. "Have you confirmed that his theory would result in light-speed travel?"

The Minister of Science sighed heavily. She feared what her answer might set in motion, but she believed in speaking the truth regardless of the consequences. "Yes. His theory has been tested using computer simulations. Professor George Anderson definitely has a working model of the Light-Speed Equation."

The Minister of Military Operations slowly let his gaze fall on everyone at the table. "I warned you they were becoming too advanced, but no one would believe me. We have to strike now, before the humans build light-speed travel vessels and make contact with the Trade Commission."

The Minister of Trade and Economics cleared his throat as a three-dimensional image of the sector of space that included Thorzalene and Earth appeared above the table. "In this case, I reluctantly agree with the Minister of Military Operations. Once the humans have light-speed vessels, they will explore this sector of the universe and make contact with the Intergalactic Trade Commission. As with all newly discovered planets, they will be invited to join as full members of the trade commission, and a new trade route with Earth will be established. It's inevitable that some of the space freighter traffic will be diverted to Earth and we will lose jobs that will never be replaced. We have to do whatever it takes to protect our economy and our way of life."

The president looked at the three-dimensional map above the table as she addressed the Minister of Trade and Economics. "I understand that we might face trade competition from the humans, but we might also benefit by trading with them ourselves. A large-scale military action is our very last option, because I don't think it's possible to hide a war from the trade commission. They'll notice."

Leaning forward, the Minister of Military Operations looked at his colleagues around the table. "If we use fusion weapons, there will be no war, just one massive strike that eliminates the humans as a threat."

The Minister of Science shook her head. "And how will we explain the nuclear explosions?"

"Years ago, in this very room, we agreed never to tell anyone that our long-range scanners detected intelligent life on that planet," replied the Minister of Military Operations. "We'll just say we decided to harmlessly dispose of some weapons of mass destruction on a lifeless planet. Most of the trade commission members are bleeding hearts;

they want planets to cut back on military spending. They'll probably thank us for being responsible citizens of the universe."

The Minister of Science glared at the Minister of Military Operations. "So Thorzalene, the planet that has always prided itself on justice and equality, is going to wipe out an entire civilization, just to keep from losing a few jobs."

The Minister of Trade and Economics slammed his fist on the table. "We're not talking about a few jobs! If planets start diverting their freighters to Earth, our transfer facilities will not be used. The consequences will be devastating. Before you start feeling pity for the humans, consider the sacrifices our ancestors made so Thorzalene could be a modern planet with a strong economy."

Irzak Sullar leaned her head back and ran her fingers through the white hair on her forehead. "What about sending a long-range patrol craft with a stealth configuration? Our technology is more advanced, so we should be able to drop off an infiltration team without being spotted. All they'd have to do is kill the professor and return home. Then we could use long-range scanners to send a signal and wipe out the data on his computers."

"It's possible," replied the Minister of Science, "but we'd have to dye their skin, use contact lenses, and make replicas of human external auditory organs. We'd also have to remove two digits from each of the agents' hands, and reattach them upon their return."

"I suppose it's too great a risk," replied the president. "If one of our agents was injured, he or she might be taken to an Earth medical facility. It wouldn't take them long to discover that his or her internal organs were very different."

The president stood and started pacing. "There must be another option. I'm not prepared to slaughter the entire population of another planet, when their only crime is progress."

"What about a probe?" asked the Minister of Science.

"We don't need to send another probe to gather information!" shouted the Minister of Military Operations. He lowered his voice, struggling to control his temper. "We already know enough about the humans. A probe is just another excuse to avoid making a decision."

The Minister of Science ignored the interruption. "We can design a probe to find Professor Anderson, and deliver a minute dose of Theroxium-Calide."

She winked at the Minister of Military Operations. "We only need a small amount. I'm sure that if someone were to try really hard, he might be able to find some Theroxium-Calide for a worthy cause."

The Intergalactic Trade Commission had banned the production, storage, and distribution of Theroxium-Calide, but the military had hidden stockpiles.

The Minister of Military Operations shifted uncomfortably in his seat. "I'll see what I can do. It's possible that when the troops were destroying the remaining stockpiles of Theroxium-Calide, that they might have missed a small amount. No one's perfect."

President Irzak Sullar wasn't comfortable with an assassination, but was relieved there was a better option than destroying the planet. "We have a plan. A probe will kill Professor George Anderson with Theroxium-Calide. When our long-range scanners send a signal to wipe out all the data on his computers, the Light-Speed Equation will die with him."

Professor George Anderson stopped in front of the restaurant. He looked around to see if his wife Carol was lurking in the shadows, ready to catch him in his sin. Believing he was in the clear, he opened the door.

As soon as he was inside the restaurant, the professor walked up to a waitress wearing a nametag that read "Francine."

"I think I'm safe."

Francine shrugged her shoulders. "Bad news, Professor, it's been really busy today, and your favorite table is taken. If you had been here five minutes ago, you could've had it. All we have left is a table by the window."

The professor knew a window seat increased the likelihood he would be caught, but it was worth the risk. He followed Francine through the glass door that separated the smoking section from the rest of the restaurant. When she tried to hand him a menu he just laughed. "I don't need that. I'll have a steak sandwich and fries, a large side order of onion rings, and a chocolate sundae for dessert. I'll also have a coffee, and please make sure I don't end up drinking that decaffeinated poison."

Francine smiled and put a hand on her hip. "When was the last time you actually gained a pound?"

"Well, I'm forty-seven years old, and I only weigh five more pounds than the year I started my undergraduate degree in physics. I was eighteen then."

"You know," replied Francine, "if I even look at a meal like that, I gain thirty pounds."

"The funny thing is," replied the professor, " I'm as skinny as a rake, but my wife's convinced I'm going to drop dead at any moment from high cholesterol. Ever since she went back to university to become a dietician she's been complaining about what I eat. This is the only place where I can enjoy a good meal in peace and quiet."

Smoking wasn't allowed in the faculty dining room, and he suspected one of the professors was a spy reporting back to his wife. She always knew when he had a hamburger and fries instead of a salad. Forty minutes later he took a final sip from this third cup of coffee, finished off the chocolate sundae, and put a half-empty cigarette package back in his jacket pocket. He walked back to the nonsmoking section and paid for his meal at the counter. He was about to leave, when he froze in his tracks. His wife Carol was walking through the front door. He deftly slipped the cigarette package out of his jacket pocket and dropped it in a plant holder. He hoped she wouldn't see it behind the wide plastic leaves.

Carol Anderson walked up to her husband and breathed in deeply through her nose. "I smell deep-fried food and cigarette smoke on your clothes. I want to see the receipt. Now."

Professor Anderson shrugged his shoulders. "Sorry. I paid cash and I forgot to ask for a receipt."

She wasn't about to give up that easily. "Who served your table?"

The professor pointed at Francine, who was carrying a tray of empty plates back to the kitchen. Carol Anderson stepped in front of Francine and pointed at her husband. "What kind of deep-fried garbage did my husband have for lunch?"

Francine looked at George Anderson as if it was the first time she'd ever seen him. "Hmmm, let's see. He was table fourteen. He had the spinach salad with low-fat dressing, a small fruit cocktail, and decaffeinated coffee, in the nonsmoking section."

Carol Anderson glared at Francine for a moment, then turned and walked out of the restaurant. There was no way to prove it, but she knew the woman was lying.

Francine smiled at Professor Anderson. "I'd hate to lose a good customer."

When George Anderson stepped outside, his wife was waiting for him.

"You're going to have your cholesterol levels checked, and you're going to have X-rays taken of your lungs. If you won't believe me that you're killing yourself with your lousy eating habits and cigarettes, perhaps you'll believe a doctor.

"Our children want you to be there when they graduate from university. I want to enjoy watching you play with our grandchildren. I don't want to show them pictures and say that their grandfather died of heart disease or lung cancer."

The professor didn't reply. There was nothing he could say to improve the situation.

After a moment of awkward silence, his wife turned to leave. "I have a class."

The probe was transported in a Thorzalene military vessel with a stealth configuration. It wasn't detected as it approached Earth, and the ship's captain reported that the probe was launched without incident. The first stage of the probe was about the size of a desktop printer.

George Anderson waved at one of the math professors as he walked across the university campus. "Hey Charlie, I've got a question for you."

The math professor raised an eyebrow and smiled. "I normally get paid to answer questions, but since you're a friend, this one's free."

"If you love greasy food and cigarettes, what are the chances of your wife deciding to go back to university, to become a dietician?"

The math professor laughed. "You shouldn't be talking to me, you should be talking to someone in the Religious Studies Department."

"Why is that?"

"Because you're cursed!"

The second stage of the Thorzalene probe was launched after the first stage passed through the atmosphere. If any scientists saw the first stage explode in a ball of fire, they would probably assume it was a piece of space debris, superheated as it passed through the atmosphere. It had been designed to self-destruct, leaving no traceable evidence that it had ever existed.

The second stage of the probe continued flying toward the preprogrammed coordinates. It was about the size of a small bird.

By the time George Anderson finished teaching his second physics class of the afternoon, he decided to accept his fate. As soon as he returned to his office, he called the university hospital.

Carol had already talked to someone at the hospital. Professor Anderson was informed that arrangements had been made for his blood work and X-rays. He was also assured that no staff member at the hospital was willing to falsify the numbers on his cholesterol report, or switch the X-rays of his lungs with someone who had never smoked. The results would be available when he arrived home from the West Coast science conference.

Professor Anderson still had some paperwork to do before he went home, so he opened the office window and lit a cigarette. Smoking had been banned on university property several years earlier, but he wasn't about to let the tree-huggers tell him what he could or could not do in his office. It was bad enough that he had to stand outside to have a smoke at home.

Stage two of the Thorzalene probe disintegrated a thousand feet in the air as it approached the university campus. The final stage of the probe was the size of a fly. It flew directly to Professor George Anderson's office.

The Thorzalene scientists who designed the probe had decided to scan the university's databases for maps and blueprints of the campus. The probe would be sent directly to Professor Anderson's office. The professor might have visitors in his office, so it was possible a student or another professor might be killed by mistake. It wasn't a problem, because Theroxium-Calide would leave no trace, and it would appear his visitor died of a heart attack. If someone else was killed by mistake, they could always send another probe.

Professor Anderson felt a slight pinch on the side of his neck and slapped the spot hard. He hated insect bites. It wasn't the pain of the bite that he found so irritating, it was the itching that followed. The last thing he wanted were flies and mosquitoes in his office. He stood up to close the window, but sat down again when the room started to spin. The first thought that crossed his mind was that he might be dying. How many times had his wife warned him that the greasy food and cigarettes would kill him? Maybe she was right after all.

He reached for his phone to dial 911, but pulled his hand back. If he ended up in the hospital, he wouldn't be able to present his theory on light-speed travel at the science conference. Perhaps it was just a headache. He decided to sit down and rest a few minutes to see if he felt any better.

Planetary President Irzak Sullar sat at the large oval table and looked at her cabinet ministers. "I just read the latest report on Professor Anderson, and apparently he's teaching classes. Why is he still alive?"

The Minister of Military Operations spoke first. "Our vessel delivered the probe to the exact coordinates and launched it without any complications."

The Minister of Science was just as quick to defend her department's actions. "We entered the exact coordinates in the probe's guidance system. All indications are that the probe delivered the Theroxium-Calide to Professor Anderson as planned. Special attention has been paid to the local media, and we detected no reports of other professors or students dying."

Irzak Sullar stared at the Minister of Science. "Well, then what went wrong?"

The Minister of Science hesitated for a moment. She hadn't thought of what she'd say if the Theroxium-Calide didn't kill him with the first dose. "Earth and Thorzalene are two different planets, and our bodies are not exactly the same."

"Thank you for pointing that out to us," replied the president. "Now, do you or do you not know what the Theroxium-Calide is doing to Professor Anderson?"

The Minister of Science shrugged her shoulders. "I'm not sure. Perhaps humans have a natural resistance to the chemical."

The president put her hands on the table and leaned forward. "*Perhaps!* Is that all you can say? That wasn't the answer I was looking for."

The president stared at the tabletop and fought to control her rising anger. "Send another probe and triple the dosage of Theroxium-Calide. I want him dead!"

The Andersons' daughter was away on a weekend ski trip, and their son was at a friend's house lifting weights. As he sat across the dining room table from his wife, George Anderson decided it was a good time to raise the subject.

"You know, Carol, I don't think it's necessary for me to get the blood work done or have X-rays taken of my lungs right now. It's just that I have so much to do to get ready for the science conference in Los Angeles. Perhaps I should get the tests done when I get home."

"Why don't you just admit it, George? You know that the tests will prove I'm right; you're a walking time bomb. I bet that your cholesterol will be at least nine point oh."

"Well," he replied, "I suppose I should have my blood checked for a different reason. I've been bitten twice by an insect that I didn't recognize."

"Well, that proves it. You've eaten so many fries, that now even the insects can smell the grease coming through your pores."

"Very funny."

Carol leaned closer and looked directly in her husband's eyes. "I'm serious. I want you to promise that you won't find some last-minute excuse to avoid the tests. I'm really concerned about your health."

The professor shrugged his shoulders. "Okay, I'll get the tests done tomorrow. But mark my words, my cholesterol levels and my lungs are just fine."

Carol slowly shook her head. She couldn't believe her husband was convinced that nothing he was doing would hurt his health. "Let's make it interesting. If your cholesterol level is higher than six, and your lungs show the effects of that filthy habit of yours, you will start following a strict diet and give up smoking. But, if your cholesterol is lower than six and your lungs are fine, I'll go to the restaurant of your choice and eat the same meal you're having . . . in the smoking section."

The professor smiled. "Get ready to eat the greasiest meal of your life."

His wife smiled back. "Not likely. Get ready to say hello to low-fat salad dressing and good-bye to your cancer sticks."

George Anderson wasn't sure what the tests would prove, but lately he'd been feeling better than he had in years. Perhaps it was because he was excited about going to the conference. It was amazing how good the combination of caffeine and adrenaline could make you feel.

It was late in the afternoon when the Thorzalene Minister of Science was called to the president's office. Normally the president would ask the minister to sit down, but today she just let her stand in front of the desk. "Our scanners picked up a message stating that Professor Anderson has canceled classes for two days."

The Minister of Science sighed with relief. He was finally dying. "Well, I guess the professor can't be feeling very well if he has to cancel classes. Apparently, the human body just has a higher resistance to the effects of Theroxium-Calide; but it is killing him. He's as good as dead."

The president stood up and walked around her desk. She stood so close to the Minister of Science that she could feel the president's breath on her face.

"Professor Anderson didn't cancel classes because of illness; he canceled the classes because he's traveling to the science conference to present his theory on light-speed travel!"

Irzak Sullar turned and walked over to a large window. "A hospital has scheduled a series of health tests for Professor Anderson before he leaves for the conference. At least we'll have a better idea what effect Theroxium-Calide has on humans."

"Should I send another probe with Theroxium-Calide?"

"Yes, if you think it will do any good."

Professor Anderson had a bad habit of forgetting what time it was and rushing to get to class. That was normal for him. But something had changed; he wasn't breathing heavily after running across the campus. It made no sense at all. Since he was still eating junk food and smoking, why was his health improving?

He'd been bitten by one of those pesky little insects again. He didn't feel sick, but what worried him was how often he was going to the bathroom. He wasn't an expert on tropical diseases, but he knew diarrhea could be one of the symptoms. He didn't live anywhere near a tropical climate, but the agent could have arrived in a crate of bananas or something.

President Irzak Sullar arranged for the results of Professor Anderson's tests to be translated and delivered to her computer as soon as possible. She stared at the results in disbelief. Moments later she started using language that shocked her assistants. They moved quickly out of her way when she stormed out of her office. They had never seen the president so angry before, and they were sure someone was going to be either demoted or killed.

A few minutes later she pushed aside a surprised receptionist and walked into the Minister of Science's office. She slammed the door shut behind her.

"Theroxium-Calide doesn't kill humans, it flushes the impurities out of their internal organs. We've made him healthier! The human we were trying to kill, is going to live longer!"

The minister tried to think of something to say. "Well, we can still use a signal to destroy the data on his computers."

"What's the point? At this very moment the planet's top scientists are listening to his presentation on light-speed travel, and there's nothing we can do about it!"

"Do you want my resignation?"

"No, you're a high-profile official. Someone at the trade commission might become curious about why you suddenly resigned, start asking questions. They might discover that we tried to kill Professor Anderson."

"But that's only one human out of the entire planet's population."

"I know, but trade commission will make it a big issue if they find out. They won't understand."

"What are we going to do?"

"We're going to lie, that's what we're going to do. First we'll pretend we just discovered that there's intelligent life on Earth. Then, we'll pretend we're shocked that the humans have discovered the Light-Speed Equation. And finally, we'll pretend we're thrilled to have them as new trading partners."

George Anderson sat in the passenger seat as his wife Carol drove him back from the airport.

"I was scared to death. There were hundreds of the world's top scientists at the conference, and my presentation on light-speed travel was well attended. I'm sure many of the scientists just went out of curiosity, but when I was finished I got a standing ovation. I was still answering questions three hours after I finished my presentation."

When they stopped at a red light, Carol leaned over and kissed his cheek. "That's amazing. When you called, you said that you were going to a meeting with government officials. How did that go?"

"Well, I'll definitely be working with our government, and they're meeting with the Americans. There's going to be a joint project. We could never afford to build a light-speed vessel on our own. It will put the British in an awkward position, because they'll have to decide whether they are going to work with the Europeans or join with us. Apparently I've convinced scientists from several countries that light-speed travel is possible, and it's going to create a lot of competition. Before I left, the Russian and Chinese delegates had a private meeting, and I'd bet it wasn't about the price of rice or vodka."

"Are you scared you might have started a new cold war?"

"I can't spend the rest of my life worrying about what might happen. It's inevitable that every new technology will be misused by someone. Jet aircraft carry families on vacation and deliver food supplies to starving nations. They are also used to drop bombs on innocent people. Countries that believe in democracy and freedom use jet aircraft, and so do countries ruled by tyrants. I can't change human nature."

"You've been talking about your theory of light-speed travel for a long time. Are you sure this is really happening?"

Professor Anderson opened up a briefcase filled with business cards from government representatives, company executives, and scientists. "Yeah, it's really happening."

As they traveled across the city, George Anderson remembered the bet they'd made. "So, what were my test results like?"

Carol smiled. "I haven't opened the envelope yet. I was hoping to see the look on your face when you say good-bye to greasy food and cigarettes."

Carol Anderson parked the car near two restaurants. One restaurant served vegetarian meals and smoking wasn't allowed. The other restaurant was the professor's favorite greasy spoon. She pointed at the glove compartment. "The envelope please."

The professor opened the glove compartment and handed the envelope to his wife. He felt unnerved by the smile on her face. He was already beginning to mourn the loss of his favorite foods.

Carol stared silently for a moment after she opened the enveloped, then looked at her husband. "These result can't be right."

When the professor read the results, even he was surprised by what he saw. His cholesterol was only 3.0 and his lungs were fine.

"You're going to have to take those tests again, George. There's no way those results are accurate."

Professor Anderson was grinning from ear to ear. "The question right now isn't whether or not the results are accurate, the question is, what are we going to have for lunch?"

Professor George Anderson and his wife followed Francine through the glass doors that separated the two sections of the restaurant, and entered the smoking area. When they were seated, the professor ordered a steak sandwich with fries, a large order of onion rings, and real coffee. For dessert he ordered a slice of cheesecake with chocolate syrup and two scoops of ice cream. As the professor lit his first cigarette, Francine turned to Mrs. Anderson, straining to suppress a smile.

"And what would you like to order?"

Carol glared at her husband, practically choking on her words. "I'll have the same."

President Irzak Sullar started at the Minister of Science. She didn't expect good news from any of her cabinet ministers, especially the Minister of Science. "How many planets did you say are capable of producing Theroxium-Calide?"

The Minister of Science looked at her data pad again, just to make sure she had her facts straight. "We are the only planet that still has facilities capable of producing Theroxium-Calide."

The president considered the possibilities. "The production of Theroxium-Calide was banned, but this is different. Even the trade commission won't oppose its production for medical purposes. We'll just have to come up with some explanation of how we found out it doesn't kill humans, but actually makes them healthier. Perhaps we'll say someone opposed to Earth joining the trade commission tried to poison an Earth ambassador and was caught in the act. It could be arranged."

The Minister of Science sat down in a chair by the president's desk and leaned closer, lowering her voice. "Of course, since we're the only supplier, we'll be able to charge extremely high prices, and the humans will think we're taking advantage of them. The humans will hate us, but we'll make a profit."

President Irzak Sullar stood and walked over to the window, watching the busy traffic in the streets below. She smiled and her shoulders relaxed. "The humans will hate us, but we'll make a profit. I can live with that."

Acknowledgments

Saying thank you to the many people who have helped on the project is a perilous venture: I am bound to forget people. To them I say please forgive me. And to those whom I've nagged, cajoled, bored, and (probably) driven crazy, very simply, thank you. No one puts up with more, or has better insights than my wife Sarah Hill.

To my business partner and friend, Jon Davis, thanks for hanging in there. A very special thanks goes to Bill Butler, my friend, former boss, best reader, and most trusted advisor. Bill, this simply would not have been possible without you. And to Jonathan Russo, agent and friend extraordinaire, thank you for having faith, patience, deep pockets, remarkable insight, and never-ending good humor.

Advice is cheap; good advice is priceless, and I have been fortunate to get some of the very best. David Stern, Charlie Deull, Stan Coleman, Wayne Kazan, Rich Heller, Martha Gershon, Paul Lima, Nathan Goldman, and Betsy Hoffman: Thank you!

My board of advisors was indispensable in getting this project off the ground and keeping it on track: Avy Kauffman; Craig Roessler; Perri Klass; Jim Simpson; and Tony Shalhoub.

Special thanks to friends who made introductions, had good ideas, and pushed things ahead when they started to stall: Patty McCormack, Anthea Disney, Richard Edelman, Randy Sherman, Paulo deOliveira, Dan Mahony, Carolyn Holmes, Sara Bailin. Chris Michel, Eric Rayman, Ali Wambold, Dick Spaulding, Rich Langsam.

To my assistant, Ben Deull, thank you! You did yeoman's work. And to my older son, Peter, one of my most trusted readers: Thank you!

To the folks at St. Martin's, thanks for having faith and for all your hard work: John Sargent, George Witte, Michael Homler.

I had dozens and dozens of readers who helped assess the more than six hundred stories that were submitted. Thank you—

Jacob Cohen, Alex Jones, Liam Alexander, Casey Barnhart, Mike Delaporte, Nick Feitel, Heather Burns, Andi Puntoriero, Carol Hightshoe, Crystal Fleet, John Pearson, Joshua Rupp, Joyce Purtle, Kirk Forster, Lania Knight, Max Wicaksono, Michelle Ryman, Mostafa Mohamed, Samantha Armstrong, Shelley Cunningham, Tracey Lord, Melanie Michael-Greer, Annette Ahtes, Tonya Saldua, Claire Armstrong, Walter Beaney, Charlotte Holley, Ellen Henry, Diana Liu, Brian Macdonald, and A. D. Floyd.

Steve Cohen
New York City
September 2006

Contributors

Russell Bittner ("Waltzing Matilda") is a former NYC-based sales and marketing executive who "sold" his way out of oblivion after a pair of towers and the industry in which he'd prospered for eighteen years crumbled. "Waltzing Matilda" was his second creative effort following one particularly memorable (and now infamous) September morning—from which, incidentally, this story takes its tone. Many more have followed onto the Net or into print, including a novel, a memoir, a couple of dozen flash-fiction pieces, short stories, and novellas, as well as several dozen poems. Only the first effort—a four-act play that takes 9/11 as its leitmotiv—remains to date both dateless and homeless.

J. Paul Cooper ("The Equation") is a part-time writer living in Calgary, Alberta. He has been involved in the film industry through writing screenplays and working as a background performer on several made-for-television movies. J. Paul has a Bachelor of Arts (Political Science) from St. Mary's University, Halifax, and is a member of the Writers Guild of Alberta.

Nancy Davidson ("Some Pig") is a food and travel writer based in New York City. She has written restaurant reviews for nymag.com, the Web site of *New York Magazine*, and covers restaurant trends for *Time Out New York* and *The New York Sun*. Her features on chefs and their cooking techniques have appeared in *Cooking Light*, and her recipes, cooking,

Contributors

tips have been published in *Pilates Style*. She has also con-
Gastronomica, *Gourmet*, *Health*, *Saveur*, and other publica-
is the author of *Killer Ribs: Mouthwatering Recipes from North
Best Rib Joints*, which profiles barbecue restaurants around the
Canada. Her fiction is often packed with food. She is currently
:ting two novels and compiling a collection of short stories.

ry Glasser ("An Age of Marvels" and "Mexico"), Brooklyn-born,
published two collections of his short fiction, *Suspicious Origins* (St.
aul: New Rivers Press) and *Singing on the Titanic* (Urbana and
Chicago: The University of Illinois Press). His work has twice been
read on National Public Radio's "The Sound of Writing," and he has
three times won P.E.N. Syndicated Fiction Awards. His fiction and
memoirs have appeared in more than fifty literary journals. He is a con-
tributing editor at *The North American Review*. Other honors include
having been a fellow at Ucross, Yaddo, and the Virginia Center for the
Creative Arts. He is the Coordinator of Professional Writing at Salem
State College in Massachusetts. He plays a wretched game of chess, bi-
cycles, and talks to himself entirely too much.

Michael Guerra's ("My Stunt Wife") most recent short stories have
appeared in *Witness*, *Hayden's Ferry Review*, and *Mid-American Review*.
He lives in Portland, Oregon, and teaches writing at Lower Columbia
College.

Ed Jesby ("Door Beast Nine Vee Bee") published science fiction a long
time ago that appeared in the old version of *Fantasy & Science Fiction*
and was collected in *World's Best Science Fiction* and *Best from Fantasy and
Science Fiction*. Lately, he retired from working for the NYPD as a computer specialist, with a lot of attention to the return of property to the
survivors of the 9/11 victims. He writes poetry and prose and hopes to
live and create forever. He has some straight fiction circulating through
the labyrinths of publishing and agentry and hopes the minotaur will be
friendly.

E. E. King ("Dirk Snigby's Guide to the Afterlife") has danced with the
San Francisco Ballet, performed stand-up and improvisational comedy
in Los Angeles and San Francisco, toured the United States with the
Nebraska Theater Caravan, and is the recipient of two International
Tides Painting fellowships and two Earthwatch fellowships. She has

worked as a teacher and as an artist-in-residence in Los Angeles, San Francisco, and South Korea. She was an advisor to the J. Paul Getty Museum and the Science Center for their Arts & Science Development Program, and was a science and art coordinator in Bosnia with Global Children's Organization. She is the arts & science director of Esperanza Community Housing Corporation, a nonprofit housing agency that provides quality housing for low-income residents in South Central Los Angeles. Her mural, *A Meeting of Minds* (121'×33') can be seen in downtown Los Angeles. She has published field reports for Earthwatch in animal communication and lesson plans on portraiture and genetics for the J. Paul Getty Museum and Science Center.

Therese Mageau ("The Adam Collection") is a writer, editor, and developer in educational publishing. She completed her undergraduate degree at the University of Michigan and holds a master's in Creative Writing from Boston University. She has made New York her home for the past two decades.

John Minichillo's ("Blind Man in the Halls of Justice") stories have appeared in *The Mississippi Review*, *Third Coast*, and *Carve Magazine*, among others. He teaches fiction writing at Middle Tennessee State University and he lives in Nashville with his two dogs. He has an unpublished novel that also ought to be a movie, and he needs an agent with the stomach to represent him.

Janet Neipris's ("The Piano") plays have been produced at major theatres in the U.S. and internationally, including the Manhattan Theatre Club in N.Y., Arena Stage, Washington, D.C., Goodman, Chicago, and at the National Theatre, London. She is the author of more than twenty plays, which are published by Broadway Plays. Her plays and letters are in the Harvard University Theatre Collection. She also writes short fiction, as well as for film and TV. Her grants include NEAs in playwriting, Rockefeller Grants to Bellagio, and an O'Neill Playwriting Fellowship. She has taught playwrights in China, Indonesia, Prague, Florence, London, and South Africa and is head of Graduate Studies at NYU's Tisch School of the Arts, Dramatic Writing. Her book, *To Be a Playwright*, published by Routledge (2005), a collection of lectures and essays on playwriting, is being used widely in theatre curriculums. She is currently working on a play about South Africa, and a collection of short stories, *Blue Hills*, about growing up in Boston.

Contributors

n Richmond ("The Good Kid") was born in Belfast and lived e throughout the worst of the "Troubles." After studying in Scotd, he returned to Northern Ireland and worked in the advertising inustry. Currently, he lives in the breathtaking Inishowen peninsula in Donegal, the most northerly part of Ireland, with his wife and son.

Jerry Ryan ("A.K.A.") is an award-winning freelance writer. He has written weekly columns for the *Courier Sun* and monthly columns for *Windy City Sports* in Chicago, *Twin City Sports* in Minneapolis/St. Paul, and *Metro Sports* in Boston, New York, and Washington, D.C. He has produced and aired weekly radio spots for WDCB-FM in Glen Ellyn, Illinois. His poetry has been published in *The Prairie Light Review*, and he won the Short-Short Story award in the national humor magazine, *The Funny Paper*. Jerry has been married for thirty-two years and has two children. With the other side of his brain, Jerry is a manufacturer's rep in the transportation industry.

Barry Simiana ("Gone to Mum's") lives and works in a small seaside village on the north coast of NSW, Australia, with his wife and son. Barry is currently president of the Mid North Coast Writers Association, as well as the Nitewriters, a local writers group. He is currently working on a series of short stories to be turned into a television series, as well as one novel completed and another underway.

Don Wallace ("The Injunction") is an award-winning journalist, novelist, and magazine editor. He is currently executive editor of *Yachting*, the hundred-year-old Time Inc. magazine. He is the author of *One Great Game* (Atria, 2003; paperback 2005), about the first-ever high school football national championship game, the novel *Hot Water* (Soho Press, 1991), which received a James Michener Prize, and a novel serialized in *Naval History* magazine, *The Log of Matthew Roving*, for which he was named the U.S. Naval Institute's Co-Author of the Year in 2002. He has written essays and articles for *Harper's*, *The New York Times*, and dozens of other publications. Born and raised in Long Beach, California, Don Wallace attended UC Santa Cruz and the Iowa Writers Workshop, married a Hawaiian surfer and writer, and helped raise a son in Manhattan, who now attends Stanford University.